"Felker-Martin's horror chops are top-notch. . . . A ballsy postapocalyptic tale."
PUBLISHERS WEEKLY

"A razor-sharp novel . . . Prepare to take a bite that will stain your jaws red."
MEG ELISON

"This book is timely, visceral, grotesque, unflinching, and unexpectedly fun, full of sex and gore and messy, beautiful humanity."
VULTURE

"Thrilling, gory, disgusting."
GIZMODO

"*Manhunt* is sublime horror. . . . You should read it and share it with all of your friends and enemies."
ROXANE GAY

"A unqiue, brain-searing nightmare that's full-on teeth and claws, and all heart too."
HAILEY PIPER

"The most unique perspective on one of the most well-trodden genres of the past several years, *Manhunt* takes no prisoners."
BUZZFEED

"Every ten years or so, a horror novel comes along that pushes the genre to terrifying new heights. *Manhunt* is such a novel. An emotional buzz saw of a book that left me shaken."
BRIAN KEENE

THE END OF THE WORLD IS NUTS.

MANHUNT

MAN HUNT

Gretchen Felker-Martin

NIGHTFIRE
A Tom Doherty Associates Book
New York

This is a work of fiction. All of the characters, organizations, and events portrayed in this novel are either products of the author's imagination or are used fictitiously.

MANHUNT

A Nightfire Book
Published by Tom Doherty Associates
120 Broadway
New York, NY 10271

tornightfire.com

Nightfire™ is a trademark of Macmillan Publishing Group, LLC.

The Library of Congress Cataloging-in-Publication Data
is available upon request.

ISBN 978-1-250-79464-2 (trade paperback)
ISBN 978-1-250-79465-9 (ebook)

Our books may be purchased in bulk for promotional, educational, or business use. Please contact your local bookseller or the Macmillan Corporate and Premium Sales Department at 1-800-221-7945, extension 5442, or by email at MacmillanSpecialMarkets@macmillan.com.

First Edition: 2022

Printed in the United States of America

For Ezra

PART ONE

MISANDRY

Trannies, your families will never love you. You are living a lie & you know it. End your miserable existence. Commit suicide now.

—Unknown troll

I

XX

Fran, squinting in the early afternoon glare, watched through her scratched binoculars as the man knelt to drink. The forest pool was dark and brackish, scummed with blooms of vibrant green algae. Skinny pines, bare-branched for a good twenty feet under the canopy of needles, surrounded it. The man's matted, filthy hair floated on the surface as he gulped down greedy mouthfuls, tilting his head back to swallow like an alligator horking down a fish.

They had trouble with swallowing, these things the plague had made out of anyone with enough testosterone in their system to put out a decent crop of back hair. Mostly they ripped their prey apart and gulped the meat down in chunks, or dug up grubs and beetles and whatever roots they could get their gnarled claws on. They'd eat pretty much anything if it came down to it. Fran had seen one choke on a tennis ball.

"Well?" asked Beth, kneeling on Fran's right.

Fran lowered the binoculars. "He's alone. Can you one-shot him from here?"

Beth was already unlimbering her compound bow. "Sixty yards," she said quietly, smirking so that the scar at the right corner of her mouth drew taut and pulled at her bottom eyelid until a little crescent of wet pink showed under it. "Which eye socket you want it through?"

"Don't be a cunt," Fran hissed back. "Just do it."

Beth's smile widened as she nocked a carbon fiber arrow and drew to the bow's full extension, the muscles in her long, thick arms standing out. She squinted along the arrow's shaft. "Lick my taint," she whispered, and took the shot.

The high-tension bowstring twanged. The arrow buzzed through the air like a thirty-inch hornet, its arc carrying it up, up, up into the branches above. The man, far downslope in a basin choked with years of rust-colored fallen pine needles, looked up from the pool, cracked and scabby skin splitting along fresh fissures to reveal raw pink flesh beneath as his face contorted into a snarl, exposing a mouthful of rotting snaggleteeth under a nose pounded flat and smeared onto the thing's left cheek by God knew how many unset breaks.

He drew a breath and for an instant Fran was sure that he would scream, that he would make that horrible fucking sound she heard ring out in choruses every night the second she dropped into REM. Then the arrow hit, punching through his skull with a distant *thunk*, and he toppled face-first into the pool and lay there, not moving. A few mourning doves cooed angrily from the branches above.

Beth touched her thumb and forefinger together and raised them to her lips, then kissed them and opened her hand, gesturing as though to let the kiss take flight like a cartoon chef just after tasting a perfect sauce. "Bella, bella!" she yelled. "Bellissima!"

Fran laughed in spite of herself, her legs going loose and shaky as adrenaline flooded her system. "God, Beth," she giggled, picking herself up to follow the taller girl out of their small brake of fiddleheads and chokeberry and down the slope. For a single blessed heartbeat she felt weightless, her nostrils full of the warm cinnamon smell of dead pine needles, her neck and back slick with sweat under her sodden tank top. It felt like summer used to feel, itchy and restless and golden. "You're such a fucking dumbass."

♀

Fran cut him open, a V incision to either side of the spine, and sliced his adrenal glands off the tops of his kidneys. Then she fished his balls out of his rashy scrotum. When she cut it open, his ballsack exuded a stink like a bath bomb infused with rancid pork. She packed his giblets into her duffel between layers of dry ice wrapped in yellowing newspaper. She tried not to look at the other things growing inside him, at the squirming tumors that flinched from her hunting knife and scalpel, hiding among bones and fleshy membranes like goldfish in the archways and battlements of an aquarium castle.

Birds gathered in the branches overhead as she worked. Crows, mostly, and the wide-winged shadows of turkey vultures sweeping in long, lazy circuits over the forest floor. A red-tailed hawk kept silent watch over the basin and its little surgical tableaux. Beth stood guard nearby, an arrow nocked, her own knife loose in its sheath at her hip.

When Fran was done, she washed her hands in the pool and dried them on the front of her bloodstained, moth-eaten tank. The dead man stared at her accusingly with one bloodshot golden eye, his face still twisted in a vicious snarl.

"You good?" Beth asked. The shadows were getting longer. The birds would draw attention. No more laughter.

Fran shouldered the rucksack and stood, knees popping after forty-five minutes spent squatting over the dead man's gaping back. She looked away from his baleful, unseeing gaze, feeling suddenly absurdly guilty. "Yeah. Let's boogie."

They scaled the slope in silence, Beth in the lead and Fran following close behind, neither of them looking back as the watchful croaking of the carrion birds became a ravenous cacophony, black wings flogging the hot summer air.

♀

A few miles from where they'd left their bikes at the forest's edge, they paused to drink lukewarm water and wolf down stale protein bars. Fran tried to imagine the taste of fresh biscuits drowning in sausage gravy, rich and buttery and shot through with a smooth, dark tang of smoke. Instead she imagined one of the dead man's tumors slithering back behind his left lung, its half-formed mouth agape in a wheezing grin.

The plague, t. rex, was as reliable as the atomic fucking clock. First, relentless hunger pangs. Mood swings. Fever. Dermal fissures that wept pus and cloudy blood before scabbing over, bursting, and scabbing again until the skin was nearly an inch thick in places. Delirium. Intense spikes of aggression. Once the initial lava flow of symptoms cooled and hardened into the shrieking, ravenous things that seethed like lice across the entire American supercontinent, something clicked on inside whatever remained of the man's brain and he started looking for something to rape, maim, and leave half-dead like those wasps that laid their eggs in living tarantulas. The good news was that pregnancy was shorter now. Much shorter. The bad news was that the babies ate their way out.

Out here on the coast, the things that had been men were scarcer, at least. They couldn't swim, so fish held little allure for them, and most of the big game had been killed off years ago. Still, sometimes one caught sight of you and before the echoes of its first scream faded there were thirty of the fucking things pelting after you on all fours through the rotting innards of a Walmart Supercenter like a pack of rabid dogs.

And if I ever run out of spiro and E I'll be one of them a few weeks later, and then some other t-girl's gonna put an arrow through my skull and slice off my balls. Oh well. So sad.

"Let's boogie," said Beth through a mouthful of protein bar as she straightened up and brushed crumbs off her ratty, threadbare hoodie. *Letsh bugey.*

"Let's," said Fran.

♀

They were almost to the forest's edge, making good time over level ground between the pines, when Fran heard voices. "Wait," she hissed to Beth, flattening herself slowly into the sparse underbrush. "Down, get down."

Beth dropped onto her elbows at her side. "I don't see anything," she whispered back. "Are you sure you're not just a jumpy bitch with clinical paranoia you'll never get diagnosed because all the psychiatrists are dead or living in, like, Monaco in some really tacky American slum?"

"Shut the fuck up and follow me. And be *quiet.*"

They wormed their way forward for a good five minutes, pausing intermittently to listen. Beth's expression sobered when they both heard a high, scratchy woman's voice shriek *"Oh my GOD!"* in a breathless titter. Other voices answered. Fran and Beth squirmed onward until finally, from the relative concealment of a patch of goldenrod growing in a clearing, they saw the TERFs.

They were a hundred yards off, half-hidden by the thinning pines near the forest's edge. A dozen women, most of them in their late teens or early twenties, a few younger, all in fatigues, most sporting undercuts, stood clustered around the bikes where Fran and Beth had left them leaning up against a rusted metal rack, a holdover from when this place had been shot through with hiking trails for rich yuppies from Boston who wanted somewhere serene to surround themselves with nature and stargaze and do cayenne-and-lemon-juice cleanses. And blow.

"Fffffuck," Beth groaned, rocking back up onto her haunches and settling into a loose, ready crouch. "It's the fucking chromosome crusaders."

Suddenly, the group of girls fell silent. They parted as smoothly as a set of drapes and a thin, pale woman of unremarkable height, maybe forty years old, strode through the divided group toward the bikes. She wore crisp fatigues and a short, tight leather jacket zipped up to her collarbones. On her forehead, dead center above the bridge of her pert little ski slope nose, was a stark tattoo: XX. Pussy certified all-natural by the Daughters of the Witches You Couldn't Burn or whatever Michigan Womyn's Music Festival bullshit the TERFocracy in Maryland bowed down to. Fuck.

"We can wait them out," Fran whispered, chin practically kissing the dirt, hair stuck to her neck with flop sweat. "Worst case is they take our bikes and we walk home. We have enough meds to get us there, I think. It should be fine. It's probably going to be fine. Hey maybe get down a little more?"

"Oh motherfuck me," whispered Beth, not even pretending to listen. "That's Queen TERF. That's fucking Teach."

Fran's eyes widened. She stared at the thin, long-haired woman currently sorting through the contents of Beth's bike basket. They called her Teach, she'd heard, because she'd been a psychological consultant at Guantanamo before T-Day hit. She was a medical doctor too, according to the rumors at the Fort Fisher trading post up near Seabrook when they'd gone to find a buyer for their excess E. Whatever her deal, and wherever she'd come from, there was no doubting she was hardcore. She got her hands on them and they were fucked. Dead. Done.

The tattooed woman said something that made her retinue laugh.

Fran watched her lips move, watched the play of muscles under her smooth face as she smiled. A cold thrill went up her spine. *God, you don't need to have a wet dream about a fucking gender-essentialist neo-fascist.* She squeezed her eyes shut, nipping in the bud her imagination's little spurt of latex tight against pale skin and thighs divided into lick-able quarters by garters edged in delicate black lace, of a hand on the back of her neck squeezing tighter and tighter until—

She bit her lip, cutting through the haze, and the world swam back into normalcy. Well, except that Beth was standing up, and she had her bow in one hand and an arrow in the other. The broad-shouldered girl was squinting. It was past noon and the sunlight seemed to be aimed right at them. The shadows were getting long again.

"What are you doing?" Fran hissed, spittle flying through her teeth. Her cock was hard, tenting the front of her stupid cargo shorts, and she was seized suddenly by the ridiculous fear that the pale woman could see it. "Beth, what the fuck are you doing?"

"Making the world a kinder, gentler place," said Beth, grinning like a fox with its head through the henhouse door as she nocked an arrow to the bowstring and drew it back level with the unscarred corner of her mouth. "I'm gonna put one through her fucking neck."

II

CROTCH ROCKET

"She moved!" Beth hollered plaintively as they tore downhill through the woods, the wounded girl's howls echoing behind them. "It's not my fault!"

Fran didn't have the lung capacity to answer. She replayed the moment in her mind. Beth's ravenous grin. The bowstring's creak. She'd loosed her arrow just as Teach knelt to inspect something on the ground, and then suddenly a big broad-shouldered girl with spiky blond hair who'd been standing behind the older woman was screaming bloody murder with three feet of carbon fiber sticking from her shoulder.

A crossbow bolt thunked into a moss-covered tree trunk a yard to Fran's left. She tried for a single absurd second to remember a tweet she'd once read about whether to run serpentine or straight when under fire, then gave up and focused on not running into trees. At the bottom of the slope they crashed through a stand of tall ferns and slid down a short drop-off of exposed clay into an ankle-deep stream running over a bed of smooth stones. Panting, Fran dared a look back up the slope.

The TERFs were hot on their heels, eight or nine of them with the kind of high-powered hunting crossbows that'd all been pillaged from sporting goods stores within a week of T-Day. Another bolt buried itself in the bank between Beth's feet. She was trying to nock an arrow, sweaty fingers fumbling. She drew and loosed too fast and the shaft buzzed over the TERFs' heads and vanished among the trees. A few of them ducked, at least.

"Forget it," wheezed Fran, grabbing the tall, scarred girl's elbow and dragging her downstream. "Just run."

A storm of bolts slashed all around them through the ferns to thud into the dirt and skip end over end off the rocks of the riverbed, trailing drops of water that flashed jewel-bright in the sun. Fran felt a hot, sharp pain in her right thigh she didn't dare to look at. The duffel slung over her shoulder seemed to weigh a ton. Her heart raced, the beat loud in her ears.

One last look showed her most of the TERFs struggling to reload and one, a stocky, fierce-looking white girl with a septum piercing, jogging out ahead of the others, crossbow held low across her body at an angle, waiting for a shot that would count.

Beth gripped Fran's hand tight. They ran.

♀

The stream wound its way through the forest on a gentle downhill slope, widening in some places into brackish shallows where pollen lay golden on the water and narrowing in others to a frothy rush where Fran and Beth had to struggle single file over slick, shifting stones. Fran's shoes and socks were soaked, her ankles raw from chafing. Her breath came in ragged gasps.

A bolt whistled past somewhere to Fran's left, struck a moss-covered rock, and pinwheeled into the underbrush. She glanced over her shoulder. Septum Piercing was a few dozen yards behind them, arms pumping, face red. The rest were still spilling down the ravine and into the stream or struggling to reload. Fran stumbled, nearly ate shit, and recovered with a lurching hop she was certain had looked incredibly stupid from behind. Her grazed leg smarted with every step.

Her dad's easy smile. His hand ruffling her hair. *Looks rough, bud. You want me to kiss it and make it all infected?*

She pushed herself harder, eyes on the rocks ahead. She'd been a runner in high school and then in college, before she'd come out. Not a good one, not like Beth had been, but she'd worked hard. It felt like three years of surviving as a prey animal in the ashes of civilization should have made her better at it, but it was hot in the jagged line of light that fell through the gap in the canopy over the stream and the stones of the riverbed turned and shifted under her feet. Her breath rasped in her lungs.

The splash-splash-splash of Septum Piercing's boots in the stream was closer now, catching up to them relentlessly. *You know what they do to trannies you stupid bitch. You've heard the stories and seen the Polaroids and unless you feel like posing for the mutilated faggot of the month inspirational calendar you'd better dig deep NOW.*

They flew across a shallow stretch where murky water swirled over waterlogged pine needles. Dust and pollen hung in the hot golden light. Tadpoles fled their oncoming shadows. Fran tried to focus on Beth's sweat-soaked back, on the taller woman's easy stride. Her legs felt like melting Popsicles. Her heart thundered in her chest. A single step misplaced. Stones sliding beneath her. She fell sprawling in the stream in the shadows of the overhanging ferns, skinning a hand and a forearm in a doomed attempt to catch herself. Her jaw hit a rock with a sharp, final *click* that sent a lance of sour pain jabbing upward through her cheek. She tasted blood.

"Stay down," said Beth. Fran, pushing herself up onto her hands and knees, fell still. Beth had her bow out and an arrow nocked. Fran followed the line of the tip to Septum Piercing, who stood frozen ten or fifteen yards upstream with her crossbow half-raised. The other TERFs were out of sight around one of the stream's bends and behind the branches overhanging the ravine, though Fran could hear the splash of their footsteps.

"Drop it," Beth called out.

Septum Piercing dropped her crossbow. She stood there as the current tugged it a few inches from her feet to catch by one arm on some hidden snag. She was breathing hard, fists clenched white-knuckled at her sides. For a second Fran thought Beth might loose. The tall girl's forearm trembled. Her fingers flexed on her bowstring. Septum Piercing stood her ground but Fran saw her bottom lip tremble, like a child's.

I don't want to see this.

The whine of a motor ripped through the stillness. Beth whirled toward the sound, arrow flying off at random into the underbrush as Septum Piercing dropped and scrambled into the cover of the ferns, snatching up her crossbow on the way. Fran lurched to her feet, dripping and dizzy with the pain in her jaw. Beside her Beth was fumbling with another arrow.

There, on the crest of the southern ridge of the defile, was Teach. She rode on a fast little Honda motorbike, the kind Fran's dad would have called a crotch rocket, slewing toward them down the slope at breakneck speed. Her hair blew wild all around the pale, pointed oval of her face and she had something compact and black in her hands, too small to be a crossbow but—

"Beth!" Fran screamed. "Get down!"

The submachine gun barked like sped-up footage of a bichon frise having some kind of seizure. Moss and dirt flew where the hail of bullets ripped into the bank. Bits of shredded fern floated through the air over Fran's head as she cowered in the stream, duffel clamped tight against her side. Through the underbrush she could just see Septum Piercing wriggling away flat on her belly. That seemed like the right idea.

All we need is enough breathing room to get up the far slope and into the trees. They won't follow, not just for two trashgirls.

The sewing machine clatter of Teach's gun let up, the echoes ringing down the defile's wooded length. The Honda's engine purred as it rolled downhill, closer and closer. Soon Teach wouldn't be able to miss if she tried. Fran looked over at Beth. The other girl lay huddled against the bank with her bow over one shoulder and her chin pressed to the mud, dirty blond hair hiding her face. *We're not going to make it,* she thought, curling in on herself as her insides filled up with the black sludge of despair.

I don't want to run anymore.

A scream rose up from the woods. It hung in the air, high and quavering, and seemed to come from all sides. Another voice, farther away, added its ear-piercing song and a white knife of terror cut through Fran's paralysis. She knew that sound. It had chased her for five years, chased her all the way from the dressing room at the Charlotte Russe at the Steeplegate Mall to this overgrown ditch where she knelt quivering, sweat streaming down her face, waiting to die. She looked up.

Halfway up the defile's slope, Teach sat on her idling bike with one boot braced in the loose earth and deadfall, looking uphill toward the men prowling out of the trees. Fear flickered across the older woman's face as she fingered the trigger of her machine pistol. They came on all fours, some still screaming, others making a kind of low, rhythmic grunt deep in their chests. It sounded like the tigers Fran remembered from York's Wild Kingdom. Her father had taken her there a few times during the divorce, and the deep chuffing sound the tigers made to warn one another off had stuck with her.

Teach gunned the bike's engine, her rear wheel throwing up a rooster tail of dirt and deadfall as it slipped, slewed, and finally found traction. The men boiled downhill in a shrieking tide, all filthy hair and scabby, flaking skin and mouths full of rotten brown teeth. Raw flesh showed under their eyes and at their joints and the corners of their mouths. Seams of it glistened like meaty lava flows between the shifting tectonic plates of their hides. Teach fishtailed up the slope and shot between two of the oncoming men and over the crest of the defile, catching air for a handful of heartbeats before landing with a crash somewhere out of sight and letting the Honda loose. The men scrambled after her, grunting and howling, falling over themselves and one another as they clawed their way over the lip.

Fran dragged Beth up and pulled her toward the far side of the defile. They climbed the slope in silence, Fran pausing every so often to look back at the trails of torn and churned-up earth on the far slope where Teach and her pursuers had gone. Beth began to laugh as they neared the top. Twice she doubled over giggling and had to lean on Fran to keep from tumbling back down the hill. Fran didn't have the energy to ask her why. Her body felt raw and vulnerable, as though someone had rubbed it all over with a cheese grater. She hardly made it over the lip.

"I'm sorry, it's just—" Beth, crawling up after her, burst into fresh peals of laughter and flopped down helplessly against a tree. She was still laughing when a crossbow bolt opened the side of her face like a Ziploc and buried itself in the trunk of the tree. Fran whirled, nerves singing. Across the ravine, Septum Piercing, standing by a toppled tree furred with thick moss, set her foot against her crossbow's arm and pushed down hard, dragging the wire back toward its lock with white-knuckled hands. Her cheeks were flushed, her short blond hair plastered to her forehead with sweat. She had a stupid collarbone tattoo, a chain of pale pink flowers or something.

Fran got her arms under Beth's and dragged her back into the brush, keeping her eyes on Septum Piercing as the other girl struggled to reload. Beth was swearing out the uninjured side of her mouth, hand clamped to the messy wound, blood pouring down her neck. She fought her way up to her feet, leaning hard on Fran. Across the ravine Septum Piercing slotted a bolt into the crossbow's nut. Fran flushed red at her grin, picturing those sharp white teeth closing gently on her throat.

You're a stupid bitch, Fran.

Septum Piercing's second shot went whistling through the trees well above them and yards to the left. "This shit is your fault, you fucking monsters!" screamed the girl, striding forward to the lip of the defile. She was tall, maybe five-ten or more. "When we catch you—"

A brief but vivid fantasy of the nose-ringed girl trailing a riding crop's cool leather keeper over her clenched and trembling ass shoved its way eagerly into Fran's imagination.

"—we're gonna leave you staked out in the sun and let t. rex peel off your fucking womanface!"

The last Fran saw of her as she pulled Beth back into the underbrush was a flash of blond and the glint of the sun hitting a stainless steel piercing.

A stupid, horny bitch.

♀

In an anime, Fran thought as she dabbed at Beth's gashed cheek and ruined left ear with a cotton swab soaked in alcohol, the crossbow bolt would have given Beth a clean, sexy scar—something to give her an edge and make it clear she was haunted by her past. In real life she had no more earlobe and a four-inch gouge in her face distressingly similar in shape to the Nike Swoosh. They sat together at a rotting picnic bench at a hikers' rest not far from the coast, Beth's legs outstretched and Fran straddling the seat.

"That fake-punk bitch," Beth growled through gritted teeth as Fran probed at the edges of her wound. "Bet she had white dreads in college. Bet she blogged about how her straight boyfriend 'felt unwelcome' at Pride. Ah, Jesus, that stings!"

"Don't be a baby." Fran took the needle she'd threaded from the first-aid kit laid out on the table's lichen-spotted surface. "And stop talking. I have to stitch it up before I lose the light."

Beth gave her a dirty look, but bit her tongue. Blood drooled in sluggish rivulets down her cheek. The hot, wet wind sighed through the trees around their unkempt clearing. The shadows of clouds and rustling leaves moved over the long grass. She set the needle against Beth's cheek just above the upper lip of the wound. The other girl shut her eyes tight, screwing up her face in anticipation.

It went quickly. Beth's breath came in quick, throttled gasps as she dug her fingernails into the rotting wood of the picnic table's bench seat. Fran sewed, pinching the wound's lips together with her thumb and forefinger while she did. The needle dimpled Beth's sunburned skin, tugging at it with each stitch. Beads of red welled up around the silk where it cut into flushed skin. It was almost comforting to work on something so definitively fixable. The world was broken, but Beth's face she could keep in one piece. She latticed back and forth until at last the lips met, wet and raw, and the wound was closed.

Fran transferred the bloody needle to the corner of her mouth, pulled the thread taut, and tied it off. She scooched back along the bench to better admire her work. The stitches were a little messy, the lips of the cut slightly puckered. Beth glowered at her and Fran smiled in spite of the dull, thudding pain of her broken tooth. "You're going to have the dumbest fucking scar."

III

THE PRIZE DRAWER

Most prehistoric people who survived to die of natural causes, the fossil record suggested, died of tooth infections. Fran had read that in a yellowing issue of *National Geographic* she found in a box in her great-grandfather's study when she was nine years old, and the fact had never, ever left her brain in the two decades since. The collapse of civilization had, if anything, shoved it closer to the forefront of her awareness. Sometimes she lay awake at night as it ran through her head again and again to the tune of the vaudeville song the old lawyer in *The Aristocats* warbled while lurching around Madame Bonfamille's parlor.

You'll die of
TOOTH DECAY!
You'll DIE of TOOTH decay!
You'll die of toooooth decay
You'll
Die
Of
Tooth
De
Cay

It was running through her head now as she trudged along the barren, crumbling black serpent of I-95 with Beth, her broken tooth aching like someone had stuffed a hot coal into her cheek and stapled it in place. It was hot and the day's aches and scrapes were pulling at her, making every starlit step an ordeal. As she walked, she chewed licorice root on the left side of her jaw, the sickeningly sweet taste coating the inside of her mouth. Shelved spiro was mostly useless now, ruined by sunlight or water or simple oxidization. So, licorice root. Spearmint tea. Some girls ate black cohosh, but it gave Fran awful diarrhea.

Winter was dangerous. The dried shit started losing potency sometime in February, usually, and even doubling up on dosage didn't always keep t. rex at bay. Two years ago Fran had come down with the shakes so bad she'd begged Indi to kill her. The dreams were the worst part, fever-sweat nightmares of toothy little tumors wriggling under her skin and seams of glistening flesh blooming around the flexion of her muscles. Her body ached. Her bones felt as though they were burning from the inside out.

And then it passed, and they hadn't talked about it since. It was just part of living now, like getting your appendix out. Except if you got appendicitis now you'd just die in agony unless you were lucky enough to know a surgeon who'd survived T-Day and wouldn't harvest your blood and sell it to bunker brats for their vampire facials. Not that it had been better when she'd been uninsured and living over Indi's garage. She ran her tongue carefully over her broken tooth, feeling the ragged flesh around it and the sharp, uneven fragments of its cracked surface.

I wonder if there are any dentists left on the East Coast. I wonder if there's any novocaine, or laughing gas.

"There's a dentist in Seabrook," said Beth, apparently reading Fran's mind. The bandage Fran had taped over the other girl's wounded cheek was crusty with dried blood. "We could trade with him, maybe. We have weed. You think he has weed?"

Fran absently transferred her wad of licorice root to the right side of her mouth. Only her absolute certainty that if a man got wind of them she wouldn't be good for much more than lying down and rolling over on her back to die kept the scream of pain bottled inside her throat. She was on her knees without knowing how she'd got there, duffel lying nearby and hands clasped over her mouth as white-hot barbs of misery crawled down through her jaw. She heaved and puked up bile and blood, both black in the darkness, onto the cracked pavement.

Beth, kneeling beside her, rubbed her back as she retched again. "Or I guess we could do it here."

♀

Beth walked her to a rusted-out minivan abandoned on the highway's shoulder just south of a cut where exposed faces of granite flanked the highway, seams of quartz catching the starlight. They sat on the car's moth-eaten floor carpeting, dangling their feet in the grass pushing its way up through the pavement, and ate cold balls from the foam case in the duffel. Fran chewed the raw, springy flesh gingerly. She scratched her own in sympathy as she choked down the best source of estrogen five years of reckless experimentation and desperate medical-library raids had been able to turn up. She could practically hear Indi's voice as she ate.

Just pretend it's one of those fancy chocolates with the gold foil. You know. A Ferrero Rocher.

She couldn't remember what Ferrero Rochers tasted like, and the pungent, gamey stink of the testicle coated her tongue like oil. How many of these things had she choked down since the last of the estradiol had oxidized? Hundreds, probably. She'd eaten more balls than she'd ever sucked cocks. The thought made her unexpectedly blue. Or maybe it was just the humidity. Sweating always made her sad.

Pretend they're oysters on the half shell.

She swallowed, fighting her gag reflex the whole way, and then sagged against Beth's side. Her jaw throbbed. It was starting to swell. "I feel like shit," she mumbled, tearing up. "I want ice cream. I wanna sleep in a *bed*."

"I know," said Beth, "but we're gonna crash in a derelict car tonight and tomorrow I'm pulling your tooth out with hand tools, so you probably shouldn't eat anything else because you'll just puke it up on me. Anyway we only have expired power bars and jerky. Oh, and balls."

Fran closed her eyes. "Can you not crack jokes right now?"

A moment of brittle silence. "Sure," said Beth, with forced good humor. "Sorry."

Most of the time, Fran thought later as she lay drowsing on the mildew-smelling car floor with her head pillowed on the duffel, things were good between them. Most of the time they worked well together, Beth the high school track-and-field star slash dropout and Fran the premed fuckup hunting their way up and down the East Coast in search of testicles to eat and kidney lobes to process in Indi's lab so they could sell nice clean hormones to the menopausal cis ladies in Manchester and Seabrook and sometimes Concord and Nashua if the roads were open. Sometimes, though, it felt like high school had never ended, like their terrible fight had happened yesterday instead of eight years ago, and Fran would wish, and hate herself for wishing, that she had two hours of highway driving and a mute button between her life and Bethany Crick.

♀

"You remember prize drawers?" Beth asked, her tone light. Conversational. It was just after dawn and she was on her knees astride Fran's lap. She had a pair of rough-jawed pliers in her hand. "Stickers. Rubber finger puppets. Those pocket mazes with the little ball bearings?"

Fran grunted her assent, oddly soothed at being asked an inane question while her mouth was full of fingers and metal. It made it seem more like she was twenty again and in a real dentist's office getting quizzed about her biochem major by a fifty-year-old man with a waxed mustache as he checked her molars for cavities.

In reality she sat with her back to the rusted-out car where they'd slept, her head pillowed on Beth's smelly sweatshirt, waiting for the other girl to rip her tooth out. At least the heat had broken sometime in the night. It was cool and breezy today, the wind blowing the salt smell of the nearby tidal marshes inland.

"I was all about the prize drawer when I was a kid," said Beth. "When we had insurance I used to beg to go to the dentist just so I could get a shot at it." She squinted, peering into Fran's wide-open mouth. "We didn't have a lot of money and I was obsessed with toys. I've always loved tiny things. Miniatures."

The plier's jaws probed gently at Fran's infected gum line. Fran groaned, her body tensing from her taint up to the base of her skull as her muscles bathed in a deluge of sour cortisol.

"When I was six our dentist got these little cars. Dragsters, cement mixers, all kinds of shit. My brother Derek got a little cop car and I was *obsessed* with that thing. I used to pretend it had tiny cops inside it, drinking tiny coffees and complaining about their tiny wives. He said there was another one left in the prize drawer and fuck, I wanted it worse than anything."

The nose of the pliers found a shard of tooth standing at an angle to the root. Slowly, her face inches from Fran's mouth, Beth gripped it and worked it free. The pain was sickening. Gray light washed over Fran's thoughts. She groaned at the sight of the bloody white sliver and Beth covered her mouth with her free hand. "You can't scream," she said. "I know it sucks."

Fran sucked in deep breaths through her nostrils, fighting the urge to bite Beth's hand and then shriek her lungs out. How long had it been since she screamed? She imagined little Beth had screamed a lot. A horrible, fussy baby with a scrunched red face and jaundiced skin. By six she must have been a terror.

"The morning of my next checkup I was practically salivating. The fuckin' adventures I was gonna have with that car." She leaned in close, dark brown eyes narrowed to slits, and nosed the pliers back toward Fran's left rear molars where the hot pulse of her broken tooth clutched at her jaw. "Finally there was one boy left ahead of me, this little ginger puke named Brian Finnerty I knew from school. I was losing my mind waiting for him to come out. I knew he'd take it first, that he'd know somehow and take it just to fuck with me." The pliers' jaws found their mark. Roots of pain unfurled down through Fran's jawbone.

"When he finally strutted out into the waiting room with that patrol cruiser in his hand, I couldn't take it. I walked up to him and popped him right in the mouth. Knocked out his filling."

Fran laughed. She couldn't help it. Beth, who must have been waiting for the opening, pulled. Tearing, sucking pain. Bone grinding against bone. Blood welling up from the white-hot absence of the socket. Threads and rags of loose flesh waved in the sluggish flow. Fran whimpered, curling in on herself, flinching away from the gory little nub of broken bone clamped in Beth's pliers. The other girl leaned down to kiss her temple, then pressed something smooth and crinkling into her limp hand. "Good job, Frankie," said Beth. "Here's your prize."

Fran looked down at it. A mini Snickers bar, the bite-sized kind people gave out—used to give out—on Halloween. Her favorite. She pressed it tight against her chest, tears threatening. Her jaw felt like someone had hooked it up to a corroded car battery and coated the jumper cable jaws with chili powder for good measure. She squeezed her eyes shut tight and imagined kids in costume running down the sidewalk through dead leaves and misting rain, the street lights coming on above their laughter.

"Thankth, Beth."

♀

Fran slept badly that night, alternately shivering and sweating, guzzling water whenever she stirred and then limping around to the back of the van to piss every fifteen minutes. Her clothes felt tight and itchy. Her skin was grimy, her hair tangled. She combed it with her fingers as she stared up at the stars through the van's cracked and lichen-spotted windshield. Her empty socket throbbed with a sick, vacant ache.

When she did sleep, she dreamed of the world that was gone, of her last few shifts at the Park Avenue Starbucks and the sputtering progress of her FFS fundraiser on Twitter. She dreamed of refreshing the page again and again only to find donations draining away, supportive comments deleted. She dreamed of the slender, elegant face she'd designed with her surgeon, Dr. Bakshi.

I was so close, she thought miserably, sitting down to a candlelit dining room table where on her plate an eight-inch cock sat crisped up beautifully under a thin drizzle of vinaigrette reduction. *I was so close to being a girl.*

Across the table, shrouded in the gloom of the vast dining room, another figure stirred. Cutlery squealed against bone china. The sound of chewing, loud and breathy, squelched beneath the sharper sound. Blood dripped onto the edge of a plate just revealed by candlelight.

So close.

The outline of the face she'd made, the one she'd dreamed of pulling down over her own as though she could step into a dream and wear it waking, leered at her through flame and melting wax. Blood and gore slicked its narrow chin, and behind its perfectly arched brows and Roman nose seethed great thick slabs of fat and bone and muscle pulsing in the dark, a huge rotten man-body hiding itself behind what she would never have.

She looked down at her plate. Blood spurted pitifully from the cock's bare head and pooled on the porcelain. The thing across the table smacked its lips, which should have been hers, and would have been if T-Day had come just a few weeks later. She'd been scheduled, hadn't she? The plague had snatched her finished self away.

Except you wouldn't have been on your meds before or after surgery, and that beautiful face would have cracked open and tumors would have grown behind it and eaten through it with their sharp little teeth, and then there'd be nothing left of you at all.

She looked back up at those red lips, pouty and full. They parted. A thin trickle of blood ran from one nostril and into its open mouth to wash over a single sharp, perfect canine. Rags of flesh between its teeth. What was it eating?

The face spoke.

"Fran, you fuck. Wake up."

Fran blinked awake. For a moment she forgot where she was and felt a sense of clawing panic in her chest before reality closed back in. The van. The heat was back, thicker and more oppressive than before, and mosquitoes whined in the starlight. Her legs were bitten all to shit. And out on the highway a set of watery headlights cut the dark, washing over their scant shelter. Beth had crept into the front of the van, hiding her silhouette behind the remains of the driver's seat. Fran stayed very still.

A flatbed thundered past them toward the notch. Someone had soldered a crude cowcatcher to its cab's grille, and a peaked canvas canopy stretched over a framework of steel struts like tentpoles ran the length of its trailer. Under the canopy's shadow Fran could just make out the orange pinpricks of lit cigarettes and the vague silhouettes of boots hanging over the trailer's edge.

"There's so many of them," Fran whispered.

Another truck rattled out of the dark behind the first, its sole working headlight flickering on and off. More boots. More cigarettes. The gleam of metal and the pale candle flames of ghostly faces under its tattered canopy. Shuttered lanterns swung there. Suits of riot gear hung from hooks like empty body bags. A third came behind it, and a fourth.

"Oh fuck my mother and forget her number," Beth hissed back, her eyes wide and frightened in the gloom.

Fran saw it dancing in the fourth truck's strobing headlight before Beth had finished her sentence. Two yard-high Xs slashed in white paint on the passenger door of the third truck's cab and repeated on banners flapping from the framework sheltering the bed. The TERFs were headed north.

IV

CHAD

They passed by Foxborough without leaving the interstate. Crows and turkey vultures circled the town in ragged spirals and perched on the eaves and chimneys of the buildings closest to the highway. Gas stations, strip malls, part of an office park crumbling under the assault of creepers and overgrowth, the slim lances of new beeches and evergreens rising here and there from the shapeless green sprawl of it. A McDonald's with a gaping, char-edged hole in its side. Bird shit clung to all of it in waterfalls of crusted white and gray and brown.

Twice they heard men scream in the distance and the second time, just after dusk, a pack of coyotes and half-breed coydogs howled in answer, their voices high and wild and lonely, rising and falling like the wails of mourners at a funeral. Fran complained about her blisters and every few hours she would start to wring her hands and sniffle and wonder aloud if Seabrook was on fire yet or if the TERFs were breaking down doors in Boston and dragging trans women out into the night like she'd heard they did in Baltimore. Beth tried not to listen.

Fran had grown up with money, back when money still meant something, and she had that middle-class brain disease that makes people think calamities can be controlled. It had been that way since they were kids. Beth knew better. No matter how prepared you were, some things just rolled over you in a hot, sticky black tide and you were lucky if they left you standing.

Beth thought again with a rush of shame and guilt of the girl she'd plugged with an arrow at the edge of the woods. She'd felt so confident lining up her shot on Teach. It would have been perfect. Right through the TERF's nose and out the back of her stupid fucking head. Someone else would have taken over, sure, but it would have felt good to ventilate that bitch's sinuses and watch her groupies lose their narrow little college-girl heads. Also she might've been able to get her grandpa's wallet out of the basket of her bike; she'd been carrying it around with her old cards and IDs out of sheer force of habit since the beginning of the end. Oh well.

Fran's voice snapped her out of her morbid daydream. "Are you listening to me?" She sounded hurt. "We need to find somewhere to sleep."

It was hot out, a muggy, oppressive kind of heat that lay over the long shadows and red light of sunset like congealing stew. Beth had peeled her hoodie off earlier and her undershirt was soaked and sticking to her back. She could feel the beginnings of a sunburn tightening the skin of her shoulders. Mosquitoes boiled in the gathering dusk and Beth realized they'd bitten up her arms and legs. She hadn't even noticed.

"Yeah," she said, scratching her forearms. "There's a rest stop in a few miles, I think. We can sleep on the roof."

A man's scream rose up from the woods again, not far off this time, and by unspoken agreement they paused to watch the birds fly in whirring coveys from the trees. Not for the first time, Beth wondered if they were lonely, those things that had been men. If they missed their wives, their mothers, their daughters and girlfriends and dominatrixes. Or maybe they were happy now, free to rape and kill and eat whomever, free to shit and piss and jerk off in the street.

Maybe this world was the one they'd always wanted.

♀

The rest stop was set back from the highway behind a brake of pine trees. A few rusted-out cars sat abandoned in the parking lot by the low, boxy silhouette of the visitor center. Vending machines lay tipped over and smashed beside the center's plate-glass doors, which were spiderwebbed with cracks and skinned with spots of lichen. The sunlight had faded to a blood-colored smear over the distant mountains.

There was a groundskeeper's shed half-hidden by sumac across the parking lot. Beth kicked the door in and, after some fumbling through the moldy interior by the scant illumination of Fran's penlight, found a folding aluminum ladder hidden behind bags of mold-speckled fertilizer. She dragged it out and across the yard back to the center, then waited as Fran knotted their climbing rope to the top step so that they could pull it up after them. The new men were stupid, but they could still use a ladder.

New men, she thought, gripping the gutter and bracing a foot against the wall. *Like Coke Zero. Same great vicious disregard for our lives, none of the socially enforced restraint!*

The roof felt like another world. Moss grew thick around the tin-plated boiler vent and spread out in a dark green carpet over half the flat tarpaper expanse, stopping at the low wooden retaining wall—half-rotten—that edged its perimeter. A line of fat brown sparrows sleeping on the south eaves eyed them coolly as they laid out their sleeping mats in the starlight. Beth thought about trying for a shot at one, but it would be a mouthful at best and they still had power bars and trail mix.

It made her think of the girl, too. The TERF she'd shot. She hadn't nocked an arrow since. Another fun thing to have PTSD about in the post-civilized wasteland of New England.

♀

Beth couldn't sleep. The stars were out, a brilliant sea broken up by the soft, dark continents of drifting clouds, and she lay staring up at them a yard from where Fran slept curled on her side in an undershirt and bicycle shorts, snoring softly.

We'd be back in Seabrook now if it weren't for me, she thought. *If I hadn't taken that stupid fucking shot.*

That girl screaming—straight bangs and big brown eyes—with the shaft buried deep in her shoulder.

Beth shook her head. She passed a hand gingerly over her face, brushing light against the swollen skin around her stitches, and wondered if she'd have time for a quick shave tomorrow. It felt stupid to still care about it. It wasn't like she'd ever passed, not at six foot two and two hundred pounds with her long horse face, broad shoulders, and blocky jaw. Why bother scraping another few days of stubble off something no one with eyes would ever think was a real woman?

She made herself exhale. A self-pitying spiral wasn't going to help anything. A shave would make her feel better. She didn't need to put any more thought into it than that. *Thanks, though, depression. This was fun.*

Minutes ticked by. Beth timed her breathing, trying to ease herself into drowsiness, to relax her muscles one by one until whichever of them held her wakeful finally unclenched. The stars turned overhead. The shadows of clouds swept over them. The heat was terrible, a smothering weight lying skin to skin with her no matter how she tossed and turned. Sweat poured in rivers over her tight, sunburned skin.

A sound jerked her bolt upright in the starlight. A muted thunder of crunches and snaps from the forest to the north. Underbrush rustling in a distant susurrus. She shuffled on her knees to the roof's retaining wall, squinting at the distant smear of Boston's lights beyond the trees. Before T-Day it would have burned like a beacon. Now it was only a pale yellow-white smudge, a porch light someone had forgotten to turn off.

The crashing grew louder. Across the parking lot, a doe burst out of the dark under the pines. She was full-out, lathered like a racehorse, her shadow sweeping smooth and fleet over the broken pavement with each bound. Behind her, mouths gaping, eyes luminous in the faint silver light, came a tide of men. They ran on all fours, callused feet and knuckles making the visitor center shake under Beth's knees. She glanced at Fran, still sleeping, and then back at the oncoming wave. Their eyes glinted in the dark like the eyes of animals caught in car headlights.

The deer ran on. Beth wondered what had happened to the rest of her herd. Torn flesh. Gristle stretched by rotten teeth. A scrap of dappled hide. A gory hoof. The men streamed after her, backs heaving, limbs scything through grit and dust and flying pine needles. They poured past the visitor center, their pack stretching out as stragglers fell behind and the doe opened up a lead. Beth dared, for a moment, to hope the creature might make it. Then the second pack came boiling quick and quiet from the woods beside the area where trucks had parked so that their drivers could catch a few hours of sleep, before.

They got the doe near the on-ramp, it sounded like, and she screamed, just once, a high, hoarse sound Beth wanted to forget as soon as she'd heard it, and then there was only the crunch of breaking bone and the wet ripping noise of the men worrying at her flesh.

♀

By dawn the pack had moved on, dragging the deer's half-eaten carcass back into the woods, and Beth had snatched a few bleak hours of sleep shot through with nightmares of screaming women whose bodies crumbled at the slightest touch. She felt greasy and faintly nauseous, her stomach clenched around a knot of half-digested power bar and jerky. She stood up and stretched, blinking bleary-eyed in the soft, wet heat.

She got her shaving kit and vaulted from the roof, leaving Fran to sleep.

A backed-up drainage cut near the west edge of the parking lot had flooded some time recently. The water didn't look bad, Beth thought as she drew closer. Not drinkable, but fine. She knelt in the soft soil of its bank and bent to splash some on her face. Lukewarm. Too cloudy to see the bottom. Her reflection swam in the brown churn. Big brick face, all scarred up and bandaged. Brick, brick, brick.

She took her razor from her belt and ran it a few times along its loose stretch, slack grown notch by notch over five years of constant travel and infrequent meals. She didn't really know if it helped keep the razor sharp, but she liked the shushing sound it made. *Stropping.* That's what it was called.

He came at her out of the cut, exploding through the placid surface in a cloud of sparkling droplets, and she saw with a thrill of terror that he was erect, his cock standing hard against his concave belly. She dropped her razor and went for her knife, but slowly, so slowly. It felt like she was moving through stirred concrete, like someone had filled her arms with steel ball bearings. Her hand closed on the knife's worn hilt.

He crashed into her and they fell together, rolling through the tall grass. She stabbed at him. He was bigger than she was and strong, hideously strong. The smell of his breath was cum and rotten meat and old, forgotten gym bags where the accoutrements of manhood festered unseen in the sweaty dark. A rat walled up dead behind new drywall. His teeth snapped inches from her face, held back only by her straining forearm. She stabbed again, hot blood gushing over her hand, and lost hold of the knife as he twisted atop her and wrapped his claws around her throat.

His filthy nails dug into her neck. She looked up at him, breathing through her teeth, fighting the urge to shrink into a ball and go away until he'd finished what the thing between his legs wanted to do to her. *I can take him. I can take this piece of shit. When he was a person I'd have whipped his ass at pool and gone home with his fucking girl.*

Warm drool dripped onto her upturned face. His nails broke skin. Her own breath hissed in her ears, thin and strangled, and she thought, for some reason, of Fran's hesitant mouth on hers, not opening, and of the other woman's soft, husky voice tickling her neck.

You make me feel so delicate.

He was going to kill her. She couldn't hold him off. He was going to kill her, and if she was lucky he'd do it before he raped her. Her forearm trembled under his crushing weight. She could see his chin and his gnashing teeth and his spit ran into her eyes, stinging and vile. Spots formed and burst like blackheads in her vision. Then running footsteps. A dull, solid *thwack* of impact. The man rolled off of her with a gurgling moan. Beth lay gasping in the mud. Fran stood over her, breathing hard, a bloodstained brick clutched in her hands.

"Are you okay?" Fran asked.

Beth levered herself up onto her elbows, coughing. "I'm great," she croaked. "I was about to focus my *ki* into the first two fingers of my right hand and liquefy his entire spine with a single strike, but you threw off my technique."

The man let out a kind of snarling whine. He was bent double, his wounded head resting against the ground, claws digging furrows in the dirt. In three somehow incredibly faggy steps—Beth had never met anyone else who minced like that—Fran was at his side. Her face screwed up in distaste, she brought the brick down on the back of his head. Skin split. Bone crunched. The brick came up, Fran's arms trembling with its weight, then down again. Up and down, hammering his face into the mossy ground.

Finally Fran stumbled away from his still form, the brick falling with a splash into the muddy water. She was shaking. Beth, still breathing hard, got up and hooked the toe of her boot under the dead man's shoulder. She flipped him over onto his back. They both stared. With his cleft chin and relatively unmarred face—the worst of the split skin and scarring confined to just behind his ears and the soft flesh under his jaw—he seemed disconcertingly normal, like a stock image of a high school football player, or a Ken doll. Beth burst out laughing.

"Oh my God," Fran squeaked. She clapped her bloody hands over her mouth. "I killed a Chad!"

V

NOT ALL MEN

Robbie knew a lot about how to fight someone bigger than yourself. The first and best way to do it was to avoid them completely, to never be where they could find you, to give them no reason to realize you existed at all. The second was to be as brutal and unfair as humanly possible. In his sophomore year of high school, he'd donned a burlap sack with cut-out eyeholes for a hood and caught Dane Kimball, the football captain, on a stretch of empty dirt road between school and home. He'd walked right up to Kimball and fired a nail gun eight times into his hand and arm. Dane had kept away from Anna and her friends after that.

It was the same with what the cis men had turned into. You had to kill them before they knew you were there, preferably during the scant two or three hours a day they spent asleep, or else when they were eating, or at a watering hole. Ideally you found one of their caves and just rolled in a Sheetrock bucket full of gasoline with a burning rag stuffed through a hole in the lid. Smoke did most of the work; you just had to stand over the cave mouth and shoot the survivors as they crawled out.

Just now, with no fuel on hand and nothing else to occupy his time, he was sitting halfway up a thirty-foot maple in the crotch of two thick branches with a sour apple gumball in his mouth, a rifle across his lap, and sixteen hundred rounds of ammunition neatly slotted into the cubby holes of a vinyl laundry organizer he'd hung from a higher limb.

In the clearing below lay the carcass of a dog he'd found, the smell of which he'd amplified with a rotten cut of venison and a liberal splash of his own piss. He was pretty sure they could smell estrogen.

The first man showed itself near noon, loping like a wolf out of the shadows under the trees. He approached the dead dog warily, snuffling at the air and snarling to itself before it thrust its face into the carcass's open flank to feed. Robbie raised the rifle to his shoulder and squinted down the iron sights. He took his time, waiting to see if another might join the first as it ripped mouthfuls of rotting meat off of the carcass and choked them down with its head thrown back, snuffling and snorting for breath. None did.

Near one o'clock he eased pressure onto the rifle's trigger on his exhale, just like he'd watched his grandfather do a hundred times shooting crows in the pumpkin field. The rifle bucked against his shoulder. The thing in the clearing gave a funny sideways leap, half its head blown off and sticky black coral ridges of brain showing through the shattered skull, and then collapsed facedown, legs kicking spasmodically at the dirt and dead pine needles. Screams rose up in the distance. Robbie worked the rifle's bolt to chamber a new round. Most automatic firearms were seized up and useless at this point, and repairing them was outside his wheelhouse, but anything they'd used in World War II you could break down, grease, and put back together in working order in a few short hours.

That reliability was a plus when you needed to kill forty or fifty extremely angry things that used to be people in the space of about fifteen minutes. He held the rifle slanting down across his thighs, swinging his bare feet idly as the sound of bodies crashing through the underbrush drew closer. It made him think of his last summer on the farm and, for some reason, of the night his grandfather, uneasy, not understanding, but with love, had shaved his head at his request with a pair of ancient clippers.

If that's what you want, tiger.

The men came out of the woods. Robbie raised the rifle. He tracked the scything motion of their long, lean arms and legs, the ripple of thick muscle under their broad shoulders. He led the fastest of them, letting out a long, slow breath.

And he fired.

♀

He walked home late that night beneath the dead and silent power lines, entangled now beyond hope of extraction with the limbs of half-grown pines. Creepers hung from the sagging lines and coiled like pythons up the few remaining telephone poles and over the rusted transformers. His cramps were coming back and he badly needed a new pad. For a moment he felt a twinge of dysphoria, a sense that someone might have heard his thoughts and sneered at them. It passed. He smiled to himself in the moonlit dark.

It felt like half-remembering a funny dream to think back on how insecure he'd been, how he'd pissed and moaned at Tess over every picture she took of him (too feminine) and every time she put her arm around his waist (emphasizing that I'm smaller than you is fucking transphobic). That venal, frightened voice inside him had shriveled up and died five years ago while he'd sat drugged in his adjustable hospital bed, chest numb and eyes bleary, watching the world burn on TV and trying not to cry because if the doctors on the news were right he'd never be able to take T again and his entire family was going to die.

Now he was the only man he knew. There were others; he'd met one on the outskirts of Manchester a year or so ago, a scruffy man in his forties or fifties named Reggie who'd been at the low point in his dose cycle when the plague hit, and he guessed fresh trans men still came out sometimes. People who hadn't known before the plague or who'd been closeted. They were out there, making their own manhood in the wreckage of the world. Sometimes he thought he should find them, link up, and hunt together, but he never did it. It was safer, being alone.

He was a dozen yards from the edge of his campsite, rifle resting on one shoulder, his gumball reduced to a malleable, crusty paste of tasteless sugar, when he heard voices. He sank into a crouch among the spreading ferns, suddenly conscious of the heat that lay like a blanket over the woods at the river's edge where he'd been staying for a week now. Mosquitoes whined in the humid stillness. One settled on his shoulder, wings falling silent, and began to drink.

". . . telling you, whoever lives here has more than she needs. Who the fuck's gonna hunt us down over some mushrooms and dried fish?"

It was a rough voice, high and strained with a hint of crackling vocal fry and a pronounced Boston accent. The speaker sounded as though she were in the middle of something difficult. The reply—which came from somewhere near his tent—was sweeter, milder. More New Haven than Dorchester. "I don't feel good about this. I want to go. We should go."

Robbie crept through the underbrush in silence. He could see a penlight's blue-white beam and the slender shadow of the person who held it trained on a second figure, much larger, halfway up the big wind-stripped pine where he'd hung his bear bags. She was rifling through the largest of them, transferring canning jars and wax-wrapped parcels to a duffel slung over her shoulder. It was too dark to see what she was taking.

He took a mental inventory of his stockpile as the larger woman zipped the bear bag back up, adjusted her duffel's strap, and began shinning down the tree. She couldn't have taken much, and he had a safety week built in. He could fish the river, gather late berries, maybe bake acorn bread if he could find eggs. The thought of shooting the intruders flitted quick and red across his mind. The big one first, then the one holding the light.

The tree climber dropped the last few feet, landing lightly and swiping sweaty hair out of her face. She had a gap between her two front teeth and a blood-crusted gauze pad plastered to one cheek. A scar tugged at the other corner of her mouth, which was soft and round in sharp contrast with the long-jawed weight of her features. Her blunt, choppy bangs were plastered to her forehead. She blew out a breath.

"Can we go now?" asked the other. She'd moved closer and Robbie could see her now, silhouetted in the moonlight. Trans, but he could only tell by the very slight swelling of her Adam's apple. With her long, straight nose and narrow jaw—a mandible shave, maybe?—she looked sad and waifish. Hunched. Elbows drawn in. A sudden pang of homesickness closed his throat and brought tears to his eyes.

When was the last time you spoke out loud to another human being? When was the last time you touched someone?

He watched them for a while as they talked, imagining the things he'd say to them, the places they might go together once they came around to the advantages of strength in numbers. He nearly stood, and then he thought of Midge and the winter after the collapse and the cabin where they'd stayed, rationing canned beans and peanuts and drinking lemon juice because Midge, who loved to read about Franklin and Shackleton and all those other idiots who got themselves and all their men killed exploring the poles, kept insisting they'd get scurvy.

The taller woman raked a hand back through her hair. She said something to the shorter one, who looked uncomfortable. Robbie thought of the day the spiro had run out. He thought of the basement and the rusted lock and the handgun buried somewhere in the woods outside of Durham. He thought of those things and watched, and waited, and didn't move until the sound of the women's footsteps faded into the soft, humid stillness of the night.

VI

DEE LICIOUS

The day after they found the stranger's camp, they cut through Middleton, heading northeast toward Seabrook on an arc that kept them well away from Boston's suburbs. Fran disliked the city. Too many cold stares through the gaps in heavy curtains. Too many empty, gutted buildings where anything might be lurking. It was a hard place, a cis place, and she'd never forgotten her friend Lizzie's story about seeing a trans girl hustler hanged on New Year's Eve from the traffic light in front of South Station. Besides, for all she knew the TERFs were there already.

There had always been radfems in New England, enclaves of sneering middle-class white women who talked a lot about performing gender roles and appropriating lived experience. They curated incestuous little social media cells where they repeated the same six talking points to the same thirty other women while cis men came sniffing around their hindquarters, venting pent-up hatred on trans women and making sure *real* women saw them doing it so they could get accredited as feminists and maybe, if they were lucky, catch a whiff of pussy.

After T-Day, it got worse. Fran could still picture the viral video of the trans girl succumbing to the virus while under observation at St. Vincent's after bottom surgery, her skin splitting along her shoulder blades in the camera's shaking frame, bloody foam dripping from her chin as she lurched through a privacy curtain and someone out of sight started to scream. She could still hear the pickup-fuzzed whisper of spotless green linen against antiseptic tile. In the year before the internet collapsed that video had been everywhere, spreading like black mold over Twitter and Facebook.

"XX" had slipped into the vernacular not long after, a way for cis women to signal safety to one another. A little shibboleth to ward off the specter of the wolf in women's clothing. And then, after a while, a catchy icon to scrawl in Sharpie on the baseball bat you kept by your bed. Or the gun under your pillow. Don't worry, citizen—I have the right chromosomes.

Boston PD and the city council turned a blind eye to the trans women who went missing. There were buildings to demolish, nests of men to root out, and a whole city falling down around them as the shadow of long-term reproductive viability whispered in their ears that time was running out, that ovaries were going stale, that any pregnancy could go wrong if some fluke of body chemistry doused the fetus in too much testosterone. Fran had heard of a woman in Vermont whose boy twins had eaten their way out of her. Who had the time to make sure the estrogen thieves were safe?

Even if someone *had* wanted to help the poor benighted transsexuals, there was Maryland and its armed and watchful Matriarchy to think about. Down there they didn't bother with trials, they just dragged your pants down and put two in the back of your head if they found a dick. There were six thousand diehard soldiers in the Maryland Womyn's Legion; not the kind of enemy Boston needed. Fran had heard rumors of TERF death squads in New York, in Connecticut, even in southern Mass. Baltimore's reach got longer every year.

Well, it hadn't mattered in the end. The TERFs were here anyway, and Boston would probably have to kiss the ring or else wind up some kind of feudal protectorate. The local XX chapters would be over the moon. *Maybe we should go west*, thought Fran, kicking idly at a loose chunk of asphalt. It went skittering over the highway, skipping up when it struck a tilted chunk of road, and spun to a halt in the sandy earth under the guardrail. *We could get through the Rockies, somehow. Make it to California by winter.*

She imagined her shoulders peeling and her shirt stuck to her back with sweat, the dry heat out there in the California desert, the molten sunsets, and the cool waters of the Pacific. It would be perfect. A chance for all of them to start over without the threat that at any moment they might be dragged out of their beds and shot against some lonely wall. *Except Indi couldn't do it. Her knees, her back. She'd fall apart before we left New Hampshire. Get us caught. Get us eaten.*

And without Indi to extract and refine E for them, they were just another pair of manhunters. No one wanted to buy bags full of ballsacks from unshowered transsexuals, but tidy glass vials of estrogen from stern, no-nonsense—and, most importantly, cis—Dr. Indiresh Varma in her office on Main Street were another story. *Maybe we could make it north, head through Vermont for Canada. We could get a car running good enough before fall.*

Lost in thought, she almost walked into Beth when the taller woman stopped dead in her tracks. In the gathering dusk a herd of goats was crossing the highway a few dozen yards on. They poured through a gap in the guardrail where a car must have run off the road, though there was no sign of one in the long, waving grass that covered the shallow slope of the hill running down from the highway to its southbound stretch. They moved in silence aside from the clop of their cloven hooves against the pavement, their kids trotting faster to keep up.

"Their ears look so soft," Beth murmured. There were tears in the big girl's eyes. Fran glanced at the tree line on the far side of the southbound, watching for any sign of movement there. A herd this big, thirty or forty animals, it was a miracle they weren't trailing a whole swarm of men. Maybe they were lucky, or all the loud goats were dead and these were the quiet, unassuming wallflowers. Fran wondered what they did all day.

The goats went over the far guardrail in neat little hops, hooves together and necks arched, and streamed uphill toward the sumac and leaning beech trees on the ridge. One, a shaggy white nanny with a dangling udder, paused to look back at the lonely stretch of road. Her square pupils looked alien to Fran, like little copies of Kubrick's monolith suspended in the amber jelly of her irises. She imagined throwing her arms around the nanny's neck and burying her face in her soft coat, inhaling the warm, musky smell of her, and knowing those strange eyes were watching over everything. *I want to feel safe again,* she thought as the herd melted into the trees and the shadows under their branches. The nanny trailed after them, last in line.

Just for a little while.

♀

Fran sat perfectly still while Beth shaved her, penlight in one hand and razor in the other. They'd camped for the night in what had once been someone's living room, a mildew-smelling cave in a tasteless McMansion off the highway. The ceiling was rotting, a huge water stain bulging at its center so that the imitation crystal chandelier hung askew, its mounting displaced and one of its chains snapped. The furniture hulked dank and rotten all around, mold colonizing armrests and cushions, whole squadrons of moths deploying from the musty drapes.

The blade tugged slightly at the skin of Fran's right cheek. Fran flinched at a jab of pain in the empty socket where her broken tooth had been, and Beth drew the razor back, leaning in close to look for cuts. Shadow flowed over the other woman's scarred and bandaged face. The swelling around her mutilated ear had gone down, at least. Out here the chances of recovering from infection were virtually nil.

Fran swallowed, trying to imagine her dry, soft-spoken therapist's advice about deflecting anxious thoughts. "Do you remember the girl they hanged in Boston? I think it was on New Year's Eve in twenty-one?"

Probably not a deflection Dr. Fielding would endorse.

"Dee Licious," answered Beth without a moment's thought. She wet the razor, dipping it into the collapsible rubberized cup of water she'd set between them, and returned to where she'd left off. "She used to be a camgirl; then she was a daddy in the South End for a couple years after T-Day."

As steel skated along her jaw, Fran tried to imagine it. Letting her beard grow. Pitching her voice low and gravelly. Holding a cis woman in her arms after a fuck and stroking her hair, telling her she'd be all right. It made her sick. To step into that vacant skin curled somewhere, dank and grimy, in the corridors of her memory—it made her think of eating her own puke.

I will never live another second as a man. Never, never.

Beth swished the razor through the water again. It clicked softly against the cup.

"Why did they kill her?" asked Fran.

Beth pursed her lips. "Jenny Greenberg told me once there was this party on the Common," she said as she brought the blade up the curve of Fran's throat, hardly grazing the skin. "They'd just zoned it clean and the city's grid was back up, mostly, so it was huge. Like, thousands of people. Jenny said Dee was there with friends, and around three in the morning Jenny heard some drunk girls saying it'd be funny to tell someone, a client of Dee's I guess, that *daddy* was there. She says she tried to find Dee to warn her, but the crowd was too thick.

"A whole gang grabbed Dee while she was dancing and dragged her out of the Common. They beat her. Jenny heard they broke her legs. Then they hung her with an extension cord outside South Station."

What did she look like?

"A client did it?"

Was she like you—a brick, never passed, never gonna?

Two slow, even passes over her right cheek. "Yeah, that's what everyone thinks. Maybe it was someone else, but Jenny heard those people talking."

Or was she like me, a beauty with a few hairs in the wrong place? Jeff Goldblum in The Fly.

"Done," said Beth, smiling.

Fran made herself smile back.

The world is over, and the only way I can know myself is by hating other women.

♀

"Do you want to fuck?" asked Fran after they'd lain in silence for a while, facing away from each other on their bedrolls, though what she really meant was *Do you want to fuck me?*

Beth said nothing, and at once the curdled black sewage of rejection began backing up inside Fran's stomach. The seconds ticked by with torturous slowness. Then the warped floorboards creaked as Beth rolled over and came to Fran on hands and knees. She always came when Fran asked, though she never asked herself. Fran didn't question this. It felt too dangerous to question it, to ask why her body was a gift to be given or received while Beth's existed only when she wanted it and otherwise remained a tightly shuttered thing, devoid of its own desires.

Beth's strong arms slipped around her from behind, encircling her waist. A hand pushed past the elastic waistband of her shorts, stroking the curls above her stiffening cock. Fran snuggled back into Beth's solid, reassuring warmth, parting her legs to wrap them tight around one of the other woman's thighs so she could grind against it.

I'm doing coke with Gabe, she thought. *We're at Element to dance, maybe to find a third, but not on Trans Night. That's another choice that I don't want to look at, because looking at it would break the glass and it would get out and everyone would know what I can't even tell myself.*

She closed her eyes and made Beth into a pair of hands. A muscled leg. Chapped lips (ignore the scar) brushing the nape of her neck with incredible disembodied tenderness. Small breasts rubbing against her back. She missed the freight train roar of coke, which she'd stopped doing shortly before she and Gabe broke up. Like her mind was hurtling down a tunnel through the dark, not trapped on the floor with another woman's hand between her legs and the hot, sticky air laying cheek to cheek against her. She missed Gabe's long, lean body against hers.

It could be a man's hand, she thought, hating herself for thinking it, and for the white-hot throbbing at the base of her cock and the arteries fluttering under the delicate skin where her inner thighs met the tense, aching muscles of her pelvis. Fingers parting her lips, flooding her mouth with the taste of dirt and sweat and sour, unwashed skin. *How many of the men I've fucked are still alive?*

♀

Afterward, Beth went back to her mat and lay down facing away from Fran. The house was alive with the sound of mice and squirrels in the walls. Little claws on joists and Sheetrock. Fran lay awake, cum drying on her inner thighs, her stomach complaining. *I want pancakes,* she thought, *sour cream blueberry pancakes, cooked in bacon grease so the tops are all golden and crunchy, like Dad made for us.*

Except he'd never made them for *her.* They'd been for the boy whose name she fantasized about deleting from her brain with an ice pick or a designer drug, whose face she'd first covered with lipstick and highlighter, then later with contouring and pale concealer and which would have vanished altogether under a surgeon's careful touch, if not for

T-Day. They'd been for the son he loved, not the daughter he'd stared at with anger and disgust across the kitchen table at the Laconia house when she'd told him her name at the end of a long, fumbling, circuitous speech.

He didn't pull me out of school, though. He could have done that, but he didn't.

Driving back to Boston that day in her little Elantra, she'd thought again and again of pushing the pedal down to meet the carpeting, of blowing through the toll booth at a hundred and ten and watching the lights of state troopers flash in her rearview as she rocketed through Acton. She'd thought about it, but that was all. It had remained safely locked away inside her, another boyhood to grit her teeth and endure. Glancing at concrete embankments as she passed them at a reasonable speed.

She scratched at the flaking scabs of cum along her thighs, wishing for a shower, for a therapy session, for making out in the back of a deserted movie theater while trash flickered thirty feet high on the screen. She wished for a thousand stupid things that would never come back. She dwelled indulgently on little miseries, on ineradicable humiliations—crying after her first lay in college, a joke she'd made about a fat girl in third grade—until unconsciousness stole in through the holes in her empty thoughts. She could still hear the mice scratching in the walls.

Fran slept, and dreamed of screeching brakes, and fire, and twisted metal.

VII

BOWSTRING

They woke early the next morning and ate smoked fish and hard acorn bread—which tasted like shit—from the stranger's camp as the fingers of pale sunlight coming through the moth-eaten drapes crept across the carpet. Afterward, Fran repacked the duffel, kneeling in front of it to rearrange its contents. Beth tried not to look at the smooth, tanned skin between the other woman's shorts and T-shirt. She tried not to think about the freckles on Fran's back or the fine cornsilk hairs at the nape of her neck.

You make me feel so delicate.

She ran her thumb absently over the bloodstained gauze taped to her cheek. The cut still hurt, but it no longer throbbed, and the ridge of scabbed-over flesh beneath was only warm to the touch, not burning with infectious fever. She always scarred like that, as though her body had known ahead of time that it was going to be torn open. As though it were prepared for mutilation. The scar at the corner of her mouth, pulling her face into a sardonic leer. The deep cut across the bridge of her nose, still scabby but stiffening fast under its soiled Band-Aid, and of course the checkerboard razor cuts on her upper thighs that once upon a time had bought her so much hell.

You think Bay Path's gonna give that scholarship to a headcase? A dish broken against the wall, a red smear of spaghetti sauce on the yellowing wallpaper. Like blood. *You're throwin' your fuckin' life away!*

They had, in the end, given the headcase that scholarship, and they hadn't pulled it until sophomore year when everything came out—her, namely, but also her thing with the coach. She could still remember how gently he'd touched her. The glistening trails of his tears down his wind-burned cheeks.

She put the thought from her mind and cleared her throat, glancing over to where Fran was still rifling through the duffel. "Oh, bellhop!" she drawled. "How's it going with those bags?"

The crack of a gunshot cut Fran's answer short. The other girl's eyes widened. *That's a rifle,* Beth thought as she scrambled for her bow, propped against the near arm of the rotting sofa. *It's not far. Half a mile.* She hefted it. Saw the frayed fibers bristling from the string near its lower V-hook. She thought of the mice she'd heard in the night, of their sharp little teeth at work on the waxed string while she slept just a few yards away. Her thoughts raced as she buckled on her quiver.

The screaming started before the gunshot's echoes faded. High and cold and somehow unmistakably randy, like a pack of Tex Avery cartoon wolves bugging their eyes out and stamping their feet. "Fran," said Beth, backing away from the windows, the door, the rotten membrane of the outer wall that seemed all of a sudden so pitifully fragile. Her mouth was dry. It was hard to talk above a whisper. "Fran, I need you to help me restring the bow. Now. We need to do it now."

Fran stared up at her, uncomprehending. The screaming grew louder. Closer. Beth stood the bow upright, forcing herself to breathe. *You don't have time to freak out. You have to restring this fucking thing. You have to restring it before the men are here.*

"The socket wrench."

Fran's mouth hung open. "What?"

"This is not the fucking time to make a point about how femme you are," Beth snarled, squatting in front of the staircase with the bow standing on end between her thighs. "Get me the socket wrench from the duffel's front pocket, then get the spare string and wax it. Now."

Fran bent over, shoulders hunched, and fished through the duffel for what felt like half an hour before passing Beth the wrench. Beth loosened the bow's limb bolts one at a time, first the lower, then the upper. She tried not to think about what would happen if the arms snapped straight. Three hundred foot-pounds of force per inch, give or take. It would be like getting slapped by a grizzly bear; she'd be lucky if it only broke her collarbone, or an arm. *Maybe it'll kill me,* she thought, fitting the wrench's head to the upper bolt again. Her palms were sweaty; she paused to wipe them on her shirt one by one. *Then I'd have nothing to worry about.*

The floor began to shake. The windows rattled. The screams were getting closer. Beth loosened the lower bolt by a second turn. Fran, sitting on the stairs, had found the polyethylene replacement string. She had one end pinned under her shoe and she was rubbing a hunk of wax along its length, her breath coming in short, panicky gasps. Her cheeks were flushed, her brow glistening with sweat. Time seemed to pass in spastic flashes.

Maybe they'll go straight for the gunshot, Beth thought, knowing they wouldn't. They'd smell girl-funk and come right through the walls. She rose into a crouch, turned the bow parallel with the floor, and set her boot against the chewed and fraying string. "That's good enough," she said to Fran, holding out her free hand as she slowly drew the bow to half extension, praying that the old string wouldn't snap. "I need you to hook it."

A low, rumbling grunt came from outside the north windows. Something rubbed against the house like a bear scratching itself on a tree trunk and let loose a long, inquisitive whine. Fran squatted beside Beth, her eyes wide, following the sound as it rounded the corner and moved closer down the east wall. All at once mice poured out from the rotten sofa, wriggling free of its fungus-covered cushions and disintegrating arms, scurrying from beneath its fetid skirts. Fran pressed her knuckles to her mouth to muffle her squeal of distaste as she picked her way across the seething floor.

Beth pulled up, shoulders burning with the strain as the bow's arms bent inward, the cams squeaking. She spoke through gritted teeth, pitching her voice low. "You see where the dud string is anchored now? Those arrowhead-shaped hooks attached to the cams?"

Fran, on her knees beside Beth, looked up at her in bewilderment, tears welling in her big brown eyes. "The what?"

I would give anything—anything—*to slap you right now. Just once, right across your perfect little face.*

"The pulley wheels, you dumb bitch," Beth hissed, watching a hunched shadow move across the gap between the east-facing window's drapes. Another scream, this one close enough to rattle the windows. Beth's chest felt tight. Her arms and back ached with the strain of holding the bow at extension. Fran fumbled with the string, hooking one loop over the upper cam's teardrop, then the other to its mate.

"I got it."

"Double-check."

Fran's slender fingers slid up and down the length of the string. Her bitten nails probed at the teardrops. "It's on tight," she said. "What next?"

A crash, flesh thudding against rotten wood. Beth looked up, squinting in the gloom at the half of the front door visible through the hall off the living room and the mud room beyond it. Another crash. The door shook. Dust boiled through a band of light out in the hall. The next scream, when it came, was so close it nearly made her flinch.

"That's not going to hold," Fran whispered.

"Detach the old string," said Beth, speaking through her gritted teeth. Her traps were on fire, her lats trembling.

"I can't get it," Fran whimpered, scrabbling at the dud string where it looped over the teardrop's hook. "It's too tight."

The door shook again. There was a dirty groan of metal tearing free of wood. Beth sucked her breath in and hauled back on the bow, not looking at the string trapped underneath her feet, not thinking about the hundreds of foot-pounds of force that, if they broke the string, would whip back at them before they even knew that they'd fucked up. Fran got the string off and flung it aside. She stood and held the socket wrench out to Beth, but her face was the color of milk, her eyes fixed on the trembling door and the splintered trim around its lowest hinge. Beth lowered the bow back to resting and rolled her shoulders, wincing at the hot ache of torn muscles. She took the wrench and sagged onto the second step of the carpeted staircase.

"It's not going to hold," Fran repeated.

"There's an attic," said Beth, tightening the bow's upper bolt. "I saw it when we came up the driveway. Go find the door." She dropped the wrench as Fran scampered up the stairs. She forced herself not to dive after it, not to drop the bow and risk torquing one of the cams. She took a breath and bent down to retrieve it. The metal felt good against her sweating palm; cool and solid, reassuring in its weight. It felt like she must feel to Fran when they fucked. Big, heavy, and threatening.

She tightened the lower bolt, then returned to the upper. Arrhythmic impacts shook the door. A framed picture, made illegible by mold, fell from one of the entertainment center's cubbyholes and broke with a bright tinkle on the floor. Muted thumps and braying from the far side of the house. The front door splintering. Claws scrabbling in the gap where the uppermost hinge had pulled loose. Fran's footsteps flew up the stairs. The mice had vanished.

Beth rose, letting the socket wrench slip from her fingers, and drew an arrow from the quiver at her hip. The door fell inward with a thunderous crash, men boiling in through the gap, clawing and biting to fight their way past one another. Beth loosed and broke for the stairs without seeing which of them she'd hit. She could hear him screaming. Glass shattered somewhere.

Your nerve is going.

The stairway was solid, the hardwood cracked and splintering but not yet spongy with dry rot. She took the steps two at a time. Something crashed against the wall on the landing below. Grunting. Hissing. Pictures of a long-dead family blurred by grime and dust. Smiling. Disney World. Graduation—cap and gown the color of blood. At the top of the stairs Fran leaping wildly for a pull-chain hanging from the water-spotted ceiling, her face a mask of desperate misery.

Beth barreled past her at a run. She jumped and caught the ring at the end of the chain, yanking it down with her in a shower of dust, dead flies, and mouse turds. The ladder unfolded with a scream of rusted hinges. Her boots hit the floor and she staggered, banging her shoulder hard against the mold-spotted wall. "Go!" she yelled at Fran. A crash echoed up the stairwell from the landing below. Phlegmy teakettle hissing.

Fran went up the ladder quickly, shaking loose a fresh shower of dust and mold. Beth slung her bow over one shoulder and followed, her nose halfway up Fran's asshole. Screams behind them. Up into the dusty gloom of the attic, the roof slanted over rotting cardboard boxes spilling panicked mice out of their nests. Something furry scampering over her arm, sharp claws scratching her bicep, and then the crash as a man struck the ladder headlong. Dry, brittle wood broke. A hinge pulled free of the ceiling with a rusty shriek and Beth dropped, her stomach lurching, and caught herself on her elbows to either side of the trapdoor, legs kicking at empty air, a humid breeze washing over her bare midriff as her hoodie rode up.

Straining to push herself up into the attic, away from the snarling, snapping things below. A low moan of black terror bubbling up from somewhere deep inside her as something grazed her ankle. Fran scrambled to her, grabbed her by the wrists, and pulled, sneakers skidding over the dusty floorboards. *Please don't let me fall,* Beth begged in silence. *Please don't let it end like this.*

Something seized her right calf. An awful weight pulled down on her and there was a bright, sharp pain that went on and on, and then she was on her back and sneezing in the billowing dust and Fran was a few yards away breaking one of the dormer windows with her elbow and kicking the glass out onto the roof. Beth sat up, the attic swimming around her, and looked at the back of her leg. Four long, red furrows ran from just below her knee to just above her ankle. Blood soaked the top of her athletic sock. She swayed where she sat. She imagined falling back into the hall below, being torn apart half-conscious, fought over like a chew toy slathered in meat juice.

A man burst up through the trapdoor, howling and clawing at the floorboards as he struggled to pull himself into the attic. He had her blood on his hands. She lurched into a crouch, the roof too low to stand upright, and one hand drifted to her quiver by reflex to count the arrows. *Eight.* She backed toward Fran, who was shouting something, half in and half out of the dormer. Glass crunched under her boots. No room to aim in here. Not even room to stand. Her injured leg felt like someone else's limb, a glitchy afterthought fizzling in and out of communication with the rest of her body. *I'm not going to die. I'm not going to die.*

Out onto the roof in the hot, sticky morning air, Fran pulling her arm over her shoulders, the beams creaking under their weight as they retreated back along the steep incline. A massive, messy bird's nest eclipsed what remained of the house's chimney. Loose shingles soft and tacky underfoot. The overgrown lawn below, sumac and fiddleheads, dandelions and clover, fat bees zigzagging through the air. The drop. A few men raced through the underbrush below on all fours, heading for the gunshot's source like chimps on the warpath, shoulders hunched and heads low, chins against their chests.

Another shot echoed. No wind stirred the trees, which were encroaching on the house's lot and on the rest of the development, built just off the highway on a sunny hillside. This one sounded closer. She must have misjudged the distance. *Please,* she thought, extricating herself from Fran and unslinging her bow as the other woman drew her knife. *Don't let it be the fucking TERFs.*

The first man prowled out through the dormer, bellowing a challenge, the raw corners of his mouth dripping nameless dark fluid. Beth put the shaft through his neck. His own momentum carried him off the roof in a kind of lazy somersault. He landed with a sickening crack. Below, the frenzied and immediate sound of feeding. Beth took sharp, shallow breaths, trying to block out the pain in her leg as she nocked another arrow. *Seven.*

Gunshot. The flat crack echoed off the hillside. Beth glanced in the direction of the sound; out of the corner of her eye, she saw a tall pine swaying. Men in the lower branches. Someone higher up. The shooter. Another man came through the dormer and she put it from her mind. This one was thin, almost starved-looking, with a thick mane of black hair swept back from his brow and running down his spine. When he screamed, she put her arrow in his mouth. The head burst out the back of his. He fell. More chum in the water.

Six.

The next one came out fast and low. She missed her shot, the shaft zipping away into the woods on the far side of the house. *Five.* She nocked another as he caught himself just short of the roof's edge, claws skittering over the shingles, and sprang at her like a mountain lion. She put the arrow through his heart. He hit the roof and rolled before the shaft caught in the gutter and he jolted to a halt, one arm swinging loose in empty air.

Four.

A big one, shoulders so broad he brought part of the window frame with him. The first arrow didn't even slow him down. *Three.* Fingers bloody on the string because she hadn't had time to find her glove. From the treeline the *pop-pop-pop* of something smaller, a handgun maybe, as she loosed again. Through his eye. *Two.* He slid boneless down the incline, loose shingles going with him. Someone's daddy, probably.

Pop-pop.

She fumbled another arrow to the string. Her leg felt as though it had been dipped in molten metal. Her boot, half-full of blood, squished when she shifted her stance. The air was thick with swarming gnats and black flies, so tiny they were only visible as moving motes, dead pixels blinking in and out of being; she imagined she could feel them in her wounds. Her scars ached. Her breath came in ragged, heavy gasps. She tried not to look at the feeding frenzy below where five or six men were tearing their own dead apart, choking down huge gobbets of bloody meat and fighting over the soft tissues of the face and belly.

"There's someone in that tree," Fran hissed. "Oh my God, oh my God, Beth, she's right at the top shooting, like, down through the branches. They're climbing after her."

Beth ignored her. A man had appeared in the dormer, half-hidden by hanging panels of wet insulation. His beady black eyes were narrowed. He hesitated on the threshold, something dripping from his scabby chin. "Come on," whispered Beth. "Come on, you stupid fucker. You leg-humping, crotch-sniffing—"

He stuck his neck out to scent the air. She got him. She did it perfectly, a shot that would have put her on the Olympic team if countries, professional sports, intercontinental travel, and ranked competitions still existed. A smile broke across her face as she watched him lurch up onto two feet, claws swiping at nothing. His eyes rolled up to show their whites and he tumbled off the roof and landed on his head with a sound like a green branch breaking. Fran was shouting something about the woman in the tree. Beth reached for the last arrow in the quiver, fingers shaking.

One.

She didn't see the other man until he was on top of her. He must have come over the ridge of the roof, come out another window or climbed a trellis she hadn't noticed. Something. His eyes were the yellow of old teeth and he smelled like rancid cum and expired deli meat and he slammed into Beth at a dead sprint. They went off the roof together, the bow lost, Fran's scream chasing them for the single nauseous, heart-stopping breath before they hit dirt.

No air. Men screaming. Knife. Yanking it free of its sheath with sticky fingers. Stabbing fast and desperate at his breast and neck. *Like top surgery,* she thought, and a braying, phlegmy laugh burst from her mouth along with a bubble of blood. She was on her back. There were bodies all around her and warm dead flesh beneath her; one of the men she'd shot must have broken her fall. The one on top of her had his hand over her face. His claws found her bandaged cheek, pushed under it and into the half-healed fissure of the scar left by the crossbow bolt. She moaned. His blood dripped hot onto her tits. Her throat. Her mouth.

He shuddered, caustic bile drooling down his chin, and she jerked her knife out of his neck and squirmed out from under his convulsing bulk. She could hear Fran screaming *no-no-no-no-no* like a scratched record speeding up. Claws tore at her hoodie. She got up into a crouch and her bad leg gave out the second she put weight on it. Then they were on her. Slavering and pawing. Sniffing at her crotch. Exhaustion broke over her in a towering black wave. Her chin in the dirt, her body crushed under the weight of the snarling men, she watched a small brown mantis pick its way along a blade of grass.

Clawed fingers slid through her hair and pressed down, forcing her face into the wet earth. Her arm and the knife were trapped beneath her body. She thought that if she could just find a way to keep the mantis in her field of vision she might slip out of herself, dissociate completely from the hard cock, barbed like a cat's, scratching at her inner thighs, from the clawed hands tearing at the seat of her shorts and the frantic, stupid flash of embarrassment that she hadn't shaved her legs in months. But she couldn't see it. She thought instead of the little cop car, a black-and-white Crown Vic, that she'd slipped into her pocket while Brian Finnerty cried, bloody-mouthed and red in the face, in the waiting room of Manchester Family Dental.

She'd taken her beating gladly when she got home, knowing the whole time that it was coming, that her mother might not care about a little boy's split lip but that she'd surely care about the embarrassment of it, the exquisitely white trash stench of pulling your child off someone else's. Maybe she was still taking that beating. Maybe the nails digging into her scalp and shoulder were still Roxanne Crick's. Maybe the agony in the cleft of her ass and the treacherous stiffening of her prick were happening twenty years ago in their house on Second Street. She still had the little die-cast car. It was on a shelf in Indi's guest room. It was hidden under a loose floorboard by the bed she shared with her little brother David.

There was a flat, hard *crack* like someone slapping bare flesh with an open palm and the man atop her spasmed. Hot fluid coated Beth's thighs and taint as the man tore free of her, the barbs of his penis ripping her open inside with a pain so hot and clean and overwhelming she could hardly feel it even as her anus clenched in terrified retentive reflex. He let go of her scalp and fell across her legs, thrashing and screaming. One of the others scrambled over her, a shriek boiling up from deep within his chest, his weight forcing the air out of her lungs in a great wheezing exhalation. Another followed. Claws scored her back just above her ass. She heard herself scream.

Crack.

The man lying across her legs had fallen still. She crawled away from him, dragging her injured leg, elbows digging into the soft ground. She saw the mantis flying, translucent wings thrumming, and the gnats and butter hoppers rising from the undergrowth around her. A dead man lay not far off, a little dribble of blood, bone, and brain laid out beside his head. Two more were screaming from atop the carcass of the big one she'd shot. They'd already eaten most of his face. His thighs were pockmarked with bloody bites.

Crack.

One went stumbling back and hit the wall of the abandoned house, an eerily human expression of shock painted across his smeared and twisted features. Deep fissures in his lips wept some kind of lymphatic fluid, clear and thin.

Crack.

He fell with a thumbprint hole in his breast. The other broke and ran, bolting like a roach into the brush. Ferns and wild brambles swallowed him. There was a thump, a grunt, and then Fran was next to her, helping her sit up, asking if she was okay, but that was all a long, long way away. Beth leaned into Fran's shoulder, inhaling the sweat and skin smell of the hollow of her neck, and closed her eyes.

I hope I die, she thought as she slipped slowly into the black oil of unconsciousness. *I hope I don't have to wake up into this again. I hope I never have to see any of it.*

Please.

♀

Robbie skinned his elbows coming down the tree, though he wasn't quite sure when or how. His flannel should have stopped it, but it was hot out and he'd rolled the sleeves up. The raw skin stung where his sweat touched it. He ran across the overgrown field, rifle slung across his back, briars tearing at his clothes. He crashed through reed-thin saplings and ferns that grew waist-high in the wet, enveloping heat. The air was thick with flies. He told himself again he hadn't shot her, that he hadn't misjudged it. *They were on her.*

He burst out onto open lawn, grass swishing around his knees, and slowed, panting. The girl—she looked a little older than him, late twenties or early thirties, big and broad-shouldered with half an ear missing and scars crisscrossing her still oddly innocent and childish face—lay unconscious or dead in her friend's arms. The men he'd shot were all around them. *Jesus,* he thought, anxiety digging its fingers into his stomach as he came close enough to see her pallor and the ugly gashes on the back of her right calf. *Don't let her be dead.*

The other woman saw him. Her eyes widened with disbelief before the "oh, right, trans men" switch flipped and she collected herself. She was pretty—petite, his grandfather would have called her—with ever so slightly crooked teeth, the front two overlapping, and freckles on her shoulders and across the bridge of her long nose. Dark hair fell pin-straight to her shoulders. "Is she all right?" he asked, not knowing what else to say.

"There's a duffel bag in the living room. It has my first aid stuff. I need to keep pressure on her leg; can you get it?"

Robbie looked down at the blood welling between her fingers from the unconscious girl's calf. He took off, rounding the corner of the house to where a man lay dead in the ruined front doorway, an arrow buried in his face just under his nose. The living room was trashed, furniture broken, rotten carpet ripped up by the claws of running men. He found the duffel bag by the wreckage of a moldering overstuffed couch. One of his own jars of canned mushrooms stared up at him from between the zipper's parted teeth.

Are you kidding me?

He ran back, trying not to let the cosmic irony of rescuing the idiots who'd robbed his campsite get to him, and dropped the bag beside the brunette. She snatched out a scrap of cloth, sniffed it, and then doused it in hydrogen peroxide from a half-liter bottle and set to cleaning the other girl's wounds. She started with the leg. Robbie squatted beside her to watch. She had steady hands and strong, slender fingers. "Get a T-shirt out of the bag," she said, not looking up from her work. She swabbed each cut with businesslike efficiency, bending low to inspect her work before setting the girl's leg across her lap and twisting at the waist to fish for something in the duffel.

Robbie stared at the thing she drew out. A surgical stapler, a white plastic rectangle with a fat handle and adjustable jaws. The girl pinched the sides of one of the gashes on her friend's calf and positioned the stapler's teeth. He felt the world start to close in. His mouth was dry. His heart hammered.

"Shirt," she repeated. "Now."

He shook himself and found a grimy shirt in the duffel, which was weighed down with unwashed clothes and layers of old newspapers over what smelled like dry ice. He sat down to work in silence, his back turned. At regular intervals the *ka-chunk* of the stapler raised the hair on the back of his neck. Black flies crawled over him. He wondered when he'd gotten so used to being covered in insects. The T-shirt, half rotten with years of soaked-in sweat, tore easily. "Sorry." He still felt a little faint. "I'm not great with open wounds. Surgery. That kind of thing."

He sounded ridiculous, he thought, his voice hoarse and high and creaky. Sometimes he muttered to himself, just to think out loud, but other than that he hadn't spoken to another living person since last February, when he'd gone through Worcester and stopped to trade for a real winter coat.

"So don't look."

Ka-chunk.

He laid the strips of cloth over his thighs, checking them against one another. The seams around the sleeves were giving him some trouble. He pulled harder. "I had no idea anyone was around. I was just trying to clear them out—the men." The seam parted with a satisfying *pop-pop-pop* of stitches ripping. "I'm sorry you got caught in the middle of it."

There was a long silence, except for the stapler's action and the buzz of flies in the morning air. They were swarming over the dead bodies. Birds, too. Crows on the eaves of the house and in the branches of the nearby trees. Turkey vultures sketching lazy circles in the air, their ragged shadows drifting over the long grass. By tonight the wild dogs and coyotes would be at the bodies, or other men would.

"I'm Fran."

"Robbie."

"I need to move her once I'm done." She held her hand out and he passed her the strips he'd torn, glancing at the injured girl out of the corner of his eye. She looked bad, her skin waxy, her eyes sunken. Fran wrapped her leg quickly, pausing every now and then to wipe away fresh blood that had welled out of her stapled cuts. "We have a friend in Seabrook we can stay with. If we rig a stretcher we should be able to make it by tomorrow morning. Will you help me get her there?"

He thought of Midge, and the gun, and the house in Durham, and the sound of the key in the rusted padlock on the basement door. *Other people aren't safe.* He thought of his sleeping bag, of the paralyzing loneliness of a silent orgasm alone in the dark. *They stole from you.* He thought of the men coming up his tree, poorly chosen, limbs too near the ground, and firing down at them between his feet, wondering if he'd picked a bad one on purpose. *You saved them; now you walk away.*

He looked the girl in the eyes. "Okay."

♀

Beth dreamed that she was running from someone. He was hard to make out, an amorphous form of hot black flame and grinning teeth, skin and clothing nebulously interchangeable. His silhouette eddied like a burning candle in a breeze. He giggled, a falsetto titter that echoed from the kitchen walls. The house on Second Street, nicotine-yellowed wallpaper and black mold creeping along where the ceiling met the walls.

Her every step was torturously slow, as though she were running through thick gelatin or knee-deep water. She felt weak. Her joints ached with a hot, sticky pain. She slipped on the peeling linoleum and fell, pitching slowly to the floor. Tiny figures watched her from the shadows underneath the kitchen table and the crack in the cupboard under the sink. Their eyes were bright as jewels. The burning thing came closer, the sick heat of him washing over her. She couldn't get up. Her arms were like dry sticks, her shoulders limp and nerveless.

I don't want it.

The little hidden creatures shook their heads and waved their hands. The thing approached and she saw with horrified fascination that the flames of his body formed a pair of new black wingtips polished to a high sheen. That was worse than anything, somehow. The way the leather creaked with every step he took. The billowing, crackling hell of him rising from those shoes. He lay down on the floor beside her, hands clasped against his breast, teeth shining sharp and crowded. His body mirrored hers precisely. The toes of his wingtips nearly brushed her feet.

Please, don't touch me.

He squirmed closer. The heat of him blew over her, harsh and dry, raising blisters on her lips, reddening her skin. She tried to scream, but her chest was tight, her throat constricted. Only a faint croak emerged. Her hands twitched limp and boneless at the ends of her trembling arms. She tried to sob, but no tears came. He reached out and took her face in his flickering hands. His fingers seared her cheeks, melting her scars, opening red fissures in her flesh. He kissed her. White tongue sliding over her teeth. The sting of lemon on an open cut.

It felt so *good.*

He wrapped himself around her, sliding an arm under her waist and another over her side. Pulling her flush against him. His leg sliding between hers, his thigh pressing hard against her stiffening cock. Tears of molten fat ran down her cheeks. The little things in the dark under the cabinets withdrew into the shadows, covering their eyes. Beth's hand scrabbled of its own volition down between her legs, pulling itself spider-like along the ravine formed by their twining bodies. The flesh of her thighs and pubis was wet and sticky to the touch. Beads of thick fluid welled up from her pores and she knew without looking that the same substance was dribbling from her cock.

Heat built at the root of Beth's sex, a raw red murmur growing louder by the moment. *Get your tongue out of me.* Her fingers crept lower, her arm still dead and limp, dragging behind her hand like a severed umbilical cord. *Please, please, no. No.*

She dug her fingers hard into the soft skin of her pubic mound, into the short wheat-colored curls that grew there, and the gummy flesh of her scrotum. The head of her penis split open against her palm, and between its weeping lips—

It was near dark. She lay on her back under a spreading tree, her head propped up on something soft, and every breath she took felt as though it put a fresh crack in her ribs. Her thoughts were slow and sticky, clinging to each other like hard candies in a jar left in the sun. Not far off, Fran sat on a rock knocking dirt and pebbles out of her ratty sneakers. A trans guy stood beside her, short and slim with a shaggy mullet under his sun-faded Red Sox cap. He had a faint mustache and a deep tan, or else maybe he was black, or kind of black, or whatever. Little crow's feet branched from the corners of his dark eyes. He and Fran were talking in low voices.

Beth wet her dry, cracked lips. "Oh shit," she croaked, the taste of blood thick at the back of her throat. "It's the last man on earth. How's it hangin', pal?"

They both turned toward her. The stranger looked caught between amusement and annoyance. Fran just looked tired. "You're awake." She offered a watery smile. "How do you feel?"

Bodies on top of her. Fingers in her hair. Beth's asshole hurt like someone had bitten a chunk out of it, and for a moment her throat closed and tears welled in her eyes. "Shitty," she choked out. "I'm sorry, Fran. I'm sorry I fell." She sobbed suddenly and then bit back a cry as the convulsion of her diaphragm sent shooting pains through cracked and bruised ribs. Her right leg felt like a bag of meat and needles. "I d-didn't mean to."

Fran came to kneel beside her. She took Beth's hand in hers. Beth squeezed her eyes tight shut so that she wouldn't see the awful look of pity on Fran's face.

"It's not your fault."

Beth whimpered and wished at once that she could put that silly, nasal sound back in her throat.

"Robbie saved us. He picked them right off of you." Fran squeezed her hand. "And hey, I got a bunch of disgusting smelly balls from the men he killed. We're way up on the hunt."

I *saved you, you cunt.*

She bit the inside of her cheek until it hurt before she trusted herself to meet Fran's eyes again. The first stars glittered through the branches of the tree. The moon was waning. "I'm sorry," she said flatly. "I just feel like garbage."

"Try to get some sleep," said Fran, her hand slipping from Beth's as she straightened up from her squat. "We'll get to Indi's tomorrow morning. You can rest there for a while, until you're feeling better. You need antibiotics and shit, I think."

Beth looked past Fran to where Robbie stood with his hands in the pockets of his old fatigues, silhouetted by the setting sun's last light. A faceless clot of boy-shaped darkness.

"Thanks, Fran."

♀

Beth drifted in and out of sleep that night, the staples in her leg waking her every time she neared unconsciousness. She fought the urge to scratch the scabby, inflamed wound. Moonlight swept in a rough time lapse over the long grass. No road. Smell of salt in the air. Not far away lay the folded stretcher they must have used to carry her. Sticks and dirty clothes. Beyond that was Robbie's bedroll, and Fran's at the edge of the tree's shadow. Beth could see her bony ankles and her long, pale toes. A stretch of almost-sleep and Fran's legs were gone. The moonlight had jumped to the edge of Robbie's pallet.

Am I dreaming?

In the silver light she saw Fran's hand uncurl at the bedroll's edge. Robbie laced his fingers through hers. One of them sighed, the sound of it soft and gentle in the stillness. Their joined silhouette undulated against the deeper darkness of the woods, two nymphlike figures twining, clutching at each other. Near-silent moans stifled against flesh. The wet, sucking glide of fingers sliding into holes. Everything fitting like it was meant to.

I will never look that right with another person.

She thought of the man grunting atop her. That was the only way she would be touched. That was what the end of the world had in store for her. They would tear and claw and thrust at her until she was nothing but a drooling hole, and then, when they figured out they couldn't knock her up, they would eat her alive, starting with her belly.

She closed her eyes and listened to the sound of fucking.

VIII

SLEEPOVER

It was just before dawn when Fran woke. A light rain fell, barely a mist under the shelter of the oak's broad leaves. Robbie's bedroll was damp. He smelled like sweat and dirt and fresh-cut grass. Fran squirmed closer to him, relishing the feeling of his arms around her and the lingering frisson of his tongue sliding slick and muscular into her asshole. When he'd gone down on her, tonguing and kissing the stiff length and soft folds of the hateful thing she called her cunt when she called it anything at all, holding her loose skin between his teeth and pressing his nose into the sticky hollows of her thighs where they met her pelvis, she'd had to stuff her fist into her mouth to keep from screaming.

"What time is it?" he whispered.

Fran pulled away, though not ungently. She hadn't known he was awake. "Five-ish," she whispered back, sitting up and running her hands through her greasy, tangled hair. Birds sang. The woods looked ghostly, the highway a dirty memory in its silence. "We should get moving."

Not far away Beth slept with her back turned to them, hugging her knees, chin tight against her chest. A single spot of blood darkened her bike shorts, just over her anus.

♀

They came out of the woods behind a lumber yard on the edge of town. Fog hung over the tall grass. Insects rose in waves before them, the buzzing of their wings low and muted in the humid air. Fran had Beth's bow and quiver, along with the three arrows she'd recovered from the bodies of the men outside the house, and the extra weight kept throwing off her stride, the bow's lower arm smacking the back of her thigh as she adjusted the duffel's strap repeatedly in a futile effort to get comfortable.

Beth had insisted on walking and already Fran saw bloodstains spreading on the backs of her ratty olive leggings where her cuts were tearing open. She moved with a stiff, halting stride between piles of moldering two-by-fours, from which delicate blades of grass sprouted like arm hair. Robbie followed close behind, though the few times she'd glanced back at him he'd looked sweaty and uncertain, all of yesterday's easy confidence melted away into the hazy, overcast morning. Now he just looked like a scruffy, skinny boy playing soldier.

Beyond the lumber yard's burned-out offices and outbuildings, past its mossy porta potties and the unreadable sign at the end of the dirt drive leading up from Sewall Street, lay a solid quarter mile of scorched wasteland where the town council had torched everything flammable and bulldozed through the wreckage. Past that was the sprawl of Governor Weare Park, its neatly spaced oaks and maples lost among choking vines and new growth saplings, the grass under their competing branches a sea of deep green waving in the sluggish breeze. The smell of salt blew through the desolation, tugging flakes of ash from the skeletons of immolated houses.

They crossed Sewall, leaving the burn zone behind, and cut north around the park. Indi's place was on Main past the town library and the start of the downtown drag, silent storefronts and barred windows, concrete barricades topped with barbed wire and broken glass. Beth was limping as they passed through the unmanned checkpoint by a narrow channel between two of the repurposed traffic barriers. Fran matched her faltering pace until they were side by side.

"You can lean on me," she whispered.

Beth looked away, spots of color livid in her pale, hollow cheeks. "I'm fine."

Fran thought of the man coming over the ridge of the roof, of the way he'd crouched down low and shaken his hindquarters like a cat about to pounce. She thought of her voice caught frozen in her throat and Beth tumbling over the gutters, tearing one of them loose with a flailing arm or leg so that it swung with a groan of twisting metal and pinched itself shut under its own weight.

I tried to warn you. Did I shout? Did I reach for you? Did your fingers slip through mine?

There was nothing but a tangle of adrenaline and fear and the sight of rotten teeth bared in excitement as the men closed over Beth, swarming and clawing with mindless insect intent. That had happened. That was what was real.

Downtown was deserted. This early, everyone would be at the power plant or inland, working on one of the town's farms. Seabrook didn't have much soil worth growing in, but there were a few strains of beans and sprouts that did all right, and one town over in Exeter was the sprawling pig-and-chicken outfit owned by a bunker brat, Sophie Widdel, whose billionaire parents had vanished on T-Day and left her with an armed security detail, a vault full of nonperishables and potable water, and the perfect sprawling underground complex to house it all. The town had to treat her like something between a CEO and a feudal baroness, which was a better deal than you got with most brats. Fran had heard there was a Gates baby somewhere in Connecticut who kept a big pit full of men in her bunker and fed them anyone who pissed her off, like Jabba the Hutt serving his dancers up raw to the stop-motion monster under his palace.

In the parking lot of the gutted CVS, they passed a pair of black girls no older than five or six throwing a tennis ball for a gangly, speckle-coated mutt. Fran smiled and waved. The taller of the two returned her gesture shyly while the other hid behind her. She wondered what it was like to be a kid in this world, to have no memory of the civilization that had come and gone before they had fine motor control, to have no knowledge of men but the slavering, screeching face of t. rex.

We outlived every dad in the world.

Lost in thought, she bumped into Beth's outstretched arm and nearly fell. Her indignant "Huh?" died on her tongue as she saw what waited for them in the square a few blocks into town. There was a flatbed with an awning parked in the street outside the town hall, the three-foot XX daubed on its cab livid in the sunrise. On the steps of the quaint white hall with its steeple and its sharp-pitched roof was a stern-looking white woman in a worn police uniform, mid-forties or a little older, and beside her, smoking a menthol and looking pissy, was a teenage girl wearing fatigues over an XX T-shirt, a rifle slung across her back. Someone had bolted huge storm-warning sirens to the eaves of the town hall and to the buildings around it. Fat loops of cable hung between them.

The fuck is that?

"Follow me," said Beth. Her breathing sounded ragged. Her face was gaunt and bloodless. "We'll go around."

♀

Indi's house was about a mile past the town hall, back toward the residential stretch of Main where the ocean's smell grew stronger and the distant booming of the surf murmured at the edge of hearing. They came toward it from Almena after cutting down Troy, making their way through the riotous overgrowth of abandoned lawns overrun by sumac and some long-dead rich idiot's ornamental dropseed run rampant. The long, feathery blades made a shushing sound against their legs as they waded through the last stretch of the neighborhood, a ghost quarter except for a few oddball holdouts Fran was sure were watching them from behind iron bars and blackout curtains.

The house sat between a paved-over vacant lot and a rocky kind of hill where a rich family, the Shaws, had built a very modern and now abandoned pile of glass and concrete in the 1970s. Indi's house was old, probably a hundred and fifty years or more, a big Victorian painted a peeling, weathered white, its roof shedding shingles, its yard kept more or less manageable by a cover crop of hardy clover, though the raspberry bushes along the rotted-through north fence had begun to climb over it. Beth let Fran take her arm without a word when they were halfway across Indi's lawn. The taller girl listed heavily against her.

There are armed TERFs a minute from here, Fran thought, looking with unease at Beth's glassy stare and colorless lips. *We'd never get away if they came now.*

She helped Beth up onto the sagging porch and glanced back at Robbie, who wouldn't meet her eyes. *The fuck is wrong with him?* She rapped smartly on the door.

He couldn't get enough last night.

The door creaked open a hair, then shut. Fran heard the chain rattling and then Indi opened it, staring out at them. Her round face was ashen, her thick black hair—shot through prematurely with gray—fell in disarray around her shoulders. "Get inside," she snapped, stepping back from the doorway to let them shuffle one by one into the coat room. She was the fattest woman Fran had ever known, her upper arms like pillows, her belly hanging halfway to her dimpled knees in two thick, soft rolls clearly visible through her faded Cannibal Corpse T-shirt. Before Fran had pulled the door closed, Indi was inspecting Beth, matter-of-factly tugging the bloody bandage from her cheek and ignoring the tall girl's yelp of protest as she probed at the puffy skin surrounding the sutures beneath. Fran shrugged the bow off her shoulder and stood it by the door. She set the duffel down and touched the raw strip it had rubbed into her shoulder, wincing. Robbie followed her lead, setting down his pack and rifle. He looked nervous, almost skittish.

"Awful work," sniffed Indi, shooting Fran a look of mild reproach. She let the bandage fall to the dirty flagstones. "You look terrible, and we have a lot to talk about. Follow me." She turned and led them up a single well-worn step into the house's cluttered dining room, her hips brushing softly against the door frame. She glanced back over her shoulder. "Who's your friend?"

"This is Robbie," said Fran, helping Beth mount the step. The other girl's face had turned the color of drywall mud, a lifeless, pasty gray. "He saved us outside town. Robbie, this is our friend Indiresh. She processes our E."

Indi brushed past Robbie's muttered greeting. "Thank you for bringing my idiots back to me," she said briskly. "Clear a seat and wait here. Read anything you like. Food in the kitchen."

Indi's office was as clean as the rest of her house was a rat's nest, the windowless north wall lined with shelves of medical texts, leather-bound volumes on endocrinology, fertility, and dentistry side by side with the water-damaged academic journals Fran had plundered from Harvard's medical library, the others occupied by glass-fronted cabinets stocked with surgical implements, rags, bottles, and bundled herbs, more of which hung from hooks set in the ceiling. In the center of the room was an adjustable examination table upholstered in stained beige leather.

Together they guided Beth onto the table. The tall girl's last few steps were erratic, almost drunk, and for a moment Fran feared Beth would faint, but in the end they got her settled on her back. Her breathing was shallow, her skin waxy. "She has an assload of open wounds," said Fran, chewing her lip and hovering over Indi as she bent to inspect her patient. "The back of her right calf is the worst. I did what I could, but we were sitting in a pile of dead men while I patched her up. It wasn't exactly sterile."

Indi was bent low over Beth's leg, keeping it propped up with a hand under the knee. "You're lucky I just skimmed new penicillin from the tank. It looks like a good batch, too. Go to the cellar. Get me four hundred milliliters and a glass of water."

"Sure," said Fran.

As she stepped out of the office, shutting the door behind her, she heard Beth say something in a small, frightened voice. She sounded like a child. "They hurt me, Indi."

And then Indi, gently.

"I know, baby. It's all right."

Beth made a sound like a wounded animal, low and strained and desperate. Fran stared at the door for a while, wondering if she should go back in, if she should tell Beth everything that had gone through her mind when she'd watched her fall off the roof and into the arms of the men below. The words wouldn't come, and so she stood there, chewing on her lip, and listened to her friend's high, thin wails of grief.

♀

Beth sobbed in the soft circle of Indi's arms, her chest aching around a hard red knot of despair. The second she'd seen Indi in the door, she'd wanted nothing but to fall against her and dissolve into a screaming, drooling mess, to let the other woman's body absorb the pent-up misery of the last week. Her stapled leg itched so badly; it was all she could do not to claw at the infected skin. Everything hurt. It hurt to think. It hurt to breathe.

"You need to hold still, baby," said Indi, pressing Beth back down onto the table. Her perfect fingernails traced the raised ridge of the crossbow wound along Beth's cheek. "I have to take these out and disinfect before I sew it up."

The swab she pressed against the wound stank of hydrogen peroxide, a cutting, acid odor. Tiny scissors snipped next to Beth's ear, the one missing a chunk where a man had bitten it off four years ago in the dead of winter. Indi drew the catgut out inch by careful inch until Beth could feel the lips of the wound sagging open around the half-scabbed gash. Her tongue probed at the inside of her cheek, feeling where the wound cut close to her mucous membrane. Another few millimeters and it would have left her breathing through a second mouth.

Hot tears rolled down her cheeks. She stared up at the ceiling of Indi's office, at the water stain by the darkened light fixture. The room was painted light blue. The ceiling was off-white. Daylight came in through the yellowing drapes. Indi scrubbed at the wound and Beth held her breath and fought down the lump of bubbling misery at the back of her throat. A fierce stinging pain lit up her cheek as Indi cleaned the cut. It felt as though a swarm of wasps were stinging her along some fault line in her body, some appetizing orifice raw and tender enough to be preyed upon. She let out a muffled groan.

"Hold still." Indi bent down close to Beth, her round face and double chin shining with perspiration, the fine black hairs on her upper lip just visible against her skin. She drew a yellowed Q-tip glistening with some kind of solvent quick along Beth's wound, then mopped at it with a folded rag. A moment later came the muted sting of the suture needle tugging at her cheek. In and out. Hot, bright flashes of discomfort. The ceiling swam. She felt as though she were being pressed flat against the table by some massive hand, the air squeezed out of her lungs, her whole awareness slowing to a nauseous, muddy churn.

For a while Beth drifted in that gray-brown haze of pain, a headache building where the bridge of her nose crossed her eyeline. Indi removed her staples one by one and cleaned the gashes in her leg. Fran came in and made Beth drink something horribly bitter while Indi talked. Beth heard herself crying, flat and miserable, like a baby wailing from the bottom of a well. They lifted up her legs, taking one each, and Indi put a swab inside her. Everything hurt. The room tilted. It came apart.

The men were waiting.

And then it was dark outside and Indi was beside her again, hips spilling from the edges of her rolling stool, glasses pushed up onto her hair and her nose buried in a book. Kerosene lamps burned in the gloom, casting flickering shadows on the walls and curtains. Indi looked up from her paperback as Beth swallowed. Her mouth was dry and cottony and tasted sour. Her head ached as though it might split down her nose and through her philtrum at any moment. "Indi, will you fuck me?"

The other woman sighed, passing a hand over her face. She had little hands, plump and perfect like a baby doll's. "You need to rest, honey. You're dehydrated, you have at least two broken ribs, you came within a quarter inch of losing your left hamstring—"

Beth slid a hand onto Indi's knee. Her arm felt as though it were weighted down with bars of lead. The other woman's skin was cool against her burning fingertips through the thin fabric of her skirt. "Please."

"Bethany, no."

The expression on the other woman's face told her this fell outside the needling push and pull of their occasional liaisons, the power games of her abjection and Indi's disdainful refusal. Beth letting her bruised dignity drop like a nightie to the floor. Indi pretending that she didn't want just that, that it was irrelevant to her that someone would approach her on their hands and knees, would beg without shame to touch the quivering hillsides of her body.

Beth rolled toward her as best she could, clutching tighter at her thigh. "*Please.*" She knew how disgusting she sounded, but she couldn't stop. It poured out of her in a dirty flood of begging even as Indi pushed her hand away, even as the other woman wordlessly held out another glass of sepia-colored diluted penicillin until Beth took it, slumping back onto the table.

"Drink this, then try to sleep."

The door swung open, then shut hard enough to shake the framed diplomas on the wall. Beth stared up at the water spot, the glass forgotten in her hands. She began to cry again in thick, snotty gasps that quickly sealed her nose and reduced each breath to a whining gurgle.

Fuck me, so I can pretend I'm a girl.

♀

Later, while Beth slept in her room upstairs, they sat together by candlelight at the hastily cleared kitchen table, eating cold pork and onions wrapped in thick brown flatbread. Fran had never tasted anything better in her life. Indi only picked at hers; she couldn't stand to be seen eating. Robbie, by contrast, wolfed his down without pausing for air. He was a loud chewer, which Fran decided to find endearing, but he still wouldn't say more than a few words at a time.

"They're all over town," said Indi as Robbie mopped tzatziki from his plate with the last of his bread. "They got here the day before yesterday. They're in Boston, too, and Manchester. Nashua. Nobody's heard anything from Nashua on the ham since Wednesday."

Fran sighed, looking out the dining room window at the overgrown hedge and the street beyond it. Farm workers were trickling back into town as the last of the daylight faded. A pair of weathered middle-aged women in faded Levis, sun shirts, and work boots, one with a little girl clinging to her from behind, rode past on horseback, laughing about something as they went. Bees wandered through the lilac bushes in Indi's front yard. It all looked like it always did.

"We ran into them out by the coast, just across the Mass border. Beth took a shot at Teach, the one who's supposed to be their den mother or whatever." She felt a phantom twinge of her desire for that woman, for the cold, bitter mommy-ness of her, and tongued absently at the socket of her missing tooth. "We barely got out alive."

Indi looked troubled. She pushed her plate away, no longer bothering with even the pretense of eating. On his side of the table Robbie was hunched defensively over his plate the way Beth sometimes did, a trait Fran had come to associate with people who'd grown up in big families. He'd taken his cap off and hung it on one of the chair's uprights. Indi's dining room chairs were metal and green vinyl, armless like all her furniture.

"How many of them were there?"

"I don't know. They had eight, nine trucks. Ballpark, maybe five hundred people?"

Fran thought of the few other trans girls she knew who lived in Seabrook, or who passed through it on the regular. She thought of Jenny Greenberg with her horsey face and tight, dark cornrows. She thought of Jenny's long arms and broad shoulders, and of skinny Allie's Adam's apple that bobbed when she swallowed, and of Princess's perpetual five-o'clock shadow. Maybe one in four of them could pass, and that number shrank to zero if the TERFs started pulling pants down. If they searched house to house it would be . . . what? A bloodbath? Mass exile? How much power could they really have up here?

"I've been thinking," Fran said slowly. "Maybe it's time we left. Whatever's going on here, it won't be good for us, so maybe we just . . . go."

Indi arched an eyebrow.

"I thought we could . . . we could hitch to Concord, trade for a car there, maybe. There's a commune in Oregon I heard about last time I was in Lowell." She felt unaccountably embarrassed, so she tried to speak faster. "They have farms, solar; they'll always need doctors and hunters. Or we could try for Montreal. It's far enough from Maryland . . ."

Indi laid a hand on hers. "Francine," she said gently. "I can't make that journey. I cannot travel three thousand miles, and even if I could there is no car in America running well enough to get me there, and no unbroken route to drive it on."

Fran thought for a long time before she spoke again. "It might start out hard, but wouldn't it get easier as we went?" Her voice trembled. "Like, wouldn't you get, you know, used to it?"

Indi's expression closed. Her mouth was a thin line. "Sophie Widdel made me an offer."

Fran felt a stabbing, anxious pang of jealousy shot through with a hateful resentment of the older woman's body, of the way its soft and helpless bulk pinned them here to Seabrook when it would all be solved if they could just *go.* She imagined a dozen different things she could say, discarding each of them in turn as Indi held her gaze, and she wondered how much of what ran silently through her thoughts had already gone through Indi's, and if it had been gentler or crueler.

I bet she hates herself in ways I can't even imagine.

Robbie, looking up at last, spoke through a mouthful of pork and bread. "The bunker brat?"

Indi nodded. "She wants an in-house doctor, someone who knows how to isolate estrogen, cover primary care and routine surgery. I was a fertility specialist before this and I also understand she wants to be a mother, so." She shrugged. "It would mean relocating to just outside Exeter. To the bunker."

"I've seen their hunting parties," Robbie said shortly. "Lot of guns." He returned his attention to his wrap.

"There's a place for you and Beth, if you want it." Indi was fiddling with the lace trim of the stained floral tablecloth. It had been her parents', Fran knew, like most of the house's decor. "I didn't mean to bury the lede."

Fran sat there for a minute, listening to Robbie chew, trying to decipher the mixture of anxiety, anger, hope, and guilt in Indi's expression. "When would we go?"

"Tomorrow. She's sending a van."

♀

Afterward, Fran and Indi washed dishes while Robbie worked the pump in the kitchen sink. Beth had rigged it up as an apology after a nasty fight over something Fran couldn't remember. That had been years ago, right after they started working together, but Indi kept it oiled and it still moved smoothly. Fran tried not to let the play of the candlelight over Robbie's muscles distract her. He worked the pump with easy, fluid confidence, the same way he'd fucked her the night before. The same way his spit-slick finger had slid in and out of her. Why was he so tongue-tied now?

He didn't ask to sleep with her when they were through, the candles burning down to stubs of molten beeswax. He asked Indi if he could stay and she said yes, of course, and showed him to one of the first-floor guest rooms. He didn't look at Fran before he left. For a moment she wanted to slap him, to drag him back into the kitchen and make him fuck her, hard, against the countertop among the remains of supper, under the twine-wrapped bundles of herbs drying on the ceiling.

In the living room she curled up on the sagging, scratchy couch and waited there until Indi reemerged from the back hall a few minutes later. The other woman sank into the ratty armchair opposite her, knees popping audibly, and let out a long, tired sigh. It was a small room, the furniture worn, the low coffee table scratched and splintering under its sedimentary layers of books. Peeling posters for the disgusting French movies Fran had never been able to sit through without getting nauseous stared down at them from the walls. *Inside. Trouble Every Day. Eyes Without a Face.*

Indi heaved a sigh, settling back into the threadbare seat. "So, you slept with him?"

Fran nodded, tears welling in her eyes.

"There's beer from Jae and Dana under the sink. Go and get two, will you?"

When she came back, Indi had her feet up on a little three-legged ottoman. They were as dainty as her hands, though swollen from a day spent standing. She took her beer and looked up piteously at Fran, batting her thick eyelashes. "Rub my feet and I'll diagnose your boy problem?"

Fran sighed, lifting Indi's feet and sinking down onto the ottoman before letting them drop back into her lap. A ripple ran through the other woman's body, which filled the chair's seat like pudding in a cup, and Fran made herself not stare. She knew it was wrong to look at Indi that way, to observe her like unseasonable weather or a strange but captivating painting. She dug her thumbs into the arch of her right foot, pressing as hard as she could. Indi exhaled, her rounded shoulders slumping.

"He's afraid of you."

Fran looked up sharply. "What?"

"Keep rubbing." Indi waved a hand at her, then took a long sip of beer. She balanced the dark bottle atop the shelf of her belly, between where her breasts sloped to its sides. "He's afraid of you, Francine. He's afraid to be close to anyone. You said you found him shooting men in the middle of the woods; not exactly a group activity. How long do you think it's been since he touched another person?"

Fran blushed, still kneading the sole of Indi's foot. She bent down so that her hair would hide her burning cheeks. "I didn't ask. I guess I figured—"

"Yes, you figured." Indi leaned back against the chair's headrest, closing her eyes. "You guessed. You assumed. You see what you want and where you'd like it to come from, not what's in front of your nose. If you want that boy to keep fucking you, if you want him to follow us out of here, you're going to need more than him feeling guilty for getting you and Beth stuck in the middle of a feeding frenzy. You're going to need to take care of him, at least a little. If he'll let you."

She switched feet, feeling the muscles in Indi's arch spasm at her touch. "I'm not moving too fast?"

"Oh, honey." Indi settled deeper into the chair, shifting back and forth inside its confines. "The world is over. Who cares how fast you go?"

♀

He was halfway across the yard before she called his name, her voice soft but carrying clearly in the cool night air.

"Robbie."

He turned. She stood by the moldering woodpile in nothing but a white satin nightie, smoking a hand-rolled cigarette. Whorls of gray-blue smoke coiled around her in the moonlight as she exhaled and plucked the butt from her mouth, holding it out to him. He went to her and took it. The tobacco was stale, but it tasted like peat and fire on his tongue. He let the smoke trickle out slowly through his parted lips.

"Are you leaving?"

He nodded, not knowing what else to say.

She took the cigarette back and took a drag. She smoked the way his mother had smoked, as though she were trying to get something from the cigarette she couldn't get in life. As she exhaled she dropped the butt and ground it out under her bare heel, and she stepped into his arms and kissed him. Smoke unfurled into his mouth from hers like a second tongue, hot and dry and aromatic. She murmured against his lips.

"I don't want you to."

The warmth of her body against his made him want to cry. It made him want to cling to her. It made him want to run until the smell of other humans was a memory he could take out in the long, dark emptiness of winter nights to hold in his cupped hands, like Peter Pan held Tinker Bell. Something to be loved, but not the way you love another person. A toy. A bauble. A memory.

You don't deserve this.

Smoke boiling between their mouths as she drew back. Hot and hungry breath washing his cheek, his throat. She nipped at his shoulder and he caught his breath. She sank down to her knees in front of him as he dropped his pack and rifle, fumbling with the fly of his fatigues, his swollen clit stiff and hot against the metal. Her mouth. Her hair between his fingers. Crickets singing in the grass around them and an owl somewhere crying out and in the distance, toward the ocean, the lights of the nuclear plant washing the undersides of dark clouds flowing over Seabrook.

♀

Beth woke to the sound of a voice crackling over the broadcast towers they'd seen coming into town. She thought about dragging the blankets up over her head, but it was warm out and her inner thighs were already sticky with sweat. The thought of marinating in her own stink held little appeal. She rolled onto her side, kicking the linens to the footboard. The window was open a crack, the smell of lilacs wafting in on a sluggish breeze. She didn't remember climbing the stairs, or falling asleep. Her entire body felt like one gigantic bruise.

"*. . . heard how many times that the world is over? I say the sex that poisoned the planet, stripped the oceans bare, and raped every woman it could get its hands on is dead, and good riddance to it! I say this is our time, that no longer will we mutilate our bodies to conform to arbitrary beauty standards! No longer will we sell our flesh to feed the misogynistic machinery of the porn industry! No longer will we be forced into whoring ourselves out to feed our children!*"

She gripped the windowsill and pulled herself up, her ribs protesting, every breath bringing a fresh wave of sharp, stabbing pains. A crowd was gathering in the street, looking up at the broadcast towers and the disembodied voice that thundered from them, static-washed and overlapping. It was early. The light was pale and birds perched by the hundreds on the rotting telephone poles and the eaves of houses. Children held their mothers' hands. Little girls, mostly, and a handful of boys born just before T-Day, no older than five or six now. In a few years they'd be castrated, or put on E, but their mothers still dutifully dressed them in blue and earth tones and junior fatigues. The last little kings of the world.

"We will no longer be beaten, we will no longer be enslaved, we will no longer let the men who wear our identities and steal our history for their own sexual gratification dictate how we live and what we're allowed to believe! We will no longer let them prey on our daughters!"

A frisson of terror slithered up Beth's spine. She thought of every time a mother had stared sidelong at her on the commuter rail, every time someone had snatched their toddler away when she crouched down to say hello. She thought of her aunt's email to her mother, explaining why her *nephew* was no longer welcome in her home or around her children.

"This is our world now! This is our America! Welcome, sisters, to the New Womyn's Commonwealth!"

"Beth."

She turned, the scattered applause and cries of outrage and derision from outside ringing in her ears. Fran stood in the doorway. She had on one of her faded floral dresses, pale blue with a pink rose print, and she'd shaved her legs. She looked like a fifties housewife.

"We have to go."

They went down the stairs as fast as Beth could manage, Fran going sidelong with Beth's arm around her shoulders. She explained what was happening on the way, speaking tersely, her shoulder-length hair already lank with sweat. Beth couldn't think of any questions. Her leg hurt. Her face. Her ribs. Her asshole. The hundred tiny cuts and scratches on her thighs, her back, her shoulders. But more than any of that, as she limped through the kitchen and dining room, out through the coat room and into the back yard where three sunburned women in jeans and T-shirts were loading boxes into a white van with rusted runners while Indi stood watching, she was afraid.

It wasn't the few who'd cheered that frightened her; it was the rest, watching with guarded expressions, not looking at those among their number who cried *Go back to Maryland, you fucking Nazis* and *Fuck TERFs!* The women who looked at each other in a way Beth didn't understand, a way sealed forever within the cold and rigid bounds of cisness but which nonetheless told her without room for doubt that they couldn't leave too soon.

That was what scared her.

The women who stayed silent.

PART TWO

THE NEW WOMYN'S COMMONWEALTH

I contend that the problem of transsexualism would best be served by morally mandating it out of existence.

—Janice Raymond

As a transsexual, I don't think of myself as a woman. Women are human females. I'm a human male who went through medical procedures to alleviate dysphoria—none of which has rendered me a woman. Sex and genetics are immutable.

—Louise Berry, quoted on the
Trans Allies page of whatisawoman.uk

I

SICUT PATRIBUS, SIT DEUS NOBIS

It was Ramona's day off, and Feather's bedroom smelled like sex and weed and Hunan Palace. The thick, sweet scent of plum sauce and the oily tang of scallion pancakes clung to their fingers and tongues. Ramona jammed half a soy sauce–soaked pancake into her mouth and chewed. "You can't get this in Baltimore," she mumbled through it, spraying golden crumbs, and laughed at herself. Weed made her stupid. It slowed everything down until her thoughts felt caught in crystallizing syrup.

Feather, their big brown eyes glassy and half-lidded, made a sleepy sound of assent. Ramona wondered idly where they kept their estrogen, if they had it squirreled away in a cool, dark cistern under the apartment building, or if they bought it from one of the city's freelance testicle collectors. They weren't *really* a tranny, not in the dangerous way; they'd had their balls cut off sometime before T-Day, so there was no chance they'd catch it even if they stopped taking their E. She couldn't imagine them like that anyway, not soft, daydreaming Feather with their doughy arms, round face, and untoned thighs. They could never have turned into one of those monsters.

She swallowed, wiped her mouth with the back of her hand, and rolled over, throwing herself across Feather's legs and wriggling around until she could straddle them. They squealed and kicked when she clenched her muscled thighs against their little belly and round hips. She bent to lick the bluish stretch marks on their upper arms, her blond hair brushing their teacup tits. The spicy musk of their armpit flooded her nostrils as they squirmed underneath her. She pushed her face down into it, lunging across their body to nip at the tender skin and sweat-damp hair.

"You taste so fucking good," she breathed.

Feather giggled. The soft, smooth press of their flesh formed a seal around Ramona's mouth and nose as they squeezed their arms against their sides. She bit down, savoring their squeal of surprise and pain. She pressed the flat of her tongue to their sweaty skin, gripping their wrists as she did. They fought her. She pinned their arms against the rumpled sheets and licked the shivering, tender skin of their armpit.

Feather shifted under her. Their little cock pressed hard against her ass cheek. She rose up, hair falling across her face, and grinned at them as they whined, straining against her. "Please?" they whimpered. "Please, daddy."

She ground against them, getting wet, growling low in her throat. "Please what, princess?"

"Kiss me."

Ramona dipped low enough to graze their softly pointed chin with her lips, then pulled away with a mocking laugh when they lunged at her, mouth open. She curled her lower lip, letting saliva gather between it and her gums, letting the resultant loogie dribble from her mouth to dangle glistening over Feather's face. She pushed her tongue against her lip and let the rope of cloudy sputum fall. It struck just above their parted lips and dripped into the dark, wet cavern of their mouth. Feather shivered with delight, their hands curling into trembling fists where they lay pinned to the threadbare sheets.

She dug her nails into their wrists, grinding harder, smearing wetness on their cock, their belly, the sweaty stretch of skin between them with its thicket of pale reddish curls. Her high was coming on in earnest now, washing her brain in a cool fizz of dissociative release. Her limbs felt loose and clean and weightless.

I'm dirty.

"You're a dirty girl," she murmured into Feather's ear, and she ran her tongue along the ridges of pliant cartilage—*pinnea, concha, helix, antihelix*, she heard in her bio teacher Mr. da Costa's voice, which made her snicker—probing at the mouth of the canal. She bit their earlobe, hard, and relished the sudden tensing of their body under hers. She growled again, low and slow and lazy this time. They let out a piteous whine that was equal parts frightened and horny, a pre-tantrum snivel that sent a filthy thrill of arousal up through Ramona's stomach.

"Kiss me, kiss me, daddy."

Their voice broke and she let go of their ear and kissed them, a fluttering warning shock of her orgasm growing at the crux of her pelvis, just above her cunt. They tasted like greasy takeout and baby powder, like lilacs and sweat and weed and pussy. She forced her tongue into their mouth, choking them for a moment before pulling back and biting down on their plump lower lip. They squealed.

I'm disgusting.

"Fucking whore," she whispered, letting their lip slip through her teeth, and spat full in their face. She let go of their right wrist and reached down between them to slip a finger between her slick lips. It was coming now. Like clawing at an itch she hadn't been able to reach in days. Feather looked up at her with those big, soft eyes, like a newborn fawn. Spit glistened on their cheek and the labial fold of their nose. They were smiling at her. She wanted to slap them, to scratch their shoulders and their soft little breasts, but she was so close and her whole body was aching for it. She stroked and thrust without restraint at her swollen cunt, her breath coming in choppy little gasps.

A blatt of static cut through her oncoming release. Her walkie, crackling somewhere in the heap of discarded clothes at the foot of Feather's bed. She thumbed her clit frantically, biting her lip, but she knew it was gone. Hot frustration bled down through the still-tense muscles of her thighs. She blew her hair out of her face, every sensation—from the slight chafing on her inner thighs to the tickle of her own hair against the back of her neck—suddenly irritating.

The walkie crackled again. An older woman's pack-a-day voice fuzzed through the speaker.

"Central for Lieutenant Pierce, Central for Lieutenant Pierce. Report to City Hall ASAP. Acknowledge. Over."

She scrambled off Feather, kicking them in the hip in her rush to the edge of the bed. "Sorry!" she hissed, though really she was angry with them. She didn't know why. She dropped to her stomach and fished through her pants until she found the ruggedized black plastic brick and clicked the PTT. "This is Pierce. On my way. Over."

"Don't keep her waiting. Over and out."

Ramona scooted off the edge of the bed, getting her feet under her, stepping into her fatigues, and yanking them up without bothering to look for her underwear. She was dripping a little, but the dark fabric would hide the worst of it. Sports bra, undershirt, putting her head through an armhole and almost ripping the worn cotton trying to get it right. Her high felt suddenly like suffocating. Her fingers fumbled with buttons and zippers. She nearly forgot to buckle her gun belt.

Feather sighed, rolling over and reaching for the piece and lighter on the stacked milk crates beside the bed. Ramona felt a surge of horny frustration at the sight of their wide, round ass. She wrestled for a moment with the temptation to retrieve the paddle from the closet by the painted-over inner door. It made the most delicious sound against their creamy skin.

Don't be a fucking idiot.

"Sorry," she said lamely, feeling suddenly awkward in the doorway of the messy bedroom. "Sorry I kicked you."

"No big," said Feather, shrugging. They held the lighter to the piece's bowl, the weed inside kindling into reddish embers. They sucked smoke, then let it stream out from their nostrils before pursing their lips to blow a ring. She wanted to hook her fingers in their mouth and yank their head up until they were staring helpless up at her, drooling on her hand. But it was over. They'd moved on from the scene, their shoulders relaxing, their manner shifting from bratty panic to an almost lizard-like calm.

Ramona picked at her right cuff, teasing a loose thread and telling herself that she didn't want to cry, that this wasn't a big deal. Just a fat hooker doing their job. "Settle up tomorrow?"

They smiled. The sunlight coming through the window and the leaves of the pear tree outside fell in dappled tatters across the goldfish sleeve tattooed on their left shoulder. "Sure, honey."

She left by the back stairs, cutting through the apartment's cramped little kitchen and taking the narrow, whitewashed steps two at a time. In the building's deserted first-floor hall she paused before a water-spotted mirror to center her septum piercing and straighten the collar of her jacket where, embroidered in golden thread, the words MARYLAND WOMYN'S LEGION XX-XIII-V stood out bold against the green.

♀

Boston's city hall was a brutalist stack of honeycombed concrete cells, recessed windows glinting between its regimented slabs. It faced a long, tiered plaza, the steps of which ran down to Court Street where the old hall and state house had been burned and dynamited and now only twisted steel and broken masonry were left. Across the plaza to the north stood the JFK federal building, webbed in scaffolding from the structural work the city had begun last year. Ramona liked Boston; it was old and earthy and the wind off the harbor was pleasantly cool. The city had none of Maryland's cloying pseudo-Southern politeness.

The plaza was mostly empty, except for the dozen or so protesters with their cardboard NO TERFS and TRANS RIGHTS ARE HUMAN RIGHTS signs who jeered and shouted at her as she hurried past them down the steps. She grinned and threw them a salute. Two Legion soldiers in secondhand riot gear stood by the hall's plate-glass front doors, one leaning against a concrete bulkhead, the other lighting a cigarette from the butt of her last. "Nice," chuckled the taller of the two, a black girl with island chains of vitiligo on her cheek, her hands, and across the bridge of her nose. Her name was Kari or Karin, Ramona thought. Something with a K.

Inside, the building was, if anything, more forbidding than its facade suggested. Light fell through skylights set into the ceiling at regular intervals, creating a grid of dusty illumination sharply demarcated by lines of shadow. Bare concrete steps rose toward reception and the elevator banks and offices beyond it. Ramona thought that it had probably bustled in its heyday, the shouts and whispered conversations of its hundreds of loud, rude Massachusetts civil servants ringing from its unforgiving walls. Now it was almost empty, just like the rest of the world.

Major Molly Lang was waiting for her by the stairs. Molly was a broad, stocky dyke somewhere in her late fifties or early sixties—"A lady never tells" was her unchanging reply when asked—with leathery skin and close-cropped silver hair. She said she'd been a cop for twenty years before T-Day, but Ramona had never quite believed that. There was something inexplicably "career postal carrier" about her. Maybe her quick, confident stride, or the orthopedic sleeve she always wore on her left knee.

"Hey, Molly," she said. "How's it hanging?"

Molly grabbed her face so quickly that all she could do was yelp and slap ineffectually at the shorter woman's strong, thick arms. Hard, squinty blue eyes magnified by scratched bifocals bored into hers. "You going up to the boss like this?"

"What the fuck are you talking about?" She pushed against Molly's shoulders, but couldn't break her grip. She hated being held like this. *Hated* it. "Stop fucking around and let me go!"

"Stupid," Molly sighed, though not without affection. "Your eyes. You look like a roadie coming off a three-day bender. How much ganja you smoke?"

Ramona wrenched herself free of Molly's clutches, staggering a little and doing her best to ignore the curious stares of the few Legion personnel and Boston council staff dispersed around the cavernous entryway. "It was just a spliff. And no one calls it ganja anymore, *grandma.*" She brushed dust off her jacket. "Do you have fuckin' eye drops or did you just want to break my balls?"

Molly chuckled, producing a yellowed plastic dropper from one of her pack's little zippered pouches. "It ain't Visine, but it should work. Two in each eye." Her expression hardened suddenly as Ramona reached for the dropper. She closed her fist around it. "Tell me you weren't with that thing again."

Ramona laughed, fighting the urge to look around to see who might have overheard. "Fuck, no," she said easily. "I told you, I just went a little dick-blind for a minute. I haven't seen it since."

Liar. Stupid cunt. She'll know.

"You've got it made in the shade." Molly pressed the vial into her palm and closed her fingers over it. Those flinty eyes narrowed, the wrinkles at their corners deepening into canyons. "My neck is out for you on this. Don't fuck it up."

"Whatever." Ramona jerked her hand away and made a beeline for the door to the stairs. Her mouth was dry. Her heart punched against her ribs. She forced herself to pause there, to control her breathing, though she couldn't make herself look back. "Thanks, Molly."

"Anytime, kid."

♀

She was sweating by the time she'd climbed the seven flights to Teach's office, her footsteps echoing stark and cold in the concrete stairwell. As she paused to administer Molly's eye drops, she kept running over everything the older woman had said to her, the tone of her voice, the look in her eyes. *I never should have told her*, she thought angrily, pushing her eyelids back and squeezing the first salty drop into her right eye. *Never should have gotten drunk, even if I am her favorite.*

Finishing, she dashed saline solution from her cheeks and finger-combed her bangs into presentability. She'd been waiting for this ever since they left Baltimore. Three years in the Legion clawing her way up from errand girl to first lieutenant under Captain Lara Rodham, who'd been killed and eaten by men in the mess after those trannies tried to bushwhack them up near Haverhill. She could still see the stricken expression on the big one's face after she'd missed Teach, plugging Annie in the shoulder with a three-foot arrow like she was fucking Robin Hood. The other women had panicked, getting in one another's way, firing their crossbows—they never used guns outside of a city if they could help it—at nothing. She'd kept it together. She'd almost gotten that big Frankenstein bitch. Opened her cheek up like a box cutter slicing through packing tape.

I want a cigarette.

She forced herself to take a long, deep breath and let it out as slowly as she could, then stepped through the swinging door and into the seventh-floor hall. Wall-to-wall carpeting the color of overcooked hamburger greeted her. The fluorescents overhead were dark—nothing nonessential came on in Boston until after sunset—but light poured in through the open office doors that lined the hall on either side. City staff watched her pass with guarded curiosity, pretending to hunch low over their desks while peering at her from the corners of their eyes. They were still nervous about the annexation, which they insisted on calling a "strategic partnership," like they'd had any choice in signing it.

It was a takeover, pure and simple, and everyone knew it. Ramona passed a conference room where a few dozen women sat taking notes from a slideshow presented by Joanne Scales, a Legion staff sergeant in drab fatigues, her long black hair thrown over one shoulder. On the projector screen behind her was a slide of a man cut open from his gonads to his chin, the filth of his cancerous insides laid bare. To either side of that ghastly incision were the bumps of his fledgling breasts.

Teach's office, appropriated after their two-day conference with the city council in the shadow of a thousand armed Legion soldiers, lay at the end of the hall behind smoked-glass doors that rendered its interior a landscape of dark blurs. Ramona took a moment to compose herself. She closed her eyes and tamped down every thought she didn't need, every feeling she shouldn't think about. Soft brown eyes and skin like buttermilk. She let it all drift away like leaves floating down a stream, then pasted on her best parade face and let herself in.

The room within had been transformed, its bare concrete walls obscured by bookshelves and the prints Teach carried everywhere she went in a long, flat black case. Gerda Wegener's sex doll portraits of her tranny wife, big Bambi eyes and pouty mouths and sleek, plump curves. Some nobody New England painter's self-portraits, spindly hands, buck teeth, horsey face bracketed by shaggy brown hair. Hundreds upon hundreds of selfies salvaged from the wreckage of the internet and printed out on photo stock like Polaroids. Bodies posed in feminine contortion, shoulders wrenched to hide their breadth, faces upturned to obscure the jut of blocky jaws and the bulging knots of Adam's apples. Dyed hair and stick-and-pokes and ragged, choppy bangs. The faces of the enemy.

There was a map of the East Coast laid out on a long oak-top desk, the working roads highlighted in blue. Beyond it Teach stood by one of three tall, narrow windows, looking out over the plaza below and the skyscrapers that flanked the downtown area where the ruins of Logan Airport lay off of the tunnels and South Station bulked dark and silent but for its sole working route, the one connecting it with Providence.

"You kept yourself together under fire," said the older woman, turning from the window so that the light blazed around her in a golden aureole. Her voice was low and throaty, her gray eyes almost colorless in the sun's glare. The XX tattoo on her forehead stood out livid against her pale skin. "I was impressed."

Ramona remembered the screams. She remembered the *shhhhhwip-thunk* of the arrow whipping over Teach's head to bury itself in Annie's shoulder, just above and to the right of her collarbone, and the screams of the men pouring down the eroded slope of the gully along which the trannies had fled. "Shoulder to shoulder," she said, almost automatically. "That's the only way the sisterhood survives. Ma'am."

Teach laughed softly, pulling her high-backed chair out from her desk. She sat and gestured for Ramona to do the same. "We haven't seen much of each other," she said. She seemed never to blink. Ramona, perched on her folding metal chair, fought the urge to blush under her gaze.

"No, ma'am."

"You're a Hollywood girl, aren't you?" Teach pulled open the desk's bottom drawer and drew out a half-empty bottle of Glenlivet and two paper cups. She poured, then pushed one toward Ramona across the weighted-down maps. "How'd you wind up in Baltimore?"

"Just for a few years." She sipped her scotch, the peaty, smoky liquor burning the back of her throat. "My dad lived out there, after he and my mom split. She got diagnosed with lung cancer April of twenty eighteen and I moved back to PA to take care of her. So, a few months before T-Day."

She could almost hear her mother's rattling, phlegmy wheeze coming from the next room, faint over the sound of *The View* or *Days of Our Lives* playing on the gigantic nineties TV set. "She died in the blackouts. My brothers . . ." A great amorphous mass of sadness heaved up suddenly from the depths of her stomach, beaching itself inside her. She blinked her tears back furiously, short of breath. "I'm sorry."

Nut up. Fucking nut up and stop crying like a little bitch.

Those big, pale eyes moved over Ramona like searchlights cutting fog. "It was a bad time for all of us, Pierce," Teach said softly, tapping a finger against the rim of her waxed paper cup. "Why don't you tell me how you joined the Legion?"

Ramona felt an overpowering sense of gratitude toward the other woman. She finished her drink in one quick swallow, relishing the warm, mellow bite as it rolled down her throat into her belly. She sniffed. "I saw you speak, ma'am. In Philly, two years after."

She could still see it. That day in Love Park by where the fountain had been, Teach up on a podium in black fatigues—she'd had an undercut, then, and worn her hair up—with Legion girls at ease around her, an informal bodyguard, and a few Maenads flanking the stage. The pop and whine of the generator they'd brought, and the feeling that had flickered to life in the pit of Ramona's empty stomach as she'd listened to the stranger.

How many times have you heard that the world is over?

"I'm flattered," said Teach. Her smile was dazzling. "How long were you with Captain Rodham's platoon?"

"A year and change, ma'am. Since I made lieutenant."

"I depended on Lara. She was a good sister. A good soldier. I'd like to think I could depend on you, in time."

Surreptitiously, Ramona wiped her sweating palms on her fatigues. "I'll give you my best every goddamn day, ma'am."

"Then congratulations, Captain Pierce. I'll expect you in the plaza tomorrow with your new command."

"Ma'am, I don't know what to say."

Teach's lips twitched into a faint smile. "Say yes." She stood and held out a slender hand. Ramona, rising from her seat, saw with surprise that her cuticles were bloody and bitten, dotted with frayed flakes of skin.

She took the older woman's hand and shook it, confident as she did that those unblinking eyes would claw right through the sockets of her skull and pry the truth out of her, that she was a fraud, a fake, a dirty chaser fucking the enemy every chance she got. She forced herself to hold a smile until it hurt.

"Yes, ma'am."

II

THE BRAT

The van rumbled down a dirt track cutting through thick forest. If nature was encroaching on Seabrook, it was dragging Exeter back into the primeval dark. Moss-carpeted fallen trees leaned against their living counterparts, strangler vines hanging from their branches like fat serpents basking in what little sun reached through the canopy of oaks and maples. Lady slippers, bruise-colored and vaginal, grew wild among the nodding ferns. Twice Fran saw deer bound away into the gloom at the car's approach, and once a fat porcupine ambling through the underbrush as though out for a morning stroll.

"Fuckin' Redwall up in here," Beth muttered. She sat beside Fran in the van's second-row seat, her face still the color of milk so that her scars looked like raw liver against it. Spots of red stained the gauze taped over her cut cheek.

The drive out of Seabrook felt like some kind of demented dream. That broadcast—Fran felt sure it had been Teach's voice, low, hoarse, and hypnotic—fuzzing the air, crowds watching the van pass with expressions still unleavened by the time it would take them to absorb the change crashing down around their ears. Fear. Pity. The kind of cold, dead hatred Fran had seen all her life hiding behind different eyes. In others, something like loss.

It's just gone. Indi's house, our work. All of it.

The duffel that held their testicle harvest, still on ice, was stuffed under the bench seat. Their whole lives fit under a seat in a van. She looked back at Indi, who was slack-faced with car sickness, and Robbie, drumming absently on his thighs as he stared out the window at the greenery of the deep woods. They hit a bump and Indi closed her eyes, moaning softly. Robbie didn't seem to notice.

Why did I try so hard to make him come with us? She watched the dappled light flow over his profile. He'd taken off his hat and his thick auburn hair was matted and cowlicked. She wanted so badly to run her fingers through it. *I don't even know where we're going, really. I don't even know* him.

In the front of the van, the driver, a tall redhead in jeans and a Bruins windbreaker, downshifted as they hit a washed-out stretch of road, the van's tires throwing up sheets of water. The skinny-fat thirtysomething slouched in the passenger seat in mirrored sunglasses and a wifebeater stained yellow under her armpits, strawberry-blond hair up in a loose bun, said "Slow down" in a tone of voice that left no room for argument. The driver did, muttering an apology, and they rattled on for a few minutes between thinning trees and then, without warning, out into a clear-cut stretch of bare earth dotted with stumps like rotten teeth. The field sloped up maybe a quarter of a mile toward a low granite ridge, above which it rose steeply through scrub pines and beech trees to a summit of bare rock.

Set into the granite's sheer face was a massive concrete bulkhead, and set into the bulkhead was a rusted steel blast door twelve or thirteen feet high and about twice as wide. "Oh, what the fuck," Beth whispered, craning her neck to squint over the driver's shoulder as they crested a low rise. Fran saw it a second later. There was a camp at the base of the cliff face, a sprawl of sagging tents and shacks made of particle board and canvas and sheets of corrugated metal. People milled through it, alone and in listless clumps, turning now toward the van as it came up the track. Fran saw laundry strung on sagging lines and people roasting corn and squirrels over open fires. Their dull eyes followed the van as, slowing, they drove through the tangle of bodies and canvas. A few people stood up from around their cookfires.

There's a place for you, if you want it, Indi had said. Was this what she meant? *Don't be a spaz; she wouldn't do this to you.*

Glass shattered against the van's driver-side door. Fran screamed and lurched sideways into Beth, who let out a strangled hiss of pain.

"Local color," said Pit Stains, turning to smile at them. Dark yellow liquid sheeted down the window. "Day laborers looking for work on our farms. They get bored waiting."

Ahead, the blast doors began to open, a sliver of gloom growing between them. A double line of women stood at the mouth of the bay just beyond the threshold, their faces made snoutlike by gas masks, scuffed plastic riot shields held in a tidy wall.

Oh, fuck me.

The guards parted ranks to admit the van. Fran could see their eyes behind the smoked plastic of their goggles. The tires made a low, contented purring sound over the smooth concrete of the bay. A dingy half-light engulfed them as they left the door behind and turned toward where a fleet of vehicles—Jeeps and vans, mostly, but she caught a glimpse of something sleek and red and European near the far wall—were parked. The sounds of the engine echoed in the gloom. They stopped. The driver threw the van in park and she and Pit Stains got out, the door alarm dinging rhythmically. Fran scrambled to follow. She blinked in the dim fluorescent lighting of the bay. The blast doors were closing, the bar of sunlight they admitted dwindling to nothing, the guards unmasked, shields coming down from ready position like a swarm of flies folding their wings.

"This is fucked," Beth hissed as Fran helped her down.

Robbie followed. He was back to watchful silence. Behind him, eyes downcast and mouth set in a grim line, Indi forced her way past the middle seat, one hip deforming against the corner of its back rest, and out the door. Fran saw the flicker of pain in the other woman's face as her knees took the shock of stepping down out of the van. Then she was the picture of composure, car sickness vanished, long black skirt twitched into place and her blouse and cardigan smoothed out with a few quick tugs. She'd been like that for as long as Fran had known her, as meticulous about her clothes, her hair, her makeup as she was careless about her house, as though she were a topiary: not quite static, but reliant on the illusion of it.

Set into the bay's inner wall a few dozen yards away from the motor pool, a huge circular pressure door like something out of a submarine cycled open with a hiss of hydraulics. Through it stepped Sophie Widdel.

She was doll-like, no more than five foot three with pin-straight blond hair and big, protuberant blue eyes that reminded Fran of a tree frog or a bush baby. She wore a navy romper and an open gold silk jacket with fitted cuffs that looked like it had probably cost more than Fran's tuition, at least back when money had mattered. Balenciaga, maybe, or Versace. The kind of thing Fran had only ever dreamed of wearing.

"You're HERE!" squealed Sophie, hopping in place and clapping her hands. Her nails were manicured, perfect ombré ovals shading from dusky pink at the cuticle to pale purple near the tips. She hurried toward them. "How was the drive?" She laughed, as though she'd told a joke. "Sorry, boring. You probably wanna see your lab? Your room? Okay, we'll just do the whole complex. Everyone calls it the Screw. You'll see why. Duh, duh, duh. Kaitlyn, can you get the golf cart?" Her gaze slid quickly along the breadth of Indi's hips. "Hmm, no. Get two. Doctor Varma can ride with me and you"—she glanced at Fran, Robbie, and Beth—"can follow. Dorothy can drive you; right, Doe?"

Pit Stains, leaning against the side of the van with an unlit cigarette in her mouth, inclined her head and transferred the butt behind her right ear.

Sophie skipped up to Indi, seized the other woman's outstretched hand between hers, wrinkled her nose, and smiled in a way Fran found completely impossible to read. "We're gonna have so much fun!"

♀

Robbie wanted to run. He'd wanted to run since waking up in Fran's arms in her narrow twin bed in the hot, stuffy room over Indiresh's garage. He'd wanted to run while Sophie Widdel's women loaded the van with books and clothes and medical supplies, and he'd wanted to run as the woman in the windbreaker drove them through the woods with Indiresh groaning and whey-faced beside him, her soft, spreading bulk looking somehow small and vulnerable in the bouncing vehicle.

Now, clinging to the safety strap in the back seat of a battered golf cart, he wanted worse than ever to bail and tear back down the long, echoing hall to the motor pool and out into the camp beyond the blast doors and to keep going until he forgot Fran's face, her voice, the furnace heat of her sleeping body. She sat beside him now, her guarded expression slowly softening as they whizzed in the lead cart's wake down a broad, arch-ceilinged hall from which countless rooms and corridors branched. He couldn't hear Widdel over the noise of the carts' electric motors, but already he'd seen a gym, a packed dining hall, and what he thought was a movie theater. Electric lights. Running water. The rattling hum of air vents sucking out waste heat. He'd expected a glorified fallout shelter; this was a company town.

I'm a courtesy tacked onto a courtesy. If I asked, they'd let me out. Why keep me?

Women watched them from doorways and the sides of the corridor. Dark clothes, mostly, though once the incongruous bright white of squash outfits on two tanned and sculpted women—twins—coming out of what must have been a squash or tennis court. A glimpse of polished wood. The sound of rubber squeaking against its hard finish. Clean sweat on smooth skin, and on past a line of chatting girls in matching floral print bikinis, towels wrapped about their waists and in beehives around their dripping hair. Beth, seated beside Dorothy on the cart's front bench, clung white-knuckled to her strap as they followed Sophie's cart down the hallway's shallow slope, staircases cut from the raw stone rising to either side of what Robbie thought was a gallery, or some kind of mezzanine. It looked like the atrium of an expensive mall.

How many people live here? He craned his neck out of the cart to look up at the faces staring down the well at them. *Two hundred? Three?*

Fran's hand brushed against his. He glanced down at her slender fingers, her delicate wrist. She had, he noticed for the first time, a tattoo on the first joint of her index finger. The female symbol: a circle with a cross depending from it. Without thinking he took her hand and raised it to his lips to press a kiss against the faded ink. The hall rushed past. Staring faces, stenciled numbers on the walls. The sound of someone crying. A blush rose in Fran's cheeks. She scooted toward him along the vinyl bench, slipping her fingers through his.

"I'm glad you came," she whispered.

Something fluttered in his chest. Too much eye contact. Deep brown flecked with darker motes and the thin red rivers of her veins. He felt giddy and slightly nauseous. He kissed her. Tongue gliding over minty teeth. Closed his eyes. Let the swaying darkness swallow him.

♀

Their rooms were small, compact cubicles branching off a side passage at least one rotation down the bunker's corkscrew layout. Beth's and Robbie's on one side of the corridor, Fran's and an empty room on the other. Doe had dropped them off as Sophie's cart sped on down the curving slope, carrying Indi away to her new lab and offices. Now Beth, lying on her back on an Army Navy Surplus cot, chewed a plug of anise root and stared up at the mural on the ceiling.

It was a man, short and broad with skinny legs and rounded, sloping shoulders. Pink petals—crabapple blossoms, she thought—stood out livid against his black skin and the coarse darkness of his hair and close-cropped beard. Part of his left calf and foot had been scraped away; so had some of his pockmarked face, one eye and part of a cheek eroded by a putty knife's rasping strokes. Beth wondered why whoever had started to remove it hadn't finished, and who had painted it to start with.

She must have loved him, she thought. The root of the man's cock, thick and downward-curving, was visible above a fan of delicate petals caught against his inner left thigh, a few tumbling over his quadricep and into the empty space of the whitewashed ceiling. It was too honest a painting to have drawn on some random subject. The slight swell of his belly, the pits in his cheeks, the wedge of tight, dark curls above his prick. *She touched him. Fucked him.*

She could hear Fran and Robbie talking outside in the hall, their voices faint. Conspiratorial. Beth traced with a mental finger the high ridge of one cheekbone, the tight curls of his beard.

Was he here, when the world ended, or did the painter bring him in her memory?

Everything hurt. It hurt so much, and she didn't know how long they'd let her sleep or if anyone would come when she needed to shit or puke her guts out or if she got thirsty and wanted water. She didn't know if tomorrow they'd throw her out to rot with the people at the gate in their canvas shantytown, or put her to work monogramming Widdel's towels.

Why the fuck are we here? Running from the TERFs? These people won't protect us.

She wondered, as sleep stole up on her, if the man on the ceiling had been alone, when he changed, or if someone had been with him.

♀

"We've had sooooo many problems with our E supply," said Sophie, drifting aimlessly along one of the theater's workstations. Her slender fingers brushed against the casing of a frictionless centrifuge in which empty test tubes bobbed. "Can you make enough for—I think it's, like, seventy? I mean obviously not just you; we'll figure out an assistant so you don't have to do it all on your own. Maybe someone from the camp, to clean at least."

"Seventy-six," said Doe, who sat swinging her feet on the counter's end beside the bulky industrial freezer. She was sucking on a bright red Popsicle, the first Indi had seen in years. Behind her the sheer concrete walls rose to a wrought-iron balustrade fronting steep, tightly packed tiers of seating. Bizarre, for a clinic, but then the whole bunker was surprising—too ornate, too big, too sprawling. It didn't feel at all like a little folly two billionaires had bought to hedge their bets against the end of the world.

Maybe they were just stupid. Overbought and overplanned.

"That's not a problem," said Indi. Her knees ached and a hot, tight knot of pain was growing in the small of her back, but if she sat now they would remember her like that forever: weak. Soft. So she stood, and smiled through it. She had a whole drawer full of different smiles for when she needed them. "Long-term we can talk about a hydroponic clover grow, producing and refining our own phytoestrogens, but for now all I need is testicles and kidney lobes. My friends brought enough for maybe a hundred and twenty doses; each dose is good for a week, so we'll need to be hunting and harvesting at scale within ten days. We'll need to discuss T blockers, too. Spearmint, black cohosh, licorice root; there are certain strains of soybean—"

Sophie snorted laughter, flashing her perfect teeth in an incredulous smile. "Like soyface? Soy-boys? That's real?"

"Not the way people talked about it, no."

The girl—she couldn't be older than twenty—made a disappointed face, then grinned and swept an arm out to encompass the whole surgery, its workstations and freezer and canvas-draped equipment. "So? You like it?"

Don't sit. Don't eat. Her back felt as though someone had knotted ribbons of barbed wire around her spine. She'd forgotten to use talcum powder before leaving Seabrook and her thighs were chafing, sweat caught between them and under the lowermost roll of her belly. She wished she was alone, free to lean naked against a work surface and let the dry, cool recycled air that blew in through the theater's vents run over her. "It looks perfect. Was it designed as a lab? It's big for that, is why I ask."

Sophie plopped down on a rolling office chair and dropped her chin onto her fists, elbows on her knees with that slumped, listless flexibility that belongs only to the young and thin and careless. "Marianne—my stepmom—wanted to train doctors or something? This whole place was supposed to be a university, like, for rebuilding and shit"—she teared up so immediately that Indi almost bent in to look for the glisten of menthol smeared under her eyes—"but after Daddy, she was never the same. She couldn't . . . couldn't . . ." She took a deep, steadying breath and drew herself up straight-backed, hands folded in her lap. "She couldn't adjust. She killed herself a few weeks after."

"I'm very sorry," said Indi, not knowing what else to say. The trip from Seabrook had left her tired and disoriented; she wanted to be left alone, to settle into the apartment off the surgery and change into clean clothes, unpack her antifungal cream, see where Fran and Beth and that quiet, mop-haired boy had landed. Everything had happened too quickly. Two days spent dithering in her empty house, wondering how long she could wait before the TERFs came knocking, how long she could stall with Widdel's people. They'd offered before, in June of last year, and she'd turned them down.

We're here because of me, she thought as Sophie stared off moodily at nothing. *We're here because they couldn't take me with them and they didn't want to leave me on my own. Because they knew I didn't want to lose them.* She hated herself then, hated herself with a cold, nauseous fire she hadn't felt since the weight had come like a tidal wave after her thirteenth birthday, swamping her sturdy child's body in a flood of soft, rich womanhood. Like drowning in buttercream frosting. Every affirmation she'd ever spat at her reflection through her gritted teeth rang hollow now. Worthless noises absorbed by her bulk and stored for mocking recitation. Telling yourself what to feel is a brick wrapped up in silk: it looks pretty, but it hurts the same.

"Oh, and the chairs?" Sophie asked with that scalding combination of pity, disgust, and studious disinterest Indi knew so well. "The furniture works?"

"Armless," said Doe, sucking on the Popsicle's stained balsa-wood stick. "Like you asked."

Indi pulled another smile out of the drawer. "Yes, thank you."

♀

While women brought in Indi's boxes under Doe's hooded, watchful gaze, snapping gum and joking as they worked, Sophie led Indi to a pressure door recessed into the theater's north-facing wall. Indi tried not to feel the other women's eyes roving over her body. "So, you're a fertility specialist." Sophie said it as though she were setting up a joke. *A fertility specialist, a cop, and a rabbi walk into a bar . . .*

"In vitro, prenatal health, premature birth care; I was a midwife before I was a doctor."

Listening to white women babble about homeopathy and healing crystals while I cleaned up their shit and blood.

"*Midwife*; that's so holistic." The girl tapped a quick sequence into a palm-sized keypad, then bent to press an eye against the ocular scanner. With a buzz, the door's locking wheel spun and Sophie flitted through, leading Indi down a utilitarian hallway sloping down in yet another spiral. She flashed a look over her shoulder. "But you helped girls get pregnant when they had a problem, like a medical problem; cysts on their ovaries."

"Yes. Many times." Bare bulbs hung from the ceiling. The air tasted dead. Indi's swollen feet protested every step, the straps of her Birkenstocks cutting into them. In the gloom she felt acutely conscious of the friction between her broad thighs. "Have you been trying long?"

They came to a second door, this one a plain slab of some dull metal. Another keypad. Another code. Locks, palm and ocular. Hidden pistons hissing. Sophie bit her lip. "Oh, there's no problem with me."

"With the right equipment I can selectively implant female embryos," said Indi. "If that's what you're worried about. Most male fetuses still develop normally, but the chance of a sharp spike in testosterone production is much higher. It's a side effect of carrying the virus. I'll monitor you closely, check levels on a regular basis. It's just a matter of time and patience."

You want to roll the dice on your own kids eating their way out of you, be my guest.

The door slid open. Fresh air washed over them, cool and sharp, and within, a dark room waited. A steel grate walkway ringed a square pit, pitch-black, surrounded by a waist-high guardrail. Sophie hurried to the rail and leaned out over it, making kissing noises and extending a hand to the darkness as Indi picked her way out onto the ringing catwalk, vertigo caressing her with its long, feathery fingers. Overhead, banks of fluorescents buzzed fitfully to life. Sophie's fish-face kisses echoed. Flat light and deep shadow washed over the pit and Indi stepped back, breath catching in her throat, and found the door had shut behind her. With trembling fingers she found its edge and dug her nails into the cracks.

This isn't real, she told herself as the lights flickered on and off. On and off. The pain in her back and knees forgotten. A shape reared up in flashing light and dark. The lights came on. Stayed on. The man rose clumsily, almost bearlike, onto his hind legs, and stretched up to butt his muzzled face against Sophie's hand. His long, slick black tongue slid through the wires and curled around her wrist. His hands were cuffed, the chain run through a steel ring bolted to the floor. It slithered, clinking, as he withdrew his tongue and nuzzled Sophie's palm, a glottal purr bubbling up from somewhere in his chest. He was big, more than six feet, with a peeling underbelly and long, sinewy arms.

"Doc, this is Mackenzie." She scratched the stripe of coarse black hair that grew along his spine before moving to the scabby flesh of his throat, dead skin flaking under her nails. He twisted his thick neck—like a tabby cat, thought Indi—to show her where he wanted it. "Kenz, this is Doctor Varma." Those big blue eyes found Indi's. A shy smile curved the rosebud lips. "She's gonna help us make a baby."

III

NEVER HAVE I EVER

Fran tapped the knife against the edge of the frying pan to dislodge the pat of rich yellow butter. It slid across the hot cast iron with a hiss, slicking the metal as it went, and melted into the tangle of thinly sliced onions. There was a brick of fresh butter still in Indi's fridge. Milk, too. Eggs. Wild strawberries. A fucking *pheasant* in wax paper. Fran had nearly cried upon opening the door. Aside from sour apples and the occasional rabbit, she'd been eating salted meat and fruit leather for the better part of two years. The bunker had *fresh food*. She wanted to tip it out onto the kitchen floor and roll around in it.

I will never be hungry again for as long as I live.

Indi's apartment was a far cry from their little dorm rooms. It looked more like something excised from a Korean luxury hotel, skim-coat walls and concrete floors, minimalist white furniture that would have looked right at home in Fran's mother's office in Watertown. A chemical toilet and recycled water shower in an immaculate black bathroom. A painting of some bold, clashing shape thingies that looked like it belonged in an advertising firm's lobby and probably cost more than a new car.

Fran plucked the balls out of the little plastic dish she'd set by the electric range and dropped them into the pan, angling it with her other hand to make sure they got an even coating of the melted butter. They sizzled, a sound like dozens of small mouths chewing at once. In the living area off the kitchenette, Beth was teaching Robbie how to play Screw, both of them slamming cards down on the coffee table and slapping at each other's hands. Fran took a pinch of salt and sprinkled it over the testicles before turning them with a chopstick, exposing their seared and caramelized undersides.

When did I become a person the quality of whose days is determined by whether she eats balls raw or fried?

Tomorrow they could worry about the rest of it, the duty shifts and placement interviews, the guards and the shantytown, the look in Sophie Widdel's big round eyes and the way Indi had come back pale and tight-lipped from her tour of her lab and gone straight in to bed, claiming she had a migraine. For now it felt good to cook, and to forget about the world outside Indi's suite. Even Beth looked relaxed, sprawled sidelong on the couch with her bad leg up on a pillow and her cards held like a courtier's fan over her mouth.

Fran gave the balls another minute before snatching them out of the pan. Hissing in pain, she dropped one in her bowl of rice and beans and the other in Beth's, then stuck her burned fingers in her mouth. The salty, faintly cheesy taste of her own skin made her think of being four years old in their kitchen at the Marblehead house, a sulky little boy sucking his burnt forefinger after touching the hot griddle "just to see."

To see what, [redacted]?

Why had he done it? She couldn't remember.

"You forget to use a fork again?" Beth drawled.

Fran, scraping the onions from the pan with a spatula, glared at her in silence, fingers in her mouth, and tipped more or less equal portions into all three bowls. She killed the range and swept dinner across the room, the odd bowl balanced on her forearm like she'd done while waitressing at the Boulevard in college. For a while after that they ate in companionable silence, forks scraping against ceramic. Fran missed the smell of lilacs blowing in through Indi's windows, but the bunker's vast and solid presence made her feel secure, and the cool light of its electric bulbs was soothing. It was after nine by the kitchen clock, one of those rimless steel circles with lines instead of numbers, when Robbie leaned over Fran's shoulder and prodded her half-eaten testicle with his fork.

"Is *that* what they look like?"

Fran flushed. It felt embarrassing for him to see her artificiality outside her body, the way she'd felt when hookups saw her hormones in the drawer of her bedside table. "Yes."

"Why?" Beth asked thickly around her own mouthful of fried balls. "Did you want some?"

♀

Weed smoke swirled pale and gray in the recirculated air, migrating slowly toward the vents up near the ceiling. Fran didn't know if they were technically allowed to smoke inside, but it wasn't like they could unpop that cherry. She smiled at that image. A fruit crushed in a pretty fist. Fingers unfolding. The cherry whole again. Tattoo of a peach with a bite out of it.

"Never have I ever . . ." Beth, sprawled on the couch beside Fran with her head pillowed on the armrest, hesitated, tongue curled up over her upper lip. She tapped the neck of her beer bottle against her teeth in contemplation. "Started a fire on purpose."

Fran laughed in horrified delight as Robbie, sitting on the floor in front of her with his head resting on her knee, tipped his drink back. Finished, he set the bottle on the floor and reached for another. He popped the cap off neatly with his teeth and grinned at her in an easy, guileless way that made her stomach flutter. She could almost see it, cinders flying through his thick, dark hair in a summer breeze. A gutted house's skeleton collapsing in on itself, red and black and flaming orange, and the wind of it flattening his clothes against his slender frame.

"Bullshit you did," snapped Indi. It was joking, said with a smile, but even Robbie seemed to feel the edge on it. She'd come out of her bedroom halfway through their dozenth round of Gin, smelling like a distillery and with a six-pack of Jae and Dana's homebrew in each hand. Since then she'd been drinking steadily. Her face was flushed. Sweat stood out on her forehead.

"I did!" protested Robbie, looking faintly hurt and extremely drunk. He blinked. "I burned down Stewart Bohannen's house. Junior year."

Fran wondered if he really meant it, but thinking was hard and Indi's weed was really good. Besides, everyone had done some fucked-up shit after T-Day. *Except he did it before.* She smothered that thought quickly, clearing her throat. "Your turn, Indi."

The older woman's huge dark eyes were wet and, for just a moment, unfocused, as though she were lost in a daydream. Her chin trembled. She stifled a hiccup with one dainty hand. The spasm seemed to pull her back into herself. Her eyes narrowed in thought. "Never have I ever prayed to God."

The rest of them drank.

♀

"If He had split the sea for us," Fran's cousin Aaron read from his well-worn haggadah, and the family in halting unison replied:

"It would have been sufficient."

Aaron turned the page, water-stained paper crinkling, and smoothed it lovingly. "If He had led us through on dry land."

"It would have been sufficient."

"If He had drowned our oppressors," said Aaron. The air was full of the smell of brisket cooked with carrots and onions. Fran, at seven, fidgeted in her seat between her thin and upright mother and her mimi's warm and fretful bulk.

"It would have been sufficient."

"If He had provided for our needs in the wilderness for forty years." Aaron's reading voice was gentle, though not monotonous. Fran imagined for a shameful moment what he might look like as a woman, with his long fingers and elegant oval face. Would he be convincing? *This was the word that occurred to her most often.*

"It would have been sufficient."

"If He had fed us manna." Would she wear her hair long? Dark, curly falls of shadow spilling over her bare shoulders—too broad?

"It would have been sufficient."

A skirt that unfolded like a dragonfly's wings out from long, bare legs—like Sailor Moon.

♀

Dear Jesus, please kill Steve. Let him die and he doesn't come home tonight, and I don't want any other stepdads, amen.

♀

Robbie's mother led the dead cicada of his girlhood through the close, sweltering air under the tent. Stained white canvas snapped and billowed overhead. Hundreds of warm bodies sweated and the white sundress she'd forced him into clung to his slick skin. His hair was plastered to his neck. People he knew from church pressed close to lay their hands on his shoulders and say how good it was to see such a pretty young woman back with her mother, how worried they'd been, how happy they were.

And then a wave ran through the crowd. Their hands drifted away. A towering, red-faced white man swayed up onto the fresh-cut pine boards of the stage. His eyes were closed, his arms raised. "Do you believe in the power of the savior lord Jesus Christ, raised up from the dead, and if you do, if you do believe, do you accept him into your heart as your personal savior? When I close my eyes I see the Kingdom of Heaven, the city of Jerusalem made of every precious stone and metal, and I know it will descend and open its gates to the righteous!"

They cried out. His mother cried out. The stench of sweat thickened in the air as they pressed on toward the stage, toward the huge man and his thundering voice. People had their arms raised up to him. They begged to be healed as he railed against pornographers and psychiatrists, death metal and online chat rooms, anime and crack cocaine. His mother pulled him onward and now in among the crowd the tongues were coming, spilling from slack mouths in torrents of liquid glossolalia, and the man was on his knees at the platform's edge where the hands of churchgoers lifted Robbie up and his mother shrieked, "Throw the devil out of her, reverend! He's got in her and he has a hold of her, so throw him out!"

Those beady blue eyes found his. Those big hands came for him, and the sharp smell of mint on the preacher's breath. He wished for his father, dead somewhere on reservation land down near the Carolina border, or for the grandfather he could hardly remember. His mother's father. The farm in Dover. Back and forth. The preacher's soft hands met his sweating skin.

And it took him. It wore him like a puppet, shaking his body and convulsing his tongue, and the words bubbled out of him. He knew that it was fake and he knew that it wasn't, that the heat and the fervor of the tent were real, and the hard, desperate need of the people around him who despised themselves and longed to be in love with something pure. And so he let it have him, and while it did, while he gabbled in tongues like a thing possessed and the hands of the crowd held him up and the preacher gripped his shoulder and held a palm firm against his brow, he prayed.

Make me a man, Lord. Take my body and burn away the parts that are wrong. Burn them out of me. I don't care if it hurts. Make me a man. Make me a man. Make me a man. He had bitten his tongue and the taste of blood was in his mouth. Make me a man. Make me a man. Make me a man.

Later, on the bus, he stared out the window through his own reflection—stab it, smash it, make it leave—while his mother wept beside him. "He touched you in there, I saw it," she insisted. "Did he take it out of you, Kitty? Did he give me back my baby girl from Satan's arms?" And through her tears her eyes were sharp, her gaze as cold and patient as a snake's. "Did he make you whole?"

He leaned his head against her breast and let her stroke his sweaty hair, and he said "Yes, mama," with as much peace as he could summon, but the prayer still echoed in his ears.

Lord, make me a man.

♀

Indi lay awake, sheets kicked to the foot of her new bed, and thought of the thing in the pit that had once been a man named Mackenzie. That odious rich kid name. Whiteness. Old money. Spoiled and unloved packs of boys like that had roamed the streets of Bridgeport in her childhood. Probably they still did, only now with less discernment as to who they preyed on.

If I don't give her what she wants, will she let us live? And if I do, what would it mean to put the future of the world into those little ombré claws? She rolled onto her side and drew her legs up against the comforting weight of her belly, filtered air blowing over her bare skin and carrying her sweat away into a world of dark, clean vents scoured bare by endless wind. *If, if, if. I'd need computers that are nothing but rust and rat nests. Software that doesn't exist anymore. Isolating embryos, testing chromosomes. And the baby. Am I going to do that to a kid?*

She closed her eyes, the room swaying around her like the hold of some dark ship. *Still drunk*, she thought, picturing again the pit and the thing and its dripping tongue wrapped around Sophie Widdel's pale, clear skin. *Where the fuck did I bring us?*

♀

"So, you were a manhunter?"

The woman in charge of worker placement, what the bunkerites called "pitching in," wasn't much older than Fran. In her cat's-eye glasses and Penn State sweatshirt, the sleeves rolled up above her elbows, she looked like a tired postgrad catching up on work over the weekend. She smelled pleasantly—her odor filling the cramped closet of her office at the bunker's midmost level—of sandalwood and something like vanilla.

"Harvesting and selling," said Fran. Slitting ballsacks open with a penknife while flies swarmed over her bloody hands. Arguing with armed premenopausal butch dykes outside Penacook over how much bear meat and block salt a Ziploc full of kidney lobes was worth. "My friend Beth did the actual hunting."

The other woman made a note on her clipboard. "And how well would you say you're known in the greater Boston area? Up through coastal Massachusetts and New Hampshire?"

"Known. Definitely known. We've been to Fort Fisher twice a year, three years running, and to Boston, Worcester, Manchester, Nashua—we trade in bulk to Lakeesha Wallis's store."

Penn State scribbled for a minute, squinting as she hunched over her board, then capped her pen with a decisive click. She pushed her glasses up onto her forehead. Fran's stomach clenched around a lump of quivering anxiety. She still felt a little queasy after last night's party, and the fluorescents flickering over the walk up from her room had made her head swim. *Maybe I'll get to help Indi in her lab. Premed isn't nothing. They won't make me dig ditches. Why would they even need ditches?*

"As we ramp up estrogen refining, we're going to want to open a new line of trade with Seabrook." The other woman retrieved a thick ledger from a drawer in her desk and set it down in front of Fran, flipping it open. Page after page of minute handwriting filled the cells and columns within. Dates. Goods. Weights. Names. "They've got fish, waste removal and disposal, freshwater springs, some master craftsmen we haven't been able to poach—we've got the medication to keep their kids and PCOS patients from going feral. Unless they want to start a large-scale horse piss concentration facility, they've got to deal with us."

"So do you want me, like, out with the hunters?"

"No, no, nothing like that." Penn State shook her head. She'd set her clipboard down. Fran could see the blank "Sex" boxes on the intake form, twin islands all-encompassing in a sea of ephemera. How many times had she dithered in the blank quarter inch between them?

"Sophie thinks you'd be a good fit to help with managing our relationship with the Seabrook city council."

Fran blinked, looking up from the sheet. "The Legion—"

"They aren't going to strip-search our people. We've dealt with them before, and we don't allow it." With a smile she checked the box next to the "F" on the form. Fran's heart leapt in joy and terror as she took it. Her token. Her proof. All at once the bunker seemed to open up around her, its blank walls limitlessly clean, its every unmet inhabitant a new best friend just waiting to be taken by the hand and led sprinting into fields of wildflowers and waving grass.

I'm going to be a woman here. I'm going to be real.

Penn State signed the form with a decisive flourish. "Whatever they might suspect about you, a suspicion is all it's going to be."

IV

SAFE SPACE

Beth liked farm shift, even in the late September heat. Since her leg had healed up enough that it no longer woke her in the night, she'd had no problem lugging pails of slops, cracked corn, and the chipped offal and bones of the animals that passed through the slaughterhouse at the north end of the compound. Indi said that soon she wouldn't even have a limp. For now, the cramping in her half-mended calf muscle wasn't much against the satisfaction of pushing herself until she had no more energy for thoughts or fears. No energy to think of Seabrook or Boston or all the friends they'd left behind without so much as a goodbye. No energy to worry that maybe someday she would ride back to the bunker for a shift change and see those long, black flatbeds parked outside.

For now, all she had to worry about were the pigs. As she stumped along the elevated walkway, a Sheetrock bucket brimming with feed in each hand, they paced her progress in the yard below like a school of grossly overgrown piranhas. Thirty-six of them, their clever, beady eyes following her and Megan and their cargo through the walkway's grating. Their trotters thumped quick and efficient against the turf. A few had gone ahead and stood expectantly around the long, shallow gutter of their trough.

Beth and Meg set down one bucket apiece and tipped the others over the rail, showering the trough and the upturned snouts of the pigs in a fragrant medley of compost and abattoir sweepings. A chorus of wild squeals rose up. Huge bodies thumped against one another as the pigs fought for pride of place and Beth went back for her second bucket. Gobbets of flesh pinwheeled through the air in a reduction of half-clotted blood and spoiled milk to splatter on the scrum below.

Meg came to lean against the rail on Beth's left, resting on her elbows. They looked down at the seething backs and thrusting snouts below. "Finally," the other girl deadpanned in a pitch-perfect Gordon Ramsay. "Some good fucking food."

Beth laughed. It was just the two of them on pen three today. They'd make a few more trips for feeding time and then drop the gate and shovel shit for the girls in composting at the edge of the farm compound—a trailer across a fenced-in yard from a compost heap sheltered by an awning of corrugated steel—to process into fertilizer. They had a minute, though. The afternoon sunlight glinted on the flashing around the slaughterhouse chimneys. The walkways bridging pens one and two stood empty, heat shimmer smearing the air around them. Sweat glistened at the nape of Meg's sunburned neck. The other girl smiled and Beth leaned in and kissed her on a wave of sudden bravery as the scent of pig shit swirled around them in the breeze.

♀

Ramona stood on the weathered front porch of the house at 33 Balsam in Arlington. The front lights were dead but the moon was nearly full and silver light washed her and her squad as they listened in the darkness, waiting for her to give the all clear. Their first night out. The inauguration of their work in Boston. Her heart fluttered. Her period had come that morning, but light. The cramps were bearable, especially through the buzz of the expired Adderall she'd snorted on her way to barracks. She raised two fingers. Made a fist.

Jules, who was the tallest, kicked the door down. Piper pulled the pin out of her tear gas canister and lobbed it down the front hall of the ground-floor apartment, clocking the first trans girl square in the nose as she burst out of one of the bedrooms. She reeled and crashed into the wall, clutching at her face. Clouds of gas billowed up around her thrashing silhouette.

"Go, go, go," Ramona barked, her voice buzzing through the snout-like filter of her gas mask. Her heartbeat quickened to a sprint. They went. Piper and Sadie first, then she and Karin, with Jules bringing up the rear. The trans girl, face bloody and eyes squeezed shut, blundered into Piper, who seized her by the arm and shoulder and propelled her face-first into the wall again. Plaster cracked. So did bone. Ramona pounded past and on into the dirty kitchen, her own breath rasping mechanically in her ears as she squinted through the smoke at the scarred butcher-block countertops, the drab little breakfast nook with its card table and folding chairs and the sachets of scraggly cohosh hanging over the sink. A crash from the hall behind them. Someone had pasted a water-spotted paper chore wheel onto one of the cabinets. *Neela: Trash, Stevie: Dishes, Veronica: Harvest, Sibylle: Pigeons.*

Not letting herself pause to wonder what the fuck kind of chore "pigeons" was, she gestured for Karin to go out through the back to sweep the porch and yard. The tall, skinny girl fumbled with the knob a moment, shooting an embarrassed look back at Ramona, before vanishing into the dark outside. Ramona turned back toward the smoke just as a wispy little elf of a trans woman came flying at her out of the darkened pantry. She had an impression of a wrinkled face, wild white hair, and the hard knot of an Adam's apple.

Ramona caught the other woman's knife arm by the wrist and for a moment they struggled over the long blade, stumbling around the kitchen in a clumsy, desperate dance. The knife caught the starlight coming through the open kitchen window. The air was cold and damp. *Did it rain last night?* Ramona drove the woman back into the counter, knocking a stack of dishes to the floor to shatter at their feet. Screams rang from the hall behind her. Flashlight beams swept the kitchen through the window over the sink. She heard voices outside.

The old transsexual's wrist broke with a sharp, dry crunch when she slammed it against the rusted tap. The knife clattered into the sink and Ramona thought of her mother's thin, brittle arms lying flat against the yellowing sheets of the hospital bed, of her brother Ben's fat little fists at the age of seven tender months, of Feather's chubby wrists and the blue veins that stood out in them and the milk and salt taste of their skin.

She flipped the sobbing freak around and cuffed her.

They went out the back down a narrow set of stairs propped up on cinder blocks and wooden pilings, Jules and Sadie leading their sobbing collars out of the front hall, Piper swaggering behind them with one hand on the butt of her pistol. In the lead, Ramona dragged the old trans woman along by her good arm. "Fucking TERF pig," the woman hissed at her through yellowed teeth. "What'd we do to you, huh? What'd we ever fucking do to you?"

She looked so frail in her panties and oversized T-shirt, all bony shoulders. Loose flesh under her arms. Skinny legs and that flyaway mane of white hair, thin and soft like a baby's. In the backyard Karin waited with a tall, blocky transsexual in ripped overalls and a striped T-shirt kneeling cuffed in front of her in the ankle-deep grass and wild raspberries. A crowd of Legion women stood just beyond the two. Molly and her platoon had come up Federal and through the rotary where it cut through Main, past the deserted shells of Chinese restaurants and nail salons. The glow of the major's lit cigarette flickered across the wrinkled landscape of her face and shone in the thick, scratched lenses of her glasses. They were here to see the job got done, to seal and witness Ramona's new command. She felt sick to her stomach. Elated and terrified.

"You've got no fucking right," the old woman snapped, twisting in Ramona's grip. Her dark eyes flashed venom. She had a deep, scratchy voice that sounded, to Ramona's untrained ear, like botched vocal cord surgery. A frog's croak. Fine silver stubble dusted her long jaw, which clicked as she swallowed and continued in an urgent whisper. "They're just kids. They're kids. If you need to make some kind of point, keep me, do what you're gonna do to me, but let them go."

Ramona shoved her down onto her knees beside the big, hunched brick Karin had caught. There was a real *thing*, shoulders like a plow horse, hairline receding at her greasy temples. Beady eyes darting nervously between the Legionnaires. *How could she think anyone would mistake her for a woman?*

"That all of 'em?" asked Molly, lighting another cigarette from the butt of her last.

Ramona peeled her mask off and flashed a wolfish smile. "Yes, ma'am. They had a little chore wheel up on the wall with all their names; we got the whole house."

"We won't do it anymore," sobbed a dark-haired girl who might have been Greek or Iraqi or something, judging by her caterpillar eyebrows and the errant chest hairs sprouting from her breast. She looked up from where Jules had shoved her to the ground. Mascara slicked her tear-stained cheeks. "We're just running low, just a little. We'll figure it out, I swear we will. We'll leave! We'll get out of the city!"

Molly took a long drag on her cigarette, double-pumping the smoke over her furrowed upper lip into her nostrils before exhaling it in a long, lazy stream. The Legion women around her were silent, little more than shadows limned with the moonlight that came through the branches of the wild crabapple in the corner of the yard. "Waiting for something, captain?"

Ramona swallowed. "No, ma'am." She caught Sadie's eye.

"You cunts," the old transsexual spat. Ramona saw in her face that she knew what was coming. Hate gouged deep lines into those pallid cheeks. An animal's hate, terrified and absolute. "You fucking Nazis. You murderers."

The others were crying.

"Line 'em up," Ramona snapped to Sadie, turning her back on Molly and the others. She was going to do this for herself. The pistol at her side felt like a bar of lead. She imagined that she heard her mother's voice. *Nothing worth doing is easy.*

The squad—*her* squad—pushed, dragged, and shoved the women—the prisoners—into a rough line near the back steps of the house. The kitchen light was on. It shone through the water spots and grime of the lone window. Ramona could feel Molly's eyes drilling into the back of her neck and she realized with a sudden, panicked jolt that someone, somewhere, had doubts about her. *Did Molly tell? Do they know? They'll shave my head and break my legs and leave me to crawl through the street and beg.*

"Ready," Ramona forced out, not turning, not wanting to face the cold expressions of Molly and her whole platoon. The old transsexual had gone silent. Her eyes were dry, her chin thrust out, her lip peeled back in withering scorn. The other prisoners huddled close around her. Den mother. To Ramona's either side the women drew their mismatched pistols. Karin's eyes were wide. Her nostrils flared with every shaky breath.

"I can't," the black girl whispered, her voice a strangled squeak. "I can't do it."

Molly's scrutiny pressed harder against Ramona. She swallowed, stepping back, and wrapped her arms around Karin from behind, taking hold of her by the wrists. She centered the old woman's mutinous expression, that cruel hatchet of a face, not one of the crying girls who weren't really there, who weren't seventeen or twenty-two, who weren't crying snotty tears on one another. "Just breathe through it," she said, her lips nearly touching Karin's ear. "That's not a woman. It's not your sister." Her own hands were numb but steady on the handgun's grip and over the other girl's finger on the trigger. "It's just a man in a disguise. We let it go, sooner or later it's going to come out of its skin." Her dry mouth. Tears stinging the corners of her eyes. "It's going to hurt us. Rape us. Eat us, if it can."

"Aim," said Molly.

The guns came up. Ramona could smell Molly's cigarette smoke, thick and stale, and the sour stench of rotten crabapples crushed underfoot, their guts mingled with the pulp of the tree's fleshy pink petals. Karin trembled against her. She thought of the big freak she'd winged that day on the edge of the woods, of the glistening edges of her unzipped cheek. Karin whimpered.

"Pigs!" the old woman screamed, spit flying, the breeze tugging at her fine white hair. "Fucking gestapo!"

Beside her, Eyebrows was whispering something to Karin's blond brick, their foreheads together. Ramona's mouth twitched. She began to squeeze, or Karin did.

Later, she thought, in a moment of terrible clarity, *each of us will tell herself the other was the one who pulled the trigger.*

"Fire."

♀

As she sat waiting on the steps of the super's trailer at the edge of the farm compound, Beth thought for the first time in months of the house on Iris Avenue in Wilbraham. The Flying Saucer Collective, a shabby two-story place right off Park Avenue where seven queers cooked communal vegan meals and brewed their own trash-can beer and fought over how to properly store sourdough starter. There was an herb garden nobody weeded and somebody's mother's old paisley shawls tacked up as wall hangings in the living room. Morning glories withering on the trellis leaned against the east wall. A real Pinterest board of a house, just unkempt enough to be chic without sliding into dereliction.

For a year and a half after dropping out she'd lived on the second floor in a filthy closet of a room, slowly dating her way through a rotating cast of roommates and friends of friends: skinny trans mascs, angry leatherdykes, demisexuals with half-ironic bowl cuts who talked endlessly about Tumblr gender discourse and whether wearing bow ties was class warfare until each half-assed relationship inevitably flamed out into brittle, silent resentment. Tension boiling around the scarred kitchen table on board game night. It was actually good that the world had ended, because now no one could make her play Settlers of Catan.

And then, three days into the nonstop onslaught of broadcast carnage in the wake of the Liverpool Massacre, Aster called a house meeting. They called it via email, which was typical passive-aggressive bullshit, and as soon as Beth saw the notification on her phone and read the subject line—IMPORTANT: HOUSING SITUATION—she knew what it meant. She was the situation. She and Venus and V's girlfriend, Tara, who'd been staying with them since the news hit. The house's three potential testosterone time bombs.

That muggy night, heat lightning flashing over the highway and the transformer towers in the cut that ran through the woods, they'd gathered in the living room to sit on mismatched furniture—a cracked and peeling leather armchair, a sagging sectional, a wool-upholstered green couch dredged up from the 1960s—and Beth watched Emily pick at her cuticles while stealing looks at V and Tara from the corners of her wet green eyes. It had started days ago, those looks, even among the hugs and tears and clouds of weed smoke. It was the look Beth would see five years later on the faces of some of Seabrook's women during Teach's broadcast, cold and hard and cis—although white Emily said she thought maybe she was two-spirit—a look that said *You know, and I know, that somewhere under those blunt bangs and that mismatched foundation you're still every bit the man you've always been, and you'll never be anything else.*

Now, waiting to be told that she was off farm shift, that she'd made Meg feel unsafe or that someone felt her attitude was inappropriate, it was that look she remembered, not Aster's circular monologue about accountability and "abusive" tones of voice and how their partner

Chase—who Beth remembered mostly as a skinny smear of purple hair and projected neuroses—was starting to feel unsafe, that Tara's night terrors were scaring them and wouldn't it just be better for everyone if they admitted they were taking a huge risk housing "potential vectors," so maybe it was best if those vectors went to the half-finished quarantine camp in Needham until things settled down and there was a vaccine?

V had shouted until her voice cracked like fired glaze, but Beth only drew back down into herself, looking from one closed face to the next with the mounting satisfaction of knowing everyone had finally decided not to pretend anymore. They hated her. She disgusted them. She was a roach scuttling across peeled linoleum. Shit smeared on the sole of a sandal. Finally, finally, they were telling her that every kiss and scene and forced and halting word of their affection had been a performance to convince themselves and each other they could love a big, dumb, ugly brick.

"Fine," she'd said the next time V paused for breath. "Fuck it. We'll go."

And they had, though V screamed and threw things and Emily scurried away upstairs and somewhere Chase was crying, their sobs high and wild and so despicably feminine. Beth stuffed clothes and meds and her squirreled cash into a ratty backpack. In the upstairs hallway, Lily, who passed and had a custom pussy and so could never contract the estrophaga virus, watched her and sniffled and hugged herself while exuding a guilt so thick and viscous Beth could feel it soaking through her hoodie and her scoop-neck tee, which she had no cleavage to fill, only an expanse of chest stippled with red marks of irritation where she'd shaved, and through the torn denim of her jean shorts and the fraying cotton/lycra blend of the tights she wore beneath them.

They stood in the front hall, the three of them and Jon and Aster, and beneath her hard-won vindication a cold terror gnawed at the pit of Beth's stomach. Suddenly she wanted very much to stay in this place where she'd never felt love, where she'd never put her art up on the walls or let herself unpack her last few boxes, where she'd played Magic: The Gathering and Netrunner with Jon (bad loser, good kisser) and gotten blackout drunk at their Christmas party and yelled at Emily for defending her cop dad (a terse, excruciatingly boring lecture from Aster about trauma triggers and verbal abuse had followed).

"I'm sorry," said Jon.

Aster said nothing, just stood there tall and thin and imperious in their sweater vest and sport coat, horn-rimmed glasses glinting in the reflected glow of the porch lights. They looked like some lost character from a Donna Tartt novel. Some trust fund kid hiding behind a cultivated thrift store image of genteel academic poverty. Their father owned the building, though they didn't like to talk about it. Beth turned back, trying to think of something cutting she could yell in parting, and they slammed the door. She was left face-to-face with the stop sign Emily had repainted pink and blue and nailed to it the year before.

THIS IS A SAFE SPACE FOR PEOPLE OF ALL GENDERS, RACES, FAITHS, AND SEXUALITIES!

She turned, shoulders hunched, and started down the front walk. Fireflies blinked over the ragged lawn. All along Iris Avenue, light fell through drawn curtains to bleed into the thickening night. The street was empty. A jagged scribble of heat lightning lit the hillside to the north. Tara, walking beside her, was crying hard enough that her breath kept hitching and rivers of clear snot pooled on her upper lip.

That was when V started in again. Beth stopped, looking back. The other girl hadn't left the stoop. "You motherfuckers!" V screeched, pounding on the door with a bony fist. She looked so angular in the soft yellow porch light, a collection of hard lines surmounted by the tight knot of her bun. Her backpack lay by her feet. "You're killing us! You're fucking killing us!" She slammed her forehead, hard, into the splintering wood.

"V!" Tara shrieked. "Stop!"

Again. Beth started back toward the house. Again. Blood on the panel's peeling paint. V screaming now, battering her fists and face against the door. Again, that sickening thud of bone on wood. And then, from above, another sound. A squeal of tortured metal and the scrape of something heavy shoved over a rough surface. Beth looked up. The air conditioner spun as it fell. Beth hadn't seen who pushed it. A hand. Curtains swirling. Bone. Blood. A sound like an egg cracking against the rim of a metal bowl. The slow, sluglike glide of the yolk over stainless steel. It looked too real. TV with the motion smoothing on, the actors' faces home-video raw and sharp. Tara screaming. Her nails digging hard into Beth's arm.

They were scared, she told herself, trying to reach back across those five long years and turn her younger self away from the sight of V's tottering body and the oozing, open gash from her ruined skull down to her chin. The fissure where her forehead used to be. *They were afraid of us, and they hated us. Lily hated us, too, and herself, and they hated Lily but they had no path to let it out. So we got it. We got all of it.*

She had dragged Tara away from that house, from that sign on the door that said they were safe, from Venus with her head caved in and her jaw split open. Two nights later the other girl took forty Klonopin in a motel bathroom and died what must have been a slow and agonizing death while Beth slept a few feet and a single wall away, and on the silent television set atop the dresser, a helicopter news crew had captured a pack of men fighting over the corpse of a little boy like dogs over a bone, snarling with their blunt teeth buried in his flesh. Or else she'd dreamed it.

The trailer door swung open. Beth scrambled to her feet, turning to face the graying middle-aged cis woman who stood on the threshold in a blue skirt and white cardigan, the frigid blast of the air conditioner swirling into the morning heat around her. "Bethany," she said, not unkindly, but in a voice that was cis and had always been cis and had never imagined anything but cisness, flat and opaque and interminable. "Why don't you come in and have a seat?"

Beth looked back at the farm, inhaling the stink of shit and soil and animal musk, of the compost shed and her own sweat, and then she turned and followed the woman inside.

♀

"It's just where they did the establishing shot," Sadie shouted in Ramona's ear over the din of the Indigo Girls blasting on the bar's speakers. "They didn't actually film the show here."

"Okay," said Ramona, who had never seen *Cheers*. The basement dive where Molly had taken them seemed like a normal pub, underlit and earthy. She glanced at the worn, polished bar and thought for a terrible throat-closing instant of all the men who'd sat there, year after year, or stood behind it mixing drinks and pulling drafts. Her father had died in a place like this. A heart attack in a booth. No one had even noticed until the owner came over to kick him out at close.

Was he cold? How long does it take for a body to turn cold?

"It's just a lot of people make that mistake. They see the sign and think—"

Ramona slid out of the booth. "Bathroom," she grunted at Sadie's quizzical expression, and without waiting for an answer she struck out across the crowded floor, sidling past Karin where the other woman stood slumped against the bar on her elbows, sipping from a shot glass, and between the Legionnaires jostling around the pool tables. One of Molly's girls, a hatchet-faced woman a little older than Ramona, the hair on the left side of her skull shaved to peach fuzz and the other side left coarse and shaggy, clapped her on the shoulder in passing.

"Good work out there." A lopsided smile from the battle-axe. Behind her, two women swaying on the water-stained tiles. Undercut pulled Ramona close and whispered in her ear. "You want an attagirl, chief said to tell you there's one waiting upstairs in 1B."

Feather's hazy stare and the soft circle of their open mouth. Their pink tongue lapping at her fingers. Ramona made herself return the other woman's smile. "Good to know."

The bathrooms lay on the far side of the bar, past the jukebox and the broken *Pac-Man* machine. Some wit had Sharpied a skirt and a long, pendulous penis onto the little figure on the MEN's plaque. Ramona ducked into the women's, pushing past Jules and Piper where they were necking on the edge of the dance floor and pulling the door shut behind her. She threw the bolt and leaned her forehead against the rough wood, counting her breaths until her heartbeat slowed. The muffled music thrummed through the door against her skin.

Get it together, you fucking infant.

She went to the sink and ran the faucet. No hot water, but after a few seconds the cloudy brown flow cleared enough that she could splash it on her face. Her reflection swam in the cracked and spotted mirror. The green dress she'd picked up from her locker at the precinct building they'd been using as a headquarters. Numbers written on the tile walls. Spiraling blooms of graffiti. A rat breastfeeding its teeming young. Lurid green and purple outlines. A cock and balls. The Cool S.

She slapped herself across the face hard enough to make her right ear ring. Again. The stinging flush as blood rose to the surface. Again, the sound in her ear rising to a mosquito's brainless whine. *Focus up, Pierce.* Three more times, quick and artless, her pinky nail leaving a minute cut near her brow. *You are not going to the bench, you're not getting benched, you're not you're not you're not.* Closed fist. Knuckles crushing cartilage against her skull. She dug her nails into the back of her neck and dragged them slowly to the hollow of her shoulder, letting out as she did a long, shuddering breath.

Enough.

She ran her fingers over the tender scratches. Relief washed over her in dull, cool waves. The tension drained from the face in the mirror, leaving only overlapping handprints in fading red and pink. She touched the outline of her palm where it burned across her cheek. The bowl of her steady hands brought water to her face. A lukewarm kiss that smelled of minerals and copper. Blood on flyaway white hair. The music had changed. Courtney Love, bleached blond hair and runny eyeliner. A bloody red hole.

Someda-ay, you will ache like I ache

Out through the door, dragging a rueful smile together like she was gluing the pieces of a broken vase. Hands slapped her back. Someone pushed a beer at her. The cold, bitter taste of it. Dancing with Jules. The click of pool cues against billiard balls as they kissed to wolf whistles and applause. Something sweet burning its way down her throat. Schnapps? A woman crying. More Indigo Girls. *Should eat something,* she thought, but didn't. *Water.* Resting her head on Jules's shoulder as they turned in place, hanging onto each other.

"The way that tranny sniveled while you helped Karin line up her shot," Jules whispered in her ear. "'Please, please, don't hurt me.'"

Someone cut the music. Ramona looked up, blinking as Molly's nasal Charlestown drawl rang through the sudden hush. The older woman stood on the end of the bar a few yards away, face flushed, beer in hand. "Where's the lady of the hour?"

Wheah's tha lady a' tha owah?

The crowd of drunken women stepped away from Ramona. Jules disentangled herself with a giggle and then Ramona was alone in the middle of the bar where they hadn't filmed *Cheers*, more than half in the bag and realizing that she *had* seen an episode, had half-watched it by her mother's hospital bed sitting up into the night while Mom detoxed from meds they couldn't afford anymore. Actors she couldn't name shouting at a fat guy in a sports coat as he hustled down the bar toward his stool.

NORM!

"I wanna say a few words about the kid," said Molly, gesturing toward Ramona with her cigarette. "Sharp as a tack, tough under pressure, always looking out for her sisters. I had my eye on her for a lotta years now, and I never for a second doubted she had her priorities"—she wondered if anyone else saw the way the other woman's expression hardened, or how her eyes narrowed as she looked into Ramona's—"in order." Molly raised her glass. The rest of the room followed suit. "To a world without cocks, and the cunts who'll get us there."

They drank. Ramona stood blushing. There was applause, and then Molly shouted, "Come and get your wings, kid." They pushed and shoved her toward the bar, laughing as they did, and pinned her right arm knuckles-down onto the scarred and polished oak. Undercut was waiting there, tattoo gun in hand, and over Ramona's laughing protests she brought the needle down to just above the blue veins at the crook of her elbow.

Ramona grinned through the dull, febrile pain of the spike flicking in and out of her forearm. A hummingbird's tongue. In bold black strokes, Undercut inked two letters—each no bigger than a poker chip—into her skin, like a stain. The chromosomal seal on her quality-control report, a little sign to tell anyone who saw her that she was a woman, a *real* woman, not some chemically altered monstrosity who had to pay doctors to saw and sand and bend her into a woman's shape.

The gun buzzed. The girls packed in around her laughed and shouted over one another as the tattoo slowly took on form. Molly watched her from across the bar, and Ramona made herself smile at the older woman's calculating look, made herself the giddy image of the mark that bloomed near the crotch of her arm, her reward for the years of service to the Legion that had brought her here to Boston, to its seagulls and driving rain, to Feather's arms and roads buckled by frost heaves. XX. Certified fresh.

The real fucking thing.

♀

Beth was crying in bed when Robbie found her. She heard footsteps and looked up from the sweaty, mucus-slicked circle of her folded arms, blinking through a haze of tears. She'd only been back an hour or so. The woman in the trailer—Joyce—had explained, in a voice that made Beth think of the special ed teachers at West High who'd concealed their burnout behind suffocating niceness, that Meg was uncomfortable with the idea of their continuing to work together, so wouldn't it be easier if Beth rotated off farm duty? They'd find her something else.

The whole ride home she'd replayed her kiss with Meg and their hookup in the shower that same night. *Did I put my fingers in her without asking? Did she pull away when I leaned in?* The more she thought about it, imagining those soft lips opening around her tongue, those long lashes fluttering in dreamy anticipation, the more she realized that no specific moment, no single touch, was to blame. What mattered was that she'd broken the silent rule. She'd touched a girl before the girl touched her, had laid her violent hands on tender skin. She should have known better. Self-pity pressed against her mouth and nostrils like a sodden rag. *I'm a girl until a real one decides I'm not.*

"Hey," said Robbie. He looked worried.

"Hey," Beth croaked, wiping her nose on the sleeve of her grubby flannel work shirt. "Sorry. Didn't know you were back."

He shrugged. "You mind a little company?"

She wanted to tell him it was okay, that he could go, but the thought of being alone in her room with the painting of the man above, the man who had been loved and remembered, stilled her tongue. She shook her head, and as he came over and sat down beside her on the bed she thought, with a mixture of jealousy and tenderness: *He's so small. He could blow away in a breeze, but not me. Not big ol' Beth in her bib overalls and work boots. Chewin' on wheatgrass an' spittin' in the wind.*

Another sob bubbled out of her, thick and choked. *She can't even cry like a girl.*

"It's okay," said Robbie. He put an arm around her and she leaned into him, hating how much taller she was, how awkward it felt to let him support her.

"Wanna talk about it?"

She didn't, but she told him. It came slow and halting at first, then hot with caustic venom, slimy with self-pity, and finally flat and dry and dead as a dissociative wind blew through her. She told him how Meg had smiled at her, how they'd kissed by the pigpens and fucked in the showers, how they'd stolen dirty little interludes all through their shift. And then the next day, nothing. Meg wouldn't look at her. Wouldn't talk to her. Turned pointedly away when Shannon came and found them in the stables and said the super wanted to see Beth.

"I don't know what I did," she whined, hating the way she sounded. "I keep going over it. I keep trying to figure it out, but I don't *know*."

"Sometimes you just have to live with that," said Robbie. "Someone's hurt, you don't know what you did, and that's . . . it. That's all there is. It doesn't make you a bad person."

Beth thought for a moment of the world that had been, of the flurries of callout posts, the texts asking her why she'd hung out with so-and-so when didn't she *know* they were problematic, that they'd broken boundaries or gaslit someone or said the word "sex" where a kid might have overheard. There had been pain in there, too. Real pain swirling through a farrago of social justice buzzwords and ruthless self-professed socialists whose politics hewed closer to Nancy Reagan than to Marx or Engels.

"I liked the farm," she said, knowing she was sulking and unable to make herself stop.

"It's not personal," said Robbie.

Beth wiped her nose on her sleeve and laughed. It was half a sob. "Then what the fuck *is*?"

♀

Ramona wasn't sure how she'd gotten to Feather's building, that pile of stone and concrete, air conditioners still lodged in broken windows like a thyroid case's bulging eyes. Her arm hurt. It itched, bad, where the bitch with the undercut had inked her. She slapped it like she would a mosquito. Not supposed to scratch. When she got her sparrows in high school—a small flock on her upper right arm—she'd had to wear oven mitts to bed for weeks to keep from clawing at them.

She'd been like that with all her tattoos. The tulips on her chest, under her collarbones. The stars on her right ankle and the dates on her left inner forearm: mother, brothers one and two. *I don't want to remember anything,* she thought, staring up at the stars. *I want to scratch it off. I want my skin back. I want my mother.* She remembered, out of nowhere, the name of the fat barfly from *Cheers.* It was Norm. That's what everyone had shouted when he hustled through the door, Boston accents ringing from the walls. *Naaahhhm.*

Why do I know that?

She was on the stairs of the apartment building, an arm slung through the banisters, laughing or crying. When had she gone inside? Someone was watching her from the door closest to the landing. A gauzy nightie. Flyaway white hair drifting in the summer breeze. She raised a hand and made a finger gun at the pale blur standing in the half-open door. "Bang," she muttered, and dissolved into gales of laughter.

There were footsteps on the staircase. Voices in the hall where the white nightgown was saying something to a big, thick blur in boy shorts and an undershirt. And then Feather was there, kneeling down beside her, belly pale and striated with deep purple waterways beneath their silver camisole. "Let's get you upstairs," they said, slipping an arm through Ramona's while other half women gathered in the hall to watch them. "Up, up, up."

She disentangled herself from the rail and looped her arms around their neck, burying her face in their little breasts, kissing the tops of them. "I don't wanna get up," she murmured into their neck as they heaved her to her feet. She bit them, not hard, just nipping their skin. "I wanna kiss you. I love you, baby."

Feather wasn't smiling when they broke apart. "I didn't pull the trigger," Ramona snarled. "Why are you looking at me like that? What crawled up your cunt and died?" She slumped against the railing, hot air rising up the stairwell and tickling the back of her neck. She laughed again, and this time she sounded ugly to herself. High and forced and stupid. She let Feather take her by the arm and lead her up around and around. Faces looked down at them from above. Trannies and butches and a few pretty teenage ladyboys came out to ask if anything was the matter, if Feather was okay, and Ramona laughed at them too and said, "She's FINE!" as they climbed past.

In the bathroom, she puked brownish bile into the toilet bowl, throat spasming and shoulders so tense that her neck ached where she knelt slumped against it. Feather held her hair. Their hand moved up and down her spine, a soft and steady pressure. "You can't do this to me," they said quietly. "You can't come here like this."

Ramona squeezed her eyes shut against the acid of her tears. She thought of Sid in eighth grade, that delicate Adam's apple, those slender fingers, hair the color of cherry blossoms. How good that pretty cock had felt inside her.

Why don't you dye your pubes pink, too?

God, Momo, you're so fucking gross.

"Are you listening, Ramona?"

White hair streaming in the dark, in the heat, as the old woman fell with a hole where her right eye had been. Ramona spat to clear her mouth of the rancid, burning taste of bile. "Shut up," she husked. She licked her lips and leaned her brow against the cool, smooth porcelain of the toilet seat. The world ebbed into gray. "Just shut—shut the fuck up."

V

DADDY ISSUES

A pool. Sometimes Fran felt like she'd been hit over the head with a mallet and the Screw was nothing but a swirling mobile of fantastic shapes shimmering just out of reach. Stars and tweeting sparrows. The smell of chlorine. The echoing slap of wet feet against white tile. The intermittent splashes as women launched themselves off of the diving blocks and plunged through their rippling reflections. She'd woken early, the lights in the main thread still dimmed when she ducked into the hall, and padded barefoot to the refectory, where she ate browned onions, bacon, eggs, and mushrooms with a fat slice of brown bread dripping with butter. The low-ceilinged space was quiet, almost empty except for the women behind the serving counter with its plastic sneeze guards and its stacks of bowls and trays. There was an aquarium set into one wall, and for a while Fran watched iridescent fish flit in and out of beds of waving water weed as snails progressed at glacial speed across the glass.

With a few hours left before she was due to leave, she'd slipped back into her room to pluck her bathing suit out of the little chest of drawers built into the north wall. Robbie shifted on the cot where he lay curled tight like a sleeping beetle. A few minutes' walk up the thread, the murmur and rustle of women changing, showering, toweling off in the locker room, and here she was at the pool's edge, watching slender figures glide over the depth markers stenciled on the tiled bottom. Curls of vapor swirled over the surface. They recoiled from her toes as she dipped a foot into the water. Warm.

Fran sat and eased herself over the edge. *When was the last time I went swimming?* The water closed over her head. She exhaled a stream of bubbles from her nose and floated, weightless, her ponytail bobbing as she rolled onto her back and kicked off of the wall. The low tile ceiling shimmered. Fran kicked lazily, letting herself rise until she surfaced with a sharp inhale. The backstroke came easily, worked into her muscles by years of swim meets and practice at the Concord YMCA. Locker rooms full of shoving, giggling boys. Speedo tight around her cold-shrunken scrotum and the shriveled root of her adolescent cock. She nearly stopped to check her tuck, still haunted by the feeling of climbing up onto that plastic diving block while parents cheered from the bleachers, their collective gaze scraping her wet skin, the chafed lines where tight nylon clung to her hips and crushed her junk against her pelvis.

The memory passed. She reached the far end of her lane and managed a clumsy flip, tile and water blurring together, and kicked off again. Her legs and shoulders had begun to burn by the time she hit tile at the shallow end. She slumped against the pool's edge to catch her breath, chin resting on her folded arms. Other women walked to and from the lockers, passing wet and dry, stopping to exchange a little pleasantry, a touch. A kiss. Fran's breathing steadied.

I could do this every day, she thought, turning to look back out over the pool at the bobbing blue and white segmented buoys, the soaked fiber cords, the timing board over the deep end, and the lifeguard sitting on a bench with a battered paperback and an iced coffee. *Is it finally over?* She drew a deep, shaky breath. *I don't ever have to run again.*

♀

It was monotonous work, disinfecting the lab. Running microfiber cloth over glass slides. The stink of solvents burning her nostrils as she transferred disorganized jumbles of instruments—she'd found an engraved nutcracker mixed in with a mismatched set of antique scalpels—from tray to tray, leaving bits of dirt and grime to float in the solutions. Indi had been at it all morning and her back was sore, her eyes watering from solvent fumes. Across the lab's wide concrete floor the short, stocky woman Sophie's people had brought in to help her—a motherly Ecuadorean woman named Mariana who spoke little English but who Indi was fairly sure had been some kind of orthopedic specialist—was cleaning out the unplugged sample freezer. *She must be from the camp,* thought Indi, looking up from the mind-numbing task of plucking each part of a disassembled speculum out of the first tray with long-nosed tweezers for deposit in the second. *Everyone else in this place is pure Wonder Bread.*

The twins certainly were. Corinne and Sylvia Slate, identically blonde, identically tanned, identically slender and toned. Corinne headed the Screw's administrative apparatus, the web of favorites and functionaries who allotted rations, assigned jobs, and oversaw maintenance requests, intercom switchboard operation, and power distribution from the compound's geothermal and hydroelectric setups. She had come down with her sister, quiet Sylvia, currently sketching in a leather-bound notepad at one of the empty work surfaces, and spent the last half hour demanding explanations for random pieces of equipment and why everything had to be resterilized and why "the work," as she referred to it, hadn't yet begun.

"Sophie wants to know why you're still prepping," said the woman, tucking a lock of blond hair back behind one ear with an immaculately manicured hand. She couldn't have been older than thirty-five. "You had a rundown on the facilities when we made our offer. It's already been six weeks. Now you're asking for new equipment, new drugs. You may have noticed we can't just order it online."

Indi sighed, pushing her rolling chair back from her workstation and moving her cracked protective goggles up onto her hair. "With semen from an uninfected donor," she began, forcing herself to speak patiently, "we'd only have to monitor Sophie's testosterone production throughout the pregnancy. Ninety-nine out of a hundred times there are no complications, no matter the baby's sex or chromosomal makeup. With ejaculant from a new man, it's a different story. When they impregnate a victim, the baby is XY. No variation. It undergoes viral metamorphosis in utero and eats its way out of the mother at three or four months. A few hours later, it can hunt for itself. In a year, it's sexually mature."

"So you'll do in vitro," said Corinne, inspecting her flawlessly tanned complexion—there was a little salon up on the presidium level, near the pool—in the mirror of her compact. "Make sure the baby's XX."

"I have what I need for harvesting and implantation, but sustaining embryos outside the womb for observation and testing, fertility treatments—I need specialty equipment, compounds that have all denatured, time, staff—"

"We got you that Dominican."

Oh fuck you.

"Corinne," Sylvia warned, not looking up from her notebook.

"Mariana's very capable," said Indi, glancing sidelong at the older woman, who, with her upper body buried in the maw of the industrial freezer, showed no sign of having heard. "But she's not specialized. I need a chemist. Experienced. Right now, without a microarray, I can't be sure whether or not the"—muzzle on his face, skin scabby and peeling, black tongue wrapped tight around Sophie's little wrist—"donor can even contribute an X chromosome."

In some ways it made it easier, focusing solely on the technical problem at hand. She didn't have to think about the snotty little child empress she was doing it for, or the people starving in the camp outside the blast gate. *There are people starving everywhere,* she told herself sometimes, when guilt crept close as she lay on her memory-foam mattress, cool filtered air blowing over her, the taste of butter lingering on her tongue. *There always were, and always will be. Being here, making a place for Fran and Beth and Robbie . . . a place for me. Is it really so bad?*

Corinne made a face and snapped her compact shut. "So what's the time frame, then?"

Are you really going to do this? Give this woman a child so that one day she can reprogram all the palm and ocular locks in this place to accept it, so that she can pass a thousand people down like a locket or an antique rocking chair?

"Give me a month," said Indi. "And get me what I need."

♀

Fran watched the coast roll by through the truck's passenger window. Most of Seabrook's beachfront houses were already gone. The ocean had swallowed them, though their collapsed hulks still dotted the beach, siding eaten through by salt, frames broken, roofs spilling into the water in ragged slopes of shingle and splintered beams. Seagulls and cormorants nested in the ruins. The city council was putting in levies; lines of pour frames interspersed with concrete monoliths.

I guess society didn't collapse fast enough, she thought. *Or maybe some Ukrainian nuclear plant went critical halfway across the world and we just don't know it yet. Maybe we're all going to get cancer, if we don't have it already. If we don't drown or get malaria or get eaten by our men.*

They pulled up to the checkpoint at the border between the town's burn zone and the downtown drag, the truck's brakes groaning as Nam-joo, the haggard bunkerite who'd walked her through what Sophie expected from the council, brought it to a shuddering halt. A broad, solid woman somewhere in her late forties or early fifties sauntered toward them and leaned into the cab, elbows on the rim of the driver-side window. She was a little cross-eyed, hair cropped to gray stubble, Legion designation picked out in metallic blue on her fatigue jacket's collar. Behind her, three other women loitered around the checkpoint's barricades in the shade of makeshift canopies, two with rifles slung and one with her hand not on but conspicuously near the butt of her pistol. The sun spilled like bleach over the broken pavement.

The woman settled her weight against the window and gave her teeth and palate a quick, low-pitched suck. "You from the bunker?"

"Kim and Fine." Nam-joo had a poker face Fran thought could probably withstand anything short of sustained artillery bombardment. Not that they had anything to hide. She crossed her legs, drumming her fingertips against her knee. Not really. "We've got a meeting with the council."

Slowly, the woman drew a stained and crumpled notepad from within her jacket. She flipped it open. Read. The corners of her mouth drew down like a bulldog's. "Well, here you are." Those crossed eyes flicked over the cab, and then the woman pushed herself back with a grunt and stowed her little book again. She held up a thick finger. "Wait a minute."

I don't know anyone on the council, Fran told herself, trying to rub a sudden cramp out of her right thigh. The muscles were spasming, as though her legs were trying to snap shut like a pair of scissors. *I hardly know anyone in town. Jenny and the rest are gone, or dead—gone; they got out and they're gone—and Jay and Dana would never turn me in. Would they? I'm as safe here as anywhere. I'm just as much a woman as any of these cunts.*

The Legion woman who'd stopped them was talking with the other checkpoint guards. Something changed hands, flashing in the light as it passed out of shadow into sun. *Even Nam-joo doesn't know. What's the point of telling her?*

A sudden thought struck her as the soldier strode back toward them, a gale of relief as she shucked a decade of hiding and hunching and scratching imperfections from her greasy, sallow skin. *No one knows,* she thought giddily to herself. *No one knows at all.*

"You're all set," said the woman, grinning broadly as she reached in through the window. In her hand she held two laminated cards, one stamped with Fran's name, the other with Nam-joo's, and both subtitled with a neat, perfunctory XX. Fran's heart skipped a beat as she took hers, the soldier stepping back from the window and waving them on through the blockade with a shout of "Welcome to Raymond, ladies!"

♀

He had a hangover, his first since he and Midge had gotten wasted on the sour cider they'd made themselves. The fall of 2018. The white light spilling through the bunker's blast doors as they screeched and rattled open dug straight through his eyes into the nascent ache squirming behind them. He squinted at the stout, gum-chewing girl seated across from him in the bed of the idling pickup, wishing he'd thought, as she had, to bring sunglasses.

Four of them sat there, and Doe, one long leg stretched out, the other crossed beneath it, her back against the cab's rear window. The crossbows and rifles were racked on the cab's roof and there was a locked strongbox bolted to the bed beside Doe's hip that he thought probably held handguns. Doe's function in the bunker's machinery he hadn't yet managed to work out. The masked and Kevlar-plated guards to the truck's either side greeted her like one of their own when she climbed up over the tailgate, and she'd smiled back with easy, wolfish pleasure. Sophie's hatchet man, probably. Someone to make problems disappear, to keep the bunker's little microclimate running smoothly.

Is this the kind of place where people disappear?

The guards parted ranks and the engine growled as they rolled out through the blast doors, suspension groaning at the thump of the wheels in the divot where erosion had eaten away the soil at the base of the granite face. Robbie shaded his eyes against the glare. Last night they played Never Have I Ever. He told them about the Bohannen house and later, while he was inside Fran, she'd looked at him as though she wanted to ask why, and how. But she hadn't.

He raped a girl. I thought I was doing the right thing. Maybe I was. Refugees watched them from either side of the narrow dirt track that ran down the hillside toward the forest and beyond that the glint of metal at the power plant and the flat dark plate of the ocean. They crouched in the mouths of their sagging tents—just tarps and canvas held up from the ground by sticks—and one woman, dumpy and worn in a shapeless T-shirt and patched Levis, stepped into the road and spat into their tire tracks as they drove away. He'd never seen someone look so angry.

At the edge of the camp a tall black trans girl stood watching them from under the laundry lines, stained sheets and undershirts flapping around her. She wore ratty cutoffs and a faded blue tank that left the scars on both her shoulders bare. Broad, livid gouges, like a bear or a big cat had mauled her. Or a man. There were others with her, crouched and standing, but Robbie couldn't seem to break her gaze to look at them.

There's something there, he thought.

The truck went over a frost heave, bouncing hard enough that he had to grab the side to keep from spilling into the bed, and by the time he looked back up at the laundry lines she was gone. His head still ached. The girl beside him offered a canteen. Water, cold and tasting of iron. He wiped his chin and thanked her, noting the way she looked him up and down, the way her small fingers brushed his.

Why am I here? Why am I in the Screw, and not out with these people? They cut north down a track that ran through a cornfield on a level stretch of ground. Pickers moved between the rows with baskets slung over their backs. The last of the summer corn, he realized. He and his grandfather had always gone for a beer at Thompson's after bringing it in. *Why am I here? Because a girl held my hand and asked me to go steady?*

Crows rose up shrieking at the edge of the field as the truck thumped over another heave. Their black wings thundered in the early sunlight. *I don't like this.* Robbie looked back over the tailgate as the dips and switchbacks of the hill bit by bit erased the camp and the swirling sheets and even the cornfield and its workers from view. *I don't like any of it.*

♀

"So we all pretty much share the dressing room and the lounge," said Dani, encompassing the cramped confines of the latter with a flick of her wrist. A bookshelf full of paperbacks and magazines. A pair of uncomfortable, expensive-looking couches in the same minimalist style as all the rest of the bunker's furniture. Beth could imagine the late Mr. and Mrs. Widdel having a passive-aggressive fight about which shade of gray upholstery to go with, the kind of argument she only knew from Fran's family and *Mad Men*. There had been no clean, cold, plausibly deniable anger in her own childhood.

"You need help taping, binding, whatever, you can just ask me or Tina. She's better with the gaffe hair, too, if someone wants a lumberjack. You're so pretty, though." She flashed a smile back at Beth, who wasn't sure if she meant it or not. "They'll probably want you clean-shaven."

They passed through the lounge and into the dressing room, a little bigger than a galley kitchen, the long mirrors on the north wall ringed in fairy lights. Men's clothes hanging from pegs like discarded snake skins. Suits and silk pajamas and sweat-smelling flannel shirts. Fake beards on dummy aesthetician heads; Beth could hardly bring herself to look at them. She slouched along in Dani's wake. The other trans girl was a little younger than her, tall and bony with jutting cheekbones and black hair tied back in a messy knot. Her breath smelled overpoweringly of licorice root.

"This is where the, uh, magic happens, I guess." Another smile, rueful and a little sad. "Sometimes they just want a dick, sometimes they want the whole deal. It's not that bad, once you get used to it." A hand placed gently on her forearm. "Have you ever daddied before?"

Beth shook her head, fighting back a sob. Tears ran down her cheeks. *All I do anymore is cry.* "I asked—" Her voice broke with a shameful, pubescent creak. "I asked for warehouse, or kitchen. I don't want to do this. I don't think, I can't, I can't—"

The cis woman in the little office. Human resources by another name. *We'll just try you out in comfort, until something opens up. Does that sound okay?*

"Oh, honey," said Dani. She pulled Beth into a bony embrace, as though they knew each other. She stroked Beth's hair and let her cry. "We'll take care of you. T for T, brick for brick."

Beth remembered, as she spluttered snotty snobs against the other girl's bare shoulder, a picture of herself that had sat framed on the mantelpiece in the house on Second Street. High school graduation. Her mortarboard askew on rumpled, sandy hair. Fran beside her, lean and pretty, neither of them out yet, but even then, put Fran in a dress and no one would give her a second look. That night, Fran posing naked in front of the mirror in Beth's bedroom, one hand cupped over her cock. *What if I were a girl? Wouldn't that be weird?*

Beth had cried, then. Burst into choking, strangled hisses of pure misery, not knowing why, the preview image from her mother's digital camera searing itself suddenly into her mind's eye. Her fingers like sausages on Fran's delicate arm. The acne-scarred expanse of her big mulish face. They'd had The Fight a few days later. After that, she hadn't seen Fran for five years. But the picture had stayed. She could see it now. Body part after body part brought into the spotlight of her memory and held up to be found wanting against a silhouette she didn't dare look at directly.

Fake. Fake. Fake.

With a steadying breath she made herself stand up straight, sniffing and rubbing tears from her eyes with the heel of her hand. "Sorry," she said thickly. "I get dysmorphic sometimes. I freak out." She dug a handkerchief out of the pocket of her black denim shorts and held it out to Dani. "I'm sorry I got snot on you."

Dani took it and plopped down onto one of the folding metal chairs. "Babe," she said, inspecting her face in the mirror with critical detachment. Her long fingers touching the corner of her mouth, the cleft of her chin, the corner of her eye. "I'm trans. I've had first dates with more crying than that."

♀

"We keep it medieval this far from home," said Doe, tossing Robbie a crossbow and a zipped canvas quiver of bolts from the gun rack over the cab. She took one for herself and slung its canvas safety strap over her shoulder, cinching it tight. "Draws less attention. You ever use one?"

Robbie nodded. All around him on their stretch of dirt shoulder at the edge of the woods the hunters were testing their strings and sorting through their quivers. Most were in camo. A few, like ball players, had smeared stripes of eye black along their cheekbones to cut through the sun's glare.

Doe jumped down from the truck. "Fisher, the new girl—sorry, kid—he's with you."

Robbie flushed. "No big deal," he muttered, fighting down the familiar prick of numb resentment. He was still spotting, and he felt suddenly self-conscious about his menstrual cup, about the faint throbbing of his lower back where his hips curved hatefully outward, bone and flesh defying clothes and ruthless regimens of exercise and, before that, a half decade of grueling starvation.

This is not your problem. He tugged irritably at the neck of his shirt, which felt suddenly itchy and constricting. *You have nothing to prove.*

The stocky girl, Fisher, flashed a smile at him. "Robbie, right?" She held out her hand and he took it, smiling in spite of himself. She reminded him, with her fat black pigtails and faint mustache, of a girl he'd kissed at Baptist summer camp. "Sam. I hear you're a pretty good shot."

They shook. "I do okay."

The group split, Doe striking out southeast with the other two women while Sam led Robbie southwest into the pine forest by a narrow dirt trail. Maybe hikers had beaten it, or hunters, or fish and game people. The familiar hush of the woods closed in around them. He could practically feel his jaw unclench. Being underground was making him crazy. The echoes, the unfamiliar people, and the sense he'd carried all his life that wherever there was money—and money had outlasted the end of the world, as a state of mind if not in fact—he would always be uncomfortable. The bunker stank of money. Of wealth. New England women idling their days away on private squash courts and the cocktail lounge down on the second thread of the Screw.

He'd heard people call it that, the Screw, for the shape of the layout. The women who lived there were mostly white. Mostly young. Mostly pretty, in a kind of Abercrombie & Fitch catalog way. He saw the way they looked at him. He always felt like a rat when he went out into the main passage, scurrying from shadow to shadow. They were trying to puzzle out whether he was white or not, whether his deep tan was just that—a tan—or evidence of something else, and then whether they wanted to fuck him. Their stares ran like a phrenologist's fingers over his high cheekbones, his strong nose and auburn hair. He knew his father was Taos Pueblo, from somewhere near the ancient city, but not how he'd died, though he thought probably that it had been his mother's brothers. He wondered if he had cousins out there somewhere in the baked arroyos of New Mexico and Arizona. Aunts. A grandmother. Maybe even a half sister with his dark eyes and long, narrow face.

Dead needles carpeted the forest floor. Squirrels watched them from the branches, black eyes shining like buttons. The pines were tall here, ancient and scaly, their lower limbs dead, their tops waving in the sultry wind. Some lay fallen across the path, moss climbing their roots. Brackish pools lay still under slowly drifting nebulae of pollen.

"How long have you been in the bunker?" he asked. They'd stopped by a narrow stream to fill their canteens and rest their feet. Clean water chuckled over mossy stones. In another life he might have hunted in a place like this, might have had someone like him to show him how to be something other than white people's version of a man. He pushed the thought away and buried it.

Sam, knocking dirt and little stones out of one of her boots, paused a moment. Her brow furrowed. "A little over a year, I guess. The last estro doc wanted more manhunters. Before that I was in the camp." She gave her boot a final thump before tugging it back over her decaying sock. "Which sucked exactly as bad as you're thinking." She sounded uncomfortable. Defensive.

"I didn't say anything."

Sam shrugged, frowning. Robbie felt uncomfortable; he'd never been good at small talk, the minutiae of navigating what you should or shouldn't say. Childhood had taught him silence was safest, his two years in Seattle a thousand different ways to split hairs and dissect language in pursuit of proving who was *good* and who was *problematic*, but at the first sign of tension he froze like a frog with a flashlight shining in its eyes. He'd done it on the walk to Dr. Varma's house, tiptoeing around the crackling charge of frustration and pain between Beth and Fran. It made him feel like he was small again, and like the outcome of that tension rested somehow on his shoulders.

“My friend’s not doing so well,” he offered after a while had passed and Sam showed no signs of getting up from her rock. “Was it hard for you? Adjusting?”

“We should get moving,” said Sam.

They crossed the stream and went on without talking for a good quarter of an hour. At intervals along the trail someone had marked trees with orange Xs, faded and dull, and Robbie wondered where that person was now. Sometimes it felt like everything around him was a cut thread. A shadow burned into concrete. He glanced back at Sam, who’d fallen behind. She was staring off into the trees, maybe at nothing, maybe at something he couldn’t see. Either way he felt sure their chance at being friends had passed.

At the bottom of a steep slope mulched deep in rotting leaves, Robbie caught a whiff of man piss in the air. He put a hand on Sam’s shoulder and inhaled deeply at her questioning look. She sniffed. She nodded. A short way on, they found the tree the feral man had marked, the base of the trunk still wet. Higher up, he must have rubbed himself against it, because bare pine gleamed where bark had flaked and fallen away. The trails left by bore beetles shone a duller silver, dead wood stiffening against the live.

It wasn’t long before they found more signs. A splash of acrid urine on a lichen-spotted boulder. Runny shit full of hair and rodent bones half-buried under soil and needles, like a dog kicking dirt over its turds. Flies already swarmed over it, their iridescent bodies a living haze of stupid, buzzing darkness. Robbie checked his crossbow again. He walked a little faster.

They spotted the man from about thirty yards off. Sam saw him first. Her expression hardened and Robbie followed her eyeline through the trees to where the thing crouched with its back to them in the shadow of a felled oak’s roots, tearing apart the bloodstained carcass of a feral cat. Sam knelt and brought her crossbow up as the man tore off a mouthful of raw meat and began to choke it down.

Sam’s shot went wide, caroming off a tree with a dull *thwack* of metal on wood. At once the man looked back at them over his shoulder, pinpoint pupils dilating hugely, and let out a crackling growl of warning. Blood ran between his rotten teeth. He dropped the carcass, still trying to swallow, and began to prowl toward them. A line of dirty yellowish boils ran across one of his cheeks and into the fold of his nose, which had been flattened and pulled left by the strain of his tightening skin.

As Sam slid a boot into her crossbow's arm and began to pull the string back to the lock, Robbie squinted down his iron sight. The man charged. He fired. The bolt took the thing high in the throat, just under the jaw, and the man fell thrashing to the ground. Blood spurted from his straining mouth. His heels dug furrows in the rich black soil and filled the air with the aromatic scent of crushed pine needles. He clutched at the steel-headed bolt protruding from his neck. *A quarrel,* Robbie remembered out of nowhere. That was what you called them, like they were a way to end an argument.

Sam walked up to the flailing creature and put her own bolt through his eye. The thrum of the crossbow's steel wire as it released echoed through the trees. It wasn't until later, as he was stuffing a Ziploc full of blood-slimed balls into Sam's little red lunch box while she heaved the dead man over onto his stomach to cut through his back for his kidneys, that Robbie thought to wonder what had happened to the Screw's last doctor.

♀

From the TERFs standing guard outside the town hall—two middle-aged white women, head to toe in riot gear, with an unmistakably suburban aura—they learned that the council was meeting up at the Shaw house, that Fallingwater knockoff on the hill overlooking Indi's house. Town hall was closed for renovation.

It felt strange to drive past Indi's without saying anything. Strange to see its windows dark and empty. There were paving crews out on Main, patching potholes and using pickaxes to break up buckled pavement. Open barrels of hot asphalt smoked in the sultry air. A few workers watched them pass and each time Fran felt a light frisson of anxiety, a conviction that they would see her and *know*; that her ever so slight Adam's apple, the single speck of razor burn under her jaw, the length of her nose would give her away. But they didn't, or if they did then no one cared.

How many of them would turn me in, if they did *know?*

They turned onto the sloping driveway that wound its way up toward the Shaw house's garage, Nam-joo throwing the truck into second as they climbed. Cut stone rose sheer to their either side. They parked in front of the big segmented metal doors with their glazed windows. There were no other cars out front. Fran looked back through the cab's rear window at the street below. How many times had she walked and biked it? *I'm not selling balls anymore,* she told herself. *I'm not some dirty fucking nobody.*

A set of stone steps cut into the rock curled up to a wide concrete porch in the shadow of the house's bulk. Below, Indi's place looked tiny and forlorn. Last winter they'd had Christmas there, the three of them smoking weed in the dead of night as snow fell thick and soft in the perfect dark outside. Another TERF in riot gear stood beside the double-paned front door, rifle held loosely across her body. She was smoking, but when she saw them coming she dropped the butt and ground it out under her heel.

"Bunker?" she asked. She was pretty, tall and dark with splashes of vitiligo mottling her skin.

"Bunker," Nam-joo agreed, expressionless as she displayed her laminated name card. Fran did the same, fishing hers out of the pocket of her jeans.

The woman—girl, really; she couldn't be older than twenty—leaned in to read them, then opened the door and went in, pulling it shut behind her. Fran listened for and heard the click of a bolt sliding home. For a while she and Nam-joo stood there on the steps in companionable silence. It was hot. She wished she'd worn something a little more impressive than skinny jeans and her lone dress-shirt, short-sleeved and with a small cum stain which, thankfully, was down low enough to tuck into her pants. She picked at the stub of a hangnail she'd spent the morning trying to bite off of her right index finger.

"Do you think I should have worn something else?" she asked Nam-joo.

The older woman gave her a flat stare.

♀

Inside, the Shaw house was as colorless as out. Their escort led them down a long, narrow hall lined at head-height with coat hooks and lit only by what sun came through the frosted glass around the front door. Past the kitchen with its black marble island and countertops—a few TERFs in uniform were eating biscuits in there—and a closed door on the house's north side. A bathroom, white tile only half-scrubbed of mold and mildew, voices audible now from somewhere deeper in, and then through a small study full of moldering legal journals, a metal desk set against one wall under a window where a dead or dormant wasp's nest grew like some strange tumor from the corner.

In the house's vast, empty great room, its plate glass wall overlooking the ashen expanse of the burn zone and beyond it the shore's rolling dunes where the wreck of the destroyer *Tecumseh*—which had run aground when its dying crew attempted to scuttle it—lay heeled over and beached, two women Fran recognized from the handful of city council meetings she'd attended were seated at a folding table with two others she didn't know, one in her late thirties or early forties, her coarse black mane of hair thrown over one shoulder and half her skull cropped down to stubble, the other tall and broad-shouldered, a swimmer's body, absorbed in conversation with a younger TERF kneeling beside her chair.

"Francine Fine and Nam-joo Kim," said the girl who'd led them in. "From the bunker."

"You made it," said one of the councilwomen. She looked tired, her large frame slumped, dark circles beneath her eyes. "Any trouble getting into town?"

"Can we skip talking about the weather?" The older TERF stubbed out her cigarette in the ashtray in front of her. "Come on, sit down. I'm not sleeping here and I don't want to drive back to Boston in the dark."

The other stranger turned back to the table as Fran and Nam-joo took their seats, her whispered conversation ended. Fran nearly froze. That short blond hair. That stupid flower tattoo. And in her nose, its belled ends shining, a septum piercing.

Ah, she thought. *Fuck.*

VI

DIRTY WORK

Indi knelt on a blanket beside Mackenzie's snoring bulk, trying to jerk him off. She wanted to do it before the Temazepam faded—she had no idea how potent it was after three years in storage, or how his metabolism would handle it. She'd strapped him down just in case. The hardest part was handling the barbs, the dozens of short, bony protrusions growing from his cock. Only with thick rubber electrician's gloves and enough Vaseline to make getting any kind of grip on him at all a nightmare had she been able to start working his shaft without fear of getting snagged and cut.

"He close?" Mariana asked anxiously. The short, squat woman leaned over Indi's shoulder. "He close to finish?"

"Yes," Indi snapped. "Stop hovering."

Mariana moved away, muttering to herself under her breath. From the corner of her eye, Indi caught the gleam of fluorescent light off polished rosary beads. *Stupid fucking Catholics. The only thing they're right about is that there's just one god.* She looked at the cock in her hand, at its thick veins and the flaking scabs and ingrown hairs at its base. *But it's not their god. Not that fussy lawyer. This is Durga's world. We're just living in it.*

He came, ropes of thick yellowish cum filling the sample canister Indi held at the slit of his cock. His huge frame shuddered with release, muscles going slack, the raw fissures in his skin oozing cloudy fluid where they'd torn in his spasm. Indi capped the tube, peeled off her glove, and let Mariana help her up. Her knees popped like firecrackers after so long on the floor. Mackenzie snored on, face twitching slightly as he dreamed of chasing cars, or dogs, or women. She felt briefly guilty for having touched him while he slept. Like she'd raped him.

"Get this to the freezer," she said, handing the canister to Mariana. "I'm going to untie him and lock up."

♀

She doesn't recognize me, Fran thought, trying to avoid eye contact with the other girl, who'd introduced herself as Ramona, without making a big deal out of it. Nam-joo and Viv, the older TERF with the undercut and the lean, hungry face, were doing most of the talking. For the most part the two city councilors—big, slumped Christina Fawcett and a skinny little gray-haired woman named Jen or Jean or something—just took notes and nodded. When she did talk, Christina forced each word out through her gritted teeth.

There's no way. Fran fought down her panic, stuffing it into the fat, coiled worms of her intestines, wiping its traces from her expression line by line and inch by inch. *Everything happened so fast that day. And if she did, what could she do? I'm protected.*

Still, when Ramona glanced sidelong at her she nearly bolted from her seat. The sound of Viv talking about crop surpluses and fishing rights and zones of jurisdiction faded to a background hum. *I thought about fucking her,* Fran recollected. *After she shot Beth, I thought about what it would be like to fuck her. What the hell is wrong with me?*

Had she fantasized about Teach, too, when they'd spotted her through the trees? She had. Garters and heels and the soft leather whisper of a flogger's head over bare skin. Those cold, unblinking eyes. She swallowed and sat up straight, forcing herself to pay attention.

". . . means we're forced to compromise our grain reserves to meet demand for poultry. If we're going to keep that supply line intact we want a thirty percent bump in what we're seeing in terms of corn and wheat."

"Thirty percent's not happening." Viv lit another cigarette and took a drag, thrusting out her lower lip to let the smoke escape in slow, fat puffs. "What's the real offer?"

"The real offer is the town cleared ground for two new fields this spring, and they're both yielding."

"Maybe they just did it for the, what's it called? Crop rotation?" Viv glanced at Fawcett, who nodded with automatic weariness. "There. See? Just stewarding the land. We can do maybe, what, five percent?" Another nod from Fawcett, who looked like she wanted to cry. Viv smiled. Her teeth were small and white and crowded.

Fran cleared her throat. The others looked at her. Septum Piercing—Ramona—had her jacket off and her elbows on the table, and in the crook of her right arm Fran could just make out a scabby new XX tattoo. She glanced down at the female symbol tattooed on her finger to keep from blushing at the taller woman's stare. "If you don't want to go to thirty, you can start providing chicken feed. Take it out of your end as part of the deal. Unless you think you can get enough protein from the eight fish global warming hasn't boiled yet."

They were quiet for a moment. Viv's expression was one of guarded amusement, but it was Ramona's that held Fran's attention. She looked suddenly unsure, her stare hooded, her shoulders slightly hunched. To Fran, trained by a lifetime of her father's brittle silences to read body language like a radar tech watching for incoming torpedoes, the other woman's change in mood was louder than a scream. She made herself swallow and keep talking.

"Thirty's cheap, and you know it."

"Fifteen," said Viv, her beady yellowish-brown eyes narrowed above the predatory gash of her smile. "We can spare that, right ladies?"

Fawcett nodded. Jean or Jen made a note.

"Done." Nam-joo scratched at her own yellowed notebook. She favored Fran with a small, tight smile. "Let's talk estrogen."

♀

The camp woman's skin parted under Indi's scalpel. *Initial incision should run from the anterior superior iliac spine to the umbilicus,* she heard Dr. Kaligian say, speaking fifteen years ago from a table beside the cadaver of a wrinkled, wizened man. *I prefer the Lanz incision, a one-third lateral cut.* Blood welled out of a thin layer of yellowish fat, which gave way with ease against the sharpened edge as she drew the blade repeatedly along the length of the incision. "Clean as I go," she said curtly, not looking up. Jane leaned in to dab at the wound with a folded cloth. The younger woman was one of the Screw's few registered nurses, a blandly pretty New Englander with pin-straight brown hair and a penchant for gossip. For all that the general clinic on the Screw's third level was housed in a spacious, well-lit suite of rooms, the nurse's voice seemed to fill its operating room from wall to wall.

"You know she's been out there for years?" Jane whispered, running her cloth over the wound's interior. "I remember she was in for heat stroke in the summer of nineteen, from working in the corn fields. She told Dr. Widdel she'd come all the way from Florida, her and her daughter."

Indi traced the cut's left lip, following its gentle oval curve. Fat unfolded, losing its smooth, slippery surface appearance as she probed at it. She said nothing.

"I'm just saying, imagine being out there like that, with *them*. It makes—"

"Forceps," Indi interrupted. She took the instrument and pushed deeper into the unconscious woman's abdomen, easing slick coils of muscle out of her way. "Now retractors, and *focus*. I'm not an anesthesiologist. I have no idea how much longer she'll stay under. If she wakes up on the table, you're closing."

Jane slipped a pair of flattened hooks of surgical steel between the fascia and pulled them back, exposing the glistening membrane of the peritoneum. The wound flexed with the woman's slow, shallow respiration. Jane had steady hands, at least. *Now if I can just get her to shut up,* thought Indi as she searched for the doubled fold of the mesoappendix, Jane sponging the wound periodically with her free hand.

Talking Doe into letting her open clinic hours to the people in the camp had taken weeks. Most of the Screw's functionaries and sycophants simpered and sniveled and offered up all kinds of cute, euphemistic phrases like "overcrowding" and "non-productives"; it made Doe's flat "What the fuck do we get out of it?" almost refreshing. The woman was a reptile, but a reasonable one. She knew giving the camp people something tangible made them more pliant in the long run. More willing to work the Screw's fields without making a stink. The woman on the operating table, weathered and leathery but no older than forty-five, had come to meet the morning's hunting parties as they drove out. Stomach pain.

What do we get out of it?

Indi maneuvered the appendix up and out through the mouth of the wound, sighing behind her surgical mask. A fat, ribbed worm of violent pink flesh. "There it is," she said. "Be ready for ligation, then we'll close her up."

♀

They drove back through the woods to Exeter as the sun began to sink, deep shadow and thick golden light flooding through the canopy to paint the forest floor. Something flitted through the gloom not far from the road and Fran remembered dreaming about deer, about their delicate bodies leaping from the edge of a cliff and falling like strange angels toward the clouds below, their long limbs thrashing at the empty air. *When did I have that dream? Where was I?*

"Not bad," said Nam-joo as they splashed across a narrow culvert, wheels throwing up sheets of muddy water.

Fran thought of Ramona, watching her warily, and of the TERFs standing guard outside the Shaw house in their worn riot gear, pistols at their hips and rifles in their arms. She thought of the guard's cheerful shout of "Welcome to Raymond!"

She smiled. "Thanks."

♀

The rest of Indi's afternoon passed in a blur of shaved ginger and chicken livers, dried cohosh and licorice root and refined estrogen in little glass ampules. The Screw's problems were mostly simple. Vitamin D deficiencies from lack of sunlight, the same cold passed around ad infinitum in the filtered air, the occasional outbreak of chicken pox or whooping cough among the bunker's hundred-odd children. A woman from the dorm thread where Fran, Beth, and Robbie lived had some kind of stomach cancer and came in once a week for weed. Her skin was like wet paper, soft and translucent, like Indi's father's had been at the end.

It felt good to do real work again, helping people instead of following complex and painstaking instructions from a Canadian chemist over the Screw's scratchy ham radio and analyzing expired fertility drugs to see if any of their compounds were still viable. People had coughs and broken bones and menstrual cramps; they needed valerian root and casts and food rich in iron. She wished she could spend all her time in the clinic. Sunday dinners were beginning to chafe. Beth was sullen, depressed about being taken off farm shift, and Fran and Robbie were becoming more and more obnoxious as their honeymoon period tailed off into tense bickering. Indi sat in her room, picking at rice and pork with onions as the happy couple picked at each other one wall away.

You could eat in front of them, she told herself grudgingly as she slipped into the clinic's back room to check on the appendectomy patient. The older woman lay stretched out under a thin blanket on a couch, her chest rising and falling slowly. *They're your friends. They love you, even if you're lying to them every day.*

The woman's eyelids fluttered at the sound of the door swinging shut behind Indi. Her chapped lips parted. "Do you know where she is?" she croaked, looking up blearily. "My Zoe?"

Indi stopped short, surprised. "I'm sorry, I don't know any Zoe. I'm Dr. Varma; I operated on you today. Do you remember coming in?"

"She was right with me," the woman croaked. She sat up with an obvious effort of will, grimacing as her incision made itself known. "It was so hot."

"You've just had your appendix out," said Indi, lowering herself to one knee to help ease the woman down onto her back again. There was no strength in the thin body. Coarse, sun-bleached hair rustled against the couch's upholstery. "Please, don't try to move. I'll see if I can find . . . Zoe, was it?"

She had her daughter with her, she remembered. *A little girl.*

"Zoe," the woman whispered, her face ashen. Blood seeped through the bandage on her midriff as she closed her eyes. "She was right with me."

Indi found Jane stripping off her gloves in the exam room, a stack of recycled paper forms beside her on the desk. They did everything on hard copy in the Screw, locking medical files in a row of huge filing cabinets down in the library. The other woman paused as she entered.

"Long day," said Jane with a rueful smile. "You going to the movie tonight? Clive Owen . . . *God,* even when Phil was alive . . ." She waggled her eyebrows suggestively.

"That woman, the appendectomy," said Indi, not particularly interested in which actors Jane might have cheated on her husband with. "She was asking for someone. Zoe. Her daughter, I think. You said she came here with a girl."

Jane's smile faded. She peeled off the glove before responding. Powdered latex popped off of her fingers, digit by digit. "It was six months back or so," she said. "Before Dr. Downey got sick. A camp girl came in pregnant. We did what we could." Jane dropped the gloves into the garbage hopper and took her foot off of the pedal, letting the lid snap shut. "She didn't make it. Pretty sure her name was Zoe."

"And the baby?"

"We got him out," said Jane with the wide-eyed, affected sobriety of someone about to share a particularly juicy piece of gossip. "He had part of her liver stuck in his teeth."

VII

THE CRADLE OF BEAUTY

"A little rougher," Amber panted. They were in the Kennedy room, the older woman spread-eagled on the huge antique four poster, her wrists and ankles held at extension by leather cuffs. The silk sheets were cool against Beth's knees and the palm of her right hand. With her left she cupped Amber's throat, her thumb against the line of her jaw. Without speaking, she quickened her tempo. It was Friday. Her shift ended in two hours, and her cock felt like molten lead.

Maybe it'll slough off of my body, she thought, taking her hand off Amber's neck so she could spit in it and rub it on the other woman's flushed and puffy cunt and the base of her own dick. *Maybe it'll drip onto the sheets and burn holes in the mattress.*

Afterward, once Amber had gone, she sat alone on the edge of the bed until her soul came back into her body. As she struggled out of her binder she thought of the summers she'd spent hooking in Boston, strange men fucking her up the ass in motel rooms, back when sometimes a man got off you if you screamed for him to stop. One year she'd worked at a cathouse in Watertown. She'd had regulars. She smiled at the memory of a fat, gentle programmer who liked to be sodomized with the handle of a hairbrush. That hadn't been so bad. She touched her cheek where first Fran and then Indi had sewn her together. The skin was rough with scar tissue and half-healed scabs.

This is a girl's face, she told herself, not daring to look into the mirror that ran along the tasteful, subdued bedroom's north wall. *This body is a woman's body. It always has been. This is just a job. It's just a way to keep from being drawn and quartered by the Knights of J. K. Rowling.*

She pressed a hand to her naked breast and drew in a deep breath. In the smudged and spotted mirror on the wall, her scars looked like someone had drawn them on. Just crude scrawls of costume makeup. She let her breath out slowly.

It doesn't mean I'm fake.

♀

Sunday dinner was pork chops cooked in butter with late sprouts and little red potatoes, because Fran liked to show off. Beth chewed without enthusiasm while Fran and Robbie chattered, playing footsie underneath the coffee table and bumping her knees every few minutes. Beth was sick of the taste of pork. She was sick of "family dinner" and of her own lies about working in the bunker's kitchens. She wished Indi weren't such a freak about eating in front of people so she could have someone to talk to, except Indi was so cold and snappish lately. Mostly she was either in her lab or sleeping. Her living room, still forested with unpacked boxes, didn't feel like their space.

Why do we eat here when she can't even eat with us?

She speared a browned and glistening sprout and crunched it. Bitter. Savory. A hint of precious salt. She wished suddenly for Dani, who she knew she didn't love. For her chapped lips and faint stubble. For a girlness she could taste and touch in safety through skin other than her own. She swallowed. Fran was looking at her strangely.

"Why are you crying?"

♀

He dug his fingers hard into Fran's ass, taking her as deep into his throat as he could stand. She had her tongue inside him. He could hardly catch a breath against the heat and pressure building in his cunt. He rolled his hips against her, feeling the bite of her cheekbones and chin, the probing jut of her nose, the caress of her soft lips. Over the curve of her backside he watched her spine shift, slow and sinuous, beneath her freckled skin. Shoulder blades angled inward and the sweaty mop of her hair on the sheets. She reached for his hand and he gave it to her and held tight as her cum flooded his mouth and her body undulated, moving like a serpent's. Her thighs quivered against his cheeks.

She pulled away, strands of mucus and jism stretching and snapping between her cock and his open mouth, and scrambled on her knees to the foot of the bed, where she went down onto her elbows to kiss him just above his swollen clit. Her hair tickled his mound and the crooks of his thighs, trailing through the wetness running out of him onto the towel they'd laid down. She licked him. Her tongue parted his lips. "Oh," he whispered, his voice quavering as fire lapped at the arc of his pelvis, questing with pale fingers for his spine. "Don't stop."

He breathed in, air enriching the taste of her cum on his lips. He was crying. When had he started crying? The wet sound of her lips closing on his clit, of her spit sucked back up into her mouth as she began to blow him. He beat a fist against the sheets and stuffed the other in his mouth, biting down hard on his knuckles. "God," he moaned into his own sweating skin. "God, God, God. Please. Please."

Make me a man.

He came with a seething snarl, back arched so that only his shoulders touched the sheets, and reached down to tangle his long fingers in her hair and force her face harder against his crotch. Tremors wracked his body. His thighs tensed so suddenly and with such force that he feared for a moment they'd cramp as a second wave broke small and quiet in the silence of the booming first. Her mouth still worked against him. Alien muscle jacked into his body's throbbing substrate. He wrapped his thighs around her head, moaning through his teeth, and somewhere in the stretched-out moments afterward, he came a third and final time, the walls of his cunt gripping Fran's fingers as though afraid she might let go until the strength went out of his legs and he went limp, breathing hard as tears rolled down his cheeks.

Fran looked up from his sopping slit, her face slick up to the cheekbones, traces of dark menstrual blood on her lips and chin and the tip of her nose. She looked like a hyena pulling its muzzle out of a carcass. "I'm sorry," he said reflexively, transfixed and revolted by those smears of red. "I didn't know."

"I don't care," she said, smiling. His blood was in her teeth, too. "I like it."

He swallowed. "Can you hold me?"

Her smile faltered. She wiped her face on her forearm. "Yeah, of course."

For a while they lay together in the quiet, Fran's arms around him, the only sound the distant rumble of the Screw's pumps and generators. *She probably wanted* me *to hold* her, he thought sadly. He licked his lips and tasted her again. *I should remember that next time.*

"Guess who I saw today?"

"Who?"

"The girl who gave Beth that scar on her cheek." She slipped her arm from under him and propped herself up on her elbows, her chin resting on her fists. "The one that looks like the Nike thing. She didn't recognize me, though."

"The TERF?" He sat up, the last of his afterglow draining out of him like dirty water through a sieve. "What?"

"It's actually not a big deal. I was just in town with Nam-joo. We had a meeting with Seabrook city council—or, I guess it's Raymond now." She laughed. "The No Transsexuals Allowed Empire."

"You said you were doing, like, trade and shipping." He knew he was being shrill, but anxiety gripped his throat in its sharp little claws and he couldn't seem to shake it. A nauseous lump sloshed in the pit of his stomach as he slid out of bed and started dressing, retrieving his underwear from where he'd kicked it onto the floor. He felt a sudden uncontrollable disgust with himself, with the pale silver scars on his chest and the stubborn swell of his hips. He didn't want to be naked anymore. "Why didn't you tell me?"

"For fuck's sake, Robbie. You're out hunting Easter eggs, Indi's in the clinic, Beth's on night shift in the kitchen; what do you want me to do, stay home and iron your shirts?"

He shimmied into his stained and sweat-smelling jeans. "There's middle ground between playing house and holding swap meets with the *fucking SS*."

"Stop yelling at me."

He paused. His hands were fists. He thought that he should probably unclench them, that he should take a breath, go for a walk. Instead he squeezed until his knuckles popped and black sludge flowed out from the ruptured blisters of resentment in his breast. "You're being so selfish right now."

"What, worried those geniuses are gonna clock me?" She sniffed. "Half of them look more like men than I do."

"Do you even care how I feel at all?"

"I should go," said Fran, her tone glacial. She threw her legs over the edge of the bed. "Sophie asked me to stop by tonight."

♀

"Nam-joo said you did, like, *so* well in the meeting." Sophie dragged Fran by the hand through the dizzying mirrored expanse of her apartment's atrium or foyer or whatever. The ceiling rose at an angle in eight trapezoidal panels to a central octagon from which a massive chandelier depended, its multicolored lights reflected and re-reflected into a sea of stars. Their reflections skidded through the dazzling gloom.

"That's nice of her," Fran said, feeling unaccountably nervous. "I just knew something useful. I heard a friend in town talking about it a few months ago."

Sophie halted. Fran stopped just short of her as the smaller girl turned back. She was wearing a black zip-front jumpsuit and a plain leather dog collar with a stainless steel ring. Fran wondered where she got her eyeliner and lip gloss and who did her beautiful cornsilk hair. "You should *never* devalue yourself like that," she said, her tone deadly serious. "You're a powerful woman now. You have to own your power. You have to believe in it and not let anyone take advantage of you."

She broke into a sunny grin, the ear-popping pressure of her stare dissolving like fog. "Come on! Let me show you around!"

♀

"I just think it's such a, like, such a fuck-you to those bitches," Sophie chattered as they careened down Rainbow Road, karts skidding over the track's technicolor film. "Like, okay, you want our shit? You wanna deal with us? You have to talk to our dickgirl and, like, recognize her humanity."

She hurtled off the course's edge into the bottomless void and let out a nasal blurt of laughter, the chocolate milk she'd just slurped dribbling down her chin. Fran, in the middle of braking through a hard turn hot on Wario's heels, set her controller down on the glass coffee table as Sophie let her own slither forgotten to the floor. "Yeah," Fran offered, smiling feebly. "Fuck them."

Sophie slumped back against the cushions. Her huge blue eyes were wide and guileless. "Wanna do Molly?"

♀

"That's just what she's like," said Beth as they slipped out single-file through the narrow gap of the bunker's blast doors, which one of the motor pool attendants had opened for them with a nod to Robbie. Her eyes were still red-rimmed from crying. "She's always been that way. If you tell her she's doing something wrong, you're a cop. If you tell her *she's* being a cop, you're a counterrevolutionary."

Robbie kicked a rock and sent it skittering down the unpaved road. The sun was setting over the forest and the valley at the base of the hill, gilding the tops of the trees where flocks of rock doves whirled and circled. There was the merest hint of a bite in the air, an omen of October. He was still angry. It writhed in his chest like something wild with its leg caught in a trap, gnawing at itself in desperation to escape. A few years ago he might have gone limp and slid back into self-pitying misery, finding someone to listen to him snivel about what a monster he was until guilt moved them to pull him close into an instantly resented embrace and tell him *No, no, you're just sick, we're all traumatized, we're struggling, you know what you did is wrong and wanting to change is what tells me you're*—and on and on until he'd vomited up all his curdled, putrid rage and could pretend he'd processed his feelings.

He still felt it, that helpless, furious panic that went hand in hand with love, but it was no longer quite so inescapable. He'd yelled. He'd been a prick. Now he was going to take a walk with Beth, who he'd found crying in her room after he stormed out on Fran, and figure out how to fix it. The filtered air sometimes made him feel tense and suffocated; outside he could think more clearly.

They turned off the road and into the camp, which had swelled over the last few weeks to spill along the base of the cliff face to the north and south. Beth handed out squares of cornbread wrapped in wax paper to the kids who swarmed around them between the sloppy rows of tents. He felt stupid for not bringing anything, guilty for storming through these people's front yard with his stupid problems, for having a cool, dry place to live while they camped in their own filth. *Calm down.* He forced himself to take a long breath through his nostrils. *Stop looking for reasons to get mad.*

"So what should I do?" he asked.

She shrugged, her scars twitching in a momentary flicker of emotion. "Break up with her."

He glared back at her, unable to keep the edge from his voice. "If you don't want to talk to me, then why'd you come?"

They walked for a while without speaking. Beth teared up, but he thought saying something would just make it worse. Around them, the camp people went about the day's last chores: skinning squirrels and rabbits, hanging ragged laundry, mending and taping and weaving as the daylight faded. Haggard women wrestled brushes through their children's hair and spat expired toothpaste into jars of dirty water.

"Sorry," said Beth as they made their way through the camp's outskirts, cutting downhill away from the granite face. A pair of sallow white women with the rheumy eyes and rotting teeth of meth addicts watched them from the mouth of a lean-to made of rusted poles and a blue tarp. "I've known Fran a long time. We have some shit; I shouldn't make it your problem."

"We're not even really, like, together."

"She know that?"

Robbie blushed. "We haven't talked about it."

Wind flattened long grass against their legs as they walked along a sandy ridge, loose earth sliding downhill in their wake. Behind them the camp was a dark blot interrupted only by the pinprick illumination of coffee-can fires and faltering solar lights. "You should just let her do what she wants," said Beth. She turned into the breeze and let it run its fingers through her sandy hair. A tear ran down her scarred cheek, its trail glistening pale gold in the last light, a buttery brushstroke of yellow over the treetops. "If you make her look at herself, she won't love you anymore."

♀

Sophie's bed was a vast lake of cool golden silk. Fran breathed in the smell of milk and lilacs. She ran her fingertips over her own face and felt the smoothness of her skin, the faint lines the wind and sun had etched into the corners of her eyes and mouth. She laughed and thought how beautiful it sounded, how good and perfect her voice had become. It sounded like bells. Like wind chimes. She loved it so much she laughed all over again, staring up in ambiently horny wonder at the ceiling, where soft recessed lighting glowed from the black marble facade.

The room was an adult's, sumptuously minimalist and dark, boring in a way only money and confidence could allow for, but within it was a half-grown teenager's tightly curled sanctuary. Beaded curtains shimmered, strung between the bed's high posts so that when Fran moved her head from side to side she saw her cloudy and uneven silhouette slide over the little spheres of polished brass. Through the curtains she could just see posters tacked to dressing screens and bureaus, armoires and freestanding sculptures. Lana Del Rey. Mitski. One Direction. A flatscreen hulked atop a faux Ionic column at the foot of the bed. Something bright was playing on it, but the sound was off.

And then Sophie was there, straddling Fran's hips and leaning so close that her silky peroxide-blond hair tickled Fran's nose. Sophie was drooling a little. "Do you top?"

Fran shook her head, blushing. She reached up to touch Sophie's hair. It slipped like water through her fingers. "You're so beautiful. I wish I looked like you. I love looking at you."

Hugely dilated pupils narrowed to black pinpricks in twin seas of china blue flecked with motes of green. Warm drool on Fran's chin. "Do you wanna eat me out?"

Slippery velvet cunt. Sticky. The zipper's hiss as it bared flat white belly and shaved mound. Black fabric slithering over pale skin. Pooling on the silk. Long nails stroked her scalp. She kissed the pink bud of Sophie's clit and imagined sucking it out of its hood of tender skin, drawing it like a snail from its shell into her own body where it might take root and change, drawing her cock up into her flesh, parting the soft curtains of her sex. She drank from Sophie. Greedy mouth on fluttering lips.

The dream of a cunt growing like a seedling in strange soil.

♀

Robbie came back to an empty room. For a moment after he flicked on the fluorescents and found the bed still unmade, her flannel still hanging from the footboard's post, before loneliness washed over him, he felt almost relieved. Part of him had missed sleeping alone. Part of him missed killing in a white haze of dissociation, missed the slippery feel of bark underfoot as he stepped from branch to branch, firing his handgun down between his feet at the men climbing toward him. That was a life without questions. Without fear.

Now he didn't even have his guns; they were locked away in an armory somewhere with Beth's bow and all their knives and the rifles Sophie's people had taken out of Indi's attic. The only armed women in the Screw were the guards and a few of Sophie's closest. Long-limbed Doe with her greasy red-gold hair and puffy lips. Nam-joo Kim, lined and humorless. The sleek, tanned twins Corinne and Sylvia with their gray eyes and catlike smiles. He sighed and began to undress, suddenly bone-tired. It was getting late. Fran wasn't coming back.

There was something in the right-hand pocket of his jeans. He tried to remember if he'd had anything in there, a notebook page or a bandana. *No.* He slipped two fingers in and found a tight, folded square of some rough fabric. *I didn't have anything.* He drew it out. It was pale and grubby, stained by sweat and ground-in dirt. It might have been a part of an old sheet, or of someone's summer slacks.

He unfolded the scrap of cotton. Inside, someone had inked a few spidery, jagged words.

Midnight tomorrow. 11-E.
Come alone.

He thought of the kids in the camp, barefoot and wild, plucking at his sleeves as they ran beside him.

♀

"You have such a pretty cunt," Fran whispered against Sophie's shoulder. The Molly's dazzling tide had started to recede, lukewarm gray water washing over her scattered thoughts. She squirmed closer to the other girl, sliding an arm over her belly. "It looks just like a flower."

"There's a woman in Tampa who still does that," said Sophie, who was sitting up with her head lolling on a heap of satin pillows, an unlit joint between her candy-apple lips, and one hand toying with a lock of Fran's dark chestnut hair. "I can bring her up here, have her do you. I mean, not, like, *do* you." She swatted Fran playfully on the arm. "Give you a *vagina*." She hissed it, like a little girl trying out a dirty word. "Would you like that?"

Fran didn't dare speak. She nodded, heart thudding wildly in her chest as Sophie's pinky nail stroked the rim of her ear, bending cartilage and flattening the fine downy hairs on her earlobe. She looked at Sophie's crotch, the sweet and gluey taste of which still lingered on her tongue. The other woman's thighs parted just far enough to admit two slim, manicured fingers. The sheets were wet between those smooth white legs.

"You don't have to stay," said Sophie, catching her glance. "I just really need something inside me, you know? I never feel done until . . ." Her eyelids fluttered. Her hand twitched between her legs. "Until . . ."

Fran swallowed, drawing her arm back and rising up onto her knees. She hitched a smile to the corners of her mouth and jacked them up with smooth, mechanical precision. This was a price she could pay. This was something simple she could do, a reward with a little catch held clumsily in the greedy glint of Sophie's slitted eyes. She bent to kiss between her breasts, to lick her navel, to press her lips against her slowly gliding wrist.

"Let me do it for you."

VIII

GENERATION Z

"You were supposed to inherit the world," said Teach from the raised concrete stage at the base of the amphitheater. She stood there, hands clasped behind her back, her black wool coat open in the October chill. "That's not going to happen."

Ramona, standing at attention behind Teach with Molly and a few other senior officers, felt a flush of guilty pride. The two hundred or so boys in the stadium seats were silent. The oldest were nearing twenty, the youngest just fifteen. Some had been raised as girls, forced into tights and dresses out of their mothers' superstitious conviction that the icons of femininity would, like garlic holding Dracula at bay, keep the virus from doing to their sons what it had done to their husbands, their fathers, their brothers. Others used cropped hair and bulky sweatshirts to offset their softening features and disguise their little breasts. A few watched Teach with close and wary focus; the rest were staring at the canvas-draped cage—which rattled and clanked from time to time—to the left of the platform.

"Somewhere between the ages of twelve and thirteen, your pituitary glands shook themselves awake. Your bodies started producing enough testosterone to make you comfortable hosts for the most dangerous, dramatic virus in the history of our species." Teach ran her tongue over her upper teeth. "So, encouraged by your mothers, you did the only thing you could do. You ate testicles. Clover. The lobes of kidneys. Drank mares' piss. And you chewed licorice root and drank black cohosh and did everything you could to keep your body from pumping itself full of something worse than death."

In the park around the amphitheater's tiered concrete bowl, a flock of mourning doves swept from one maple to another in a rush of iridescent feathers. A few of the boys looked up at the disturbance, but most kept their eyes on Teach. A few mothers sat in the audience. More waited back at the trucks. This was something for the sissies, the ladyboys, the not-quite-men who were all that remained of the patriarchy. Ramona had seen Teach speak to them before, in Philly and in Baltimore and once in Long Island, across the Sound from the haunted wreckage of the city, and the mothers seldom came. Maybe they didn't like it, thinking of what else their sons might have been.

"A male body is a time bomb," she continued. "The male temperament inclines you to toss that bomb from hand to hand, to take foolish risks, to behave without thought to the greater consequences. No matter how real your girlhood, if you tell yourself you've had one, may feel, you have been raised as men. You have been raised to brutalize, to steal, to disregard the women who raised you and sacrificed their own lives to protect yours." Her breath plumed in the cold air. She leaned forward over the podium. "You may think that you've remade yourself, that believing in your own womanhood makes you a woman, but between your legs is a weapon of war that has terrorized us for a hundred thousand years."

Some of them were getting up and leaving now. The Legion women at the exits would note their names. Ramona remembered doing that in Rockaway, making sure the kids who left saw her with her notepad. Making sure they knew that they were being watched. She scanned the faces of the crowd, thinking back on those other boys, frightened and angry and resentful as they fled the movie theater where they'd held the rally. Acne and baby fat. Greasy hair and blackheads. They might have been the same crowds, unstuck from time.

Just make a list, Molly had told her that morning over trail mix and instant coffee in the ruined lobby of a Marriott. *Most of them wise up, check in with our people, take the deal.*

What about the rest?

They know the stakes, kid. You want something to be sad about, think what the ones we don't get do to your sisters.

"You can go, of course," said Teach, her deep voice mild. "You can tell yourself, 'What does this transphobic cunt know?' and walk out of here. Never think about me again. But Boston asked for my protection, and I take that seriously. When you lose your access to the herbs that keep you sane, or you harm a woman, or you start displaying symptoms of t. rex, you will cease to be a citizen of this commonwealth, and I will not hesitate to put you down like rabid dogs."

More were leaving now, nearly half the crowd hurrying up the cement steps to the park. Someone shouted "TERF!" and a water bottle whipped through the air and burst against the edge of the stage, but Ramona didn't see who'd thrown it. She drew herself up. *You think we care about that stupid word?* She imagined Feather, sixteen and awkward, their body shapeless in baggy clothes. Were they here? Were they leaving now? *Why don't you say it to my face, then? Come back here and call me a fucking TERF.*

The shrouded cage shook. The women flanking it looked nervously at one another.

"I'm offering you a chance to earn what you've taken as your due. In the Maenad Corps you will prove by defending this, our sacred bond of sisterhood, that you deserve to be a part of it. Serve with distinction and you earn the right to a new legal name, to our hormones, and to surgery to neutralize your body's threat and bring you as close as medicine can to womanhood. Sergeant Kilroy, would you please step forward?"

A slim, flat-chested young officer stepped smartly out of line. She had thick black eyebrows (Ramona didn't think of the Greek girl, crying against her ugly friend, who Jules had shot a month ago) and a nose like the prow of a battleship. She wore her hair back in a tight, severe bun.

"How long have you been a Maenad, Sergeant?"

"Three years, ma'am." Kilroy's voice was beautiful, soft and fraying at the edges. Like torn linen.

"And you're second in command under Lieutenant Fried, am I right?"

"Yes, ma'am."

Teach nodded, satisfied, and turned to the women guarding the cage. "Would you pull that tarp down, please?"

They did. Canvas fell, folding stiffly onto itself. The muzzled creature within blinked at the sudden light and hurled himself against the bars. He let out a strangled, seething whine as still more boys fled their seats. Others leaned forward in morbid fascination. The man was hunched and starving, but even so the empty purses of his breasts were plain to see, the deformed cauliflower scarring along his cheekbones and his tapered jaw clear evidence of where surgeons had cut into the bones beneath his face. Infection often threw scar tissue into overdrive, producing ropey, knotted masses of tough skin. His real face had bubbled up along the lines of his attempted self-feminization.

Teach jumped down lightly from the stage and rapped her knuckles against one of the bars. She ignored the *clang* as the man slammed his muzzled face into the steel a bare inch from her hand. "This called itself Camilla."

The crowd was in full flight now. Only a handful remained in their seats, though Ramona couldn't tell if they were terrified or fascinated. Both, probably, as she'd been when she saw the same sight in Philly. Sara. Her monster. Silicon moving in spongy mantles under his grayish skin, which hung in rags from raw pink flesh where his dermis had grown too tight and burst.

"Maybe you think you don't need the sisterhood, you don't need the Matriarchy. I can understand that. You've survived without us until now." She turned back toward the audience, the thing in the cage climbing the bars behind her, bashing its bruised and bloody head against cold metal. "But before you decide to walk out of here and set yourself against us, think about this."

One slim hand dipped inside her coat—Ramona watched the crowd tense—and drew out a crusty, half-wet tampon by its string. She raised her voice to drown out the disgusted groans. "Every woman—every *real* woman—has already bled a thousand times for nothing." She made a fist, crushing bloody cotton.

"Imagine what we'd do to defend what we love."

Sergeant Kilroy, as real as fake could be, stood smiling at attention at the platform's edge, the nearer end of the path that led to the huge, misshapen thing battering itself against the bars a scant few yards away. Ramona felt a strange sort of pride toward Kilroy, a surge of sisterly affection mixed with loving pity. *Look at her,* she thought. *She gave up everything for us. Abandoned manhood. Her body. Her gender.*

What a special thing.

♀

Afterward, once Teach had shaken hands with the remaining boys and the junior officers had taken down their names and addresses, the party cut across the park and over a small creek by footbridge to the curb where a black town car idled. Molly opened the rear driver's side for Teach as Ramona climbed in opposite her. Pigeons seethed in the street and perched in noisy rows along the eaves and sills of nearby buildings. They pulled out, Molly and the driver's voices muffled by the smoked glass of the car's partition, and the birds rose in shimmering waves around them.

"I think you really had them," said Ramona.

Teach said nothing. She was looking out the window at the warehouses and depots of the waterfront, which little by little gave way to apartments, burned-out restaurants, and looted husks of corner stores. Across the Summer Street bridge, the ocean pounding under them in hypnotic white whorls and Boston Harbor laid out to the east past another bridge, collapsed, a heaving slate-gray chop interrupted by a string of half-drowned islands where the wrecks of sea forts and summer homes sank slowly into saturated earth. Then through the dead lights and back into the city, past the south end of the docks where rusted ships sat sunken and crooked between rotting pilings and collapsing piers and a small fleet of barges and container ships waited at anchor for the boats ferrying the city's latest crop of salvage. In among the buildings, jungle of brick and concrete, down narrow connecting roads named after revolutionary generals where carts of knockoff handbags and lucky cat souvenirs with their upraised paws moldered, crushed back against graffitied walls. At an intersection, teams of city laborers rolled derelict cars onto a carrier to be hauled away for scrap while Legion women stood around, watching the connecting streets. Protests had been getting louder. A woman in Molly's detachment had been hit in the teeth with a brick on patrol near Back Bay station while they were out of town.

For a while they drove in silence. On the corner of Beach and Harrison, Ramona saw two women in headscarves and heavy skirts and aprons jointing a man's carcass strung up by its ankles from a frame of welded fence posts. A bucket of offal lay by one woman's feet. They paused in their work as the car passed them. Blood dribbled from the dead man's mouth onto a stained brown tarp weighted at the corners with rubble. Ramona wondered what a man's flesh tasted like.

They skirted a massive pothole half-flooded with groundwater and she caught sight of the rusted sign for Kneeland Street. Faded billboards and murals. Mock Buddhist tourist trap architecture squashed up against ancient brick apartment buildings plastered with rotting signs for third-floor bubble tea places and nail salons. Chinatown. Ramona's heart skipped a beat. *She can't know. There's no way she could know. Molly would never—*

Teach leaned forward and pressed the intercom as they took the corner. "Pull over. We'll have lunch here." She released the button and settled back into her seat, those pale, unblinking eyes unreadable. "It looks good, don't you think?"

"Yeah," said Ramona, her mouth dry. The driver pulled up to the curb outside the weathered green-and-gold facade of Hunan Palace with its gilded dragons at the upper corners of its doorframe, about two blocks from Feather's building. How many times had she been in there on her way to their apartment?

Inside, the owner ushered them toward a corner table. A smiling younger woman took their coats. There were only a few others in the place, a table of three and another where a tired middle-aged woman was occupied with helping a frail older one spoon up her steaming broth. Through the tinted front window Ramona watched Molly and the doughy, slump-shouldered driver, standing together on the sidewalk, light cigarettes from the wavering flame of Molly's BIC. They stepped back under the eaves as a thin, leaden rain began to fall. It was warm inside. A space heater stood by the wall not far from where they sat, and hissed faintly as the girl brought their tea and poured it. The gentle sounds of chopping and the hiss of steam echoed from the kitchen, underscored by quiet conversation. The other customers avoided looking at their table.

Teach seemed content to sit in silence, sipping at her tea. Ramona wondered what her real name was, and which rumors were true. Had she really broken Al-Qaeda operatives, working up through their chain of command with jumper cables and looped tapes and bodies held in place by rope and polished wood until blood pooled in burning joints and anything she asked for slipped from trembling lips? Had she been Janice Raymond's lover, sucking on those bony convent toes in the dark stacks of UMass Amherst? She rode a motorcycle and fired a gun like someone brought up to do both, but her voice was as accentless as a newscaster's. She might have come from anywhere.

The girl returned. A bowl of steaming rice. Bok choy in melted butter. Moo shu pork, Mandarin pancakes, and a little jar of plum sauce, the scent of which made her instantly sick. Other dishes followed. The tired woman by the door had brought her elderly companion up onto her feet. She was helping her into a worn coat, a slow and evidently frustrating process which so engrossed Ramona that she didn't realize Teach had left their table until the woman cut across her field of vision in a swish of black and approached the two.

Ramona caught only a few snatches of the conversation. Teach had her coat, which she must have retrieved without Ramona noticing, folded over one arm, and with serene confidence she helped the old woman out of her threadbare camel hair and into sleek black wool, which she then buttoned herself with deft fingers. Belatedly, Ramona stood, but no one took any notice of her. ". . . and tell her she's to take you home."

The weary-looking woman took the other—who, Ramona supposed in a sudden needle's stab of grief, must have been her mother or grandmother—by the arm, gave Teach a tearful thank-you and goodbye, and led her out through the front door, the bell above it ringing as it swung. They shuffled down the steps toward the driver, who dropped her cigarette and crushed it under the heel of her shoe. In the span of a few moments both women were tucked safely into the back seat and the town car had pulled away, leaving Molly alone in the drab, dirty rain.

Teach hung the dirty coat over her seat back. She sat down and speared a piece of green bell pepper with her fork as Ramona resumed her own seat hastily. Those pale, unblinking eyes flicked up. "Do you know why we're taught to hate old women?"

"Ma'am, I apologize, I should have—"

"Do you know why, Pierce?"

Ramona swallowed. "No, ma'am, I don't."

"Because they're of no more use to men—can't cook, can't fuck, can't breed—no use at all, but they remember. They remember the rapes, the beatings, the cracked skulls and little arms yanked out of sockets. They remember, and men know it, and if you can't rape a woman, if you can't kill her, slap her, shout over her every word, then you have to face her, and you have to face the things you've done."

Ramona thought of her own mother's body, winnowed down to sticks and cold, bruised skin by cancer, and of the stooped and reed-thin phantom of her nana in the hospital years earlier, lifeless gray hair and sunken, nervous eyes. All the men in her family had died young, had never lived to see their women get old or to face the things that they'd inflicted on them. She felt a hot surge of frustration at the unfairness of it.

"They'll live like queens," said Teach, the lines at the corners of her mouth drawn suddenly down with furious intensity. "Once the city's been swept out and centralized we owe it to them to give them comfort. Respect. I don't care what they say in Maryland. I will see it done."

Ramona picked at her bok choy. "I'd never thought of it that way. It makes sense. Honoring them."

"Another question. Don't look so nervous, Pierce. I'm not trying to fool you. Do you know why I wanted Seabrook?"

Ramona swallowed. Something about that trip still didn't sit right with her. "The power plant?" she ventured. "If we can reconnect the lines—"

"I have no plan to reconnect the lines."

"The manhunters? A lot of them move through there. Valuable supply to control, and—"

"It's much simpler than that." Teach smiled. "I think you can see it from that postmodernist dump."

A hulk beached on the glittering sand. Guns draped in dried seaweed. Gulls nesting among antennae and radar dishes.

"What, that boat?"

As soon as she'd said it, she understood. The railroads were all well and good, but the coast was both lifeline and fortress. A hundred fractious little city-states, from quaint, salt-smelling Seabrook down to the malarial floodlands of Miami, all of them tenuously stable after the long years of vicious swarm-fighting which had followed T-Day. Next came power. Control. Supply lines and trade agreements. Strong states swallowing up the weak, nascent ideologies nourished or else smothered in their cradles. If the Matriarchy could put real firepower on the water . . .

Teach's smile widened. "There," she said, plucking a dumpling from the plate between them and popping it into her mouth. She sucked grease from her fingers. "Now she has it."

♀

The Screw ran six levels deep into the hard, cold granite, starting at the motor pool and its double airlock and decon valve and moving on through UV greenhouses, security, the front offices for trade and "participation," the squash courts and the swimming pool and the indoor basketball court, residential A, security, the kitchens, fungal beds where farmers used processed shit from septic two levels down to grow designer mushrooms in the dark, Sophie's thread-spanning apartment, and the cisterns, and just above the surgical theater which served as Indi's lab, there was a square little afterthought of a library, a three-story shaft full of tightly packed shelving.

It was quiet when Robbie arrived a few minutes before midnight, ducking out of the deserted central spiral and down a narrow corridor past the empty reference desk. Banks of darkened fluorescents wired to timers hung above each row in the stacks. The floor was carpeted in cut gray berber. In the far-right corner a narrow staircase led down to the second floor, which, since the stacks on the first ran one through ten, was where the note he'd found finally led him. Nowhere else in the Screw was ordered like the stacks. Robbie took the stairs. A lone bank of lights buzzed below, visible through the rails. He reached the bottom of the shaft and looked down the eleventh row.

A trans woman stood under the buzzing fluorescents at the row's end. She was tall and lean, her head shaved down to black stubble. She wore a long black skirt and a mustard-colored cardigan, and on the back of one dark, long-fingered hand was a tattoo of twining beach roses that wound up past the cuff of her sweater. Her dark eyes held the wan light strangely, like prisms. "You're Robbie."

"Nice to meet you," he mumbled, not quite knowing what else to say. The thought that this was some kind of perverse loyalty test had crossed his mind more than a few times. He had a knife he'd taken off one of the women at the blast doors hidden up his sleeve. "I got—"

She shook her head to silence him, an almost imperceptible gesture. "I'm Zia. I run the stacks. Have you been down here before?"

Robbie shook his head.

"You can help me with reshelving. It's all alphabetical; there, on the spines." She tapped one, indicating the peeling yellow-white sticker near its base. "I lock up at ten. Then maybe we can get that coffee?" She flashed a dazzling smile.

"What—oh, yeah, right," said Robbie, suddenly uncertain. "But—"

"Later," said Zia, her voice suddenly tight, and with that she vanished back into the stacks, leaving Robbie alone with the handcart and its complement of well-thumbed paperbacks and graphic novels. He looked them over idly, pulling one at random off the cart. *New Moon*. The Mormon lady's vampire story. The rest was mostly young adult stuff, too, the kind of thing he'd read before the end of the world took all the appeal out of stories about beautiful teenagers being brave or hugging fascists until they turned good.

He scanned the shelves for a minute and then began slotting books back into place. He'd always liked that part of library work. Match the letters and the numbers. Click the physical object of the book into its appointed space. Minutes passed. He was replacing the last volume of some candy-colored superhero glurge when the fluorescents flickered, dimmed, and died, and Zia, armed with a penlight's narrow blue-white beam, came and found him. "Sorry," she hissed, sotto voce. "Cameras. Doe doesn't watch *all* the recordings, but she can read lips."

Robbie imagined the gray, heavily lidded eyes of Sophie's chief lieutenant following him across the motor pool, tracing the movements of his mouth and jaw to pluck his words out of the distance. It felt true. "Okay," he said. "Why did you plant that letter on me? Why do you want to talk to me?"

"I'd usually wait," she said, stepping closer. She was a full foot taller than him. "Take my time, see what you're made of. It's just that your friend isn't working out as a daddy, so I think they're going to sell her to a chain gang."

♀

Feather watched her from the bed as she laced up her boots. It was too warm for the season, the breeze that blew in through the open window salty and humid, and their tawny skin was dewed with sweat. They lay on their back, their own bruised breasts cupped in their hands.

"You had a boyfriend before, didn't you?"

Ramona looked up from her feet. "What?"

Feather rolled onto their side, tugging the sheets over the stretch marks that glistened on the swell of their hip. "It's just something about you. Even when you're here, I feel like you're hiding from me. Like you're waiting to go back to something real."

She tugged her laces taut and tied a bow. Her throat felt tight. "You ever think that's because you're a whore?"

"You said you loved me."

"Yeah, that's right," simpered Ramona with a sudden guilty surge of venom, her voice syrupy sweet. "I love you, baby. Let's get married. We'll get a little house in the suburbs, adopt a couple of pandemic orphans. I can get you on my insurance and we'll find a doctor to chop your cock in half and ram it up inside you so we don't have to worry about getting dragged out of our beds at three in the morning and shot in the goddamn street! Are you out of your fucking mind?"

Feather sat up, tugging the sheet up to cover themself. They had such stupid eyes, Ramona thought. A cow's eyes, dumb and soft and vacant. "Why are you being like this?"

She was on her feet now, advancing on the bed. "I have *never* been with a fucking *man*."

"Oh no?" Feather's voice dripped cold contempt. They didn't flinch as she loomed over them. "You've never had a cock inside you?"

"You're a woman." Sid's pink hair in her fist. Reena's thighs parting for her mouth, revealing the tender thing taped back between them. "I love *women*."

Feather laughed. "I'm not, though. And you can't even look me in the eye." They slipped out of bed, wrapping the sheet around themselves. Their doughy body seemed regal in the sweaty morning light. "I know what they're doing in the city."

She stepped toward them. "You don't know shit."

"You're killing people."

"But my money spends, right?" She was standing too close to Feather. She knew it, but she didn't step away. "You'll take my ration cards and my street passes. You didn't have a problem with that chromosome cert I got you."

Defiance flashed in those big cow eyes. "I never asked you for anything."

"*But you took it*, you fat fucking parasite." Closer, almost nose to nose, Feather just a little shorter than her—she liked that, she liked it so much—and her breath whistling through her nose like an angry boar's. "You took it, and then you find the balls to say I seem like I fucked men?"

Didn't you, though? Didn't you hide behind all those boring boys, and even later, in college, with the other cis women, weren't you still hiding? All that tedious, joyless sex while you were daydreaming about what you really wanted.

"At least I'm not a fucking Nazi."

Ramona put her fist through the wall next to their face. She stared at their profile, turned away from her, nostrils flared and color in their cheeks. A few pale flecks of plaster stuck to their sweat-dampened skin. She pulled her bloodied knuckles free of the ruined Sheetrock and stormed out of the room, her heart a solid red weight in her throat, her breath coming in thready, hissing gasps around it. The edge of the door in her hand and the shuddering boom as she slammed it shut on their tear-streaked face and the pink gash of their mouth, opening around a shuddering sob that chased her down the stairs and brought the other hookers scrambling out onto the halls and landings, some with clients crying after them from the tenuous anonymity of their rooms.

"What the fuck are you looking at?" she screeched. Her hand was on the butt of her automatic, though she didn't remember moving it there. She stabbed a finger at the nearest of them, the same tall, long-faced thing who'd stood over her that drunken night, that snotty-looking whore with her cancerous beauty mark and jutting chin. "Get back in your *fucking* holes!"

"Don't come around here anymore," said Beauty Mark. "They don't want to see you."

Ramona had just opened her mouth to snarl something back at her when she stepped on her own shoelace and pitched headfirst down the stairs, thumping and coughing as the steps pounded the breath from her lungs until she fetched up with a crash against the landing just to the left of the front door, her whole head ringing and her body so sore and tender she felt sure for a moment she'd broken something. She staggered to her feet and lurched down the last few steps, reaching up with shaking fingers to find blood on her upper lip. One last look back at the women—the things—on the staircase and looking down at her over the banisters, and then she turned and limped out of the building into the sullen heat.

♀

Indi stared at the sample vials slotted neatly into the brick of black Styrofoam on the freezer's second shelf. Vapor swirled around them. The freezer's hum was loud in the empty lab. She shut the door and locked it with the little key she wore around her neck. On the far side of the lab, Mariana was disinfecting the operating tables, gray hair pulled back in a loose bun that flopped back and forth as she scrubbed at the stainless steel.

I should burn this whole place to the ground, thought Indi. *I should poison that girl and all her little soldiers and her rich, beautiful friends, and that man in the pit. None of this is worth a place to live and a few creature comforts. Fresh butter. A good mattress.* She gnawed at her left pinky nail, worrying a sliver of thin keratin loose. *If I left, would they let the others stay?*

"Nasty habit," came a voice from the doorway leading out to the main hall. Doe stood there, slumped against the frame. She had a lit cigarette in one hand, though Indi had asked her a dozen times not to smoke in the lab, and a thin trail of cadmium haze wound through the air in her wake.

"Put that thing out," Indi snapped, tucking her key into her sports bra as she turned her back on the freezer. "I have enough problems keeping this hangar sterile without you flicking ash everywhere."

The other woman took a long, spiteful drag and exhaled it in slow puffs as she ground the butt out under the toe of her scuffed Converse. "The microarray you wanted," she said, smoke still trickling from her nostrils. "The glassware, the HTF. We'll have them by the end of the week. Making a big push south to strip the clinics on that list."

Indi felt naked in front of the other woman. She'd been working all morning in frayed shorts and an undershirt, and Doe's long, lean body made her painfully aware of every place denim and ribbed cotton bit into her flesh or clung tightly to heavy rolls. She forced herself not to hunch, not to suck in her belly—it only made them more contemptuous if you tried to hide what couldn't be hidden. *That's why you're dressed like this, idiot,* she reminded herself fiercely, fighting the urge to pull her shirt down over the sliver of soft flesh between its hem and the waistband of her shorts. *Fat is a weapon. Disgust is armor.*

"Is there anything else?" She took off her glasses and rubbed the smudged lenses on her shirtfront. "You could have used the intercom."

"Sophie needs you." Those gray eyes slid like molten grease down to Indi's sandaled feet, then back up. "You might want to change."

♀

"I don't believe that," said Fran. They were sitting in the dark, she on the edge of his bed where the light from under the door showed Robbie her silhouette, he in the metal folding chair set in the corner. "I'm sorry, I just don't. It's ridiculous."

"Why would she lie?"

"Are you naive? She probably wants our rooms. If we make a problem and get booted, she gets a shot at getting *her* friends inside. We're only here as a favor to Indi."

"So they didn't ask for labor at your last sit-down?"

She hesitated, then let out a snort. "The *town* did, not Boston. It's salvage and road repair."

"People are getting sent up the coast somewhere. Zia showed me a list of names, and Beth was on it."

"And where'd she get this so-called list?"

"She has someone in Boston. An informant. She says they're shipping people out from there, too. Fran, they're sending trans women they arrested." His voice broke. He thought of the men he'd seen cutting brush and breaking rocks on so many different roadsides, the black men, the native men like him, and of the articles he'd read about prisoners in California fighting wildfires for a buck fifty a day—what was different now?

"You're honestly blowing this so far out of proportion. What they're doing down there, whatever it is, did you think it wouldn't be horrible? The world's dead, Robbie. It's not our fucking problem."

"It *is* our problem," he said, knowing he sounded dramatic. "Them, the people outside, the people in Boston and Concord and Worcester. Every dyke and freak and faggot in the world is my fucking problem, and they're yours too, Fran. You just can't see it. I know the world's dead, but that means we get *more* of a say in what happens to the people left in it, not less."

"Oh you're *so* radical," she sneered. She was crying now. "I'll talk to them. I'll make sure Beth doesn't have to rake leaves or pour cement. Am I using my privilege right, Daddy?"

His heart closed like a fist. Long black hair blowing in the wind. Long, slender sunburned hands. Had he seen him, once? Maybe in a dream he had. His voice shook when he said, "Don't call me that."

"Then don't fucking tell me what to think." She tipped her head back, sniffled, and rubbed the heels of her hands against her eyes. It was a while before she spoke again, and when she did her voice was thick with tears. "I'm sorry. I'll just—I'll talk to Nam-joo about it. I'll see what's going on." She took a deep, shuddering breath. "I didn't mean to flip out on you like that."

"People could die, Fran. Beth could die."

"I really don't think so."

He stood. He couldn't listen to her anymore, couldn't keep trying to drag her through her own discomfort. Without a word he strode toward the sliver of light under the door.

"Are you leaving?" She sounded small, almost frightened.

He paused, his hand on the doorknob. "What do you think Sophie would do if men got into the camp?" he asked, not turning. "Don't answer. Just think about it. Will you do that?"

He felt her tearful nod. Heard her swallow. "I will, I just really think you're taking this too ser—"

He slammed the door behind him.

♀

"Oh my God I'm *so* sorry to drag you up here," said Sophie as Indi slid out of the golf cart, parked at the mouth of a branch passage on the Screw's third thread down. They weren't far from the day clinic and the hydroponics farm. A few guards—in plainclothes, not riot gear—stood around chatting, but their eyes stayed on the sparse foot and cart traffic moving up and down the thread. A chill slithered up Indi's spine as one of the guards hit a switch and a segmented steel partition slid down from a recess in the concrete ceiling, plunging the whole passage into gloom.

"It's no trouble," Indi forced herself to say, flashing her best approximation of a smile as Sophie seized her arm and guided her toward a door set halfway down the hall. "Where's the patient? What, exactly, is the matter?"

"It's not, like, a huge deal." Sophie pushed her glasses up her nose with a finger manicured in glittering gold. "Just a few women in labor."

"What, more than one?"

A guard opened the door for them. A low moan bubbled out, silencing Indi as Sophie drew her onward through an airlock bracketed by curtains of heavy strips of black rubber and into a long, low-ceilinged space lined with narrow cots. In each of the cots lay a woman, all of them heavily pregnant. There were close to twenty of them, Indi guessed, and about a third were soaked in sweat and thrashing violently, held down only by canvas straps and guards in ponchos. Jane was there, ear to a teenage girl's rounded belly, and the Screw's other nurse, a stocky older woman named Pam who kept to herself and reeked of stale tobacco smoke, knelt between an unconscious woman's legs with something swaddled in her arms.

It took Indi a moment to spot the first corpse. She was a kid, no older than seventeen or eighteen, with big ears and a constellation of freckles. Someone had thrown a blanket over her midriff, but the long, inexpert incision bisecting it vertically was still visible where the blood had soaked through the thin wool.

"So just pitch in wherever you want," said Sophie, raising her voice over the groans and screams of the women in labor. "If you think—"

Indi hit her. She knew even as her palm met the girl's cheek and rocked her little head back like a speed bag that it was a mistake, that it might be the last one she ever made, but that didn't keep her from following up with the back of her hand before Doe and a short, thick-bodied guard wrestled her away, wrenching her arms behind her back.

"What the fuck did you do?" Indi screamed. "What the *fuck did you do?*"

"I wanted to know if he could make a girl," Sophie sobbed, blood dripping from her chin as she straightened up. "What was I supposed to do? Sit around and wait?" Her big blue eyes glistened with tears. "I'm trying to start a family, and this is from *before* you were here. How was I supposed to know about your tests and your micro-thing?"

"It won't make a difference." Indi felt her throat might close, that her thoughts might flurry faster and faster until neurons began to burst like blown-out spark plugs. "Even if he can sire a girl, it *doesn't make a difference* until I can test the embryos!"

The woman Jane was tending to let out a piercing shriek, convulsing against the canvas straps restraining her. Blood, perhaps from a bitten tongue or cheek, poured from her mouth as she thrashed. The look of guilty embarrassment that flitted across Sophie's face as her eyes darted from Indi to the screaming girl was somehow worse than the cold anger it hardened into. "You should get to work," said the younger woman, sniffling. "Once one starts, the rest seem to get excited."

Across the room, Pam was on her knees wrapping her kicking, hissing bundle in a sheet of plastic while Jane cleaned blood and afterbirth from the mother's thighs. Not a child. Not a boy. A man. How much of the host had it eaten before they got it out of her? How long would she last now, waxy-skinned and staring numbly at the wall?

"Come on, you fuckin' whale," Doe growled in Indi's ear as she steered her away from Sophie and toward the nearest cot. Toward the wide-eyed, shivering teenager whose sweat and water had already soaked the sheets. "Go save a life."

♀

They answered when she knocked. She hadn't thought they would. She knew she didn't deserve it. It was late and the fairy lights above their bed danced through their preset patterns, dead bulbs interrupting their cluttered constellations. Outside the window the city was a sea of black stippled with little points and squares of light. Their soft face was guarded as they stepped aside to let her in, though they made no move to take the flowers she'd traded for at a kiosk on Lagrange. Baby's breath and bleeding hearts. She held out the bouquet. They said nothing.

"I'm sorry," she breathed. From where she stood she could see the hole she'd punched in their wall, an empty black wound through which anything might slither. She'd had a few drinks at that place, the bar that wasn't from *Cheers*, before coming over, and her head was swimming. "I'm sorry, baby."

You should send me away. I'm nothing.

"I'm sorry."

She dropped the flowers and fell to her knees, looking up at them through a veil of stinging tears. "I'm sorry," she blubbered, and it sounded half an accusation, petty and aggrieved.

Why would anyone love me? Garbage. Stupid. Ugly.

She lurched forward and pressed her cheek against their belly, left bare by their sequined cami. "I'm sorry," she sobbed into their warm, familiar skin with its mingled smell of weed and cum and milk. "I'm sorry. You're the only good thing in my life."

They pulled her to her feet. They took a double fistful of her uniform and kissed her, ignoring the snot dribbling over her upper lip, the drool on her chin. They kissed her and the tension went out of her shoulders as though a wire between them had been cut. A sugary sweet cascade of endorphins. "Baby," she murmured as they broke apart. "I'm s—"

"I don't want your flowers," they whispered in her ear. They drew her back toward the bed and sank down onto it, pulling her after them, still sniffling, to straddle their wide, soft lap. "I don't want your apology. I don't want you to say you love me. I won't believe you."

Ramona opened her mouth, tears falling from her chin to run glistening down their cheeks, and they set a finger to her lips. "I want you to tie me down." They took her hand and brought it to their small, fat breast, crushing her fingers together around their nipple until a single bead of blue-white milk dewed from the dark skin. "And I want you to make me scream."

With her free hand she cupped their throat, thumb pressed in its hollow, feeling the downy hairs that grew there. Headlights washed the room as a car passed, rumbling over broken pavement. The fairy lights swayed overhead, and in the distance thunder rumbled in the clear, cool night as Ramona slid a spit-slicked finger into them and they breathed a word in her ear and cut her to the quick, as though she'd slipped in the kitchen and slashed her palm open, in one bright, sparkling second.

"Daddy."

IX

FREON

It's all volunteer," said Nam-joo around a mouthful of half-chewed apple. "They need muscle to clear roads, cut lumber and firewood. They'll trade us specialists, send them to stay with us a few months and rework our ventilation system and our hydroponics." She swallowed and wiped her mouth on her sleeve. "After that, we swap back. Not a big thing."

Fran picked at the cuticle of her left thumb where a translucent rag of skin had separated. "But the trans women—"

"Won't have much fun," Nam-joo finished for her. She tossed the gnawed core out the window. It bounced off the tar at the edge of the road and went pinwheeling into the sawgrass that grew in the ditch beside it. "Sophie'll give them a little extra. Rations. Picks in the theater. Gym time. Even it out."

Outside Fran's window the sand and grass of the town limits gave way to blackened earth and blowing ash as they drove into the burn zone. She chewed her lip. *What do you think Sophie would do,* she heard Robbie say. *Don't answer. Just think about it.*

Nam-joo looked at her as they went over a frost heave and the rumble of broken pavement gave way to the smooth hiss of resurfaced road. The shadows of clouds skidded over the burned earth. "Someone been pissing in your ear?"

"No," said Fran. "Just wondering."

♀

"Shave and a haircut" jolted Robbie from his nap and brought him blinking and sniffing to the door. He opened it, expecting Beth, and instead found himself face-to-face with Sam. She blushed prettily at the sight of him in nothing but his boxers. "Shit," he swore, snatching his denim jacket from the peg beside the door and buttoning it up as quickly as he could, eyes smarting from the sudden light. The sheepskin lining, musky with years of his sweat, felt warm and reassuring against his bare skin and around the numb ridges of his surgical scars.

"I'm so sorry," said Sam, cheeks still blotchy with embarrassment. "I had no idea you were—"

"Not your fault." He shook his head. "I thought you were someone else." His own blush spread belatedly over the bridge of his nose. "Do you want—can I help you?"

"Doe asked me to get you. We're headed out."

He gripped the doorframe tight to keep any hint of an expression from his face. "I'm not on shift today."

She knows that. What is this?

An apologetic smile. "We're doing clinic raids. We need an extra pair of hands. I'll cover for you next week?"

He risked a glance over her shoulder and caught a flash of black at the end of their little hall. Security. Two of them. "I would," he said slowly, "but I'm supposed to meet Beth soon."

"So leave her a note," said Sam, flashing a forced smile. "Come on, are you that whipped?"

They're going to take me out into the woods, he realized with a sudden brutal clarity that sliced away the last cobwebs of sleep. There would be no rebellion for him, no linking up with Zia and her crew within and without the Screw to liberate the women it was sending north to be worked to death by TERFs on some industrial project. *They're going to put me through something, something to make sure I stay loyal.*

"Sure," he said. "Give me a second—I'll get dressed."

He kicked the door shut and dove under his bed, scrambling over the concrete floor without regard for his bare knees. *Or,* he thought as he used his teeth to rip a strip of electrical tape from the roll he'd stashed and wrapped it tight around his stolen knife to strap it to his forearm, *they know I talked to Zia and they'll just kill me, and leave my body out there for the dogs, and the turkey vultures.* He'd tried to find Indi last night, to tell her what was happening, but she hadn't answered her door and the public clinic wasn't open.

He struggled into an old, paint-stained sweatshirt and a pair of shapeless jeans. His reflection, pale and harried, looked back at him from the mirror by the door. He made himself take a breath. Another. And another. His composure was all that stood between him and the forest's scavengers. He exhaled and gripped the doorknob.

And the other men.

♀

Vivian led them down the beach, waves flattening out over wet sand before retreating, leaving only a silvery sheen and a few flecks of foam in their wake. Fran watched a crab scuttle sidelong through the rushing surf. The ocean was calm today, sparkling and trackless, and seagulls whirled over the breakers where they tumbled clear and ponderous into the shallows, the mass of the water beneath them no longer enough to support their weight. Dissolution. The hiss of water over earth.

Ahead, the TERFs' work crews were scrapping the USS *Hyannis*, taking her apart screw by screw and loading the resultant detritus onto the barges they'd pulled ashore in the predawn light. Hydraulic cutters whined. Rusted steel crunched and sparks flew in short-lived jets where women severed struts and whatever you called the little walls around the deck with acetylene torches. Most of the pilot house and radar tower were already disassembled and loaded away, and a crane jacked up on bricks and shale strewn over the sand had one of the deck guns swinging from its arm.

"We'll have shipping running up and down the coast," Viv shouted back at Fran and Nam-joo. "Rye, Portsmouth, Bath—we'll start in Boston, come up through here!"

They have people that far north?

"Fuel?" Nam-joo shouted back. She'd stayed behind a few minutes at one of the checkpoint shacks near town, then rejoined them later, jogging down the beach. It gave Fran a bad feeling, just like the destroyer's sharklike silhouette.

Viv smiled. "Trade secret!" They were in the shadow of the ship's aft section now, welders and wreckers in safety harnesses hanging from the rail above with their boots braced against the destroyer's hull. Sparks struck the sand around them like little kamikaze fireflies. "Important part is, you send pork, hormones, whatever up the coast, we bring you pharmaceuticals—we've got a contact in Canada, still has a couple intact factories and supply networks. Sedatives, benzos, heavy-duty antibiotics. Get that little clinic you've got up to speed."

They walked through the relay lines of women in coveralls and heavy gloves passing scrap down to the barges, stopping every now and then to wait as slabs of metal—some still glowing at the edges—went from arm to arm ahead of them. The shadow of one of the deck guns swept over them as the crane swung it clear of *Hyannis*'s bulk and toward a waiting truck bed. More women waiting to guide it in, lash it down with canvas straps. Intact and lethal under its snakeskin of flaking rust.

What do you think Sophie would do?

In the barges women stacked and sorted, distributing salvage so as not to upset the flat-bottomed craft. There were others, fully laden, which had already put out and were moving up the coast, against the current. They'd picked a bad time to launch. They were wasting fuel. The figures on their decks toiled in silence, rendered indistinguishable by distance.

Think about it.

♀

There was a knock at the door of the Kennedy Room. "I'm not taking anyone right now," said Beth from the little bathroom where she stood at the sink, dabbing concealer into the furrow of the scar that cut across her left cheek. Dani mixed it herself—out of what Beth didn't know—and it looked like the real thing, but you had to redo it every couple hours or the color started to go off, like a bruised apple. One of her clients had said it made her look like she had a case of necrotizing fasciitis.

She heard a key in the lock and turned from the mirror, panic and anger churning in the pit of her stomach along with her meager breakfast. A hard-boiled egg. A handful of wild blueberries. "I said I'm not taking anyone!"

Tumblers turned with a solid, satisfying *clunk* and Sylvia stepped into the room. She wore a flowy white sundress, straps crossed over her tanned and perfectly sculpted shoulders. She and her twin looked so effortless, like they'd sighed and just sort of slumped into their perfect shared form, but Beth had seen them on the squash court and at their laps in the pool, back and forth, back and forth, until even she lost count. Like sharks.

"Sorry," said the blonde, looking around the room with an expression of mild distaste as though she'd just noticed a coil of dog shit on the sidewalk. "Everyone's going up to the theater. There's some kind of leak here. Freon or something."

It wasn't until she was dressed and halfway down the hall back to the main thread, a few of the other girls ahead of them, that Beth remembered the day her mother's fridge had died, the moldy chemical smell that had hung in the air above that spreading puddle of dirty meltwater. She inhaled deeply through her nose. Nothing. Just the same flat, recycled air. She glanced back at Sylvia. A smile. A polite nod.

They're going to kill us, she realized with sudden unfeeling clarity. *This was the bottom of the barrel. My last chance to be useful. I blew it. They're actually going to kill us.*

"Shit," she said, pretending to stumble. "Shoelaces. Sorry."

She knelt to redo the knot, trying to listen for Dani's voice, to see who else was around. *Think of something, you stupid bitch,* she thought furiously. *Think of something, think of something, think of something.*

"Can you hurry it up?" asked Sylvia.

Before she could psych herself out of it, Beth reached back, grabbed the other woman by the ankle, and yanked her leg out from under her. Sylvia went down like a Looney Tune slipping on a banana peel, except Sylvester the Cat's skull had never made a sound like that—a sickening, gravelly crunch—when it hit the floor, and Porky Pig had never groped weakly at his murderer's throat and face while being strangled, had never let out a ghastly, rattling whimper as her thumbs crushed his trachea.

This is a fucked-up thing to think about while you're killing someone, Beth reflected, squeezing with all her strength against the thundering pulse in the sides of Sylvia's throat. *Thufferin' thuccotash! Thith ith thecond-degree moider!*

She started laughing just before the light went out of Sylvia's eyes. The other girls—the other *daddies*—were screaming, and someone was running. Beth laughed and laughed until her stomach hurt, ignoring the shouting voices, the cries of terror, and then something pierced her back and she pitched over on her side, current roaring through her body, and pissed herself. Someone kicked her in the kidneys. She saw white. Red. *Ah-buh, buh-duh, th-that's all, folks!*

Black.

♀

It took them most of the day to reach the seventh clinic. First they hit a collapsed bridge near Hollis and had to drive an hour down washed-out backwoods roads while Doe and Sam, who was driving the big, rusty contractor's van, argued over a tattered atlas. Then they had to kill the engine and wait for a pack of ten or fifteen men to pass through the suburbs of Leominster, the stale smell of their own sweat blossoming in the gloom as they played euchre on a folded sheet and Shane, the girl who'd shared her water with him on his first day with the hunters, held a disintegrating copy of *The Silence of the Lambs* about three inches from her nose and sounded out each word in silence, lips moving like two plump, pink worms.

Of the first six clinics, two they'd found burned to the ground, one looted to bare boards—and from the other three they'd scrounged a meager pile of glassware and ampules of phenol red, calcium chloride, and other chemicals from Indi's list. Most would be useless, rendered unstable by time, heat, sunlight, and simple entropy, but a few might be potent, and more might still have uses unlockable via medical degree and autoclave. Robbie was reasonably sure it was a real errand, and reasonably sure he'd be knifed and left in a ditch when it was done.

The seventh clinic was the biggest, a sprawling wreck in the pine barrens just outside Northampton where once upon a time rich, white suburban women had come to get pumped full of hormones and have their eggs hoovered out of them and shotgunned back in once fertilized, to lay broods of three or four or five plump little grubs who could grow up to carry on the family pill addictions and fight over grandma's bequests and major in philosophy at expensive liberal arts colleges where they learned to care very much about the poor and the downtrodden and also to never, ever touch them or engage them in conversation.

College, Robbie's grandfather had often said with scorn, *is where they teach you how to get an NPR subscription.*

Sam parked the van in the ruined lot where witchgrass and wild mustard choked what was left of the pavement and nettles grew from clumps of browning lawn grown wild and spilled out of their medians. A slender pear tree thrust up through the rotted-out staves of an abandoned planter. Robbie saw the shriveled leavings of its blossoms lying in the dirt around it like the wings of mayflies. When they piled out the back of the van a cloud of insects rose up from the underbrush and swaying milkweed, which were shedding their last silky seeds. It was hot. Robbie swigged filtered water from his canteen and wondered how to kill six women with a knife and one crossbow bolt.

If I can get Doe's gun, maybe. Maybe.

They crossed the parking lot, heading for the front entrance. The whole place looked like an upscale spa under its heavy coat of climbing ivy. Whitewashed facade. Glazed windows. Doe, lean and hungry-looking in her Red Sox windbreaker and grimy jeans, .38 snub nose holstered on her left hip, led the way. "Fisher, new kid—" She glanced at Robbie. "You got a last name?"

"Diller."

"What, like Phyllis Diller?"

"I guess."

"Huh." She scratched her chin. "You two take point. Me and Yoshida and Jennings'll be right behind you. McCutcheon, Doherty, you stay back here. Watch the tree line."

The two older women nodded, turning back toward the forest. Robbie and Sam jogged on ahead to the rusted-open doors and sidled through into deep shadow, flicking on the penlights taped under their crossbows. The narrow blue-white beams swept over mossy tile and a decorative stone fountain where the bones of koi fish lay mired in dried algae. In the angled beams above was a songbird's nest, abandoned for the fall, and on the front desk a huge gray tomcat, all jowls and scars, was licking himself in a shaft of sunlight that fell through a hole in the roof.

"Jesus," said Sam. "Look at the size of his balls."

They went through the waiting area with its moth-eaten designer chairs and moldering whitewashed walls. Beveled glass doors, one broken off its hinges and leaning at an angle against the frame, and then a long hall lined with soundproofed doors. Some stood open. Some were cross-hatched with splintered claw marks, and the acrid stink of piss told Robbie men had marked here recently, unless the gray tom was particularly ambitious and well hydrated. *I could pick an open room,* he thought. *Stab Sam, duck inside, shoot whoever comes through first and take their cross.* He glanced sidelong at the stocky girl beside him, her straight brown hair up in a loose bun, sweat standing out on her wide forehead. She couldn't be older than twenty-one, twenty-two.

I could run. Go out a window. Would they let me go?

Through an open door, he saw a skeleton slumped in a rolling chair, a sunroof in its cracked and yellowed skull. The gun might still be nearby. *It won't work. Not after five years.* The soft, careful footfalls of the three women behind them echoed down the hallway. Robbie's back itched between his shoulder blades, as though in anticipation of a bolt. *Will it hurt? When it goes into me, will it hurt, or will there not be time for that?*

They picked their way through a fat wedge of sunlight falling through a rent in the clinic's exterior. Greenery spilled through the gap, tomatoes black and wrinkled on their drooping vines. Bees droned lazily among dead flowers. *I could fit through there,* he thought. *A few prickers, a couple of scrapes, and I'd be gone. I can last as long as I have to, out here.*

Longer than Beth on a TERF work crew.

Than Indi, working with that psycho bunker brat.

They pushed through heavy skeins of cobwebs bagged down by dust and long-forgotten insects and into the lab space at the back of the building. Dead computer towers. A locked industrial freezer on the far side of the long room with its rows of work surfaces laden with journals eaten through by dry rot, autoclaves, microscopes, and other shit he didn't understand. Dusty light fell in pinpricks and splotches through a trio of skylights mostly overgrown by moss. Petri dishes lay under drifts of dust and grime.

Longer than Fran, when someone tells, or guesses.

The others followed at Sam's signal from the doorway. Doe led them in. Vicki Yoshida, tense and irritable and skinny, her black hair shaved on the sides and standing up in a messy rooster's tail at the center. Peanut Jennings, who must have been almost seventy and whose real first name he didn't know. Dust sifted down from the ceiling, hanging in the golden sunlight. He made himself inhale and set his crossbow down on the nearest workstation, though his hands shook as he did it. Close in was the only way he might have a chance. They'd make a pincushion out of him if he took the time to line up a shot worth taking. He flicked his wrist to loose the knife he'd hidden up his sleeve. His fingers steadied on its worn, scuffed grip. When he turned back, Doe was almost on him. She had her crossbow up, the light that fell through the skylights dappling her in liquid shadows. He'd missed his chance. He'd never really had one.

"Sorry it had to end like this, kid."

"Okay," said Robbie. It seemed like a dumb last word, but he couldn't think of anything else. He kept picturing Fran's legs under the gauzy hem of her nightgown in the backyard of Indi's house. He kept imagining the smell of her down there, the soft arch of her half-hard cock against his cheek.

That was when the man came through the skylight. First he saw its blurred outline through the cracked and lichen-spotted glass. A hand. A chest. Then it was plunging through the air, a mass of hair and muscle and torn skin, and shards of broken skylight rained down with it as it landed square on Doe's shoulders, claws tearing through her windbreaker, teeth snapping at her throat. They fell in a tangle of limbs. The crossbow went off, the bolt punching through Peanut's right arm. Robbie flung himself over the workstation, skidding through the dust, and grabbed up his crossbow to chance a wild shot at Sam. He missed, tumbled off the Formica in a shower of dust, and ducked as she fired back at him. The quarrel skewered one of the dead computer towers with a brittle crunch.

Robbie broke for the exit. He clipped his shoulder on the corner of a workstation and skidded on peeling linoleum. A knife flashed at the center of the lab as Yoshida threw herself into the melee between Doe and her attacker. He saw, from the corner of his eye, the second man come out of the freezer. He had an enormous cock—ten or eleven inches—and what looked like some kind of fungal infection scaling his breast and part of his throat, the skin flaking and greasy almost to the left-hand corner of his mouth, reddish-brown leopard spots mottling his sunburned complexion around the fissures at the corners of his mouth and on his shoulders and elbows. He yawned hugely and stretched like a cat.

Out into the hall and Robbie ran straight into a sprinting Donna McCutcheon. By pure reflex he set his palm against his knife's grip and slammed it hard into her breast. She came up short, eyes bulging, staggering along so that they turned in an awkward circle, like a drunk couple lingering for too long on the dance floor. He yanked the knife out. She fell, her hot blood soaking his hands and the front of his hoodie, and he saw Midge's face and the furrows she'd clawed into the basement's dirt floor. His breath hitched in his throat. From the lab came a man's scream, wild and furious, and the crash of heavy equipment knocked to the floor.

Sam staggered out and nearly tripped over McCutcheon's body. She was covered in blood. He grabbed her hand, not caring that she'd tried to kill him all of ten seconds ago, or that he'd tried to do the same to her a moment earlier. He dragged her down the hall, away from the sounds of tearing flesh. She stared at him without recognition until, as they passed the hole in the wall, she seemed to come to herself, tearing her hand from his and backing into the clinging thorns and rotten vines. "No," she whimpered. "No, no, no."

"Stop fucking around," Robbie hissed. "We don't—"

A man hurled himself into the breach behind her, scattering dead foliage and broken masonry, clawing at the crumbling edges of the hole. He got one scarred and scabby arm around Sam's throat and hauled her up and off the floor. Her heels drummed against the wall. Robbie lunged, swinging his knife at the man. The blade met a descending forehead and rebounded. Tingling fingertips. The man bellowed, blood running into his piggy little eyes, and heaved back with all his strength, and Sam was gone, though Robbie could hear her screaming, her voice high and thin and completely deranged, and her blood glistened on the hole's sharp edges.

It went on and on. It wouldn't stop. It seemed, until it did, it never would.

♀

The ultrasound screen shivered with dark visualizations of the younger woman's innards. Gossamer folds of flesh. The obscure darkness of her organs. White static snow intruding at the margins and along the inner curves of Sophie's cunt. Slowly, carefully, Indi slid the hollow point of the syringe through the vaginal wall and up toward the gelid shadow of the girl's left ovary. She'd thought Sophie might whimper, given that she was on a cocktail of expired Vicodin and benzos rather than real anesthesia, but the girl didn't make a sound. Her whole focus was on the screen, the reflection of which squirmed and quivered in the depths of her blue eyes. In the corner stood a woman in riot gear, one hand resting on the butt of a Taser.

If you weren't a coward, you'd poison her. Slit your wrists tonight.

The needle pierced the ovary. A whisper of resistance as it slid into one of the fluid-filled sacs inside the delicate organ. Indi drew back the syringe's plunger, sucking the eggs within up into the suspension fluid in the canister. "Almost done," she said. "Just focus on your breathing if you start to feel nauseous or light-headed."

"It's incredible," Sophie whispered. The entire length of the appointment she'd acted as though the maternity ward had never happened, as though the scabbed-over cut on her lip had come from nowhere at all. Indi had slept in a little room off her apartments the past night, armed guards at the door. "We all look like that inside, now. Everyone in the world."

Indi ejected the full canister of cloudy follicular fluid, capping it with rubber and setting it carefully in the sample wheel she'd set on her instrument table. "Well, almost." She depressed the plunger and thumbed a fresh glass tube into place, screwing it in tightly. It began to fill as she set her thumb against the plunger's base and eased it back. A hungry vacuum drawing the motes of a score of little future Sophies out into the light. *Don't think about that.*

From sedation to retraction and the swabbing away of the thin trickle of blood which welled up from the wall of Sophie's vaginal canal, the entire extraction took less than fifteen minutes. *Every day I am making a choice,* thought Indi as she set the sample wheel onto its shelf in the freezer. *Every day I decide I matter more than the people outside this place. More than the girls she killed because she got impatient waiting for her little dream family.*

Eleven women dead in the space of a few hours. Indi up to her elbows in slippery gore wrestling those *things* out of their mothers, first crying because they still looked like babies, then dry-eyed and deafened by the screams, gloves shredded by sharp teeth and little claws, trying to repair the minute bite marks and lacerations the things left behind them as, like clockwork, Pam disposed of the little bodies, silencing them in wet folds of bloody fabric and a crinkling plastic caul. Indi had wanted children, once, but Vikram had said no, that it wasn't the right time, and wouldn't she be at a higher risk for complications? She had thought of it then, holding the single girl-child in her arms as guards dragged away the other women. Chaff from the camp and the surrounding countryside. Travelers picked up by the Screw's hunting parties. One baby girl, red-faced and crying.

She taped a gauze square over Sophie's puncture wound. "We're done."

"Take Dr. Varma back to her room, Louise. No visitors." Sophie looked sadly at Indi from the vantage of the examination table, effortlessly poised despite her paper gown. "It's just until we've had a chance to rebuild a little trust."

Indi stared at her, ears ringing. She wondered if she could kill the girl before Louise—approaching now across the bare concrete—got to her, if she could grab hold of Sophie's hair and ram the syringe like an ice pick through an eye socket. Then she thought of Fran, and Beth, and Robbie, and of the guns that would follow them now, barrels tracking their every movement against her good behavior. She forced a smile. "Of course," she said.

♀

"All right, so a hundred and sixty laborers, six-month contract, and in exchange we get your hydro people, a team to install your gray water recycling system in the Screw, and two mycologists, all for the same period." Nam-joo peered over her little rectangular glasses at the sheet of scratch paper before her. "We expand our farming operation, you provide us with the raw materials for barricades, we grant an exclusive license to trade on our behalf on the East Coast, and we supply your Legionnaires while they exterminate all men within the borders of the township and surrounding areas. That everything?"

I will have a cunt, thought Fran, sitting in silence beside the older woman. The Shaw house was silent around them. On the beach, work continued apace around the disintegrating bulk of the *Hyannis. I will have a cunt, I will, I will, and I'll never be hungry again or sleep outside or have to pretend with Beth. It's going to be better. It's going to be—*

"Perfect," said Viv, tugging off her right glove with her teeth and offering Nam-joo her hand. "Let's fucking celebrate."

♀

Robbie staggered out the clinic's front door, stepping over Reena's body where it lay curled on the threshold in the arms of another corpse—a man, his teeth buried in the back of her neck, a crossbow bolt through his left eye socket. A dozen yards off, two more men were fighting over what was left of Sam in the shade of a stand of beeches. Flesh stretched and tore between their rotting teeth. He watched them, breathing hard. The van stood unattended across the expanse of the parking lot. Thirty yards of waving grass and wildflowers shedding dry, dead petals in the wind. *I can make it.*

From somewhere back inside the clinic came the booming report of Doe's revolver. A man screamed again. Another answered from the tree line to the north. No more time to think. He shoved his knife into its sheath and launched himself toward the van. No cover. Witchgrass hissing against his jeans. His own breath rasping in his ears as he saw Sam yanked again and again back through the hole in the wall. Blood on broken brick and concrete. An eagle swooped low over the field, passing by not far from him, and he wished, with the same terrible, helpless fury with which he had once wished to sleep and wake up as a boy, to shuck his skin and leap after it into the sky, to be wild and alone and friendless. Free.

The van's rear doors were open. He leaped inside, nearly braining himself on the car's roof. The gray tomcat hissed at him from underneath the passenger seat, eyes gleaming like jewels in the dark. He covered his mouth to stifle a yelp of hysterical fear and crouched down to catch his breath, not daring to believe he'd made it. The keys were still in the ignition. The lockbox where Doe kept her handguns lay forgotten under the bench that ran the length of the van's left-hand wall.

"You coming with me?" he asked the cat, who only hunkered down and made a low, warning kind of *yraowl* sound. He chuckled and turned back to pull the doors shut behind him. Doe stood there, snub-nosed revolver pointed squarely at his chest.

"Too bad," she rasped. Her ginger hair was matted and spiky with blood. Ugly gashes glistened on her throat and shoulder. She held her right arm tucked under her left and the sleeve of her windbreaker was soaked through and dripping. The van lurched as she climbed awkwardly up into it. Her breathing sounded like someone inflating a wet burlap sack and then squeezing it flat, but the click of her .38's hammer echoed hard and flat and definite from the blank white panels. "Thought you might . . . have the brains . . . to run."

He threw himself at her without a word, his hand flying to the hilt of his knife, and the shot, when it came, was as loud as thunder.

X

NEUTERED AND EXEMPTED

Beth woke to the smell of her own vomit. She didn't open her eyes at first, reflecting instead on the virtues of plausible deniability. *I am not lying in my own puke,* she thought calmly. *I did not murder Sylvia. I am not in line waiting for the gas chamber.* Except that thought made her think of Steve, her mother's second husband, who everyone had said was so handsome, such a good guy, what a catch. She remembered his shit-eating grin. He'd loved a good Holocaust joke.

What's the difference between a Jew and a pizza?

She hadn't answered him then, as he leaned over her with a hand on her eleven-year-old thigh. She remembered that. He just liked to hear himself talk; it was better if you let him.

A pizza doesn't scream when you put it in the oven.

Between the stale, boring trauma of having been molested by a dollar-store white supremacist and the exciting new life-ruining possibilities of whatever was happening to her now, she chose novelty and opened her eyes. Her half-congealed upchuck greeted her. Her cheek rested in the puddle. It was in her hair. She spat, levering herself up on one elbow. She was at the back end of the aisle running down the center of a bus, her wrists zip-tied together. Women filled the worn bench seats, some looking back curiously at her, others carrying on with idle talk.

"You're awake."

She almost wept at just the sound of Dani's voice. The tall, wiry woman sat on the outer edge of the rearmost seat beside Sharice, a big, quiet woman who worked as one of the Screw's other daddies. Beth coughed, worming backward from the stinking puddle. "What's going on?" she wheezed. "I dreamed someone was screaming."

Dani had a black eye, her left. "They brought you in and dumped you on the floor. You killed Sylvia Slate?"

"Stupid fucking name." Beth spat to clear her mouth. She ran her tongue over her teeth. Her head hurt. Her back hurt. Her stomach felt like a lead brick. "What is she, a porn star? I mean what's going on here? Why are we on a bus? I'm guessing they're not driving us to a production of *Jersey Boys*."

Dani let out a mirthless laugh. "We got traded. Sold. Whatever. We're going to work for the TERFs."

It took a moment to sink in. While it did, the bus's front door groaned open past the iron cage someone had welded to its inner frame. A blast of chilly night air—the bus's windows were painted over, the only light the tube fluorescents built into its ceiling—swept in ahead of a middle-aged redheaded woman with bags under her eyes who seemed to be in the middle of a shouting match with someone standing outside.

". . . said I'd bring the full eighty, so that's what I'm bringing!" she hollered back over her shoulder in a thick Down East accent. "These Maryland bitches are hardcore, and I'm not gonna show up saying the dog ate my homework. Take it up with Queen Munchkin, you got such a hard-on."

Hahhhhd-on.

The second woman came up into sight as the driver took her seat. That face. The long, straight nose. Blunt honey-blond bangs and gray eyes red-rimmed with crying, pouty little mouth twisted in a snarl of rage. Sylvia's face.

Fuck.

"I'll take the heat with Her Majesty," Corinne growled, staring straight at Beth down the length of the aisle. "Just give me that thing." Her hands closed into two trembling, manicured fists. "And a gun."

♀

A crowd waited in the square outside City Hall. It was raining, though only lightly, and Ramona had to fight her way through their packed ranks on her way to the front steps. She'd overslept after coming back to the dorms from Feather's and woken hungover and feeling greasy to the crackle of Kilroy telling her to come in early. She was already late, and now this. "Will you fucking move it?" she snapped at a clutch of older women in rain slickers, who took one look at her scowl and bloodshot eyes and parted ranks to let her pass. That was when she got her first look at the scene unfolding in the shadow of the hall, that ominous concrete heap. Legion women lined the steps. Molly and her people. More stood in front of them at ground level in the ravine between opposing tiers of cut gray granite, one with an automatic in her hand. Molly. And in front of them, kneeling handcuffed in the rain, were three whores from Feather's building and one already lying dead, the back of her skull blown in. "No," Ramona whispered.

"Captain?" Karin, trailing after her.

She swallowed, gripping the rusted rail set into the stairway. "Nothing."

An acne-spotted Maenad on the steps read from a yellowed pocket notebook as Molly stalked to stand behind the next woman in the kneeling line. "Jason Cohen. One count rape by omission of biological sex, one count preserving a known vector for the estrophaga virus, thirteen counts aiding and abetting in the preservation of such vectors. Last words?"

"Fuck you," she sobbed.

A gunshot. The wet smack of the body falling face-forward onto the concrete pavers. Blue hair fading into brown at the roots fanned out in the rain around the ruined head. Molly's boots splashed through a shallow puddle. The handgun came up a bare inch behind the next girl's skull. She was crying, the woman. Ramona had seen her before.

"Anthony LaRoche. One count trespassing in a women's space under false pretenses, one count possession and distribution of narcotics in opposition to the survival of the species. Last words?"

She shook her head, eyes squeezed tightly shut. Bang. The trans woman shuddered. A second shot and she collapsed, her long legs kicking madly, the worn-out treads of her sneakers scraping against wet concrete. The crowd watched. Ramona felt them learning. Hardening. It was the knowledge that there was a way to survive that held them back, not the machine pistols on the steps or the sharpshooters on the roof of City Hall, making themselves conspicuously visible in their neon-yellow hooded rain ponchos, cigarettes glowing, smoke whipped away by the wind each time they exhaled.

They dragged Feather into line from one of the armored cars parked up by the hall before Ramona realized what was happening. The world slowed down. They were in one of their nighties, a shimmery silver thing that showed the bottoms of their plump ass cheeks, and their bare legs were bruised and scraped. It was Molly's people hauling them. Feather met her gaze, just for a moment, as Rachel forced them down onto their knees.

"Saba Farahmand. Three counts rape by omission of biological sex, thirteen counts aiding and abetting in the preservation of known vectors for the estrophaga virus."

An absurd pang of jealousy. *Three?*

They didn't look at her again. It would have been enough, if they had looked at her, to split her open. It would have been enough to tell everyone what lay between them. They could have called Ramona's name and dissolved the whole square into a riot. Or at least ensured she joined them kneeling down there in front of the silent crowd. The thin, twitching slit of the Maenad's mouth seemed to encompass the whole world.

I draw my gun.

"Last words?"

I shoot Molly between the eyes. Rush down. Throw myself between their body and the firing squad. Shoot into the crowd.

Their voice was cold and flat and dead. The wind picked up, driving the rain with greater force; Ramona missed whatever it was they said. The shrill little pop of the gunshot echoed through the square. What a stupid sound. What a stupid, boring way for a life to end. Beside her, Karin looked sick. "Don't puke," Ramona said without thinking. She bit the inside of her cheek to keep from spitting out the rest. *If you puke, they'll know.*

Feather lay curled on their side. The rain beat down on their smooth skin where Ramona's mouth had left an archipelago of bruises two nights earlier. *Don't tell me you love me. I won't believe you.* She fumbled a cigarette from the case in the pocket of her fatigues and lit it with trembling fingers, to have something to do. The Maenad was calling another case. Another name. More women being dragged out to the gulley where the dead lay bloodied. Feather's big brown eyes, soft, like a cow's.

A hail of lead, and we die in each other's arms.

♀

It was so easy to cross that bloody stretch of concrete and mount up the steps, exchanging hellos and the quick, forceful gripping of arms that had become the norm among the sisterhood. So easy to tell Karin to wait in the cavernous, echoing lobby with its empty desks and rectangular pools of rain-slashed daylight. She seemed to fly like a zephyr up the stairs to the seventh floor, boots hardly touching the steps, soaring down the hall to the doors of Teach's office where a pair of Maenads stood guard, P-90s cradled in their arms.

They opened the doors for her and she went in. Teach was at her desk, Andrea Kilroy leaning over her shoulder to point at something laid out on it. The Maenad straightened and saluted, fist over her heart. Ramona did the same. Teach's gaze flicked up to meet hers. Rain beat against the long window behind her. "Glad you could join us, captain," she said with a hint of gentle reproach. "Run into traffic?"

Ramona blushed. "The crowd outside, ma'am. I let myself get distracted."

Teach scribbled something in the cloth-bound composition book laid open on her desk. Its pages looked clean and crisp beneath the cover of her scratchy, indecipherable handwriting; the first new paper Ramona had seen in weeks, probably from one of the little mill towns along the Merrimack. "Yes," she said. "Molly's people found, well, I don't know what you'd call it—a hive, let's say, of male prostitutes in womanface. But that's not why I called you here." She flipped the page and smoothed it down gently. "I want you in Raymond tomorrow for the labor signing. Shake hands. See how things are coming with the brat's people. She's been compliant so far, but a degenerate like that . . . you can't be too careful."

Ramona wondered idly how much longer she could last before she started screaming, before whatever was churning under this glacier of cool calm broke out into the world and dashed itself to bloody hamburger against whatever was closest to hand. A hundred trans women watched them from the walls. Dead eyes. Judgment. Lili Elbe looking back over one pale shoulder, blue iris faded like a pressed flower. "I'll drive down tonight," she said.

"You'll have company. Vivian has made it clear to me she isn't cut out to continue managing our interests in Raymond. I've decided Sarah Jane Spiers will take her place." She tapped the butt of her pen against her chin. "Break the news to Vivian and bring her home, if you'd be so good."

"The doctor's really going to stick with naming the town after herself?"

Teach sniffed. "Some of the Matriarchs are stuck in an obsolete paradigm of government. They still think in terms of territory. Ownership. Masculine thinking. But the world has changed, Pierce." Her pen scratched in the silence. "Power now is a fluid thing. It comes from understanding. From nurturing. The mistake we made before the plague was to rely on print media and academic discourse—insular, sterile parts in the machinery of human society. Things in which most women rightly evince little interest.

"Our sisterhood, what we're building here and up the coast, will outlive every lecture series, every textbook. We're making a womb, the strongest thing there is, and once we've solved the fertility problem it will carry our new world. A world without rape. Without wife beaters. Without borders or nations or races. A world where women, after a hundred thousand years of terror, can be safe."

Here and up the coast, Ramona thought. *Not in Maryland. She knows the Matriarchs are scared of her popularity, afraid she'd pull a Caesar on them. That's probably why they let her take Boston and the coast. She wins, their territory grows. She dies, they don't have to worry about her anymore.* She dug her nails into her palms. *Which one do I want to happen?*

Kilroy turned to look out the window, though before she did, Ramona thought she glimpsed something like jealousy in the Maenad's eyes. No womb. No womanhood. No future. Just a little card, kept in a pocket close to her breast in case anyone was checking papers, that read "XY—NEUTERED & EXEMPTED" above her names—natural and conferred, and the serpents of the Matriarchy, tails entwined, framing a white sun in fallopian coils.

A quick, precise jab of the pen's nib to dot an i. "That will be all, captain. I'll await your report."

Ramona saluted, fist to breast, and turned to stride across the empty room toward the heavy oaken door. The eyes on the walls seemed to follow her. Shaggy hair. Little budding breasts. Those strange self-portraits. Teeth barely showing between chewed lips. A beauty mark beside a long, straight nose. A pit yawned somewhere inside her. Something important had fallen into it—something special—and now she lay crouched beside it, waiting for the sound of impact. Marsha P. Johnson, smiling and a little cross-eyed, in a crown of flowers, real and silk, in a framed print by the door.

Stop looking at me. There was nothing I could do.

The scratch of pen on paper halted. "Oh, and Pierce?"

She paused, her hand on the doorknob. "Ma'am?"

"No one thinks any less of you. Women have certain urges." The pen resumed its scratching progress. "But with an eye toward the future, I would consider investing in a good dildo."

♀

"I loved my sister," said Corinne. She walked a yard or so ahead, hauling every now and then on the rope she'd tied as a crude collar around Beth's neck so that Beth had to lurch forward clumsily over the exposed roots and treacherous deadfalls of the forest floor, without her arms for balance, or else strangle. Dawn had just begun to break. "I loved her more than anything in the world. This fucking wasteland, this *pit*, scuttling around after my ex-boss's psychopathic teenager so I can be sure I'm right there to tell her how important and special she is while she gets stoned and watches cartoons and screams at us because the hard drive with her favorite cached YouTube videos got corrupted. I did it for Sylvia. So she could have a place to live. So I could see her. Touch her. Now I have no one." Her voice broke. "Nothing."

"She was gonna—" A swift jerk of the leash and she stumbled forward down the sloping forest floor, rough linen biting into her throat. She coughed. "Kill me."

Corinne rounded on her, eyes bulging, a vein in her forehead standing out so dramatically Beth took a half step back on pure reflex and choked herself again. "Six months of *compensated manual labor*," Corinne bit out as Beth gagged and spat, "is not a *death sentence*."

"Oh, you think they were gonna send us back once we were done putting a new wing on the Judy Chicago Memorial Museum of Interesting Vaginas?"

"Don't look at me like that," Corinne spat, points of color blazing in her cheeks. "I don't give a shit about any of that weird uterus worship. I have trans friends."

"Your sister was taking me to die."

Corinne hauled on the rope with a scream of pure frustrated rage, dragging Beth downslope at a stumbling run. Beth tripped over a half-buried rock and went sprawling, skinning her shoulder against the rough bark of a pine tree. Beth thought she felt her left pinky break beneath her as she levered herself awkwardly up into a sitting position. It felt as though her veins were full of thick, dark venom. "You know she came to see me a few times," Beth rasped, spitting bloody mucus. "Got herself a little daddy fix. What a fucking ass she had. I mean I guess you've got it, too, but I can see the appeal. You two ever, you know, I don't have my hands free, but you remember *Game of Thrones*, right?"

Corinne's little black wedge toe hit her square in the mouth. The back of Beth's head bounced off the tree trunk and she saw stars, strobing points of black and red and green, in the moment before the smaller woman threw herself on top of her and began raining blows down on her face and shoulders. "Easy!" Beth shouted through a mouthful of blood. "I'm not into the rough stuff, baby! This how you used to fuck her?"

"Cunt bitch," Corinne screeched. "Fucking whore!"

"You blow your father with that mouth?"

Wild gray eyes bulged horribly, red-rimmed and bleary. Slender fingers found Beth's throat and squeezed. One hand fluttered to her face, as though to spare Corinne the sight of her. The fine lines of her palm.

I wish my hands looked like that.

"This is how she looked," Beth hissed through the other woman's fingers. They slid away. Rejoined their mates at her neck where her pulse raced and jumped. The world began, slowly, to narrow, darkness eating at its edges. She swallowed against the viselike grip. "When I killed her, this is how she looked."

She thought suddenly of Indi's laugh.

And then the other woman was scrambling off of her and Beth was coughing hard enough to tear the lining of her throat, blood drooling from her split and mangled bottom lip. Corinne listened, silent, as somewhere in the distance a branch broke. Leaves rustled. Someone was running through the sparse autumn forest. The rapid crunch of old pine needles underfoot. The woman yanked a pistol out of the waistband of her jeans, tried to fire, fumbled with the safety, and finally got off a shot. It was still dark under the trees; Beth couldn't see what she was firing at. The racing footsteps didn't slow and Corinne raised the gun again, aiming carefully this time.

Maybe it's a man, thought Beth. *At least he won't try to make me feel bad before he kills me.*

She kicked the other woman in the back of the leg, just below the knee. The shot went wild, and as Corinne rounded on her, Robbie burst out of the brush uphill and hit the slim, tanned woman like a train. They tumbled together over Beth's legs, rolling downhill in a knot of teeth and hair and clawing hands to fetch up with a sickening thud at the base of the hill where it rose into another, a flat defile not so different from the one she and Fran had fled down late that summer. Robbie was on top. He had a knife. It was over quick.

"We've got to stop meeting like this," Beth croaked as he came up the hill toward her, pausing only to collect Corinne's fallen automatic and stuff it into the waistband of his jeans. He reached her, limping a little, and knelt, and she thought she'd never again in her life be so glad to see someone. "I killed her sister. Can you tell me what the fuck is going on?"

"We moved in with slavers," he said, untying Corinne's hasty knot and pulling the collar from around Beth's neck before turning his attention to the zip ties. "They packed up the camp people. Most of the transes in the Screw. They're selling them to Boston for some big project. The guards at the bunker tear-gassed the camp when someone figured out it wasn't just day labor. Then they started shooting people. Set a few tents on fire."

"How'd you get out?"

"I didn't. I was up in Northampton raiding fertility clinics. I guess they knew I'd been talking to people in the camp, that *I* knew about the labor thing." He slid his knife between her right wrist and the zip tie, the metal warm against her skin. The temperature of Corinne's heart. "Doe tried to kill me."

"The fuck? What happened?"

♀

The gunshot blew out his left eardrum. He felt the soft, wet implosion. A *pop* as it depressurized. Then a white heat in his shoulder. He put the knife through Doe's wrist. It slotted in perfectly, clicking against bone, and he twisted the grip. The gun flew out of her hand and went off when it hit the wall, putting a hole in the roof. The cat yowled and swatted at their feet as they staggered past the seat together. He ripped the knife out of her. She screamed. Clawed at his eyes. Somewhere nearby, men were roaring. They would be here soon.

The thumb of her good hand found the hole in his shoulder, worming through his powder-burned hoodie and into raw, bleeding flesh. He must have made some kind of sound. Her twisted face was his whole world. Her teeth bared in a spit-slicked snarl. He got a hold on her hair and banged her head against the wall panel. Once. Twice. She lost her grip on him and he brought a knee up hard into her stomach, doubling her over. He chanced a look out the back of the van as she retched at his feet. Men were coming. Three of them loping through the windblown grass. The leaves had changed. All pale yellow and warm orange and deep, bloody red. When had that happened?

He grabbed the back of her windbreaker, dragged her to the tailgate, and threw her out. He paused for a moment, watching the men close in, then kicked the gun out after her and slammed the doors. Threw himself into the cab and scrambled awkwardly behind the wheel. Started the van with fumbling, bloody fingers, not yet daring to look at the bullet wound in his shoulder, which hurt as though someone had pushed a heated wire under his skin. The cat lay curled placidly in the passenger seat, trauma forgotten.

He saw her moving in the water-spotted rearview as he pulled out of the parking lot. She got up onto her knees, bad arm limp at her side, one eye swelling shut. For a moment she stared after the van, the gun coming up as though she meant to try for one of his tires. Then she closed her eyes and shoved the barrel up under her jaw. There was a deep, throaty *bang*. The top of her head came off like a cheap toupee.

She collapsed onto her side as the men converged on her, and through the press of their malformed bodies, just for a moment, her red-gold hair caught the sun and burned bright as a torch.

♀

"She missed," he said shortly, cutting the ties and sliding his knife back into its sheath. "Come on. We should get out of here."

Beth rubbed her chafed and tingling wrists and wiggled her fingers. The pinky felt more like a sprain than a break. Robbie helped her up gently. "God," he breathed as the light that filtered through the canopy found her bruised and aching face. "She really did a number on you."

"I was trying to get her mad." Her head still ached abominably, and her right eye had swollen to a slit. She was afraid to touch her nose to find out if it was broken. There was blood drying on her upper lip. "I thought maybe I could, I don't know, headbutt her or something, if she got close enough."

I wanted her to get it over with and kill me. I'm so sick of crying and begging all the time. The world's not going to get better.

He nodded. "Let's go."

"Robbie."

He looked back questioningly at her and she took his hands, noting for the first time the dried blood crusting the right shoulder of his hoodie, and stood on her toes—the slope put him a few inches taller—to kiss his cheek. In a flash he was hugging her, crushing her against his strong, narrow chest. He pressed a kiss to the crown of her head and she let him hold her close among the falling leaves and relished the illusion that, if only for a little while, she was safe.

"Thanks," she said against his unwashed sweatshirt, which smelled of gasoline and sweat. "For saving my life."

They broke apart and to her surprise she saw that Robbie was crying, tears pouring down his smudged and grubby face. *It would be extremely inappropriate to ask him if he saw someone littering,* she told herself. *That's an inside thought.*

"I haven't had a friend in a long time," he said. His voice trembled. His eyes were bright, tears clinging to his long, dark lashes. Beth thought he might kiss her. She wasn't sure how she felt about that, but in the end he just squeezed her hands and then turned to lead her uphill through the trees and falling leaves.

They came out of the woods not far from the bus where it sat parked on the edge of an old logging road, along which a throng of what looked like a hundred women milled in anxious, orbiting clusters of tears and arguments and low, hushed conversations. There was a van, too, one of the Screw's big white ones, like the kind contractors drove, and around it stood another group, mostly young and in fatigues. She didn't recognize them. They seemed to be listening to a tall black trans girl with buzzed hair and an AK-47 on one shoulder.

"Who's that?" Beth asked.

"Her name's Zia." He led her toward the van through the fringes of the crowd. Some of the women paused to watch her pass, eyes widening at the sight of her bruised and battered face. "She's got a plan to raid the Screw. I'm going with her. Getting Indi out. You coming?"

"Where's Fran?"

"Safe in Seabrook, at least for tonight." His voice was suddenly hard, his jaw set. "She blew me off when I tried to tell her what was going on."

Beth couldn't think of anything to say. The leaden weight that settled in her stomach was familiar, but not something she could voice. She thought of Fran watching her fall from that roof at the end of summer, the day they'd met Robbie. She thought of Fran's slim body in her arms.

You make me feel so delicate.

"Okay," she said. "Let's go get Indi."

XI

OFF-DUTY

Fran sipped her bitter, yeasty beer politely, watching Nam-joo dance with the TERFs and the city council people. Septum Piercing—Ramona—was lurking by the seafood table. She looked drunk and pissed off about something, her expression sour, her chest flushed and blotchy. She'd come with a tall, statuesque brunette who was currently lighting Nam-joo's cigarette for her by the bar's restaurant's front window, the lighter's flame dancing in the glass. All told there were maybe fifty women—Screws, TERFs, and Raymonders—in the Lighthouse, the town's best restaurant and the only one that had managed to dodge the pre-plague council's draconian zoning laws to get a view of the ocean, even if it was only from the back patio.

"What's a girl like you doing all alone up here?" came Viv's smooth, smoky voice. Fran jumped, nearly dropping her drink. The older woman had snuck up on her where she stood by the bar. She was close, one foot on the floor, the other on the brass heel rest of the stool she'd sunk onto. With her undercut and shaggy forelock, chin propped up on a fist, elbow on the bar, she looked like a big cat sunning itself on a rock.

Fran swallowed and reached up to fiddle with the topmost button of her dress, a fitted black challis with half sleeves and a high collar. "Oh, I'm just not much of a partier."

"But you'll dance with me, surely, if only to avoid the appearance of rudeness?"

"Sure." She gave her best approximation of an easy smile, the thought of her body close against a TERF's both exhilarating and disgusting. "Just keep your hands at ten and two, officer."

"Captain," said Viv, leading her out onto the polished dance floor to scattered applause and a piercing wolf whistle from the end of the bar. A few other couples were out there already, dancing awkwardly to Goldfrapp's crackling Eurobeat. "Not that I'm trying to impress you."

"No," said Fran, mock serious. "Of course not."

"But supposing, just hypothetically, that I were." That lazy smile widened. "Where would you suggest I start?"

♀

The camp was burning. Robbie saw bodies in among the tents, and people staggering out of the thick, choking smoke. There would be men here before long, fighting one another over these heaps of cooked meat and twisted limbs. He stopped the van not far from the Screw's scorched blast doors and unclipped the walkie from its rest beside the busted air conditioner dial. The cabin stank of smoke and blackened pork. He clicked the transmitter. Three long. Two short. Two long.

A moment of breathless anticipation before the doors began to open. The women in the back of the van released their breath nearly in unison. "Good work," Zia whispered. She had a clipped way of speaking, low and quick and urgent. He nodded, his voice caught in his throat. Five years between Midge and the women he'd killed today. Doe in the rearview, pulling a trigger into which he'd slipped her finger. Corinne under him, scratching and hissing, dead leaves and pine needles stuck to her skin, tangled in her silky blond hair. He'd seen her swim once, her breaststroke easy, fluid, that hair unbound by any swimming cap so that it trailed behind her like a comet's tail.

He put the van in drive. They rolled slowly toward the widening gap, smoke stroking the windows with phantom fingers. How many times had he driven through this place? How many times had he turned away from the unease he felt at seeing these wan, starving people in their shabby tents, telling himself there was nothing he could do, that he was just one person in a larger system, the same way he'd watched Ferguson and Standing Rock and thought, *Well, what can I do?*

Except this had been right on his front stoop, and if he was just one person, well, there were probably all of two or three million of those left in North America. *You always could have done something,* he thought as the van bounced over the speed bump at the motor pool's threshold and passed through a loose clump of gate guards in full riot gear, faces smudged with soot, blood drying on their plastic shields. *You were just afraid to be uncomfortable.*

"About time," snapped the gate captain, striding toward them as the van groaned to a halt in its usual spot between a cloth-top Jeep and one of Sophie's unused and flat-tired Porsches, a sleek silver lump of expensive steel. She was a big woman, the captain, a hulking fortysomething named Mercer with a tattoo of an eagle gripping a globe in its talons on the back of her neck. Robbie waited until she was close enough to realize through the streaked and ash-caked window that it wasn't Doe behind the wheel. Her deep-set eyes went wide just as he popped the lock and kicked the door open with both feet, pistoning a hundred and sixty pounds of steel and plastic straight into the woman's face. Bone broke. Skin tore. She went down as, behind Robbie, Zia and the others threw the van's back doors wide and opened up on the gate guards as they withdrew from the entrance. The echoing boom as the bunker sealed itself swallowed the sound of their opening salvo, but he saw, climbing down from his seat, the harsh and fleeting shadows cast by overlapping muzzle flashes.

Mercer screamed as he bent her arm behind her back and dragged her with some difficulty to her feet. He pushed her forward, out into the open, from between the cars as soon as she could walk. The thunder of the blast doors faded into the *boom-boom-boom* of an automatic shotgun, the crack of rifle fire, the undignified pop of automatics. He tried not to see the guards scrambling for cover. Lying dead on bloody concrete. One sat blinking at the crossfire's edge, her guts spilling out into her lap, her hands idly stroking a length of perforated intestine. Another crawled toward the van, legs dragging, a wide snail's trail of blood behind her as though someone had swept an enormous paintbrush over the floor of the motor pool.

Robbie shoved Mercer toward the airlock door that led to the Screw proper. She was sobbing, unsteady on her feet. He kept his knife at the small of her back. The suddenness of their transition from silence to carnage sang through his nerves. He felt both numb and completely exposed, as though his skin had been peeled back to reveal the twitching flesh beneath. The gunshots slackened. Stopped. His bad ear started to ring as he pushed Mercer against the wall beside the door's scuffed keypad. "Open it."

Her trembling fingers tapped against the keys. The lock clicked. The door hissed open with a *whump* of pressurized air escaping. "Led be go," Mercer blubbered, looking back at him over her shoulder. "Blease. I did whad you—"

He stabbed her in the neck just below the curve of her jaw, ignoring the blood spatter that misted his cheek and the side of his throat, and jerked the knife out, wiping it on his sleeve as she fell to her knees and slumped against the wall. She pressed a hand to the gash, pulling at its livid lips as though to close it up again. Blood pumped between her fingers. Her lips were white, her face as pale as milk. She mouthed something unintelligible. Red spittle dripped from her split lower lip.

He went back to the van and got his rifle.

♀

It was so much easier to drink than it was to think about tomorrow. And why shouldn't she enjoy herself? What did she have to feel bad about? Someone had cut a tumor (her heart) out of her chest and now all her worries were over. Ramona was free. Teach's golden girl, forgiven for getting her dick wet—well, for getting someone else's wet, anyway, and here to act as the chief's eyes and ears in the city formerly known as Seabrook. She was made. Set. Minted.

She wanted to die. No. Not really, she didn't. That was just the beer and gin and crème de menthe talking, their liquid voices sloshing up from the depths of her uneasy stomach. What she really wanted was to already be dead. That, she thought as she swayed back toward the bar along the edge of the dance floor, slurping a fresh oyster off its pearlescent shell, would be such a relief. Maybe then she'd stop seeing the scrapes and bruises on Feather's chubby thighs, the cut across the bridge of their nose where someone must have hit them with a baton, or the butt of a gun. Maybe then she wouldn't think about their mouth on her painfully stiff nipple, sucking gently, and their round baby face relaxed in exquisite peace.

"'nother beer?" she slurred, dumping herself onto a stool and doing her best to focus her eyes on the woman tending bar, a wiry little fairy with spiky gray hair and laughing eyes. Just now she was pouring a draft for one of the city council women. Fawcett, the big black woman with the slumped, defeated shoulders.

"With you in a sec."

A sudden squeal of laughter drew Ramona's attention to the far end of the bar, where Jules and Sadie were rocking with mirth at something one of Molly's women, a five-foot-nothing Legionnaire named Monica Sprat, was saying. ". . . things these fucking freaks say when you're about to do them, I swear to God I'm not making it up. Swear to God." She flashed a huge, shit-eating grin. "It looked right at Molly, like square in the eye, and it fuckin' said, 'I want my Daddy.'"

Gales of mirth. Sounds of good-humored disgust and disbelief. Ramona looked away as though Sprat's voice had burned her. The bartender was refilling her glass but just the thought of drinking it made her want to vomit. She staggered away from the bar, nearly knocking over Major Spiers and the dykey bunker negotiator, who were swaying slowly to "Tiny Dancer," and through the dining room where women sat chatting around unset tables in the dim light of colored glass light fixtures. They looked like aliens in their little pools of blue and red and yellow.

She slipped out the back door and into the night, the wind whipping at her open jacket and her hair. The cold salt air tasted clean. It brought tears to her eyes. Teach at Hunan Palace, biting into a hot dumpling so that pinkish meat juice trickled down her chin. *She took me to the restaurant. Our restaurant. She was telling me she knew.*

A few dozen yards away, past the amorphous shadows of the picnic tables on the sand-strewn tiles, waves shushed over the beach. It was a cloudy night, the air damp and cool, a few stars glittering through in patches of bare sky. Almost November.

She took me, and I understood, and I didn't do anything.

As her eyes adjusted to the wan starlight, she saw that two other women were already on the darkened patio. One sat on a picnic table. The other stood in front of her, hands on the first woman's hips. Long and lean. Starlight catching black and silver stubble on the side of an angular skull. Viv. The other woman's hands were tangled in her hair and they were locked together at the mouth in what seemed to Ramona like a contest to produce the most disgusting sound imaginable. They hadn't noticed her, or didn't care. Music blared through the restaurant's walls.

Hold me closer, tiny dancer
Count the headlights on the highway

She thought of her father, dead in his scratched and peeling bar booth, and how he'd always insisted on bellowing, "Hold me closer, Tony Danza," when that song came on. She'd laughed at that. Her mother, thin and tired even then. Her brothers. A warm pack around her. Rabbits in their burrow. The other woman lifted her face to the sky as Viv sucked on her neck. It was the bunker girl, the one she'd had a weird feeling about at that meeting a few months back. Fran.

I knew what it meant, at Hunan Palace. I let them die.

Then all at once she knew where she'd seen Fran before. Sweating, half-shaven, at the bottom of a defile in the woods while her big brick friend held an arrow trained on Ramona's heart.

♀

Mackenzie slept, muzzled and sedated, on the cool black silk sheets of the bed in one of Sophie's guest rooms, the walls and doors already rent by old claw marks from past visits, the carpets stained by his excretions. A trail of dribbled piss and saliva led back across the room and out through the apartments, where Mariana and a few other staff knelt scrubbing on their knees beside buckets of hot, bleach-smelling water. *I could have made something good here,* thought Indi, watching the other women clean effluvium off Sophie's floors. *Passed on a few skills. Taught teenagers how to set bones and remove appendixes and culture penicillin.*

Instead she was supervising the transport and medication of a cannibal troglodyte because Sophie wanted him close when, after Doe's return, she conceived. "We've always been really, like, intimate and not afraid of our bodies," she'd offered in a confidential whisper. "He used to spread me and just *inhale*, because that's where life comes from."

She had paused, as though expecting Indi to gush about the pussy's beauty and symbolic power, then gotten bored and wandered away to the flat-screen television set in the middle of the great room's empty, vaulted gloom, opposite an antique sofa and a low glass-top coffee table. That was how everything was in Sophie's rooms. A little island, insular and without context. She was still there, naked from the waist down and scratching irritably at a little red spot between her right thigh and her vulva. "I'm ready for my shot," she called, not looking away from the television, where *Pride and Prejudice* with Keira Knightley blared at a volume that would surely have raised Jane Austen's eyebrows.

"I'll be right with you," Indi said quietly, locking the guest-bedroom door. No word from Fran or Beth or Robbie. She tried not to think about what might have happened to them because of her. Because she'd slapped the child now scratching herself in the blue glow of the screen. She thought of the baby, Mackenzie's only daughter, swept off to who knew where, and with trembling hands unclasped her medical bag and looked inside. Her father had given it to her when she completed her residency at Concord Hospital. Black leather, a little creased now, and steel fasteners to bind its jaws. How her mother had rolled her eyes telling her about their trip to the custom leatherworker. *The man said you're sure you don't want the gold-plated clasps? And your father told him why would I? She is a doctor, not the Sultan of Oman. I want her to use the bloody thing.* She remembered the tears in his dark eyes as he'd said, *I'm very proud of you*. Now it held Sophie's fertility treatment, a syringe of expired clomiphene to stimulate her ovarian follicles. She held it up, squinting in the low light to check for bubbles, and then made her way to lower herself slowly and awkwardly, one hand braced on the couch, down to the floor at Sophie's side.

The girl drew up one bare leg and planted her little foot on Indi's shoulder. "Remember," she said, not looking away from the television. "If I get sick from this, Doe's going to kill your friends and shoot you in the stomach."

I'm going to die in this place. In this also-ran little dystopian cult. A teenager whose parents shorted medical stocks is going to kill me for not getting her pregnant. "I remember, Sophie."

The foot withdrew. Indi pinched the slender woman's belly, chose her spot, and gave her the injection. "Be *gentle*," Sophie snarled. She slapped

Indi across the face the second the needle was out and the gauze taped into place, just hard enough to humiliate. "I'm going to be in a delicate condition soon. I don't need you *jabbing me*."

Indi stood with a sharp grunt of effort and turned from the couch, not wanting the younger woman to see her expression. Her whole face tingled. She felt an overwhelming urge to grab hold of the girl and shake her. To pull her hair until she bawled. "Of course. I'll be more careful. I'm so sorry."

Across the room, the security light above the barracks-side entrance burned green as someone accessed it. The door hissed open and a tall, solid woman in riot gear stepped through and made a beeline for Sophie. Indi backed slowly away from the couch, the television, and their island of blue light. "There are people moving down the Screw," said the guard, stopping short and folding her arms. "Ten or fifteen of them. Camp people. Armed. They shot their way through the motor pool and the gate guards."

"So kill them," Sophie snapped, though beneath her surface irritation Indi sensed a wriggling, ratlike panic—the unthinking terror of the very rich when something unclean looks like it might touch them. "Lower the bulkheads and send in Doe and her girls. We still have dogs, right?"

"Dorothy didn't come back. The camp people used her van to get inside the bunker."

"All right," said Sophie, still jittery but apparently unfazed by her right hand's disappearance. She prodded at the needle mark on her belly, tracing the red-spotted gauze with a long fingernail. "Then *you* get in there and kill them. Get it done and you can have . . ." She cast about for an appropriate carrot, then slapped her thigh. ". . . her apartment!"

The woman blanched. "That won't be necessary—"

"I'm offering you a *gift*, Louise. It's something *special* to me, and, like, if you don't want it that's fine but it makes me wonder where your priorities are. If you just want to *fling it back into my face*, imply I'm sick to offer it, that's fine. That's totally fine."

As Sophie's tirade escalated to a punishing screech, Mariana, wiping soapy hands on her apron, appeared at Indi's elbow. "Doctor," she hissed, taking hold of her hand with surprising strength. "I need you to come with me."

"In a minute, Mariana. I've still—"

A flash of frustrated rage narrowed the older woman's eyes. "*Come-mierda*. No 'in a minute.' *Now.*"

It hit her in a flash, then. The other staff were gone. The door to the guest room was open, just a crack. Indi looked back at Mariana as though seeing her for the first time. Dark hair. Thick eyebrows. A high widow's peak and a fierce, broad face with a great hawkish jut of a nose. *Jesus, I have been so incredibly fucking stupid and racist about this woman.*

On the television, Mr. Darcy declared stiffly that he loved Ms. Bennett as Sophie got up onto her knees on the couch to scream in Louise's tight-jawed face.

"Okay," said Indi.

♀

The woman stuck her head around the corner of the checkpoint just ahead of dry storage and Robbie squeezed the trigger and took off an ear and most of her jaw. He shot the woman who exposed herself trying to catch the first one, too, once in the shoulder and again right through her nose after she fell screaming to the floor. Not far beyond the checkpoint, one of the Screw's golf carts idled, warning lights blinking on and off, driver collapsed dead against the steering wheel and her passenger lying sprawled on her back in the middle of the Screw with one foot still draped over her seat.

Robbie's body sang with waves of adrenaline and cold, numbing sickness. A few steps to his left lay the body of one of Zia's people, a pretty girl in her mid-twenties, long black hair fallen across her expressionless face. One of the guards had shot her twice from the moving golf cart before Zia got her. Now the firefight had come down to patience and the exploitation of minuscule errors. It wasn't so different from shooting men. You just had to decide they didn't matter. You went away from your body; used it, like you'd use a can opener, to complete a direct and specific task.

The corridor was silent for a while, except for the fading echoes of gunshots and the quiet growl of the idling golf cart. He and Fran had ridden in one of those things on their first day in the Screw. Fran had taken his hand in the back seat, her thumb stroking his palm, a little smile on her face. Maybe it was the same cart. Maybe the women in it had smiled at each other, had held hands as they drove through this bizarre little SkyMall dictatorship.

I'm no better than they are. I ate their food, I followed their rules, I swam in their Olympic standard pool. One night he and Fran had even gone to see *Love Actually* in the little movie theater, making out in the back while Hugh Grant stammered and sweated. *It's an accident I'm even on the right side of this shit. I would have sat and twiddled my thumbs while they sold Beth to a chain gang.*

"Throw your weapons out," Zia shouted from her place beside the bulkhead opposite Robbie's. "Walk out one by one and we'll make sure you get a share from storage. No one else has to fucking die over nothing."

"You're sealed in," someone shouted back after a short pause. "You didn't see the blast doors come down, genius? Not to mention without Sophie you won't even be able to get into storage. You'd need that little brat's palm print and eyeball, and she's locked away thirty feet under us."

Robbie kept his eye to the rifle's scope, forcing himself to keep his breathing slow and even. He tried to think of it like he was playing *GoldenEye* in Jesse's basement, just a low-poly Pierce Brosnan avatar scooting through a maze of vents and corridors.

"Yeah," said Zia, grinning. "We're working on that, too."

♀

At the crack in the bathroom door, Indi watched over Mariana's head as Mackenzie came out of the bedroom, prowling on all fours with his head low to the ground. He made a sound like a hungry dog, a hoarse, plaintive whine that trailed off into a cavernous yawn. The stripe of thick reddish hair that ran the length of his spine stood on end as he stretched, hindquarters up and foreclaws kneading the carpet, and then raised his nose to sniff the air. The muzzle had left deep scars, long ago healed into cartilaginous furrows and ridges, pressed into his jaw and mouth, but his eyes were as blue and lively as a little boy's.

I wish that it had changed their eyes, thought Indi. *I wish they didn't look at you like that.*

"Indi?" came a panicked shriek. Sophie's voice, which sounded so horribly young and alone. *"INDI?"*

Like they're still in there.

Mariana shut the door and threw the bolt just as the man exploded into motion, racing past them like a hound after a hare. Indi set her back against the door and closed her eyes. Something heavy and breakable toppled with a shattering crash. The television, probably. The dull thump of furniture upended onto carpet. Wild, screeching sobs and a low, stomach-clenching *chuff* like the sound a tiger makes when you're getting too close. Indi could almost feel the man's huge, muscular weight coiling to spring. She found Mariana's hand and gripped it tight at the rough, breathless smack of flesh on flesh. The hollow *bonk* of a skull striding the floor.

"No, no, no, no! Down! Off! Please, Kenzie! Please!"

And then, in a voice that scaled up and up until it was a barely intelligible shriek that could have cut a straight line through a pane of glass, "*What if Daddy sees? What if Daddy sees? Get off me! Get off me or he'll make you go away again!*"

He must have put a hand over her face, mercifully, because whatever she screamed next came out only as a muffled, strangled wail. An almost lovingly tender crunch of bone and sinew snapping. Flesh tearing like rotten leather. Mariana pulled her hand from Indi's and went to the toilet, kneeling beside it to fumble under the tank. She drew out a compact revolver and stood up, her expression grim as she peeled duct tape off the cylinder.

Indi stared at the gun, her ears full of the sound of Mackenzie swallowing in the other room. *Hork, hork, hork.* Like a heron with an oversized fish. "What are you doing?"

"Palm and eye," said Mariana, tapping her own. "For locks." She thumbed the revolver's safety off and unbolted the door. "Before he eat."

♀

The blast doors groaned up into their slots not long after the guards surrendered. A ragged cheer came from Zia and the others, but Beth didn't feel like cheering. Everything since Sylvia and Corinne had only wound her tighter and tighter until she felt like a spring about to crack and split apart under the pressure stored inside her body. She kept looking at the dead women lying further down the ramp by the blinking, growling golf cart. And then Indi limped into view below, another woman trailing after her. Beth flew down the echoing corridor and crashed breathlessly into her friend, gathering the shorter woman into her arms and crushing her close.

"I thought you were dead." She hadn't realized until she said it. "Indi, I thought you were dead."

"They hurt you," Indi cried against her chest. "They hurt you because of me. I was trying—I thought . . ." She gripped the back of Beth's flannel tight in both fists. "I'm sorry I brought us here. I'm sorry, I'm sorry."

The other woman gave Beth a nod as she passed by. She had something under her arm. A Ziploc, and inside it, a grisly little sphere trailing wisps of nervous tissue and a hand cradling it, its fingers limp, sheared off at the wrist—Beth closed her eyes. She held Indi close and rocked her gently, taking as much of her weight as she could. "It's all right. You can just sew me back up again. Don't cry, Indi. It's all right."

Zia and her friends, or coconspirators, or fellow trans militia, or whatever they were, had come prepared. They went into dry storage with surgical precision, empty duffel bags over their shoulders, as others emerged fully laden. A short way down the Screw, the other half of the crew were looting the weapons lockers while Robbie and a short, squat woman with a shotgun kept watch over the central avenue and the half dozen guards lined up shivering against the opposite wall in underwear and sports bras. A few people had come out of the residential threads to watch, mostly in silence, some shouting questions.

"It's okay," Beth said again, stroking Indi's hair and planting a bloody kiss on her friend's forehead. "It's okay. We're getting out of here. We'll go get Fran.

"We're going to be okay."

♀

Ramona stood and stared at the two women making out on the picnic table while Elton John sang about lying down on linen sheets. *Viv doesn't know,* she thought, her drunken mind chewing its way reluctantly through the unpleasant thought. *She doesn't know, or else she's playing with her.* She took half a step toward the shadowed couple, then paused as Fran broke the suction of their kiss.

"Wait," said Fran, reaching down to take Viv's hand off her thigh. Ramona's heart flew up into her throat. "Wait, wait. I can't do this. Stop."

Viv grinned. "Please. I can smell how bad you want it."

"I have a . . . a girlfriend."

Viv snorted laughter. "Oh fuck you," she purred playfully, leaning forward to kiss Fran again, to lick the arch of the other woman's neck. "You're really gonna leave me with my cock in my hand? After the eyes you've been making at me all summer?"

Her fingers slipped into the fork of Fran's thighs. Ramona saw the trans girl struggling, heard her hissing, *no-no-no*, and then the sound of a zipper. Viv jumped back as though she'd been burned, clutching the hand she'd forced into Fran's lap against her chest. "You bitch," she squeaked, her voice high and tight. "You cunt piece of shit. That's rape. Fucking tranny. Fucking monster. Undisclosed fucking genital rape."

Fran was crying as she frantically zipped her jeans and did up the buttons with trembling fingers. "Please, I'll leave, I'll never tell anyone, I'll get another job at the bunker. It's fine. It's fine. I'm sorry. You're right. This was so awful of me but please, please—"

Viv lowered her hand, suddenly expressionless. "Shut up," she said. "Shut your fake fucking Barbie mouth." She was silent for a long, long moment as Fran sniffled and shivered, still sitting like a child on the picnic table's edge, her slim legs dangling above the patio. Ramona started toward them, crouching down, trying with all her drunken presence of mind to place her feet carefully and without sound. Twelve feet. Eleven. Ten. The wind picked up, sweeping sand over the bricks.

"All right," said Viv as Ramona came up behind her. The other woman's hand drifted to the automatic holstered at her hip. Elton John was still singing. It felt so real, he said, and Ramona found that it did, that everything had become clear and sharp and definite.

Viv's hand closed on the pistol's grip. "Fuck it," she said. "I'll make it quick."

Ramona darted forward and seized a handful of the other woman's hair. She tugged her knife out of its sheath. Viv grunted, twisting, and drove an elbow back into her ribs. Once. Twice. Fran, eyes wide, clapped her hands over her mouth to stifle a shriek as inside the restaurant Sir Elton, who must now be licking himself in a London alley full of other men, mouth bloody and claws ragged, scraps of flesh caught in his teeth, flew into the final chorus.

Hold me closer, tiny dancer.

Ramona stuck the knife into the side of Viv's neck, and the rest of the older woman's sentence, whatever it was, gurgled out through the ragged slit as she jerked the blade back toward herself through muscle, skin, and tendon. She tore it free and stabbed Viv again, this time in the chest. The taller woman took a double fistful of her shirt and hung on grimly, jaw set and eyes bulging, as blood sheeted down her throat. Ramona twisted the knife. Viv's grip went slack. She folded up and fell.

"Hold me closer, Tony Danza," Ramona muttered, half-numb. She knelt and wiped her knife on Viv's jacket, leaving a dark streak of blood.

"What?" Fran stared at her like she'd grown a second head. The trans girl's voice was reedy with terror. "What? Why?"

"Go," said Ramona. "Get out of here. Now."

The other girl scrambled down off the table and skipped over Viv's outflung arm with a whimper of fear, never taking her eyes off Ramona until she was well clear of the patio. Then she put her head down and took off up the beach at a flat sprint. Ramona watched her go, breathing hard in spite of the clean air and the soft, soothing sound of the waves.

What the fuck did I just do?

PART THREE

TERF WAR

Internally, I'm thinking, of course trans girls all love and fuck each other. Who else will? When I first learned the term *brick* for those square never-will-be-passable trans women, it was auxiliary to an explanation for another term, *masonry*: as in brick-on-brick love—only bricks get stuck to other bricks.

Except what do you do with the meanness of the word *masonry* itself—it was other trans women, the only ones that bricks could supposedly trust, who came up with that hilariously cruel slang. Brick-on-brick betrayal. But we have to understand each other well to be so cruel.

—Torrey Peters, *Infect Your Friends and Loved Ones*

I

LIGHTHOUSE

When Fran reached the Screw, it was already burning. A few women stood outside it in the smoldering wreckage of the camp. She joined them, staggering uphill, feet blistered in her evening flats after a long night of creeping through the woods and side roads, too afraid of TERF kill squads to risk a direct route. Smoke guttered out of the half-open blast doors. The dull orange glow of flames flickered within. She smelled gasoline and cooking flesh, a stink like pork left too long on the grill.

I'm never going to have a cunt. Tears rolled down her cheeks as she watched flames lick at the opening. A fiery red slit. Her cock still burned with the memory of Viv's fingers finding it, worming through her unzipped jeans to caress its stiffening length in the half-second before disgust curdled the other woman's hungry expression, in the split second before Ramona staggered drunk out of the dark and stabbed Viv in the throat. That gaping wound, slick and pinkish red where the starlight touched its ragged lips. She imagined setting her lips to that fragile gash, tonguing its depths, kissing beads of sweat and blood off the wet landscape of its interior.

"Fran!"

Robbie came toward her from the north side of camp through the stinging smoke. He had blood on the side of his face, and more crusted the shoulder of his hoodie. It was one of hers, actually. She took a panicked half step toward him, then stopped short. He hadn't opened his arms for her. He stopped not far away, looking relieved, but not much more. The familiar leaden pressure of rejection squeezed Fran's throat. *Did I lose him?*

"What happened?" she asked.

He told her. His voice was flat, his eyes averted. The fertility clinic. The men and the fight with Doe and the mad drive back to Exeter where he'd met up with Zia's people. Beth and the twins and the chain gang and the bus in the woods. When he talked about shooting his way into the Screw to get Indi, his shoulders grew so tense, his neck so rigid that she wanted to run to him and hug him close. Instead she let him talk until his words dried up while around them ash blew in the chilly predawn wind. Until all he had left to say was a dull, cold "I told you."

She swallowed past the lump in her throat, casting around desperately for some reason she hadn't believed, for "Robbie, I—"

"Apologize later." He *did* look at her, then, and the anger in his pinched mouth and narrowed eyes silenced her as quickly and as totally as a slap. "I have a car hidden downhill. Not far. We have to go before the TERFs get here."

"What?" Viv whispering in her ear on the dance floor. Viv clutching the front of Ramona's shirt as blood ran down her chin. Teach in the woods, her huge pale eyes retracing the path of Beth's arrow to find them standing in among the waving ferns. "Why would they come?"

"Because we helped half the workers Sophie promised them escape," he said, watching a woman Fran had seen once in the gym pick through a pile of greasy ash that might have been a tent. "And if they haven't figured it out already, they will soon."

"What happened to her?" Blond hair and hungry mouth. Chocolate milk on plump pink lips. "Sophie, I mean."

"Dead," Robbie said shortly, turning and starting back through the wreckage of the camp. Fran followed him in silence, looking back toward the city only once as approaching headlights flashed and shivered through the trees in the forest below.

♀

They took the van and the two pickups Zia and her people had come down in northwest along a muddy logging road on which they became mired twice and had to get out to lay down planks and heave the rusted vehicle out of dark, sucking muck that spattered them as the tires spun. Then onto Route 125, cutting back northeast through Raymond and Epping, where there was an uncleared jam at the exit for Route 4 that forced them to rumble offroad down a steep hill overgrown with briars and leafless saplings draped in strangler vines.

Beth, with a thoroughly stoned Indi snoring softly against her shoulder, watched the rusted-out tangle of cars go by through one of the van's tiny cross-hatched windows. They were jammed in rail to rail, a landslide of metal from back when the roads were intact and people had thought there was somewhere to run to. Princess, a trans girl she knew who'd used to grow weed with her partners on a little farm outside Seabrook, had told her once that at the Canadian border there were rivers of abandoned cars, miles and miles of them left to rust and ruin by frantic women who'd found themselves caught between checkpoint guards and an oncoming swarm of men.

It made her think of V's broken skull, remembering the early days of t. rex. Of Tara seized up stiff, eyes staring at nothing, stinking of piss and vomit in their motel room's bathtub. Back then it had seemed like there was no bottom to the horror, as though passing houses where men had turned and killed their families in the night and now rampaged around inside, smashing furniture and shattering dishes as they tried to find a way out of their mausoleums, would be all she ever did for as long as she lived. It had never stopped. Not really.

They hit level ground with a grinding scrape as the van bottomed out for a moment, wheels spraying gravel and loose chunks of pavement before it thumped back onto the road just past the edges of the pileup. Beth imagined being caught in that, trying to worm your way through tangles of hot, twisted metal and broken glass, trying to herd your screaming kids, maybe with a broken arm dangling at your side, as the men who had been your father, your brother, your husband, your son, every man you'd ever fucked or kissed or held or screamed at, closed in from all sides in an unthinking avalanche of teeth and muscle.

She rested her head atop Indi's. Half the other women in the back were sleeping, too. There had been a lot of crying at the start of the trip. Two of their group had died in the Screw. The tall black girl, Zia, had held one of them while she choked on her own blood. Would this be the same as the bunker? Running away from yet another home, relying on strangers to do something other than torture and exploit them? She pressed herself deeper into Indi's malleable and reassuring warmth, inhaling the weed smell caught in the other woman's thick black hair, the scent of sweaty armpits and unwashed skin. She kept thinking of Sylvia's hands clawing feebly at her face, of the fat sludge-gray bubble of depression that had popped inside her chest when she realized Corinne was really going to kill her. At first she'd thought the woman was taking her into the woods because she didn't have the nerve to pull a trigger, but if she hadn't to start with, Beth had talked it into her.

At least it would have been over, she thought, closing her eyes. *At least I wouldn't be so fucking tired all the time.*

♀

They jounced and rumbled down a logging road that cut through the woods to the north of the Screw, low-hanging branches scraping their sides and hissing against the Jeep's cloth top. The sun was coming up, and in the distance Fran could hear the raw, wild calls of men emerging from their dens to the smell of smoke and burning meat heavy on the wind. She hoped they'd go in search of that, rather than the roar of the Jeep's engine.

She looked at Robbie as his profile emerged from the predawn gloom. He was angry with her, she knew, but he'd waited. He'd been there. "You stayed behind for me."

"I had no idea where you were," said Robbie, shifting up as the rutted track began to climb. "I was torching the motor pool to keep it away from the TERFs. We were gonna send some of Zia's cis girls into town for you tomorrow."

Her lip trembled. She felt a sour, burning kind of misery at the back of her throat. *Don't cry.* "Oh."

He glanced at her, that high brow furrowed, his black hair escaping in strands from the knot at the back of his head. "Why *did* you come back?"

"A TERF tried to kill me," she said spitefully, attempting not to relish the unassailable position of her victimhood too much. "She was trying to fuck me, all over me. I couldn't get her off, and then she put her hand down my pants. Another girl saw it happen and stabbed her right in front of me. In the neck."

The venom drained from her as she recounted the story. Her fingers tingled. Her own voice sounded far away and thin. The thumps as the Jeep took each frost heave and rut seemed to jolt up not through her body but into a dumb sack of meat and bone. Robbie looked horrified and furious, his mouth twitching.

"Go ahead," she said numbly. "Tell me it's my fault."

"It's your fault."

"Well, what about you? What happens to the other people in the bunker now?"

"They got shares from the storerooms. Medicine. Herbs and hormones for the people who needed it."

"There were kids living there." She couldn't seem to shut up, though digging at him only made her feel worse. "Babies."

He wouldn't look at her. Leaves and needles slapped the windscreen as they plowed through an especially thick brake of vegetation, roots knotting the track with twisted ribs. "That place was sick, Fran. They're better off in a normal town."

"It was *safe*."

"You know Beth wasn't working in the kitchens, right?"

Yes. She was always crying, and I knew. "No. What?"

"She was a daddy. They took her off farm detail because a cis girl hooked up with her, then got cold feet about it. So they put her on a rotation where she'd dress up in boy drag and fuck middle-aged women."

Fran started to cry. "I mean, if she'd said something, if she'd told us maybe I could have—"

"You're being hateful."

She punched her own thigh, wishing for the first time since her early twenties for the gentle endorphin wash of dragging a safety pin's sterilized point down her inner forearm. Flare of pale, sickly pain. Release. "Why are you so mad at me?"

"I'm not—" Robbie gripped the steering wheel hard enough that his knuckles went white. He took a deep breath as they toiled up a muddy slope onto the highway, skirting a derelict army troop carrier, its canvas slashed and sun-faded, its tires flat and skewing to the sides as time and weather bowed it. "I *am* mad at you," he said at last. "A couple cis women smile at you and suddenly Beth's shit on your shoe? I tell you

Beth's headed for a chain gang and you won't even fucking admit something *might* be going on?"

She said nothing. A hundred rejoinders flashed through her mind, but she discarded each in turn. *You don't know me, what I've been through. How dare you fucking judge me? You have no idea what it's like to be a trans woman here, to be hunted and hated and played with like a sex doll.* Some of it was true, maybe, but none of it really mattered. He was right. A pretty girl had given her a card with "YOU'RE CIS" printed on it and promised her a boutique pussy and that was that. She'd closed her eyes and plugged her ears. "I'm sorry," she said at last, her voice small.

He was silent. The trees on the sides of the highway were turning, leaves tumbling through the early morning sunlight. The ones in town were still mostly green. She rested her cheek against the window and watched the signs on the side of the road blur past. Roads rendered impassable by wrecks and New England winter. Towns burned off the map by "controlled resource denial" bombing runs in the government's last days as Pelosi and Ivanka fought over the dying federal body, D.C. carved into a neo-feudal civil war between factions that formed and collapsed on a daily basis. She slept, and in her dreams she lay on an operating table while Indi and her father stood on either side of her. Her father was naked, and though she wanted to look away her eyes were glued to the dark, curly hair between his legs, the curve of his circumcised penis.

Indi was at the foot of the table. Had she been there the whole time? People watched them from the shadows, whispering to one another. "Hold still," said her friend, pushing her skirt up around her hips. "If we're going to make them match, I need you to hold very, very still."

Fran woke to the smell of the ocean and the juddering rumble of the Jeep crossing a stony stream. Or, no, not a stream. The ocean lay outside her window, four or five feet from the road's edge. A tidal channel, then, and far across the water a forested shore, the tree line broken here and there by neat little white houses now falling into the sea.

"Where are we?"

"Portsmouth," said Robbie. "We're out on the north hook of New Castle Island. That's Maine across the Piscataqua."

A concrete fort built back into the rough, rocky slope of the coast stood behind a mossy, birdshit-spattered brick wall, its rectangular bulk interrupted by a pair of raised semicircular platforms and a narrow observation roost with only a single slit, facing the sea, for visibility. The twisted skulls of men hung from poles set to either side of the drive. It looked straight out of *Saving Private Ryan*. Probably it *was* from World War II. Beyond it, the spit of land stretched from the main body of the island to a chain-link fence and, past that, a few wrecked sheds and outbuildings and a stretch of crumbling wall. At the end of the point stood a lighthouse, whitewash salt-eaten, widow's walk rusted and sagging on one side where a support strut had come loose or rusted through. Beth and a few other girls were waiting in a cleared gravel yard not far from the water. Seabirds soared on the rising thermals and dove like falling lawn darts down into the waves.

♀

Teach led Ramona along the pier past a crew of city women loading barrels onto a flat-bottomed barge. "Siphoned diesel," she explained. "We agitate it to see what's still viable, then strain out settled detritus. Amazing how much fuel you can dig out of a few square miles of suburban wasteland. Land Rovers. Jaguars. The midlife crisis of the American male finally produces a usable result."

Circling seagulls cried. Their watery shit slapped against the jetty not far ahead. At high tide the water rose almost even with the concrete surface; now it lapped at stones crusted with barnacles and mussels and draped with slimy seaweed. A trio of harbor seals watched them from open water a few dozen yards away, wise and inscrutable with their whiskery mustaches and big, dark eyes. Ramona wondered what it would be like to live like they did, diving down into the silent dark, your whole body suited almost perfectly to your life.

"Beautiful, aren't they?"

"They are," Ramona answered, coming to a halt as Teach stepped to the pier's edge to watch the seals vanish one by one into the slate-gray water. Her black hair was down today, the wind catching at loose strands. She'd acquired a new coat, navy wool lined with pale silk, since giving her last to the old woman at Hunan Palace, and she looked a little like an Old Hollywood actress with her loose scarf and fitted slacks, her pale skin ever so slightly sun-kissed.

"You kept your head in Raymond," said the older woman. "Not how I'd have broken the news to Vivian, but you can hardly be blamed for guessing a few drinks would soften her up. Still . . ." She shook her head. "How's the arm?"

"Healing," said Ramona. The truth was she'd done too good a job slashing herself up believably—the whole arm was stiff and the cuts itched enough to keep her up at night. But she'd seen Viv use that knife before; mere nicks and scratches would've raised questions. She flexed her hand and grimaced as the motion tugged at scabs and stitches. "Doctor Fleming says I'll be all right. Might lose some mobility in my pinky."

"Shame. Though considering Vivian's knife work I'd say you got off easy."

She knows! screamed a tinny little voice at the back of Ramona's mind. *She knows! She knows! She'll kill you!*

"I'd tend to agree, ma'am."

Teach laughed bitterly. "So, a drunken stabbing, our allies in the Widdel bunker up in smoke, half our Raymond labor force in the wind, and my hand-picked replacement to manage the town goes over my head and requests a transfer back to Baltimore, making me look like an ineffectual idiot."

"Ma'am, it could have happened to any—"

Pale eyes flicked toward Ramona, hair blowing across them like lines of static crawling up a TV set. "You'll have to learn to allow me my little bouts of self-flagellation, major, if we're going to be working together so closely."

Ramona blinked. Her palms felt suddenly damp. There was a sour taste at the back of her mouth. "Major?"

"I'm putting you in charge of our work in Raymond. The scrapping and transport of USS *Hyannis*, manhunting, the recruitment of suitable labor. You've done well with cleaning out the city. The rest is pickup. Scavenging. You'd be wasted here."

"I'm honored, ma'am." She was, in a way. It felt like one of those rare moments when her mother had looked at her with undisguised pride, with a kind of rough hope and ferocious love. It made her want to cry. "I won't let you down."

I want my daddy.

"That bunker," Teach mused, still watching the water where the seals had gone down. Seagulls now rested there, rising and falling with the gentle waves, beaks buried in their feathered breasts. "Whatever happened there, it isn't the first time we've lost a New England asset to sabotage. I want you to find the people responsible." Her voice was calm, but Ramona saw the tendons flex as her left hand became a fist. "Make them understand what it means to cross the Legion."

II

THE BEAUTIFUL PEOPLE

No electricity at Fort Dyke, which is what Zia and her people had renamed the coastal battery they'd scoured, bleach-washed, and occupied eight months ago, before Zia and Mariana had infiltrated the Screw. Eleven women lived there in a musty communal bunkroom. Thirteen now, with Robbie the only man. Their lucky fourteenth. Bilbo Baggins to their company of dwarves. There was so much estrogen in there it was practically sloshing ankle-deep on the floor. And Fran. Fran was there, too.

In the three days they'd stayed on the rocky spit of land, he'd made a point of being where Fran wasn't as often as possible. Walking along the stony shoreline with Beth. Drinking stale instant coffee with Indi at the custodian's house, where Leda and her kid lived with the four Fort Dykers whose chronic shit and disabilities made roughing it in a bunk bed untenable. There was the lighthouse, too, where they stored their computing equipment and the diesel generator. An older woman named Rachel who had awful night terrors slept there most of the time with her wife, Keesha.

There was plenty to do. Fish to smoke, bird shit to scrape, traps to check, chamber pots to lug off into the woods where the contents were tipped into long trenches filled in square by square and marked with mold-speckled orange surveying flags so whoever dug the next one didn't accidentally scoop up a big shovelful of shit. But no matter how intently he ignored Fran's miserable looks and threw himself into whatever chores he could take on or invent, the Screw came creeping after him on bloody feet. Doe getting up on her knees in the rearview. Corinne clawing at him as they tumbled down the hillside. The gate captain, Mercer, and her final nasal plea. *Bleeeease.* He heard it in the dead noise of his ringing ear, the one Doe had blown out before he killed her.

At dinner on their second night, served early and dispersed over the sprawling, ramshackle bulk of the custodian's house, he sat alone at the foot of the narrow steps leading up from the kitchen to the second floor and stirred his fish chowder without enthusiasm, wondering about taking bricks from the old fort's sea-facing wall to repair the barricade around Fort Dyke. Snatches of conversation drifted in from the living room, where Beth was rubbing Indi's feet and a few of the older women were knitting, wooden needles click-click-clicking in a peaceful rhythm. Someone was talking about Grace, the girl who'd died beside him in the Screw. The gray tomcat who'd stowed away in the bunker's van lay dozing on the back of the couch. He saw Fran come in through the front, talking with a short, chubby cis girl with a shock of violently purple hair, and drained the rest of his bowl, leaving it in the sink on his way to the back door.

The sun was sinking over the tidal river to the west of the spit, bloody orange light rippling over the water. The wind had picked up, bringing spray from the breakers with it, and the bullet wound in his shoulder was aching miserably in the cold and damp. That morning, it had been so stiff he'd had to dig the pommel of his knife into it just to unwork the knots. Indi had told him he was lucky, that if it hadn't been a through-and-through it could've made a mess out of his whole arm, but that didn't make it feel any better. He went quickly down the rickety back steps and started toward the laundry lines. He could start bringing things in before the wind got worse.

He was carrying an armful of moth-eaten linens back to the fort when Zia stepped out from the shadow of the tumbledown maintenance shed and fell into step beside him. "Lotta sheets," said the tall, angular woman, flicking open her lighter and touching flame to the end of a hand-rolled cigarette clamped in her teeth. "When we vote tomorrow I'll be sure to bring that up. 'Boy can lug a sheet.'"

"Whatever you all decide, it's nice of you to let us stay this long. I just want to pitch in."

She blew smoke out her nostrils. "Bullshit. You feel bad about the bunker. It's eating you."

His shoulder throbbed. "I've killed people before."

"Oh, was it super great for you then, too? Just BLAM"—she mimed shooting a kneeling figure—"and then afterward you were really well-adjusted?"

Robbie's ears burned. Part of him wanted to slug this near-stranger, another spur-of-the-moment decision he'd made to throw his lot in with people he didn't know, chasing a sense of belonging he didn't deserve. Midge lay at the end of that road. The gun. The cellar door. The choked, glottal slobbering sound that had come up through the floorboards all that endless night. "You don't owe me anything," he said, his voice wooden. "I'm not staying, one way or the other."

She put a hand on his arm and drew him gently to a halt, though his shoulder pulsed with hot, dull agony and his nerves sang out, telling him to run, to drop the sheets and pillowcases that belonged on bodies worthy of gentleness and rest. "Nobody ever got anything from a boss by asking nicely," she said softly. "Someone has the power to make things better and they keep not doing that, sooner or later all that's left to do is put two in the back of the greedy bitch's head. Shit, you're an Indian, right? You know what happens when you wait for the people holding the whip to grow a heart, or you listen to the nice white people who coordinate their protests with the cops."

Her hand slipped from his arm and they went on together without speaking for a while, boots crunching in the gravel of the car yard. The waves boomed against the shale on their left as they came into the shadow of the fort with its ragged flags—trans and gay—snapping in the wind from a pole atop its observation tower. Robbie thought about the night he'd tried to leave Indi's, after he'd helped Fran bring Beth home. After they'd fucked in the woods with the moonlight spilling over their unwashed skin.

"This is a good place," said Zia. "I mean, we've got our bullshit dyke drama and whatever, we're all fuckin' traumatized and sick and they don't make psych meds anymore where we can get at them, so that can get a little rough, but we're a family, too." She flicked the butt of her cigarette out over the rocks and into the breakers in an extraordinary arc. "You seem nice, Robert. So do your friends. Most of us want you to stay.

Honestly, the TERFs keep moving north and we could use someone who knows how to shoot.

"Just do what you have to do to put this shit to bed, or you'll be no good to anyone."

♀

On their second night at Fort Dyke, after the quiet funeral for the two girls left behind in the burning Screw, Beth went to Indi's room in the custodian's house and knocked just after sunset. She slipped inside at the other woman's husky "Beth?" and saw Indi sit up in her bed, huge shoulders naked and smooth in the moonlight, ribbed green bedspread held to her breast with one hand. "What is it? Is something wrong?"

"No," said Beth. "Can I sit?"

Indi patted the edge of the bed and Beth sank down, one leg under her and one still touching the warped floorboards. "I've been running around after Fran for three years," she said, tearing up the moment she began to speak. "I kept thinking I was in love with her. Maybe I was. Am. But I think mostly I just wanted her to . . . make me real, the way you're real when the beautiful people look at you, and talk to you, and let you fuck them.

"And then Corinne took me into the woods, and I thought I'd never see you again. I thought I'd die out there without even getting to say goodbye." She let out a little sob, then held up a finger to silence Indi as the other woman opened her mouth, probably to say something comforting. "Let me finish, or I'll never get it out." She took a deep, shuddering breath. "I love you, Indi, and I want to go where you go, whether it's here or wherever, and rub your stupid tiny feet and fuck you every fucking day."

She stammered to a halt, unable to meet Indi's eyes, unable to think anything but that she'd broken the rule. She'd offered herself as though someone might want her, as though she didn't have to wait to be asked before her touch transmuted from invasion to caress. And then Indi's arms were around her and she was falling back into the tangled sheets and blankets under the other woman's soft, enveloping weight. Indi's lips found hers. Their teeth clicked awkwardly together for a moment before their tongues met, gliding over bone and the soft ridges of their palates. Beth gripped fistfuls of Indi's sides. She twisted and pressed her lips to the older woman's neck, running her tongue along the velvet crease where it met her buried collarbones.

You feel so good, she thought, palming one of Indi's breasts and tweaking the dark nipple between thumb and forefinger. It stiffened. A muffled groan against her shoulder. *I don't care if you love me, as long as I get to be with you.*

Indi pushed two fingers past her lips and Beth's eyelids fluttered with the sleepy ecstasy of that sense of fullness. In and out. Drool running down her chin as she moved to follow Indi's hand, to prolong the slow fucking of her mouth. Her breath came in shallow pants. She kneaded Indi's breast as her free hand slipped between the rolls of her waist, fingers walking gently over tender skin. "Am I hurting you?" Indi whispered, pulling her fingers free to stroke Beth's cheek and leaving a warm streak of saliva down almost to her chin.

Beth wriggled, smiling. "Not enough."

♀

"Fuckin' bullshit!" Leda cried from across the firepit, where stacked driftwood burned just above the tide mark in a circle of dark stones. She had a low, lazy-sounding voice, all vocal fry. Her six-year-old, George, sat curled asleep in her lap, his breath stirring his long brown curls where they fell across his little mouth. "There is no fuckin' way, Steph."

"I'm telling you I saw him," said Steph, who was tiny and doughy and had something distinctively trailer-parky about her under the purple hair and lime-green tights and the DYKE knuckle tattoo on her left hand. "He was in a ShopRite in Norwalk, like, six months after T. Day. He was looting beans."

"Steve fucking Martin did not survive the apocalypse."

Fran, wrapped in an old wool blanket at the edge of the circle of firelight, ran again and again through the feeling that had raced up from the pit of her stomach into her throat when she'd held that laminated card with its little XX. She'd had a few puffs of the joint they were passing around, hoping it would mellow her out, but instead it seemed to have stuck her in a short, deep rut. She kept imagining her fingers inside Sophie, the times she'd put her cock in the other girl (*because she promised you a cunt*), and then the body. Dead.

Zia leaned forward into the firelight, grinning evilly. "Fuck Steve Martin. Have the new girls heard what happened to the Harry Potter lady?"

Most of the women around the fire groaned, though a few straightened up attentively. Beth shook her head, blushing at being made the center of attention. Her bruises were fading from dark purple to brown and yellow, as though someone had spray painted her for autumn camouflage. She sat leaning against Indi's side, hands in the pouch of her hoodie. It felt so fucking weird to sit on the rocky beach as the stars came out, swapping stories about what had happened to the world's celebrities when the big one hit. It felt like the end of the world was prowling the limits of the firelight, waiting for the embers to go out.

"Okay, so, first off she ended up being a crazy TERF, like, super intense. When the news about t. rex started, she hired a bunch of woman contractors—remember Blackwater, those sickos in Iraq? She had them all up at her castle in Scotland with a bunch of her rich girlfriends and they were all drinking wine, kissing her ass, planning out how to rebuild society. They had their sons, husbands, whatever, in some kind of hermetically sealed guest house she'd had built special in case of germ warfare or something."

Robbie sat down next to her. She hadn't seen him coming down the beach. Her stomach clenched as he said something to the older woman, June, on his other side and then turned to listen to Zia's story. *He hates me. I had a chance and now it's done and he hates me and I have nothing. I have nothing at all.*

"So, they get exactly one day into their girl-power retreat and then it turns out one of the friends has PCOS and doesn't know it. She flips in the middle of the night and starts ripping into the other guests before someone knocks over a lamp or something. I guess they'd been stockpiling diesel and kerosene." Zia mimed an explosion with her hands, fists coming together before unfurling into spread palms. "Anyway, the Blackwater bitches who survived the blast looted what was left of the place and bugged out. Left everyone else to burn alive, and finally the whole castle collapsed. Real *Masque of the Red Death* shit."

A log popped somewhere in the fire. Sparks eddied from its shifting architecture. Fran imagined the beams of that old castle coming down on her, crushing her body like Mrs. Danvers in *Rebecca* because she wouldn't let go of a dream of a woman who couldn't be loved, or touched, or known. She imagined the heat searing her skin. The breathless moment of impact. Everyone around the fire sat silent, as though thinking the same thing.

Robbie's hand found hers. Her mind raced even faster for a moment, trying to parse the strength of his grip, the way he slid his fingers into hers, the set of his jaw in the firelight. And then the flurrying thoughts fell away. She squeezed his hand and shifted closer, resting her head on his shoulder. "I'm sorry," she whispered.

"I know," he said. "It's okay."

"What happened to the men in the guest house?" asked Indi, accepting the joint from Steph and taking a dainty little hit.

"Oh, the locks and air filters all seized up when the castle's generators blew," said Zia. "They must have suffocated, but a girl I met who came over on the *Saffron Spirit* from Aberdeen a few years ago said when she and her friends went to pick the place over, they heard something scratching at the walls from the inside."

♀

Beth and Indi walked down the beach hand in hand, Fran and Robbie a few dozen yards ahead of them. The crumbling wall of the old fort, raised during the Revolution, lay on their left while the river sighed in and out over the slate and the dark sand on their right. "What do you think they're talking about?" asked Indi.

Beth shrugged. "How hard it is to be conventionally attractive?"

Indi laughed. She caught a glimpse of motion in the shadow of the ruined wall. A dimpled white curve of backside. A dark hand gliding over it to slide a finger up into its crack, and a soft, hitching sigh of pleasure that the wind stole as it whipped in off the river. Zia and Steph? She smiled. Her father had always said salt air was the best aphrodisiac, no matter how often she begged him not to say "aphrodisiac." He'd been matter-of-fact about sex. "Try a man out before you marry him," he'd said to her more than once. "Leave chastity to the Christian girls."

And she had. As her body bloomed and swelled she threw it at whoever would condescend to take it. First to the boys at high school who'd fuck her, but not hold her hand, then to the white girls at Dartmouth-

Hitchcock who let her eat them out and told her that her skin was like caramel or coffee or sandalwood, though they never called her beautiful. Not exactly. She'd married Vikram during her residency more out of despair than anything else, accepting his tedious conversation and whining, needling methods of manipulation as a fair price to pay for his willingness to be seen with her in public. She remembered how he'd pissed and moaned when she told him Fran was coming to stay in the spare room over the garage.

She's a family friend, Vik. Our mothers taught at the same high school and she's transitioning, having a rough time at home. I want to do this for her.

So what I want isn't very important, then.

It must be nice, arguing with the bitch version of me you spin out of thin air whenever I don't do what you want.

In the end, after he spent a week huddled in their basement in a plastic decon tent while she and Fran did what stockpiling they could in between barricading windows and doors, he'd caught the virus, as she'd known he would, and begged her through chattering teeth to be with him, to give him something to end it and to lie with him while it happened. She'd stood there at his bedside, watching his sores redden, his skin stretch tight over pockets of lymph and settled blood, and thought of how he never remembered how sensitive she was where her belly met her groin, how he watched her mouth with faint disgust whenever she ate, when she could make herself eat, and how he hovered at her shoulder in the supermarket and asked, again and again, *Are you sure you need that?*

So she gave him his morphine and left, zipping the plastic tent behind her as he crawled out of the bed, trailing sheets and blankets, reaching toward her, moaning her name, and she went upstairs and had a coffee and a piece of tiramisu while he died. Later she and Fran had buried him under the compost heap in the backyard, so he could nourish something for a change. She'd hardly thought about him since, except when she couldn't eat, or when someone nagged her about something meaningless.

Beside her, Beth stooped, straightened, and sent a flat stone whirling out over the water. It skipped twice, silvery ripples unfolding over the river's dark surface, and vanished into a gentle wave that broke over the shingle and raced up the shore to kiss their bare feet. Bitter cold.

III

NATURAL WOMAN

Zia had her gauges out. She was dabbing at the piercings with a wet rag. "The short version is, we'd like you to stay."

It was just before breakfast at the custodian's house. Zia sat at the long Formica-topped kitchen table with its overflowing ashtray and stout eggplant salt and pepper shakers with a tall, heavyset enby named Linden, Indi's friend Mariana, and a hunched, rail-thin trans woman named Persephone with buck teeth and long, shaggy black hair.

Beth's heart raced. She sat opposite the Fort Dykers, Fran on her left and Indi on her right. Robbie stood by the stove, ripping noisily at a hunk of fresh brown bread with honey. He paused, open mouth full of half-chewed mush. Beth wondered if he breathed through his nose that loud when he sucked cock. Fran looked pale. Indi's expression was carefully neutral.

Zia worked her left gauge back into its hole, her distended earlobe squeezed between her thumb and forefinger. "You'd better hear the long version before you answer."

Mariana spoke to the younger woman in rapid Spanish, then made an unmistakable neck-wringing gesture. Zia leaned forward. "I don't know a non-psycho way to translate that, so I'll be blunt," she said. "We'd like your help killing TERFs."

Sylvia staring up at her, face turning purple, snot leaking from her flared nostrils as she tried desperately to suck air into her lungs. V's head with that gory red notch bashed into it. The man on the top of the roof crashing into her, bearing her down in a lover's embrace. She still couldn't take a shit without a stinging reminder of that day. That moment. The mantis crawling up a blade of grass. Teach's lantern eyes moving unerringly to find her through a hundred yards of underbrush and new-growth pine.

"You're fighting them?" asked Fran, turning a little pale. "There are what, twenty thousand women in the Legion?"

"We've been nibbling at them as they move north. Picking off scouts. Trapping roads with IEDs." She replaced the other gauge and set her hands on the table. She had a burn scar on the back of one hand, a smear of shining, waxy melted skin. "Fran, this Pierce TERF who saved you when you got outed"—Beth looked at Fran, her stomach turning. Why hadn't she said anything?—"Our plant in Boston says she's just been put in charge of the Legion's work in Seabrook after Teach's first pick went back to Baltimore; some kind of internal conflict between Teach and the Matriarchs."

"Probably feuding to the death over whether to spell it w-o-m-y-n or w-o-m-b-y-n," muttered Indi.

"Would you meet with her? See what she can do for us?"

Fran darted a nervous glance at Robbie; Beth could practically hear the gears in the other girl's skull turning. "I'll do it," she blurted suddenly, cheeks coloring. "Just tell me what you want. I'll get it."

"I'll fight," said Beth. She felt a momentary flicker of pride in herself for how steady she sounded. Under the table she gripped Indi's hand as hard as she could. *I will never fucking leave you.* "I'll do whatever it takes."

"Me too," Robbie said quietly.

Indi nodded. "I can convert the great room into a clinic if you can loan me a few girls to shift tables."

Beth's heart beat hard against her breastbone. She felt, for the first time in her life, what she'd longed to feel since the day she'd watched through the just-cracked bedroom door as her sister Debbie and her friends giggled and painted nails and whispered cutting gossip, an ache in her chest she wouldn't put words to for a decade and change. She felt sisterhood.

Linden, who maintained the fort's little library and kept the minutes of its innumerable meetings, laid a map of New Hampshire out on the table. They did it with almost cartoonish fussiness, smoothing the rolled paper with the flats of their hands and setting mugs on the corners after wiping their bottoms clean with a little handkerchief they produced from the pocket of their slacks. "Our Boston friend," they said, "also tells us the reason Pierce was sent to Seabrook is that Teach considers her both degenerate—a chaser—and an efficient killer driven by self-loathing to show she's twice as brutal as her sisters. She's here to clean house and prove herself. Kill everything between us and the TERFs up in Bath."

"We'd like to give their first hunting parties a warm fuckin' welcome." Zia flashed a wolfish grin. "We'll thin them out. Get them shaking in their Doc Martens."

Mariana slammed a fist on the table hard enough that Beth jumped a little. She bit out something venomous and raised her chin running her fingers up her throat and then flicking them in a throwing-away motion. Zia translated. "She says there may be a lot of them, but they're the same stupid white women who thought pussy hats could overthrow the government. They're complacent narcissists used to publishing unreadable papers and letting men do their dirty work.

"She says when it comes to blood, they'll be worthless."

♀

Indi crossed the courtyard in the sea wall's shadow, toward the chicken coops and the wire run where the hens pecked fruitlessly at the hard earth. All morning she'd been thinking of the lone little girl born in that nightmare maternity ward. Surely even Sophie, that broken, dead-eyed reptile—*a child's plaintive screams of "Indi, Indi!" through the bathroom door*—wouldn't have killed a baby. Someone must have taken her. Kept her safe.

Indi unlatched the back of the first coop and plucked warm eggs speckled with straw and chicken shit out of the nesting boxes within. In a matter of minutes she'd cleaned out the four ramshackle coops and nearly filled her wicker basket. Last night, with Beth's face between her legs and Beth's cum drying on her tits, she'd thought of the woman then, too. A girl, really. A teenager. By the time she'd thought to look for her they'd already left the Screw behind. *Maybe she died in the camp*, she thought as she started back toward the whitewashed house, its clapboard siding weathered and salt-eaten, its gutters bent under the weight of whatever leaves and airborne detritus the wind had piled there over the years. *Maybe she rolled into a river, like Mouchette.*

Indi set the eggs down on the house's weathered back stoop and, turning, lowered herself carefully before letting her body drop to the second step, which groaned under her weight as she settled back to rest. She wondered idly what it would be like to sit without a constant background hum of *will it hold me, will I fit, will it hold me, will I fit.* It felt like that on top of Beth, sometimes. Was she hurting her? If not, how long until she did? What if she got fatter and hurt Beth then, lulled into a false sense of security by prior enthusiasm, by the other woman's hoarsely eager panting under her, by her bright eyes and the hands that kneaded and held her overspilling flesh as though there were not enough of it?

She fished a cigarette from the tarnished holder Fran had given her years ago, a yellowing picture of some white lady pasted onto its inner lid, and smoked in silence for a while. *Everything is a war,* she told herself. *At least this is the right side. At least you're not harvesting a teenager's eggs to help her have a little* The Omen *baby. And Beth is safe here. Fran and Robbie are safe. As safe as anyone gets, anymore.*

On her left, George ran out of the house's shadow with a sparkling laugh, streaking from the front door with Leda following behind, bleached dreadlocks coiled over one shoulder like a heavy knotted rope.

♀

Ramona hated Raymond. She hated it so much she could hardly think straight, so much it made her want to scream. All the bougie seaside shit, the empty storefronts, the sugar shacks and oceanfront spas. And the restaurant. As she paced the full-length window in the living room of the Shaw house she worked a finger through the blood-speckled bandages Piper had wrapped for her that morning to dig at the flaky dead skin and dried blood of one of her self-inflicted cuts. She was sick of her sling, even if Jules said it made her look rakish, whatever the fuck that meant, and she was sick of being fussed over and swabbed with hydrogen peroxide. Maybe she'd feel better if she just cut the arm off. That had been her mom's sole joke, whenever one of them whined about a nick or scrape. *You want me to cut it off?*

Want me to break the other one? You'll forget all about it.

She glanced out the window toward the shrinking wreckage of *Hyannis* and started at the sight of Karin's reflection in the doorway at her back. "Don't sneak around like that," she snapped. "You gave me a fucking heart attack."

The tall, thin girl blanched apologetically. "Sorry, major. Just thought you'd want to know Jules handled that situation downtown. The t-girls in the old library."

"You don't sound too happy about it."

Karin gave her a long, opaque look. "Is it something we should celebrate, ma'am?"

Ramona flopped down into one of the Shaws' stupid modernist chairs, as expensive-looking as they were uncomfortable, and bit back a hiss of pain as she banged her cut elbow on one of its metal arms. "Don't," she spat as Karin started toward her. "If you spend one more second fussing over me I swear to Christ I'll put a bullet in your kneecap."

That's good. Scream at your staff. Piss your whole future away over some stoner eunuch who didn't even love you.

Karin stood silent, eyes downcast, face flushed. Ramona forced herself to take a steadying breath. "Anything else?"

"There's someone from the Screw here to see you."

"She can have five minutes," Ramona snapped. "But if she's here about the farms, you can tell her to fuck off. They're ours now."

Karin left. For a minute Ramona sat stewing in the bad smell of her own temper tantrum and watched the bright sodium flare of arc cutters take *Hyannis* apart at the joints. How the fuck had that thing got so far up on the shore? It must have been going like hell when it ran aground, swarming with changed men, the handful of women in the crew either dead or barricaded in a single cabin while the massive engines thundered and the deck rolled beneath their feet. Maybe they'd prayed.

She heard footsteps in the front hall. In the window a woman's reflection swam out of the dark mouth. Slim and lanky, sandy hair around her shoulders and in soft, feathery bangs creeping uncut toward dark eyes. Fran flashed a nervous smile. "I hope you don't mind," she said quietly. "But I really think we should talk."

♀

"Thanks for coming," said Rachel, hopping aside to let Beth in through the lighthouse door. The air inside was damp and cool, morning light slanting in through high, narrow windows above. Shadows lay heavy on the older woman's lined and wind-burned face and the wrinkles in her unwashed linen pants, tied off just under the stump of her right leg. She moved quickly on her crutches. "Dr. Varma said you might be able to give us a hand with a little programming problem."

The lighthouse's ground floor was a rat's nest of cables and scavenged electronics in various states of assembly. On the far wall, in a chair under the rusted spiral stair, Persephone sat hunched in front of a trio of mismatched monitors surrounded by computer towers. Somewhere out of sight a generator whined. A sprawling, unmade bed lay beside the entire setup, its tangled sheets and blankets smelling of sweat, sex, and something delicate and floral.

Beth flushed, still befuddled from sleep. "Uh, I know, like, super basic Python and Ruby, but I'll do what I can."

"One of our people in Boston got this to us last week," said Rachel, swinging herself down onto a scarred piano bench beside Persephone's chair and leaning her crutches against the wall.

Beth peered over Persephone's shoulder. A fat packet of torn, stained, and recycled paper spilled across the desk beside the keyboard, every page dark with printed diagrams. Code jammed the monitors in a dozen overlapping windows, complex and alien. "What am I even looking at here?"

"Military computer system," said Persephone in a whiny, resentful voice that immediately drove Beth insane. "Nothing wireless. Hardened—ruggedized, I guess it's called. So you can't knock it out with an EMP or a surge."

"Not military," said Rachel, bending over to scratch her stump. Beth had heard from one of the other Fort Dykers that she'd lost the leg in Iraq. "Naval. Gunnery hardware and software for some kind of battleship."

"This is way, way past anything I've worked on."

"I *told* you," Persephone groused, twisting strands of greasy hair around her finger. "We're wasting our time. We're just going to have to work harder."

Beth diplomatically ignored this, scooping the printed packet off the desk and thumbing through the opaque diagrams. "I did do a little free-lance web security back in college, though. What are you trying to do?"

Rachel's eyes gleamed with mischievous delight. "Find a way to wreck it."

IV

THE ELEPHANT

Fran looked smug as she stepped out of the hall's shadow and into the sunlight spilling through the wall-length window. Pleased with herself, like a cat lapping up spilled cream. "I think you'll want to hear what I have to say."

"Are you out of your fucking mind?" Ramona hissed, scrambling out from behind her desk. She crossed the floor between them in three long strides and grabbed the trans girl by her slender throat, a thrill of excitement pulsing in the long muscles of her thighs as that self-satisfied smile flickered and vanished. She pushed until Fran's back hit the wall. It felt good to come close to hitting her. Good to hurt someone so easily. "You want to get us both killed?"

"No one's going to know," Fran husked, clutching uselessly at Ramona's hand. She was up on her tiptoes. "Not unless you make a scene and give it up."

Dead tranny in my office? Who'd say a fucking thing?

Ramona let go of the other woman's neck with a snort of disgust. Panic came stealing back in as adrenaline bled away in caustic dribbles. She rubbed her knuckles. "We have nothing to say to each other. Get the fuck out of my office."

"You saved my life."

"I was drunk," she said bluntly. "It was a stupid mistake."

"You knew who I was. That day in the woods, with the men. And you still saved me."

Ramona glanced toward the empty doorway. Karin was out there somewhere. Jules. Piper. Sadie. Any of the two dozen Legion women or the new Maenad detachment stationed in and around Raymond. One pair of ears in the wrong place and she was as good as dead. She had a chance here, a chance to prove that Teach could rely on her, that her nasty little predilection was no more than that. Some of the women fucked their Maenads, she knew. She could do that. Pick one of the pretty ones, soft and sweet with big doe eyes and a little belly marbled with pale stretch marks.

A new one. Cauterize it. Tie a tourniquet.

Fran gave her a look she didn't like, a look that gave her a sneaking suspicion her expression had betrayed her. "Who'd they take from you?"

Ramona did hit her, then. She punched the other woman square in that wide, smirking mouth and then she was kissing those lips, soft and flushed, and her nails were scraping the fine hairs on the sides of Fran's throat as she forced a thigh between her legs and felt the stiffness of her tucked prick against it.

Stupid, she thought viciously. *Stupid, stupid, stupid.*

♀

He broke from the edge of the woods at a run, arms pumping, grass whisking over his sneakers and the legs of his jeans as he sprinted across the pavement toward the hulking black silhouette of the semitruck parked near the weigh station. Three guards. One, on the far side of the trailer not far from a stand of sumac, already dead with Veronique's knife in the back of her neck, lit cigarette tumbling from her suddenly slack lips like a little falling star. Chloe racing toward the second somewhere out of sight up near the cab and the stabbing glare of the headlights.

The third TERF caught sight of Robbie as he came up on her. Her eyes widened just before he rammed his knife up through her jaw. He yanked the blade out and caught her as she fell, lowering her twitching body to the ground. By the time the TERF gurgled her last bloody breath, Steph was already up on the truck's rear running board and picking the lock on the gate. In the shadows under the truck he saw someone wriggling wormlike next to Chloe's boots on the far side of the vehicle. Lock and chain slithered down to pavement. Women scrambled out, hair matted and tangled, the stink of piss and shit unfolding like a soiled flower into the night air. Some of them were crying. One, hair-thin scratches on her naked thighs, screamed at nothing before Steph got a hand over her mouth. Workers bound for whatever the TERFs were doing up north.

"It's okay," she whispered. "It's okay. We're not hurting you. Nothing's going to hurt you."

Robbie stood there, knife in hand, breathing hard as he looked down into the dead woman's face.

♀

There were seven of them. TERFs in dark fatigues, five with crossbows and two with compounds. One had a bait bag at her belt, blood soaking through the rough canvas to stain her pant leg. Sitting high up in the branches of a gnarled pine, Beth thumbed the transmit button on her walkie-talkie twice in quick succession. She had pine pitch in her hair and a splinter under her left thumbnail that was driving her insane. She'd been chewing the same plug of licorice root for so long that her mouth had gone a little numb and tingly. The construction worker's harness securing her to the trunk had started to chafe her waist after four hours up the tree.

The TERFs were right under her. The one in the lead was a chinless white woman with faintly jaundiced skin and a stupid smirk on her narrow face, like she was Kraven the Hunter out for Spider-Man's ass and not a probably alcoholic divorcée doing what amounted to taking a big stick and going down to the basement to bash rats to death. One of the others had a little charm bracelet of finger bones and teeth she must have cut off dead men. The walkie, its speaker gutted, clicked faintly twice in answer to Beth's signal. She clipped it to her belt and slowly, carefully retrieved her bow from the crotch of the nearest bough. Zia's looters had grabbed it on a whim. The familiar worn grip felt good in her hand. Her mistake had been trading it for the Screw's poisoned gift of safety and security, routine and convenience. Better to shit outside than be declawed.

The real answer to her signal came a bare few seconds later when the distant *whump* of an explosion startled birds to flight. Below, the TERFs turned back toward the sound. As she nocked an arrow, took aim through the pine's sheltering limbs, and drew back to the corner of her mouth, thighs clamped tight around her branch, Beth heard one of them say something about a car. She loosed. It caught the one with the bait bag high up in the left thigh. She went over, and to her credit she had the presence of mind not to scream. Beth watched her face turn purple with effort, tendons standing out in her neck like cables as she dragged herself over the forest floor, hands clawing at dead needles and soft humus. It didn't matter, though, because the one Keesha nailed through the stomach with a crossbow bolt from a tree set back from the far side of the game trail started shrieking like a banshee about half a second later.

Chinless cast about wildly for something to shoot as two others got Thigh Wound to her feet and started hauling her back the way they'd come, shouting for the rest to follow as the first harsh screams rose up from the deep woods to the northwest. One woman, a thin forty-something blonde, took off alone at a run, her Legion sisters yelling at her to come back, to get back here Paula, you stupid bitch, but she was gone. Beth wondered if any of them would make it back alive to the fire-bombed hulk of their truck. An afternoon cull, picking off men in twos and threes before winter set in and dwindling food supply drove them into packs, then hordes. Leaves and pine needles flurried through the air as a stiff wind blew through the trees.

The TERFs hadn't made it far when the men came at them, two on the right and a larger pack snarling and slobbering somewhere just out of sight on the flagging group's left. Chinless brought her crossbow up and fired too early, the bolt burying itself in a tree with a low thrumming sound. The men on the right flank broke from a thicket, three huge specimens trailed by a clutch of yearlings, teenager-slender rape spawn with mouths full of rotting baby teeth and milky eyes weeping rivers of crusty conjunctival crud. Beth thought of Leda's little boy, George, and his screams of delight as he ran in and out of the freezing surf along the shore outside Fort Dyke. She thought of what Indi had sobbed to her near dawn a few days ago. The man in the Screw and his clutch of bastard boys.

Two of the surviving women—the gutshot with the wedding band

and the sad eyes and one of those who'd dragged her—got to their side-arms and shot themselves before the men closed with the hunting party. Crossbows twanged. A man went down, floundered in the deadfall like a landed fish. Another staggered and kept coming, bolt protruding from his shoulder like a cancerous growth. He got to the shooter as she struggled to reload, knocking her sprawling in the dirt and ripping out her throat with a convulsive heave of his muscled back and neck.

Beth swallowed the chewed licorice root and spat a stream of dark saliva through the gap between her two front teeth, not watching where it fell. She slung her bow over her shoulder, took her walkie off her belt, and clicked the transmitter twice as the last woman's screams rose to a glass-cracking pitch and then, abruptly, ceased.

♀

Fran looked up at the ceiling. There was a water stain above the bed, dark at its center and fading to a light yellowish-brown at the edges. Ramona had two fingers deep inside her. The pressure of it, the ecstatic too-fullness, made her want to cry in a distant, hazy kind of way. No lubricant but spit. Those short, blunt nails. Stupid tattoos on pale skin. Flowers on her collar. Sparrow on her arm. Fran had almost screamed with hysterical laughter when she saw the XX on the other woman's forearm as it pumped between her thighs.

How close is the nearest person who would kill me if she saw? Fran wondered. She bit her lip hard enough to draw blood, though she barely felt it. *Is she in the front hall?*

Ramona's nails scored lines along her throat. The other woman spat into her open mouth.

The great room?

The blotch on the ceiling seemed to have grown. That wasn't possible. Fran took fistfuls of the starched blue cotton sheets. She was so hard it hurt. Harder than she'd been in years. A terrible ache, bone-deep and pulsating. She didn't want to come. She felt as though her cock would tear, as though its bare head would split around the white pearl of her semen.

Is she outside in the corridor, her hand on the bedroom door?

Yellow water damage. Eyes? This part of the house was newer, she remembered. The Shaws had built it for the woman's parents, who never came to stay. A guilty daughter move if ever Fran had seen one. She wondered what Mrs. Shaw had been like as a girl, and how she'd disappointed her parents.

She's inside me, she made herself think, *pressing up against my prostate. Making me—making me—*She let out a little sound, a quiet cry of anguish and regret. Her hips rose trembling from the sheets. *Oh, God.*

♀

The claymore went off with a blast that set Beth's skull to ringing even through her big red plastic earmuffs. The pickup came apart as though a great fist had come up from the earth and punched it between cab and bed. Bands of twisted metal flew. Smoke swallowed the wreck as it skidded over humped and buckled pavement, a wave of dust, grit, and churned asphalt billowing ahead of it.

Zia walked up to the first woman to crawl free of the remains, knelt down on her back, and drew her knife across her throat in one smooth, brutal motion. Beth watched. She couldn't hear the knife cutting the woman's flesh. She couldn't hear Zia's footsteps or the skitter of steel over stone and hard-packed dirt. The rest of the ambush party rose up from the brush of the forest's edge to watch the wreckage burn.

♀

In another life, Fran reflected distantly, she might have written overwrought teenage poems about Ramona's back. She'd written a few for Celine McKenna in high school, though she'd never showed them to anyone. Stately, plodding odes to a body she'd wanted more to hollow out and crawl inside than fuck. Ramona had broad swimmer's shoulders and a few faint scars down by the gentle belling of her hips, close to her pale, faded stretch marks. A puberty that had gone just as it was meant to. Muscles shifted to either side of the channel of her spine, a riverway down which another Fran's long finger might have drifted. This Fran's hands were busy scrubbing cum off her thighs with a dirty rag.

"All right," said Ramona, not looking at her. "I'll help you."

♀

Indi hated the steps to the cellar. Narrow, creaking, one wall open and the other draped with veils of dust-choked cobwebs. The split boards groaned and bent under her feet. The whole house was a pinched Victorian nightmare of narrow doorways and steep steps, its every aperture and angle hostile to her body. Still, there was nowhere else the testicles would keep. They floated in the gloom under the solar lights, packed in sea salt in chipped mason jars.

Orchiectomy, she thought, staring down the rows of shelves stacked with balls and hand-milled grain and salted fish and the supplies they'd looted from the Screw. *Long-term it's the only way we can sustain this kind of population. Have to stagger the operations, make sure we're foraging wide enough to get us through the winter. Have to do George's before puberty, too, but that's delicate. I'll wait to bring it up.*

It was funny, she thought, that people treated her flesh like a public resource, a reservoir for all their insecurities and emotional dysfunction, when it was she who had *their* insides at her fingertips. She had seen the fragile bird wing tremor of a heart's last beat, parted skin, muscle, and fat with a flick of her wrist, cupped a cyst-pocked kidney in her palm. She had seen inside them all.

♀

They started back toward Fort Dyke, down the scar of a long logged-out hillside where transformer towers stood rusting, their cut cables swaying in the wind, crows perched on their struts above alluvial fans of dried bird shit. Beth saw a pack of stray dogs lope past through the undergrowth. She watched their hungry muzzles track the scents of the six women for a while before they vanished one by one into the dead sumac and scrub pine.

It was just past noon when Leda gasped, stumbling to a halt over loose earth and shifting rocks and raising a hand to point toward the verge of the forest uphill from where they walked. Beth followed the other girl's trembling finger. Her mouth fell open. She must have gotten out of York's Wild Kingdom, or maybe the Franklin Park Zoo, though how she had survived five New England winters in the open she had no idea. Her wrinkled hide was scarred, her eyes ancient and sad. Beth felt a lump form in her throat. She choked back a sob. The elephant seemed to watch them for a time, so huge she felt like something out of a dream, or like a god come down to earth to walk among the mortals she had shaped from clay.

She curled her trunk around a low-hanging pine bough and in one quick motion stripped it of its needles and its smaller branches, which she transferred to her mouth with the ease of lifelong practice. Her ears, holed and tattered at the edges, waved like sails as she dipped her huge, tusked head, the sound of her chewing like millstones grinding, and turned back toward the woods. In a moment her earth-shaking bulk was gone. Only footprints remained.

"No one's going to believe it," said Zia. There were tears in her eyes.

V

RADICAL CONSENT

"I let her do it," Fran mumbled. "I thought if I didn't she might turn us in."

Indi dabbed a cotton ball soaked in hydrogen peroxide against the scratches on her neck. It stung. "Shhh," her friend said gently. "It's all right, baby."

"I'm not upset," said Fran. She could hear voices outside: Beth and the others returning for the night. She closed her eyes, her mouth thick with the taste of the valerian tea Indi had given her. "It wasn't that bad."

She could still feel the spit on her face.

♀

There was a staircase, an old-fashioned square stairwell stretching up out of sight. Ratty patterned red carpet on the steps. Then there was a room, and the smell of plum sauce and fried scallions. She was naked on the edge of a sagging bed, two fingers inside herself, and someone was sucking on the toes of her right foot. She didn't want to look.

Her mother's withered wrist draped limp over a pillow, the case cheap and almost papery, like the ones in hospice. A giggle came from the far side of the hospital bed. *I had to fight with that thing to get it to go up and down. Second-hand piece of shit.* She stepped closer, trying to pull her fingers from her cunt, mortified at the thought her mother might wake and see her playing with herself. It wouldn't come out.

A sound like chewing, and still that tittering child's laugh. Ramona moved around the corner of the bed. She saw the boy crouched in its shadow, mouth sticky with his brother's blood. She woke from the dream so violently that she punched the wall in furious panic before her sleep-gummed eyes had focused. Cursing and sucking her scraped knuckles, she dragged herself out of bed and across the just-brightening floor into the attached bathroom where she splashed cold water on her face. Her eyes were bloodshot, her breath noxious.

You're drinking too much, she told herself as she peeled off her undershirt and dabbed halfheartedly at her reeking armpits with a soapy cloth. *Someone's going to notice. The Maenads love reporting on us. Any excuse to stick it to a real woman. Or Karin, who you've practically been begging to realize you're having some kind of drawn-out public meltdown.*

She sucked her teeth, tasting cigarette smoke, bile, and the syrupy licorice sweetness of Fran's mouth. *What the fuck are you doing, you dumb bitch?* She turned the tap off and stared at her reflection in the mirror over the sink, watching drops of water roll over her blotchy, broken-out skin. *They're using you. That cunt is using you, just like the last one did.*

You're going to get yourself killed.

♀

Fort Dyke had been built to defend against a sea invasion, then rebuilt along the same lines when the World Wars ravaged the globe and ratcheted American paranoia up to a new high. None of its planners or commanders had envisioned a future in which their entire gender went irrevocably insane, or one in which the country devolved into ten thousand warring tribes and fiefdoms. Hence the new land wall for which Beth had been laying bricks since just before dawn. A short way down the trench knelt Dani, working in her shirtsleeves with sweat streaming down her face. She'd come the day before with a few other Screw survivors.

It felt strange to work beside Dani again. It made Beth think of the painting over her bed. The man someone had loved. It made her think of the cheesy and vaguely maritime Kennedy Room and the little dressing closet with its mirrors and fake beards and sweat-smelling wardrobe, its packers and dildos and bottles of expired cologne. What a faggy, girly place to put on cishet drag. That had been a little comfort, in its own way. The silliness of it.

The crew broke for lunch just after eleven. Rachel and a short, stocky woman named Frida, who lived in the house, brought out deviled eggs, smoked and salted fish, and jars of pickled green beans from the cellar. Beth ate slowly, resting her back against the old sea wall where someone had cut back the moss and grass. The new wall was taking shape quickly, brick sunk into a concrete bed and sandwiching rammed earth and rock. When it was done they'd put up the ramparts Steph and Leda were building. She got the impression things were moving faster than most of the women knew, the sense that events had begun to tilt inevitably toward carnage.

It felt good to see it coming. In the Screw she'd been too caught up in her own misery, too preoccupied with daily life to imagine being happy, or getting even. Now she had her bow back. She had an enemy to hurt and a way that she could hurt them. She thought of Fran, reaching for her or not reaching for her, on the roof of the abandoned house. *It will be different this time. I'm not alone anymore.*

Dani sank down next to her onto the trampled turf and shyly, gently laid her head on Beth's shoulder. They sat like that in silence for a while, watching the shadows of clouds scud over the yard and the wall and the fort's mossy and decrepit bulk. The sound of the surf breaking against the shale and pitted stones washed over them in a slow, easy rhythm as the wind sighed through the ruined stonework of the sea wall. Their breath, predictably, stank of onions and garlic and the sulfurous vapors of boiled eggs.

"I'm glad you're here," said Beth. "Back to it?"

Dani stood and dusted off her knees, grinning broadly. "Bricks laying bricks," she giggled, and skipped away before Beth had finished groaning.

♀

"We found her leaving a packet under an old mailbox at the edge of town," said Jules as she led Ramona down a freshly cut and leveled dirt road running out through the burn zone toward Raymond's abandoned lumber yard. It was near dusk and somewhere in the gloom a barn owl had begun to hoot, a high and lonely sound that set Ramona's teeth on edge. "Frequencies, troop strength and movements, barge routes and manifests. A few hours later a tranny came out of the woods to collect." She snapped her gum and flashed a self-satisfied grin. "We bagged it. Piper and Sadie are working it now."

Ramona said nothing. The tendons in her neck felt like cables. Her shoulders ached. She couldn't seem to unclench her fists, even though her nails were drawing blood. Three weeks of sabotage and ambushes had left her worn down to her last fraying thread. Three weeks of fucking the shit out of Fran at least gave her something to distract herself with when her officers brought her news of a patrol slaughtered in the woods, a cargo truck blown apart on Route 93, all of it because she was blabbing her sisterhood's secrets to the first pretty girl who'd made eyes at her.

You must not really be a person at all, she thought as she and Jules cut through trampled undergrowth and a ragged wall of saplings into the overgrown lumber yard. *People believe in things. They have morals. Principles.*

They passed two older Legion women standing picket by what was left of the yard's offices and skirted a heap of decaying sheets of particle board to where Karin knelt gagged and handcuffed in the dirt, one eye swollen shut, another guard standing behind her with a crossbow in her arms. *If I were smart,* thought Ramona, crouching down to look Karin in the eye, *I could make up some reason to keep her alive. I could convince Jules we could use her as a double agent, get her out of here. She never had the stomach for it.* If, if, if. A dozen lies crawled to the tip of her tongue before scrambling back down her throat, too convinced of their own inadequacy to emerge.

"All right." Ramona's mouth was dry. She straightened up and put a hand on the butt of her pistol. She licked her dry, chapped lips. From a shed not far off came a muffled cry and the sound of leather striking flesh. A flat, sinuous crack like the sound Jules made when she snapped her gum. They were torturing a woman in there. *A woman? Yeah? Better make up your mind about that, dipshit. Better make it up real soon.*

Karin looked up at her without emotion. Blood had dried to a scabby crust on her upper lip. Another strangled cry came from the shed. "I knew there was something wrong with you," Ramona heard herself say, her voice echoing and distorted in her ears, as though heard from a long way off. She kicked the other woman in the stomach, knocking her sprawling in the dirt. Karin gasped like a landed fish. "Fucking tranny-lover." She stepped back, knees weak, her face stiff as a mask. "Get what you can out of her. Shoot her with the other one tomorrow."

Jules curled her tongue and spat her gum into Karin's hair, where it stuck like a wrinkled little barnacle. "You got it, chief." She smiled. "I know how to treat a girl right."

♀

It was low tide and Robbie was digging for clams on the mud flats when he saw Steph come pedaling along the coast from the south road. He set his bucket down and waved, but she didn't see him. A cold wind scoured the flats and whipped froth from the edges of the breakers. Robbie shivered, watching her brake hard outside the growing length of the land wall and ditch the bike without a second thought.

Something's wrong. Really wrong.

By the time he'd wiped his feet clean on the grass and made his way back to the courtyard, half the Fort Dykers were gathered there and Mariana was on her hands and knees by the front stoop of the custodian's house, making a sound like a wounded animal while Fran knelt beside her with a blank, dissociative look on her face, rubbing her back. Robbie slowed, at a loss for what to do. Zia stood not far away. Her expression was grim. He slunk toward them, eyes averted from Mariana. Her misery felt almost physically hot, dangerous to look at.

"They got one of our people." Zia's voice was rough with grief and anger. "They got Luz, down by Seabrook. Mariana's sister. They came up from Ecuador together after T-Day."

Mariana screamed again, forehead pressed against the earth, black hair fanned out over the trampled grass and soil. Robbie watched her knuckles whiten as she dug her fingers deep into the dirt. Her bare feet were arched as though she meant to launch herself into a sprint, toes clenched and trembling.

"Our plant in Raymond, too."

"So let's go," said Robbie, desperate to do something, to do anything but stand there in a circle of awkward, terrified silence and listen to the sound of Mariana's screams. "Let's get them out. What are we waiting for?"

Zia shook her head. "This isn't Robin Hood." She took off her glasses and swiped the tears from her cheeks, thumb and forefinger tracing the edges of her mouth. "If we go after them, they'll kill us. Capture us. The only way this works is to get them to come here."

"I could—"

"My mother was born in Nigeria," Zia snapped. "Abacha arrested my father before I was born. I know what happens when you try to rescue people from the government on your own. You die. You fucking die, and nobody's any better off because of it." She jabbed a finger at Robbie's chest. "You want to spend your life, wait until it's going to mean something."

Mariana screamed again, the sound so violent it made Robbie flinch away from her and clap his hands over his ears, wondering in horror how anyone could survive making a noise like that, wondering if he *did* want to die. He backed away from the pulsing white-hot sun of the kneeling woman's loss and staggered out through a gap in the half-built wall to where he'd left his clams, the pearlescent strips of their shells catching the thin sunlight.

It couldn't last, he thought as he sank down onto his haunches and buried his face in his hands. *It was never going to last.*

♀

The door of the shed in the lumber yard stood open like a crooked mouth, its frame leaning with the rest of the rotten structure. In the moonlight Ramona couldn't be sure whether the black stain on the threshold was blood or just some creeping mold. She nodded to the guards on duty, who saluted as she went past them and ducked into the shed's near darkness, her gas lantern hissing gently. Dim amber light swept over the interior.

Karin lay curled against the far wall, hands cuffed behind her back, a thick rope tied tight around her neck. She was still gagged, though some wit had gotten Jules's gum out of her hair by cutting through a swath of it, leaving part of her scalp shorn to stubble. Tufts of tight, dark curls littered the floorboards, gathered here and there into banks and drifts by the wind that keened through the chinks in the walls.

Ramona squatted in front of the other woman. She waited for Karin's eye, the one not swollen shut, to open. It stared at her in mute judgment until she reached out and plucked the gag from her mouth. "Why'd you do it?" she asked, unsure of whether she wanted a reason of her own or an excuse to break Karin's jaw. "You know what this means for me? For the rest of the detachment? For Teach?"

The beaten girl licked her dry, cracked lips. "What we're doing to them . . ." Her voice was a ragged croak not much louder than a whisper. "It's just the same shit men did to us before."

"They *are* men."

"No." Karin's eyelid fluttered shut. "They're not, and I think you know it." She was silent for a moment. Ramona could see she was working up to something, but when she spoke it still struck like a slap in the face.

"Will you kill me?"

Ramona nearly fell. Shaking, she grabbed the spit-soaked rag off of the floor and jammed it back into Karin's mouth. She tied it hastily, then rose to her feet so quickly that the blood rushed to her head and dark spots formed and burst at the edges of her vision. The lantern's light swept deep umber shadows into the shed's corners. The grip of a shovel, its blade rusted away to nothing. A pile of bags of fertilizer overrun by some kind of creeping vine. She took a step back toward the door.

The look of desperation on Karin's face as she strained after Ramona, gurgling around the gag, made her want to scream. It made her want to draw her gun and—what? Shoot her? Shoot herself? She shook her head in mute denial, thinking of her mother in that shitty secondhand hospital bed, of the dry leather creak of her breathing. Fragile wrist against sterile blue sheets.

Please, Mona.

Her groping fingers found the doorframe. "Teach is coming up tomorrow morning," she said, her voice flat and dead. She felt so hollow inside she was half-afraid she might collapse in on herself, like a burning house. "She has half the Boston garrison and two of the new Maenad detachments." She stepped back over the threshold, feeling with her foot for solid ground. "She'll kill you in front of them before we head north to wipe out the insurgents."

She shut the door and slammed the bolt home. The guards saluted her again on her way back toward Main Street. The wind was picking up and dead leaves blew in rustling clouds over the caved-in roof of the yard's offices and the heaps of abandoned planks and timbers sinking back into the earth. Ramona shoved her hands into the pockets of her coat. Her heart felt like a rock in her chest. She felt a deep and humiliating fear of the dark, the way she'd feared it at seven years old, standing at the top of the basement steps and looking down into the hungry black.

At the intersection with Main Street, the other prisoner dangled from the bough of an old oak, her limbs slack, face dark and swollen in the moonlight. One of her shoes had slipped halfway off her foot and dangled pitifully from her toes, swaying back and forth as the wind stirred the body. Ramona passed through the dead woman's shadow and on into the howling night.

VI

COCHLIOMYIA HOMINIVORAX

The next day they held a funeral for Luz after a manhunter named Jenna Losa, big and soft over thick cords of muscle, came through to trade her insulated chest of balls for a knapsack full of pickled veggies, fruit leather, and salted fish, and told them she'd been hanged at the edge of the Burn Zone. Her English was rough, but Leda had grown up in Manchester and spoke a little Kirundi. She worked it out in the end.

When she heard, Mariana had tried to take a gun from the armory and one of the trucks. Zia and Beth had wrestled her down until she lay sobbing in the courtyard, the Fort Dykers close around her. She'd let Indi dose her with valerian tea once they got her inside and now, standing at the corner of the old sea wall, she looked like a walking corpse. Mariana stared with vacant horror at Steph's sketch of her sister where Zia had pasted it up with a dozen others above a heap of rotting flowers and candle stubs. It pissed rain on their little assembly. The sea boomed out of sight beyond the wall. Indi, standing between Beth and Fran among those who hadn't known Luz well, shifted from foot to aching foot as the service wore on.

There'll be no one to sketch us if this place doesn't win, she thought as one by one the Fort Dykers shared their anecdotes and memories. *This will be it, and pocket by pocket the rest of us will follow until it's just the Cisterhood forcing little boys into their little crossdresser Hitler Youth and finding reasons to accuse each other of masculine-coded behavior. They'll win, and they won't even like it.*

Steph was talking, one fist clenched in the fabric of her skirt, the other curled between her breasts as though she were holding something delicate against herself. "When we went out fishing she used to take the bait fish out of the bucket and make them talk," she said in a choked rush. "Wiggle them around and do a funny voice. She used to . . . used to . . ." She dissolved into sniffling sobs. Zia put an arm around her and drew her close.

Others spoke. Persephone mumbled a story about Luz doing her laundry when she couldn't get out of bed. Rachel said simply that she and Keesha never would have met if Luz hadn't brought her to the fort. A few were silent, but most of them said something. Most of them had known this woman, dead and gone now. Indi thought with a bittersweet pang of regret that every time she'd heard the words "queer community" used like a cudgel or posited as some benevolent given, every argument she'd had about lesbian utopianism or gay communes or whether or not sex should be allowed at Pride parades—*fuck you, of course it should*—on one of her scrupulously locked and hidden Twitter accounts, no one had ever had any idea what that meant.

Community is when you never let go of each other. Not even after you're gone.

Beth's hand slipped into hers. She squeezed it tight. Funerals always made her want to fuck. She was already wet, her cotton boy shorts soaked through where they touched her cunt. She looked sidelong at Beth, that long jaw and crooked nose, those scars like canals running through her sunburned skin. Her sandy hair and stuck-out ears. How many times had she sewn that face back together? How many times had she held its bloody pieces in her hands and pressed them into that strong, earnest shape? *I love her,* she thought suddenly. *Stupid. She's what, twenty-eight? Twenty-nine? A baby.*

She remembered how annoyed she'd been when Fran came back with Beth in tow in the middle of a scorching summer three years before, how ugly and obnoxious she'd found Beth at first. Scared of everything. Cringing and apologizing constantly. Looking at her with the kind of furtive, mournful hunger she'd always associated with the most deeply self-loathing chubby chasers. When had things changed? When Fran was obsessed with Cynthia Bouchard and Indi and Beth got drunk together one night while she was out? She remembered *The Devils* playing on the TV, unreliable solar cutting in and out and a bootleg DVD, the picture watermarked. Vanessa Redgrave licking blood from the wound in Christ's side as a crowd jeered at her deformed spine, as she staggered in circles flailing her fists and screaming, "I'm beautiful, I'm beautiful."

They'd fucked that night for the first time, Beth turning toward her as the nuns screamed and cavorted among clouds of incense smoke, the film grain shifting as it cut to restored footage. Beth's face, ear already notched but cheeks still unscarred, nose unbroken, so vulnerable in the flickering gloom. Piles of books sliding from the coffee table as one of them kicked its edge in their laughing, clumsy struggle to find a position that worked. Dark, tense silence when Indi's fingers brushed Beth's throat, then wrapped around it.

Can I hurt you?

Mariana spoke last, haltingly and mostly in Spanish. Fran translated quietly for them as Indi gripped Beth's hand as tightly as she could. "She says they came here together from Ecuador when the secret police of the new state started disappearing transsexuals." Her brow furrowed in concentration. "Something about the border; I missed it. A raft."

Mariana made a small gesture, as though she were throwing something away. Fran swallowed. "She wishes they'd died together, too."

♀

Two hundred women and half as many Maenads stood at parade rest east of Main Street in the center of Raymond's burn zone. Tidy blocks of twenty each. Ash drifted on the cold morning breeze where the marching ranks had kicked it up. In front of the silent crowd, Karin hung naked against the trunk of a burned-out tree, tied flat to its cruel splinters and rough, sooty knobs with doubled cords of nylon looped under her armpits and thighs and across her midriff.

Ramona stood beside the trussed girl. In front of them, facing the assembly, Teach paced back and forth, ash whisking in her wake, her coat's high collar turned up against the chill. "This traitor," she said, her voice echoing in the zone's blackened emptiness, "sold out her sisters for a degenerate subspecies of autogynephiles." Spit flew. Her teeth clicked together. "Men who take sexual pleasure in stealing our bodies. In wearing our skin."

Jeers and boos rose up from the crowd. Ramona spotted Molly at the head of her platoon. Jules and the others with Ramona's command. Part of her wanted them to charge the tree and rip her limb from limb, to sense what she was too chickenshit to spill: that she was unnatural, a tranny-loving sack of shit still sucking the dead patriarchy's cock. She wished they'd stone her. Shave her head, like they'd shaved Karin's. She looked so small without that mane, her sleek skull scratched and bleeding.

"Let's see what she has to say for herself."

Teach turned and untied Karin's gag. The girl spat full in her face. Ramona froze as Karin snarled, "Fuck you, you evil—" and Teach backhanded her with vicious swiftness even as the watchers gasped in horrified delight. A string of bloody saliva slapped against the dirt. Karin worked her tongue against her cheek and spat out what looked like part of a tooth. "—cunt."

Teach dabbed under her eye with a handkerchief as Ramona wrestled the gag back into Karin's mouth, her hands clumsy, almost numb, her vision narrowed to a shaking tunnel. "You seem not to value your connection to your sisters," Teach said mildly once Ramona had stepped back. The cut was so sudden Ramona almost fell fighting the urge to recoil. One moment Teach's palm was flat against the soft curls of Karin's pubis; the next blood was sheeting down the black girl's thighs and she was screaming through the dirty cloth stuffed deep into her mouth, convulsing as much as she could in her restraints.

"I'm going to demonstrate to you," she roared over her shoulder as the crowd began to stamp and scream, baying for blood, "just how vital that connection is."

Karin's eyelids fluttered. Her head swayed.

"Smelling salts," Teach said briskly, winkling the knife into what looked like the hollow of Karin's pelvis. Ramona fumbled the vial from her pocket, cracked it one-handed, and brought it up under her friend's nostrils. There was a strangled sort of grunt. Karin's eyes opened wide. "You know," said Teach in a lower voice, one just for her and Ramona, as she dug the knife deeper into welling blood and squirming flesh, "in college I had a professor who referred to the ovaries as 'undescended testes,' like a woman is just a man who hasn't finished taking form. An unfortunate teratoma on the Herculean body of mankind. Do you know what a teratoma is, Pierce?"

Ramona shook her head. She was crying now, unable to stop herself.

The salts slipped from her fingers and fell to the ash. The crowd's thunderous bellowing would draw men, sooner or later. She watched the spotters at its edges readying their crossbows, but there was no fear in it. Teach wouldn't cut it too close. The men were just the cleanup crew.

"It's a rare form of tumor. I knew a man, years later, who had one removed, and I was fortunate enough to observe the operation. My aunt was on the board at Inova Fairfax, the best hospital in Virginia." She cut something off the exposed bone. A little bubbled clump of gory flesh. She held it up in her palm and inspected it. "When they conducted the biopsy, they found milk teeth, part of a spinal column, and some clumps of thick black hair. Cancer, dreaming it was human."

Karin let out a little sob. She was breathing fast, blood pumping out of her at a terrifying rate. Ramona hadn't known about the drop where the other girl had left her stolen documents. Was her whole outfit riddled with snitches? Rotten, top to bottom. Teach had trusted her. *Still* trusted her. Karin beat her shaved head, cross-hatched with little nicks and scabs from her ungentle shearing, against the tree's burnt trunk as Teach pulled something slick and glistening out of her. A membranous mass of bloody tissue. The sight of it made Ramona's stomach cramp in sympathetic terror as the crowd's screams rose to a fever pitch—someone's shrill, repeated screech of *"Take that, you cunt"* drilling into her like a diamond-tipped bit—and then Karin's body jerked, piss dribbling down the insides of her twitching legs, and went limp. Her head sagged against her breast.

I don't want this to happen to me.

Teach wiped both sides of the knife on Karin's cheeks and stepped back from the corpse, slipping the blade back into its sheath. "No life without a womb," she shrieked to the crowd, raising her bloody fist into the air as Karin's uterus slipped out of her wound and slithered to the ground. "The sisterhood, forever!"

"Forever!" they screamed back. In the distance, lost in the crowd's thunder, Ramona could already hear the screams of hungry men.

♀

"Eleven votes to abandon the fort, split into separate groups, and head west. Thirty-six votes to keep fortifying and defend." Zia took off her reading glasses and folded them, then tossed the yellowed note card aside. The kitchen of the custodian's house was filled to overflowing, women perched on counters and sitting on the floor with their backs to the old, cracked cabinets. Fran stood in the corner by the pantry door, a sick top-of-the-roller-coaster feeling growing in her stomach.

"No one has to stay who doesn't want to," continued Zia. "I don't make decisions for you. This isn't an army. It never will be. But—" She paused to swallow, as though fighting to get the words out. "I'm staying. I'm fighting. They know where we are; it won't be safe for us until they're fucking dead."

"If we bring them here," said Mariana, speaking rapidly in Spanish as Zia rushed to translate for the others, "we can beat them. Pick them off in the woods, lure them into the old minefields, torch their trucks. Numbers won't matter once we have them in our territory. Stay and *fight,* God damn it. For Luz and Sanam and Paulette, for Gina and Mirsa and everyone else these miserable fucking Nazis have killed. Kill them. Kill them all and piss on their corpses."

There was a pause. A few women—Addison and Laurel's little clique of normies who'd come in with the bunker exiles—looked disgusted and horrified. Fran's heart fluttered. Her mouth was dry. *I don't want to be in a war. I don't want to. I don't.*

"We have *options,*" cried Laurel, a skinny gray-haired woman in her mid-fifties who Fran knew only from sharing shifts cleaning the chicken coops and helping with laundry day at the river further inland. "We can hide, we can *talk to them.*"

"No," said Zia. "We can't. They're killing us. All of us."

Addison, no older than thirty and even thinner than Laurel, her milky right eye hidden behind a patch, cleared her throat. "I think there's been more than a little alarmism about what may or may not be happening in Boston."

"One of them tried to kill me a few months ago, before we came here," Fran blurted. She caught Beth's eye across the room. "And they tried to kill me and Beth this summer."

We tried to kill them first, but that's beside the point.

Indi, seated at the table, looked around the room, then shrugged. "I say we do it. Lure them in and rip them apart."

Addison flushed angrily. Laurel said nothing. Most others murmured in agreement. Fran found herself wishing Nam-joo had come instead of these milquetoast people, women she'd seen only in passing in the Screw, traveling to and from the squash courts and the refectory in little knots of straight-haired cis isolation, all cold stares and brittle faces. The end had left them stiff and fragile, unable to accept that the suburbs were gone, that there was no more escaping the mob, no more pretending floors and toilets scrubbed themselves and reading about black people in monthly book clubs the way you'd read about the construction of London's sewers or the history of the fur trade, as a kind of boutique curiosity, instead of actually talking to them.

The rest was bickering over how soon they needed to finish the land wall and whose turn it was to clean the armory. And then, finally, little by little, it ebbed. People went out into the fading sunlight or upstairs to carry on their own insular versions of the conversation, or to fuck or cut or drink; something to clear the tension. Fran felt sick and drained, painfully conscious of her newness at the fort, her inability to intercede or help. Indi, charismatic and blunt, had stepped easily into its dynamic. Beth had her jokes. She and Robbie could fight. What did Fran have? She felt like a vestigial sixth finger waiting around to see what the rest of the hand would do.

When the room had nearly emptied out, Zia cleared her throat. "Leda—"

"Oh *fuck* you." Leda, sitting on the counter by the huge, tarnished samovar, snarled, lips peeling back from her crooked teeth. "I'm not leaving. I am not a fucking invalid."

"Thanks for that," said Linden, one of the fort's original members, their tone dry as they bounced the haft of their cane against their knee. Fran crept toward the back door.

"George needs you, Lee," Zia fired back. "You go inland tonight."

Leda was on her feet now, fists clenched. "What are you going to do? Drag me?"

"You're making a scene," said Zia.

"So?" Leda screamed back, spittle flying. "You think I fucking care? You think it matters to me?"

"Lee—"

Fran slipped out of the room. Beth was waiting for her in the back hall with the coats and rain slickers and boots. Sunlight slanted through the beveled glass of the back door.

"I'm a shitty fucking mother," Leda screamed, her voice so raw it made Fran's throat close up with sympathetic grief. "He'd be better off." The sound of a fist thudding weakly against something. Countertop, or someone's back. "He'd be better off."

♀

Sometimes, when Indi couldn't sleep, she thought about *Cochliomyia hominivorax*. The New World screwfly, the same one from Tiptree's "Screwfly Solution," which humans had sought to make extinct by releasing tens of thousands of sterile males year after year during breeding season and leaving the species to fuck itself into gradual oblivion. She wondered sometimes if that's what had been done to Earth. A voraciously contagious designer virus slipped into a water supply, and let the rest sort itself out. But who could have done it? If it was anyone it was America, except the feeble old white eugenicists in Washington would never have used *men* as the vector. Would never have risked their precious carcasses, pumped full of teenage blood and transplanted organs.

She looked over at Beth, snoring softly beside her, and at the grimy window on the far wall. The sky was overcast. A few stars glittered in the dark where the clouds parted. Was there someone out there waiting for the human race's clock to finally stop ticking? Some galactic real estate agent who'd just shelled out to have the place tented for sapient life before the new clients moved in? The news, back when news still existed, had squealed a lot about North Korea and Iran and biowarfare. Horseshit.

The wind sighed, the custodian's house creaking as it settled, and Indi looked out into the scudding dark and thought of screwflies laying eggs in living flesh, of maggots feasting on blood and tissue. *We looked at ourselves, and that's what we saw. Just a wriggling mass of parasites chewing at whatever they could get into their mouths.* She imagined someone cracking an ampule next to a circulation vent, or maybe leaving an aerosol mister in a restroom at a fast food joint or in a subway car. *Who hasn't thought that we should be exterminated? Who hasn't imagined doing it?*

I guess someone finally did.

♀

Once upon a time there had been a billion-dollar industry dedicated to teaching women how to make men chase them. *Cosmo* quizzes. Pinterest fashion blogs. Makeup tutorials sprawling across YouTube's algorithmically sorted wasteland like popup housing developments. Perfumes scented with the barest traces of rot and rut and stinking civet. Now all you had to do was blast Meek Mill out a speaker in the bed of your truck and you could pull a few hundred in a matter of minutes. Chum the highway with rotten meat scooped from a bucket and flung out over the tailgate and you'd start drawing stragglers who caught the scent, and as they got closer they'd hear the music or the sound of the engine. Some of them would start screaming. In an afternoon you could pull a thousand of them out of their burrows and dens. A bellowing horde of Pepé Le Pews chasing the scent trail of a Drake verse and some rancid pigs' blood.

Alyssa loved kiting detail. She'd been on one of the cross-country crews that pulled the horde down on Detroit in '20, back when the Matriarchy was still getting its feet under it. Now, kneeling in the bed of a battered Ford pickup as Layla cruised down 93 doing a sedate ten miles an hour with occasional bursts of speed to keep them ahead of the tide of diseased flesh gathering in their wake, she felt that same thrill. Men drooled out of the woods singly and in twos and threes. Sometimes a whole pack emerged at once, snapping and screaming, to follow the trail of chum Alyssa scooped out of a Sheetrock bucket full of roadkill and rotting chicken shreds and dumped over the truck's tailgate every half mile or so.

She liked to look back at the surging wall of men behind them and see the frustrated rage in their eyes, almost the way Billy had looked at her when she said the wrong thing or dropped a glass or ate something he'd wanted for himself. There was something oddly comforting about it, something that gave her a case of the giggles just like she'd used to do when Billy got that look on his face. Nervous, knowing something bad was coming, but happy, too, because being hit was so much better than being afraid. Once it happened it was over, no more anxious worry, and sooner or later he'd cry with his face in her lap and tell her how much he loved her and say how her mother would see the bruises and get nosy, how he feared she'd go gossiping and poison everyone against him, and she would stroke his hair and shush him gently, promising she wouldn't, feeling like a god as she held his whole life in her hands.

She felt like that now as she brought the horde looping to the west. They'd drive about a day inland from the thinned-out woods of the coast where hunting kept male numbers in check, then turn back toward the northeast and head for the sea fort Teach's aide had marked on their atlas after the execution. One of Major Pierce's people, that black girl named Karin. She'd felt almost ecstatic watching it, as though someone holding a live wire had kissed her on the mouth.

One of the men broke out ahead of the body of the oncoming wall, baying with frustrated rage as Layla tapped the gas and roared ahead, leaving it to fall back among the others. Alyssa smiled and scooped another trowel full of chum out of the bucket. The horde would be the anvil. Teach was headed north to get the hammer.

VII

GALBRAITH

They're kiting men out of the woods," said Tandeka the herbalist in her brassy South African accent, only slightly muffled by the enormous bite of blackened fish she was in the process of wolfing down. They were huddled around the table, Robbie and Beth and the rest of the fort's fighters and hunters. "I saw them. They were headed west, and north toward Concord; twenty trucks on different routes. I don't know how far they'll go before they turn around, but they could have a few thousand tailing them before they get back to you."

Robbie felt an icy calm descend on him. All his days spent killing in the woods, mowing through meat with mechanical disinterest. He had his rifle back. If he'd spent his time preparing for anything since the end of the world, shooting a bunch of screaming cis idiots was it. He glanced sidelong at Beth. Ever since she'd started fucking Indi the two of them went around with stupid secretive smiles on their faces, like everyone didn't know. He'd sit on that wall for a week and shoot every man who came inside half a mile of Fort Dyke if it meant Beth got to keep smiling that dumb, dopey smile.

"You staying?" asked Zia. "I'll make it worth your while, and you can add a few TERF ears to your collection."

Tandeka tapped her fork against her front teeth, eyes narrowed in thoughtful deliberation. "Jenna Losa here?"

"She was. She left the day before yesterday."

Tandeka nodded slowly and stroked her jaw, considering. "All right. You take me on through the winter, I'll help you break the eternal legion of menopausal white ladies with bad dreadlocks or whatever they're calling themselves now."

Even here, at the gates of hell, thought Robbie, *dyke drama reigns supreme.*

♀

Indi kissed the scar that cut in a clean arc from Beth's left ear down under her cheekbone. Some of Fran's sutures had puckered the skin, but she'd gotten to it soon enough to stave off the worst of it. Most of the cut was relatively smooth, the skin between its lips of scar tissue no longer angry red but a soft infant pink, as though the wound had cut back through the calluses life had beaten into the younger woman's skin, back to something clean and small and wondrously new.

"I love you," Indi whispered in her ear. Beth blushed a bright cherry red. "I love you." She nipped the younger woman's earlobe gently, tugging at it before she let it slip from between her teeth. "I love you."

Beth arched her spine, breathing hard as she tried to wriggle her bound arms into a more comfortable position behind her back. Her eyes were bright, her hair damp with sweat and fanned out over the pillow. Indi licked the surface of Beth's right eyeball, tasting salt and something faintly bitter and acidic, as though she'd pressed an orange peel against her lips.

Gently, knuckles white where she gripped the headboard, she lowered herself onto Beth's face. A faint gasp escaped her as the other woman's nose pressed up against her dripping cunt. Her asshole clenched, a quiver running through the rolling flesh of her hips and thighs as she settled her weight across Beth's mouth and shoulders. Her knees ached from kneeling, but the tongue tracing the cleft of her pussy kept her muscles taut and her joints locked. She tried to breathe in time with the motion of Beth's mouth against her, with the wet glide of her fat cunt over scarred skin and plump lips. She could almost feel the negative of that strong, beautiful face pressed into her body.

Please, she prayed as her lips parted and a moan spilled out of her like water. *Please, great Rati, don't take this away from me.* She remembered her one trip to Delhi with her parents, the summer of '96, sweltering air, rank sweat in the creases of her huge, alien body, and her uncle Krishnan—who her mother had come back to talk out of abandoning his family to live as a *sadhu*—rocking with laughter on the steps of that huge, dirty temple, his filthy black-soled feet kicked up, his begging bowl clattering away as he held his stomach and cackled under the rumbling clouds. Behind him, a relief of Kama and his consort Rati, she of the sword and the sigh and the bright-colored parrot, entangled in the naked bodies of their supplicants, the goddess astride her lover, her legs locked together at the small of his broad back.

Let me stay here forever. Let it go on forever. I don't want to feel anything else. I don't ever want to feel anything else.

Indi stuffed her hand into her mouth and screamed as her whole body spasmed, red fire clawing up through the foundation of her stomach to coil around her spine and stiffen her nipples to painful hardness, and as she slumped against the headboard, breath coming in ragged gasps, and her spit-slick hand fell from her mouth to stroke the tiered fall of her belly, she felt Beth smile against her.

♀

When they'd taken the watch together, Fran had thought he had something he wanted to tell her. It had been his idea, after all. She'd hoped at first, pathetically, that he might want to take her back, even if only for sex, but by their third hour sitting in not-uncomfortable silence on the windswept walk of the land wall, she realized that it was something else. *I'm not going to cry about it*, she told herself. *I want everyone to love me. Sometimes they don't. And I fucked up so bad with you, Robbie. I'm sorry.*

They sat huddled under a musty wool blanket, passing a thermos of hot soup back and forth as they watched the dark, swaying body of the forest bend and groan with the wind. The few hundred yards of rocky ground between wall and woods was featureless in the velvet night, but Fran knew Zia and Rachel had spent half the week burying landmines looted from the armory in Manchester. An owl hooted somewhere, a mournful sound, and then, just as Fran began to doze, Robbie started to talk.

"I was staying with my friend Midge when things started to get really bad," he said. He was silent for a while, and when he spoke again his voice trembled, thick with tears. "She was helping me. I'd had top surgery. My grandfather died the year before, I'd just broken up with my girlfriend, and I hadn't spoken to my mother in a long time, so I didn't have anyone else.

"We got out of town after a few months. Everything was falling apart. You remember what it was like. I went into a CVS and I got all the estradiol and spiro I could find, and we went north into the woods. Midge's dad had a cabin up there and the driveway was about a half a mile long so it wasn't like anyone was going to trip over us by accident. We were safe, for a while. We read her dad's Stephen King novels and played Scrabble and marbles and cards. We kissed, sometimes.

"In January we figured out her spiro wasn't working. Something was wrong with it. We were already snowed in and she kept getting this low-grade fever. She had lesions on her arms. She doubled up her dosage, but it wouldn't go away. She made me . . ." He stopped for a moment, nearly breathless with the weight of the truth caught in his throat. He swallowed. "She made me take her to the cellar. There was a bike lock.

"I tried to get into town, but it was too far, and the storm was getting worse. The snow . . . I had to go back. My fingers were numb. I thought I'd lose the tip of my nose. I listened to her change. All that night I lay in bed, snow piling up against the walls, and I listened to her screaming in the cellar. In the morning I went down and shot her. That was about five years ago, and I thought I'd never have another friend as long as I lived."

She took his hand and held it for a long time as the wind howled and the ocean boomed and crashed at their back. He was so capable; she hadn't seen the frightened, vulnerable man behind the rifle that had saved Beth's life, and hers. Indi had told her. *He's scared,* she'd said in the living room of her lost house, cluttered and smelling of mushrooms and mildew and home. Fran hadn't listened. She'd seen what she wanted to see.

After a little while he pulled the blanket up to his chin and leaned his head on her shoulder. "Thanks for asking me to stay."

♀

Maine was cold. The November wind cut straight through the thick wool of Ramona's coat and uniform as she trudged along the coastal trail a few steps behind Teach. They'd come up through Kennebunkport and past Derry to the coast of Bath, where slopes of crumbling rock ran down to surging breakers and, ahead, vast stretches of virgin sand across which the ocean breathed in its slow tidal rhythm.

"This place makes me miss Cuba," Teach sighed, looking out at the bay. "The water there, you didn't even shiver walking in. It felt like a warm bath. Do you like to swim, Pierce?"

"I was on a team in high school, ma'am."

She'd thought Teach would be disappointed in her, that the disaster of her tenure as Raymond's governor would have exhausted the older woman's interest in her as a protégé, but it seemed only to have sharpened it. *Maybe she sees herself in me*, Ramona thought, a dull, leaden numbness spreading through her body. *These problems she's having with the Matriarchy. The chance that they'll risk recalling her and stripping her of rank—maybe she feels better that we're both embattled.*

She straightened out her pack with a shrug of her shoulders, trying not to feel the weight of the little single-board computer—a Raspberry Pi—Fran had given her a few days earlier. What it was for she had no idea, but she'd promised to take it with her wherever she went. To keep it close, safe inside its plastic and oilcloth wrapping. She looked sidelong at Teach.

She gave me everything, and I sold her out for a piece of ass.

Teach drew a deep breath through her nostrils, squinting up at the seagulls circling over the bay. "I love it. Floating there, surrounded by the same dark depths we crawled out of at the dawn of time. The first womb we ever knew." The wind blew her fine black hair across her face as she looked back over her shoulder, smiling. "My mother died when I was very young. Sometimes I think I've spent my whole life reaching back for her."

Ahead a long finger of rock and soil lined with straggling pines stretched a few hundred yards into the dark water. A rocky pier stuck out from its tip. They walked toward it for the better part of half an hour, Ramona cinching the straps of her backpack as they began to chafe her under her arms, her feet sliding in the gravelly sand. They were nearly there when she finally noticed the low, rumbling roar at the edge of her hearing. Teach smiled at her again as a ship came into view around the jut, visible at first in flashes through the swaying pines and then emerging, long and sleek and violent, her gunmetal hull calligraphied with the XX up high on her gunwale near her prow, just ahead of the ship's name.

"The *Galbraith*," said Teach, breathing the word like a prayer. "Five hundred feet, nine-ton displacement. She's got a pair of five-inch guns, a two-incher, and three automated point defense turrets, anti-surface and anti-air missile batteries, and a computer targeting system so precise she could shoot the candles off a birthday cake without touching the frosting. I don't know a damn thing about ships, Pierce, but I do know this: nothing still floating can touch her."

Ramona stared, rooted to the spot. It looked like a shark. A bullet. A butcher's cleaver. Even the broken antennas atop its pilot house and the ugly lines of bad solder on its flanks couldn't disguise what it was: a thing for killing. *We've been playing soldier,* she realized with a sudden, sickening lurch. *We've been dicking around like a bunch of neo-Nazis with our walkie-talkies and our hand signals. This is real war. This isn't fucking around anymore.*

She's actually going to kill every last one of them.

"Once the horde has them penned in," said Teach, her eyes fixed and unblinking, her smile so strained that deep lines cut the corners of her mouth, "we'll come down the coast and open up with the big guns. They won't last long."

She's going to kill Fran.

They met the ship at the pier's end, spray misting their coats as the destroyer, which up close rose towering above them like a wall of slate and rivets, let down its boarding ramp and Kilroy came to greet them with a crisp salute. "Welcome aboard, ma'am," she said to Teach. "Captain Roach is ready to depart."

"Perfect," said Teach, flashing her teeth. "Get Pierce's things, won't you? She'll be in the cabin next to my stateroom."

Kilroy took Ramona's bag, swinging it up over one shoulder, and followed close behind as they climbed up toward the deck, toward the massive guns and milling Legion women, the armed Maenads and the mismatched launches hanging over the ship's sides. *This is a nightmare,* thought Ramona. *I'm going to wake up any second and I'll be back in Feather's bed, and I'll do it right this time, I'll desert and take them to New York and find somewhere for us, be a manhunter or a guard or something, anything but this, I don't want to go to war, I don't want to see more people die, I don't want to see Fran die, so please let me wake up.*

Her boots struck the deck. Teach and Kilroy went on ahead of her as a few women hurried to bring up the ramp, collapse it, and fit it back into its slot in the hull. She looked back at the pier and the Maine forest beyond it, wild and trackless and cold.

Please.

The ship's horn blew an earsplitting blast as the great engines thundered to life somewhere far beneath her feet.

Let me wake up.

VIII

MORAL MANDATE

The men came out of the woods just before dawn a few days after Tandeka arrived to warn them. There were only a few at first, scurrying like roaches across the swath of burnt and blackened earth as Fran scrambled down to where the wall met the fort's concrete bunk to ring the signal bell. Robbie watched them come from where he knelt draped in a blanket on the creaking walk of the new land wall, his heart fluttering in his chest. He could hear others running in the courtyard behind him. Women on the ladders. He sat up, blinking sleep from his eyes, and settled his rifle on the wooden ramparts. He squinted down the sights, picked a target, led it, and put a round cleanly through its bellowing face as other women joined him at the ramparts, fumbling with their guns, some still in pajamas and T-shirts in spite of the morning chill. A ragged, rippling wave of gunfire. Limbs went out from under charging bodies. Puffs of dirt rose from the barren ground. Robbie shrugged his blanket off and worked the bolt, ejecting a smoking cartridge.

A wave of screams rose from the tree line, a moving wall of noise so loud it felt like a slap as it broke over the wall. The scavenged wood and bricks shook beneath him, and the body of the horde broke from the shadows under the old pines. Thousands of them. More than he'd ever seen in one place. For a moment he froze in place, unable to imagine how he could begin to choose where to shoot. What was the point? Like firing at a landslide.

Then Steph plunked down beside him, sweaty and flushed, and opened up with the M60 they'd looted from the Screw. The gun sounded like a car door slamming about thirty times a second. Smoking shells fountained from its ejector, pinging off the bricks as Steph swept the barrel back and forth. Muzzle flash strobed in the predawn gloom. Men came apart. Robbie sucked in a deep breath and ducked back down to his sights. He fired. He worked the bolt. He fired again. Bloody skin and rotten teeth.

The forefront of the charging wave barreled on into the minefield. Detonations tore the earth and flung towers of flame and smoke into the sky as shrapnel and ball bearings shredded flesh and pulverized the bone beneath. Still they came on, pounding through the carnage and the drifting towers of smoke, racing toward the wall.

That was when the trucks roared out of the woods, three huge semi cabs plowing through saplings and thundering over the rocky, uneven ground. Driverless. *Steering wheels must be jammed in place*, he realized. *Bricks on the accelerators.* Men vanished under the huge tires. Others scrambled, shrieking and yelping, out of the way. The leftmost drifted from its course, funneled by a flat tire or the lay of the peninsula or some other quirk of fate out onto the stony beach and into the surf. The right-hand truck went up in a spectacularly sudden fireball as Steph hosed it with armor-piercing rounds. The middle truck came on. Bullets punched through its grille and hood. Shattered its windscreen.

It's going to hit.

"Get down!" Robbie screamed, lurching to his feet. "Get off the wall!" His legs tangled in the discarded heap of his blanket. He toppled. Fell. The ground rushed up at him and smashed the breath out of his lungs. Something popped inside his chest with an awful white burst of pain. He retched and inhaled, sucking air, clawing his way up onto his feet, rifle still miraculously in hand, women landing all around him, legs threshing the air as they arced over his head. He turned.

A tremendous, hellish crunch of metal against brick. Then, silence. The wall came apart. Bricks spun mutely through the air. Dirt pelted Robbie's body in hard pellets and clumps. Someone nearby, a shape staggering through the smoke, fell as shrapnel tore through her like a scythe. He stumbled over something soft and saw a flash of Steph's purple hair. Broken bone and blood. *Fran was down at the end,* he told himself as he pawed at his rifle with numb, trembling fingers, trying to slide the bolt again, looking back at the shadow of the hole in the land wall. *She was nowhere near. She's safe.*

"Make a line!" Zia was screaming at the top of her lungs. She had a long, ragged cut up near her hairline and blood sheeted down her face. "Make a line, make a line, make a line!"

What the fuck were we thinking? Robbie wondered, dazed. There was blood on his right hand. *We're going to die here.*

And then the men came through the breach.

♀

Ramona could just see the fort from where *Galbraith* floated at anchor half a mile off the coast. Plumes of smoke drifted over the low spit of land with its wartime heap of an emplacement and mismatched walls of brick and concrete. Beside her, Teach stood with one hand on the gunwale and the other planted on her hip, inhaling deep lungfuls of clean salt air. She'd been standing like that, the crew frozen all around her, for almost half an hour before she turned back toward them, a secretive smile on those thin, perfectly arched lips.

"Gunnery, find your range."

The massive barrels pumped, fire and smoke leaping out from their muzzles as the deck rocked back under the force of their recoil. The shells carved furrows along the surface of the sea. A breathless moment. Then, impact. Fire stitched along the coast. Thousands of pounds of rock and earth hurled into the air in grayish columns. Smoke rolling over the piled stones of the fort's sloping foundations. Ramona couldn't breathe.

Which shell will kill her which one which one which one which one oh God what have I done what am I doing who am I who am I?

The deck rolled again. Smoke and fire. Teach laughing into the wind. The deck crew cheering, screaming, pumping fists. Wolf whistling.

Feather.

I'm sorry.

♀

Fran dragged the screaming trans girl across the yard, trying not to look at the tide of men pouring through the breach in the land wall, or at the dazed and bloodied women struggling to make some kind of firing line. "My leg!" Dani shrieked, her raw voice penetrating even the high, whining pitch the truck's detonation had smashed into Fran's skull. There were shards of brick sticking out of the other girl's right thigh and calf.

"We're almost there," said Fran, her own voice a watery smear in her ears. "Just hang on, honey. Indi'll fix it. You'll be okay. You'll be okay."

And then, from somewhere out on the bay, came a sound like muted rolls of thunder overlapping. Fran caught sight of something dark far out on the water, a long, sharklike shape wreathed in smoke and flames.

Oh Christ, oh fuck, oh Jesus no no no.

Chunks of the sea wall rained down around her. Huge scars cleaved the trampled turf. She couldn't hear again. A stone the size of a tire buried itself in the dirt a foot from Dani's injured leg. Fran hooked her arms under the other woman's and hauled back, pulling as fast as she could, limping toward the custodian's house, where Rachel waited at the back door. Persephone was running toward them, her long, lank hair blowing in the wind, her face pale and pinched with terror.

♀

"People always think of the divine feminine as nurturing," Teach said between salvos. The sound of cannon fire still echoed across the water. "A big soft mommy cow to be raped and bred. But our foremothers bit through their own umbilical cords. They smothered their deformed infants. They killed the wounded on the battlefield. The screams of childbed, the hot blood of the menstrual flow—those things are the goddess. People don't understand."

She shook her head as the guns thundered again, smashing another section of wall to rubble and ripping into the soil beyond.

"It's our turn to do a little raping and pillaging." The huge blue eyes burned like live wires into Ramona's above the spit-slick teeth, the sharp canines. "Don't you think?"

Ramona's feeble smile and nod seemed to satisfy the older woman. Teach turned toward the Maenad who'd been running messages for her, a pimply, hunching creature with buzzed hair and sullen eyes, and said: "Why don't you tell gunnery to see what they can do to that little house there?"

♀

They fell back toward the fort and the custodian's house in no formation at all, firing wildly at the men still pouring onto the base. Beth caught sight of Robbie for a second not far off in the smoke and writhing bodies, then lost him when a six-foot man came howling at her on all fours, black tongue dangling, jaws agape. She fired the automatic Linden had pushed into her hand when she'd stumbled out of Indi's room that morning, the alarm bell clang-clang-clanging across the yard. The man fell to the torn and smoking soil, clawing at his gushing chest and throat. *There are so many of them.*

A few yards away two more men squabbled over what looked like parts of one of the Screw's refugees, who Beth had watched take a bad fall off the land wall and crack her head. One of them had his claws hooked through her eye sockets, dragging her after him as the other snapped at his throat and wrists, trying to scare him off the meat. Beth shot at them. Winged one, then put a round through the bridge of his nose when he turned to hiss at her.

She glimpsed Fran through a gap in the smoke. She was dragging Dani toward the back porch of the house. Why was there rock falling out of the sky? Flecks of stone and earth. *What the fuck is out there on the bay? I can't hear. Fucking explosions. Fucking eardrums. What the fuck is happening?*

Something smashed through the house's east wing like the walls were made of tissue paper. Beth felt as though her spine had been severed, as though someone had reached into her chest and yanked her heart out with a single tug. Splinters blew on the stiff sea wind.

Indi.

♀

The first salvo fell short, hurling turf and stone into the air. The second went through one of the old house's wings. "There goes another brothel," Teach snarled. "The things these people do to themselves.

That's what they think it is, being a woman. Selling your body. Suckling like a tick at the rest of society. It makes me sick, the way—"

A harsh cry interrupted Teach. "M—woman overboard!"

Ramona turned to see Jules jogging toward them. "It's Kilroy, ma'am!" the tall girl shouted. "She blew right past me and went up over the rail!"

"Why would—" Teach's eyes widened. She whirled back toward the bustling deck around the guns. "Boats!" she screamed. "Get to the boats, God damn it! Get to the—"

Galbraith heeled violently beneath them as her starboard side tore open like a blister under a ragged thumbnail, metal shrapnel blown out in a hundred-foot fan into the water. Flames licked up the hull to kiss the gunwales as part of the deck collapsed into the twisted breach, women spilling down into the water or the gnashing metal mouth of the ship's wound. Ramona's body reacted with easy confidence. She dragged Teach clear of the widening gap. She called for the others to head for the boats. Fire suppression. Abandon ship.

And while she did, she imagined Kilroy's slender body flying through the air to plunge knifelike into the rough sea. She imagined the trail of silver bubbles that would have unfurled behind the younger woman as she reached the nadir of her dive and began to kick hard toward the surface. She imagined Kilroy going down into *Galbraith*'s guts and rifling through her bag, plucking out that little brick of electronics, the Raspberry Pi. Where had she plugged it into the ship's nervous system? What had it done? Mistimed a firing sequence? Made the engine rip itself apart somehow? It didn't matter.

It was done.

The ship was dead. Ramona had known, and she had let it happen.

IX

DEADNAME

The boats cut through the breakers, picking up speed as they pulled away from *Galbraith*'s sinking bulk and made for the stretch of rocky shallows in the shadow of the fort's east wall. Jules and Sadie sat beside her, pupils dilated, knees bouncing. They'd spiked up while the wrecked destroyer's crew lowered them toward the heaving iron water, bending together over Jules's knife to snort crushed Adderall off its blade.

"Ride of the fucking Valkyries!" Jules shrieked into the wind, her honey-blond hair whipping around her grinning face. "Someone put that fucking song on! Someone hook up an iPod and *blast* that motherfucking joint!" She threw her head back and let out a long, loud wolf howl, then burst into laughter, lolling back against the launch's low gunwale so her hair trailed in the spray.

Teach stood in the prow of the boat, swaying easily with the shuddering impacts as they crested each wave and bottomed into the trough between it and the next. She had her compact little machine pistol, the TEC-9 with its ventilated barrel and banana clip, and a combat knife sheathed at her hip. A revolver holstered on her leg.

What am I thinking?

The boats hit the beach and crunched ashore in the shadow of the ruined sea wall. The others scrambled over the sides with ragged cheers. Fifty or sixty survivors of a crew of a hundred and twenty. Her hand drifted to the butt of her pistol as she rose from her seat, feinting as though she meant to follow Jules into the shallows. Ahead, Teach still stood looking inland, hair blowing in the wind.

Why didn't I just let her die when the deck collapsed? Watch her slide into the breach.

Ramona drew her sidearm, breathing hard, and raised it in a trembling hand to point at the back of the older woman's head.

♀

Beth forced her way through the house's jammed back door, loose shingles and gutter slime raining down on her as she banged the heel of her hand against solid oak until it gave enough for her to wriggle through the gap ahead of the men on her heels. She staggered down the hall, trying not to look at the ruins of the kitchen and pantry, the charred boards and licking flames. *She's alive,* she told herself. *She's alive, she's alive, she's alive.*

Indi stood at a sheet-draped table in the living room, pulling shards of brick out of Dani's leg while the trans girl sobbed. Fran and Persephone tried to hold Tandeka down on one of the couches as the blood-soaked woman thrashed. Beth sucked in a deep breath, relief washing over her. *Thank you, thank you.* Someone grabbed her shoulder and she nearly screamed before she registered that it was only moon-faced Linden with her bow and quiver. "—found these in the dorm. TERFs are landing on the southeastern part of the beach. Everyone else is falling back into the fort."

She traded them the automatic. "Men at the back door," she said, since clipped sentences seemed to be the order of the day. *Keep joking. Keep joking. Nothing can kill you if you're laughing.*

She ran down the front hall and out into the bitter morning cold, nocking an arrow as she went down the wide porch steps. No men on this side, yet, but there were women in riot gear pouring through a gap in the ruined sea wall. White XX symbols daubed across their breasts. A light rain had begun to fall, and out in the bay some kind of battleship was sinking under a pall of thick, oily black smoke as little explosions lit its gaping innards. Firecrackers popping in the dark.

♀

Teach must have seen Ramona from the corner of an eye. She moved like a snake, falling flat across her bench seat as Ramona fired at empty air, and then the other woman's own gun was in her hands. Ramona hardly heard the bark of the revolver over the booming of the waves. A white-hot poker slid straight through her Kevlar vest and into her stomach. Blood soaked her uniform just below her ribs. She shot back. Missed and blew a passing seagull into blood and feathers—she thought of Randy Johnson's fastball obliterating that bird in midair—and Teach's second round caught her in the leg as she heaved herself up and lurched at the smaller woman.

They went over the gunwale and crashed into the surf together, Teach clambering atop her as Ramona swallowed a mouthful of salt water and began to hack and cough. The agonizing sting of the salt bloomed like smoke through her gunshot wounds. Sharp rocks cut and stabbed her back and buttocks. A fist slammed hard into her face as she scrabbled for purchase on the front of Teach's vest. A wave broke over them. She spluttered.

Teach pressed the revolver hard against her forehead. The mouth of the barrel was still hot enough to blister her skin. The older woman stared down at her, eyes bulging, face a rictus of disgusted rage. Black hair trailed wet in the surf and adhered to Ramona's cheeks and nose. "Why?" Teach snarled, her voice strangled. "You ungrateful little whore. *Why?*"

"Kill me, you fucking cunt," Ramona laughed, blood dribbling down her chin. Her stomach felt like someone had packed it with hot coals. She saw Feather, just for a moment, looking wide-eyed up at her in bed, spit glistening on their cheek. "I deserve it. Everything I've touched since I met you turned to shit. I want to die, so kill me already. Nut up and kill me, you fucking pussy piece of—"

♀

The fort was a labyrinth of blood and flesh. In the dormitory, Robbie stabbed a TERF in the back of the neck and left her gurgling on the floor, stepping over her body toward the next in the cautiously advancing line. Men shrieked, their cries ringing from the walls. It drowned out the sounds of his footfalls as he crept up on a broad-shouldered redhead, wrapped an arm around her face to smother her cry of alarm, and cut her throat. She looked at him in confused terror as he lowered her gently to the bare concrete. Her two squadmates still advanced ahead, pistols raised and trained on the east door to the seaward munitions locker where some of the fort had come down under bombardment.

Men came through it, five of them in a scrabbling pack, claws and faces red with gore and one with a huge scrap of bloody scalp held in its teeth, wisps of blond hair plastered to its throat and jaw. The TERFs started firing, but it was pure panic. They winged one. Dropped another. Three of the survivors bulled into the taller of the two women as she dropped her reload, the clip slipping through her trembling fingers. The fourth already had the other screaming on her back as he climbed onto her, howling in triumph. Robbie fell back through the bunks, some of them fallen, boards splintered, pallets shedding foam through olive drab upholstery. He crouched to retrieve a fallen automatic, checking the clip—eight bullets—and slamming it back home. The men were eating now.

Up the nearest steps and through the bloody radio room where TERFs and Fort Dykers lay tangled with the wiring, a few still moaning. In the hall beyond he found Mariana, a wild cut sheeting blood across her face, reloading a revolver with three dead TERFs staggered ahead of her where she must have shot them down. The cries of the men grew louder behind them. There was a great crunching, rumbling crash as some part of the fort collapsed, shaking the floor beneath their feet. They hurried on without a word, turning back only when the click and scrape of claws against concrete became a din to fire into the raw tide of shrieking mouths and reaching hands.

This is what you want, they seemed to cry. *Make me a man, Lord, yes? Wasn't that you? Wasn't it? Wasn't it?*

On through the gutted command post with its slit view of the stony beach where bodies lay in the pounding surf. Beth, glimpsed going up the rusted stairwell to the roof and behind her, running back down through the deserted west armory to the half-flooded laundry, and drifts of dead men—one only wounded, black tongue lolling from slack jaws as he crawled piteously toward them—on the steps of another stair along with two dead TERFs. They stopped again, Mariana panting as she reloaded, and Robbie darted down the steps, pausing only to shoot the wounded man as it reached for him with a whine, and plucked the dead TERFs' guns off their bodies. Hooting cries rang up from the laundry down below, and from the hall they'd taken.

Splitting skin and rotten teeth came roaring down the corridors as somewhere a machine gun chattered, high and thin.

♀

Fran raced across the fort's mossy roof to where Rachel lay bleeding by a handful of dead men, three shot and one with a knife jammed through the top of its skull. She was tired. Her legs felt like bars of molten lead as she knelt beside the older woman and got her arms under hers. "Okay," she said, more to herself than to the half-conscious Rachel. "Okay, here we go on three. Gonna get you back to Indi."

When she straightened up, Rachel dead weight in her arms, Teach staggered through the door to the observation tower, hands bloody, half her coat soaked through and her hair dripping wet, and slammed the door behind her. Something banged against it from within. She smiled hugely as she raised the same blunt little Uzi she'd had on her that day in the forest. A typewriter clatter. A horrible red looseness in Fran's stomach. Her right hip. Her thigh. She fell against a pile of rubble, her hands slipping from Rachel's.

Oh.

Metal clanging. More gunfire. An arrow zipped past. She could hear someone screaming her name, but it felt as though it must be from a long, long way away.

♀

Indi put Persephone's guts back inside her. No time to check for perforations. No time to resterilize her hands. There was only her against the tide of shredded flesh that poured in through the house's doors. The entire west wing of the house had collapsed in on itself. She was almost sure someone had been inside it when it came down. Maybe they were trapped in there, alive and slowly suffocating as fire sucked the oxygen from their lungs. She stapled her assistant shut and turned to Linden, lying on the couch, but they were gone.

Outside, the sounds of gunfire and the screams of men.

♀

Beth hit the concrete on her knees beside where Fran lay, not far from Rachel, who Fran didn't think was breathing anymore. Teach had fled across the roof and down through one of the crevasses in the fort's ruined east wing. "No," Beth moaned, pressing her hands against the parts of Fran that didn't feel like anything anymore.

Fran watched her do it. She felt as though something important had come loose from her and floated away over the sea. "I was a bad friend to you," she said.

"Don't say that," Beth sobbed. "Don't say it. I'm going to get you back to Indi."

"No," said Fran. She felt calm, though tears poured down her cheeks. "No you're not, baby." She took a deep, hitching breath. Something shifted in her belly that should not have moved. Cold and slippery. "Can you kiss me, Beth?" she asked, her voice small. "Will you kiss me, please?"

Beth kissed her.

She realized that in some way she would never unravel, in some strange and hazy confluence of gentleness and violence and self-mortification, Beth was more a woman than she'd ever been. She tried to say it, but what came was, "You're beautiful." She stroked the other girl's cheek as they broke apart, her fingers leaving smears of blood. "Bethy, you're so beautiful."

Beth's tears fell on Fran's upturned face. They felt warm. "I don't want to do this without you."

"It's okay," said Fran. "You'll be all right."

"Don't leave me. Please, Fran. Please."

"Shhh," said Fran, reaching out to cup Beth's face in her hands. Her arms felt so heavy. "I love you. You're my sister." It was hard to breathe. "Tell Indi and Robbie. Tell them . . . tell . . ."

Red. Black. The sun had moved, and Beth was gone. Fran was shivering beside Rachel, who was dead. She could see the beach from where she lay at the roof's edge. A stocky woman with short, spiky gray hair limped down the rocky shore toward the boats, a few TERFs in uniform straggling after her. They pushed one of the launches out into the waves, most scrambling aboard while two others got it turned around so that its blunt prow pointed away from shore. A pretty redhead about Fran's age took the tiller and the engine roared to life. The women in the surf were shouting, crying out, reaching toward those in the boat as it slewed out against the current and the pounding breakers.

They don't even love each other, she thought. The boat cut through the glittering reflection of the sun on the dark water. It was coming up, washing the fort's battlements in blinding radiance. It hurt to breathe. Black spots danced at the edges of her vision. *They're men.*

She let out a long, shuddering breath. She couldn't seem to draw another.

They're just men.

♀

It was going wrong. Everything was going wrong. *Galbraith* was sinking. Kilroy and Pierce had turned on her. Molly nowhere to be found. And that big freak bitch, the one who'd taken a shot at her in the woods on that hot July day, was here. She'd got the other one, but the sight of that scarred face on the roof of the fort had rattled her enough to run when the bow came up. To *run*. Her. The woman who'd broken the back of the Baltimore transsexuals in the early days, when it had been just her and Dr. Raymond and a few dozen sisters who saw the chance the virus represented.

The Maenads had been a mistake. She saw that now. She'd been too soft on them, too willing to believe that the right social pressures and incentives could override a hundred thousand years of baked-in slavering pig rapist instinct. But Pierce? Had it really been over that doughy degenerate thing she'd had shot, and if so, then why had Kilroy given her that brothel full of freaks? Hadn't they been in it together? Traitors everywhere. That whole generation, poisoned beyond salvaging.

She could still make it back to the boats, though. She still had loyalists, women who must be falling back too, wondering where she'd gone and how they could come to her aid. That was the sisterhood. That was their strength. They would never abandon her. She came around a massive chunk of ruined wall and nearly stumbled into a seething pile of men tearing at a woman who lay curled on the ground. She screamed, bringing her gun up. The TEC-9 cut through the pack like a sickle through wheat. The thing that remained looked up at her. "You saved me," it croaked. Not a woman at all.

She stumbled back with a low groan of horror and sprayed lead into its face and tits, ripping through all of some poor plastic surgeon's work. Had anyone seen? She stared wildly around the courtyard and for a moment her heart leapt at the sight of a blessed XX daubed across a suit of riot gear. But it was only a corpse. One among many, men heaped all around them in drifts of scabby, sickly flesh. Some still whining and dragging themselves over the bloody soil. Her girls, her beautiful girls, so many of them dead, and the beautiful *Galbraith* sunk, and all of it ruined. She wanted to scream and tear her hair and cry. She wanted to suck on her revolver. And then she saw him.

Another man knelt there by the sea wall, his hand on the hilt of a knife buried in the chest of one of her girls, who lay on her back in the dirt. Kate Quinn, who had been with her since Bethesda in the wake of the first outbreaks. The man wasn't one of the things, but a man like men used to be, thin and of middling height with long, straight black hair, dark reddish skin, and a high forehead. He saw her, yanked his knife out of Kate's chest, and broke into a dead sprint. His sneakers splashed in the growing puddles.

She shrieked at the top of her lungs, ejecting the spent banana clip from the submachine gun and yanking a fresh one from her belt. She slapped it home and brought the gun up, whipping a line of fire across the courtyard and the wall of the gardener's shed behind which the man vanished at a run. Glass shattered. Splinters flew. It wasn't a man. It was a dirty little brainwashed traitor, one of those pitiful women conned into abandoning her gender to grasp at the straws the patriarchy dangled just out of her reach. Sawed into, T-poisoned, and spiritually mutilated.

She crossed the courtyard slowly, pausing twice to shoot oncoming men and pump more rounds into the shed. Glass shattered. Sawdust flew. Finally the little traitor lurched out from behind the ruins. She'd winged him—he was bleeding heavily from a deep groove on his right arm, struggling to hold up some huge boxy power tool. What, did he think he could take her with a fucking cordless drill? She laughed.

And then it came up, and she realized.

Nail gun.

It made a funny chuffing sound, little blasts of pressurized air escaping its corroded muzzle. Something plinked against the pitted stone beside her head. Again. Again. Dark, pointed flashes rebounded from the granite and went spinning off into the blinding dawn light as the boy sprinted past. And then a dull, quick jolt of pain in her right arm. Another. And another. A line of little agonies scrawled from her bicep to her throat. Her breath came in a desperate wheeze. Her left hand moved to feel the roughened iron studs protruding from her flesh. Nails. A fucking nail gun, like she was a contracting job. Drywall. Somehow, the indignity stung worse than the metal in her body.

"Fucking traitor," she shrieked, muscles convulsing around the nails stuck in her throat so that her voice emerged as a slurred, buzzing croak. "Fucking faggot piece of shit! I'll kill you! I'll kill you!" Firing at everything. Filling corpses full of lead. Cutting down someone, she didn't know which side. Men screaming as the fingers of her injured hand stiffened into claws on the trigger. Lurching through the rain toward the dubious safety of the fort, a rear entrance into a kind of arcade. At least she'd be dry. She could catch her breath and try for the beach again. She'd make it. She would. She could still salvage this.

She thought of the thing her husband David and his brothers had kicked half to death behind that little bar in Arlington, of its weave coming out in her hand and the swollen, bloody ruin of its bony face. Who could ever have believed it was a woman? Who could want to be something like that, unless it was for camouflage, for hunting. She thought of the freak at the academy, Alice Prince, whose dirty secret no one knew until she'd ferreted it out. And before her there'd been her selfish faggot brother, that disgusting thing wriggling nylons up its hairy legs, melting their parents' brains with his lies about how trapped he felt, how wrong his body was, bankrupting them for surgeries to pinch and squeeze and mold his flesh into grotesque new contortions like something out of a dirty horror movie. Her mother's voice delivering the words that had crushed her utterly, finally, irrevocably.

My beautiful daughters.

♀

Beth was coming down from the observation tower when Teach staggered out of the rain into the fort's landward arcade at the foot of the stair, five yards below. She was white-faced, one arm hanging limp at her side, her machine pistol dangling from the other. Beth drew to a halt and nocked an arrow, moving with dreamlike slowness and surety. She drew the string back to the scarred corner of her mouth and let a long, slow breath escape her as Teach stumbled to the wall and leaned against it, a puddle forming under her. Blood and water.

"Hey," Beth said hoarsely.

Teach turned. There were roofing nails embedded in her cheek, throat, and shoulder, slick with blood, and her black hair was plastered in whorls to her brow and neck. Blood diluted by rainwater ran over her milky skin. Her eyes widened.

Beth let her fingers slip off of the bowstring.

The arrow caught Teach in the mouth. Bloody chips of tooth enamel flew. She jerked back, one eye rolling up into her head so that only pale sclera showed, and slid down the wall until she came, twitching, to rest, one leg folded beneath her and the other stuck straight out. She'd left a long, dark smear of blood along the concrete. Her good eye followed Beth as she came slowly down the steps, letting her bow drop with a clatter.

Beth turned to face the gagging thing, bracing herself against the sides of the door. Rain lashed her back. Teach smiled at her around the splintered shaft. Her thin, bloodless lips twitched. "Branden," she croaked, the word slurred and horribly babyish on her split and bloody tongue. "*Bwannnden.*"

No.

She slammed her boot into the other woman's grisly smirk. The arrow snapped. Bone gave between wall and hardened rubber. Beth drew her leg back, cocked her knee, and kicked out hard again. A gurgling laugh came from the ruined face. The lone remaining eye, pale and unblinking, stared at her through a mask of blood and broken skin. Her knuckles popped where she held tightly to the doorframe. She brought her leg up a third time. The woman's hand came with it, fingers clinging weakly to the gory sole, and still that horrible wet grunt of a laugh, *huh-huh-huh*, and black blood pouring from the ruined mouth.

How did she know?

Beth jerked her foot away from Teach's feeble grip, then drove it back down like a piston with a final awful crunch. She turned and lurched out blindly through the door into the rain, suddenly desperate to get clear of that dead, staring eye. She fell to her hands and knees and vomited onto the bloody flagstones, heaving and retching until there was nothing left to come up. Until there was nothing left at all.

How did she fucking know?

Robbie held her. He was kneeling at her side while she keened in the bitter, blowing rain.

Oh, Fran. Oh, God.

EPILOGUE: GARLAND

Beth fell asleep that night as soon as her head hit the pillow, and when she woke thrashing, half-tangled in the sheets, and began at once to sob, Indi stirred from her own exhausted sleep and held her, her tears falling hot onto Beth's brow and cheek. They kissed and Beth thought how good the fine, dark stubble on Indi's upper lip felt against her mouth, how right her salty tears were as they dissolved into her saliva.

"You taste like licorice," Indi whispered.

The ocean of that soft, fat body in her arms, clawing for release, and afterward her own voice, muffled and congested in the dark. *Not fair. Not fair. Not fair.*

♀

Robbie couldn't sleep. By the wrecked wing of the caretaker's house he sat among the dead. There were others around him. They clung to the bodies covered in sheets, whispering in grief-choked voices, keening low and urgent. A woman he didn't know screamed and beat her head against the muddy earth. There were still men out there in the night, but there were guards on the wall and floodlights bathing the forest verge and the wrecked trucks and bodies in their sodium-white glare. It was safe to feel the day, now. He gripped Fran's hand where it stuck out from beneath the bloody sheet someone had used to cover her.

Are you leaving? she'd asked, standing there in her nightgown in Indi's backyard.

He closed his eyes, crying now in silent, gulping sobs.

I don't want you to.

♀

Beth crossed the lawn just after sunrise. The others were burning the dead men and TERFs, dumping kerosene on stacks of bodies. By the sea wall, a few Legion survivors sat huddled together under armed guard, uniforms crusted with blood and salt, faces scratched, bruised, cut. Robbie had come to get her not long after dawn. One of the prisoners wanted to talk to her, he'd said. The one Fran had fucked.

Zia and some of the others had found Ramona Pierce shot up and half-drowned by the rising tide, a hole in her head, and brought her into the custodian's house, thinking to let her die in comfort. Instead, impossibly, she'd lived. She lay on a narrow canvas cot in the surviving part of the house, Robbie's gray tom curled up in the crook of her arm.

"You look good," Beth joked from the doorway to the living room, beyond which she didn't feel like stepping.

"I'm sorry," croaked the pale girl in the cot. The scabbed-over bullet hole in her skull looked like someone had used one of those hydraulic cow-slaughtering things on her. Stupid fucking tattoos. Dumbass septum piercing. She paused to take a labored breath. "Are you the one . . . one I shot? The woods, off the highway . . ."

Beth tapped her scar, a funny ringing in her ears. "That's me. You have something you want to say?"

"This place," Ramona wheezed. "It's . . . I don't know. It's peaceful." Tears glistened in her eyes. "I think . . . someone I loved . . . they would have been really happy here. I thought maybe, once I'm better—"

"No," said Beth. The force of her own voice surprised her. She straightened up, folding her arms. "No. I'm grateful, for everything you did, for the risks you took—but I don't want you with me. With us, here. I don't want to be near you."

Ramona propped herself up on one elbow, though it cost her visibly to do so. Rage and self-pity warred across her bruised and battered face. "I gave up . . . *everything*," she said, her voice cracking into a pained sob. "You have . . . no idea . . . what I lost. What I sacrificed . . . for *you people*."

"You really don't get it, do you?" Beth turned, heading for the front door. "You're lucky we don't fucking hang you."

♀

"Do you remember how your mother screamed when you got your nose pierced?" Indi asked, slipping her forceps into the ragged red mouth of a wound. It helped to talk, she found, when you had to work on something that had been someone you loved. She scrunched up her face in mock disgust, digging deep for her best impression of thin, neurotic Willa Fine with her gray bob and her nasal Brooklyn accent. Cold, bloody skin shifted against her fingers. "'They won't let you be buried in Upper Valley with that hole in your face! Is that what you want, to be apart from me and mimi and your uncles *forever*?'"

Her laughter threatened to become a sob as, with a gentle turning of her wrist, she eased another bullet from the ruin of Fran's pale, flat stomach and deposited it in a dish set by the dead girl's head. She forced herself to breathe in deep and dipped the forceps' jaws in a small bowl of alcohol, swirling them to dislodge any tissue, then slid the instrument back into one of the bullet holes. She had already removed Fran's bowel, torn to ribbons by the storm of lead that had cut her down. It lay coiled in a trash bag by the bloody couch. A cool, damp wind blew through the room from the gaping hole where *Galbraith* had shelled them. She dropped another bullet in the dish. The pancaked metal clinked against the bloody porcelain.

"I think that's all of them," said Indi to the empty living room. "Goodbye, baby."

♀

It took her and Robbie a long time to dig the grave. The ground was rocky and roots coiled through it, old and gnarled and vital. She hacked into them with the shovel's rusted edge, tore and twisted them apart, flung them off into the undergrowth. Twice she had to stop and let the grief that built up in her breast pour out of her in sobs she stifled with her hands. The whole time Fran lay wrapped in bedsheets at the edge of the small clearing they'd chosen. Mushrooms scaled the trunks of the old oaks. The bare branches cut the morning light into a thousand broken shards that fell over dead pine needles and soft moss.

"It's not your fault," Robbie said to her the second time, laying a hesitant hand on her back. "It happens. It just . . ." His own voice grew thick with grief. "It just happens."

It was past three when they lowered her together into the rough rectangular hole they'd dug, Beth standing in it, unable to keep from looking at the layers of humus, stone, and loose, dry earth they'd dug through, the worms squirming confused into open air, the grubs dreaming in their soil cocoons, as though it were the secret history of time itself. Robbie slid Fran down to her little by little, the sheet trailing from her long, slim body so that an arm fell free. Fran's chipped pink nails brushed the dirt as Beth lowered her to rest and scrambled up out of the hole before real horror could sink in.

"You sure you won't stay?" she asked as they stood together, their backs to the grave.

He shook his head. "My dad . . . he was Taos Pueblo, from New Mexico. I want to see if they're still out there. If I have family. Mariana's headed the same way and said she can show me how to get there; we're leaving after this."

"What's so hard about it?" she joked, unable to keep her voice from breaking a little. "You just walk until you fall into the Grand Canyon."

He hugged her, the crown of his head tucked neatly under her chin. They stood like that for a minute before he said, "You'll say goodbye to everyone for me?"

"Sure." She held him tight, thinking how brave he'd looked when he'd run toward her down that wooded hill and tackled Corinne headlong, like a quarterback. "Don't get killed."

"Never have." They broke apart, he not quite meeting her eyes, and she felt certain, white-hot loss gripping her heart and closing her throat, that they would never meet again.

"I'll see you, Beth."

She watched him go until he was no more than a thin spike of shadow in the distance, lost among the trees and veiled by the dust that hung in the golden light. "See you, Robbie."

♀

Beth lay against Fran's cold body as the sun began to set, her head resting on the dead girl's shoulder. She hadn't been able to bring herself to fill in the grave, or to go get Indi and the others. To put dirt on Fran's still face, on her white dress and freckled shoulders. "I don't know what's going to happen next," she whispered. Fingers of shadow moved over their skin. Jags of light and dark. "I'm scared. I wish you were here."

She kissed Fran's pallid lips and pulled the body closer, pressing her face into the hollow of the other woman's neck. "I love you," she breathed in a voice that trembled at the weight of all the different ways those words were true. "I love you so much, Fran, you stupid bitch." She closed her eyes, squeezing them shut tight against the acrid tears that burned at their corners, wrapping her legs around Fran's to be closer, to touch her one last time. Every breath was a hitching, desperate sob. Fran in her sundress in the door of her room at Indi's house. Fran screaming at her in back of the high school. Sucking her dick in a mossy clearing they'd found one day while they were supposed to be hunting. Fran laughing. Fran crying. Fran in her arms.

Fran, beautiful before she was ever a woman, posing with a hand over her cock in front of the dirty mirror in Beth's bedroom, a tentative smile on that slender oval face, framed by falls of sandy hair. The most perfect thing that Beth had ever seen.

What if I was a girl?

For by my side you put on
many wreaths of roses
and garlands of flowers
around your soft neck.
—SAPPHO, FRAGMENT 19
Anne Carson, *If Not, Winter: Fragments of Sappho*

ACKNOWLEDGMENTS

I'd like to thank my parents, who never took my books away no matter how much shit I pulled; my grandparents, who read to me long after they'd have liked to be asleep; and my sibling, of whom I am so very, very proud, as well as my dynamite agent, Connor Goldsmith, my incomparably patient and insightful editor, Kelly O'Connor Lonesome, and all the people at Tor Nightfire (especially Emily! Hi Emily!) and Jordan H., Sarah, Laura, Kristin, and Dakota, as well as my thoughtful and diligent authenticity readers, Cameron, Jordan, Sarah M., Devii, and James. Huge thanks to cover designer Esther Kim and sculptor Sarah Sitkin for making such a gory, slimy treasure. Julia, thank you for being my sister, my best friend, and for helping me figure out how to make this book as gross as possible. Vince and Alice, for your invaluable feedback, for movie nights and trans normality. Hazel, for endless Magic games and teary heart-to-hearts. Josh, Dana, Julian, Huey; all my beautiful nerds who keep my imagination roaring along and my heart full and pumping. Bill, my mentor, whose words of encouragement and confidence in me have carried me even when I wanted to take my ball and go home. And Sam, my love, for supporting me with such earnest dedication even though you can't read any of the gross splattercore shit I write. For your patience, I will say this here so that it endures forever in the vaults of the Library of Congress: you are Batman now.

A special thank-you to Torrey Peters and Alice Sheldon, whose work inspired this book and next to whom I hope against hope I might measure up, at least a little.

And to every trans woman I've ever loved, to all your perfect shoulders and the arches of your necks, to your lovely wrists and fingers, to your cocks and cunts and lips, to the feel of your skin against mine and the sound of your voices, low and urgent, in my ear; all of you are in this thing, in one way or another. I could never have written it without you.

♀